LEXIE
AXELSON

PRETEND

CREATURE

Pretend Copyright © 2024 by Lexie Axelson

All rights reserved.

No part of this book may be reproduced in any form or by any electronic or mechanical means, including information storage and retrieval systems, without written permission from the author, except for the use of brief quotations in a book review.

This book is a work of fiction. Any names, characters, places, or incidents are products of the author's imagination and are fictitious or used in a fictitious manner. Any resemblance or similarity to actual people, places, events, or establishments is purely coincidental.

First Edition: July 2024

Paperback ISBN: 979-8-9906844-1-6

Copy Editing and Proofreading by K. Morton Editing Services

Cover Design by Jaqueline Kropmanns

To all the hurt souls, you are more than your scars and mistakes. Every day is another opportunity to grow, heal, and learn.

Just keep going.

And to my dark romance besties who want a fictional, unhinged, masked military man to wrap his dog tags around them, Daegan Hannibal is yours.

Content Warnings

This book is intended for mature, adult readers 18+.

This series is about *fictional* Navy SEALS.

This story contains content, themes, and situations that may be triggering for some readers, such as graphic violence, stalking, degradation, PTSD, mentions of suicide, mentions of death, mentions of post-partum depression, torture, sadomasochism, and graphic language. Please visit the author's website for a complete list of content warnings.

This contains sexually explicit material such as blood play, knife play, bullet play, breath play, CNC, spitting, and breeding.

www.lexieaxelson.com

Content Warnings

This book is intended for mature audiences.

Playlist

Sober Thing by Cody Jinks
A Little Piece Of Heaven by Avenged Sevenfold
Yellow by Coldplay
Skin and Bones by David Kushner
Stargirl Interlude by The Weeknd ft. Lana Del Rey
Blue Jeans by Lana Del Rey
Black Beauty by Lana Del Rey
Until I Found You by Stephen Sanchez
Wildest Dreams by Taylor Swift
Paint It Black by The Rolling Stones
Take Me To Church by Hozier
Nightcall by Kavinksy

Playlist

Prologue

Daegan

"ANOTHER DAY...ANOTHER SCAR UNLESS *you have a breaking point.*" He slices the side of my face again with a thick, unsharpened blade. It's incredibly dull, which forces my captors to press down harder. The knife cuts through the side of my brow down to the bottom of my eye. A stinging, burning sensation ripples as it breaks through my skin. My teeth grind hard to stop myself from giving in to what they want.

No grunts. No emotions tethered from pain. I won't give them anything. Information. Intelligence. My name. They're going to be sorely disappointed...I don't have a breaking point.

A roar of laughter escapes my dry throat as he cuts me. My captor goes rigid, and he stops, gripping the handle tight in his hand and adjusting his posture. His eyes widen like he just saw something that scares him.

My blood drips down my face and onto my chest. I'm showered in red. I hum as the blood glides down onto my abdomen. My favorite color.

His wicked smile fades into a menacing frown. He narrows his brows at me, flaring his nostrils, and slices the same side of my face again, but this time it's fast and less torturous. "You think this is funny, Creature?"

I laugh harder, leaning against the pillar I'm tied to. I rest my head, chuckling softly. I'm naked, cold, and beaten to shit. So yes, I think it is pretty funny how they think I'm scared about having a few scars on my face. They just made me more deliciously handsome.

"It is funny, actually," I tell him, with a grand smile curving onto my bruised face.

He punches me in my stomach, the impact forcing my lungs to give out, and I scrunch over as far as my body lets me. I cough as I struggle to breathe the air that was forced out, the chains around my wrist grinding against the metal. Damn, he got me good. I'll give him that. Still, he's weak, and I'll show just how funny his tragic undoing will be once I get myself free.

"Why is that?" He leans down, getting into my face. One of my eyes is closed shut, and I'll be a lucky bastard if I can still see from it after all this is over. Eh, I guess I only need one eye to snipe, so I should be fine. I shrug my shoulders, tilting my head to the side as I talk to myself. I regain my strength and focus on the dead man standing before me and smile, flashing my bloody mouth. He's puzzled, but then I spit onto his face.

He flinches as he gets sprayed with red, closing his eyes, and I smirk.

"Because I don't have a breaking point, dipshit. Oh look, you've got a little something on your nose...if you let me out of these chains, I can get that for you." I purse my lips. One of the captors in the corner behind him breaks into a roar of laughter. The man I spit on whips his gaze from me to him and glares. This causes the laughing man to clear his throat and look at the floor.

PRETEND

He wipes his face clean with his hand, pouting like a child who got their favorite toy taken away. He walks to a table full of weapons laid out a couple of feet from where I am. Walking up and down, he smiles with satisfaction because he's found another tool he wants to use for his sick pleasure of hoping to break me. He grabs a machete and holds it to my throat...

I jolt up, panting hard, escaping the nightmare I dream about every fucking night since I escaped being a prisoner of war. The alarm I have scheduled on my phone rings loud, dragging me out of the shadows I endure when I close my eyes.

I'm covered in sweat, and my bed sheets are damp. My chest heaves up and down, desperately to flush out the darkness I was trapped in. I rub my hand through my dark hair as another attempt to drag myself out of the dreadful memories. I never sleep well. I'm always in and out of sleep. I'm used to this. But after being tortured and suffering life-lasting injuries...it's worse.

Sweat drips down my chest hair onto my stomach. I have the bedroom fan off because I dislike seeing it before falling asleep. The wings remind me of a helicopter, and it takes me back to Iraq. I can't sleep without the lights because it reminds me of the dark bedroom I stayed in when I was captured.

I look over to the clock on my nightstand, and the time shines bright. It's one in the morning, and I'm still trying to catch my breath. I passed out after a long day at work and the gym. I clear my throat and sit up, throwing my legs over the edge of the bed. My heart skips a beat at the thought of one person who has driven me to the point of no return.

ALESSIA

A brush of cold air wakes me up from my heavy sleep. I hum, squinting through heavy eyelids, sleep slowly fading as my muscles come alive. That's when I noticed I had fallen asleep listening to the storm outside. I left the window open because I like the white noise it provides. Rain is peaceful to me. Something about the sound of water falling, winds blowing, and thunder striking that has me relaxed. I do this every time a storm rolls by, even if it is only for a couple of minutes.

My arm stretches out in hopes that I will find my boyfriend and ask him to close the door for me. But the bed is cold, and my fingers meet nothing but more blankets, and I groan in familiar disappointment.

He's probably out drinking again with his friends.

I turn to my side, trying to muster up the strength to stand up and shut the window. There's barely any visibility in my dark bedroom, and the moonlight from the storm that's plagued the sky slightly creates dim lighting.

I open my eyes, ready to pull the blankets off me, and my heart falls to my stomach. Thunder strikes and my blood runs cold when I see a tall, massive figure dressed in a skull mask standing in the doorway.

He doesn't look panicked. His hands are at his side, and he tilts his head amusedly.

PRETEND

My mind instantly eliminates the possibility that my boyfriend is the one in the cryptic mask standing there, because Jack is only 5'8 and lean, but this person is well over six feet tall, and he's taller than the door frame.

I scream, a short gasp of a scream, and adrenaline kicks in as my eyes widen. I scramble for my nightstand, headed for the lamp, tearing my eyes from the intruder.

I find the switch and fall off my bed when it turns on. My body lands with a short-lived thud. I spring towards my firearm, grabbing my Glock that's hidden underneath my bed. I point it at my door with a tight grip, switching off the safety.

But the man isn't there anymore. He's gone. Just as fast as I noticed him watching me, he disappeared like an actual ghost. I'm left with a heaving chest, one hand clawing at my blankets, questioning if it was just a bad dream or an actual invasion.

1

Daegan

Three Months Ago

I BECAME A NAVY SEAL at twenty-eight years old, and the adrenaline I get when I'm about to jump out of a plane never changes. I'm thirty-four now, and my dedication to this career has become an obsession, always striving to do more and to be better.

I was working for one of my step-brothers, Graves. He runs a private security company. The services that Graves provides make his job title an understatement. It is a very abnormal private security company. He also does various other businesses; I haven't asked what they are.

But I craved more. I wanted to do more. Joining the Navy was my *'more.'*

We're high in the sky, ready to bring hell on a mission I'm the center of. Somebody will be in my crosshairs, and I'll wish them a good night. Another high-value target. Another evil soul that won't be able to hurt another person again. And we're jumping in this time.

Oh, what fun.

This is my favorite. Jumping in the middle of the night as darkness surrounds me, getting lost in the stars as I float and fly down like a dragon, ready to unleash fire.

Everyone has jumped. Rooker, Lopez, Grim...except Kane. I'm smiling big underneath my mask as he hesitates to walk off the plane.

"You good Bane?" I coo deep and wickedly.

I haven't been on SEAL team executioners for long, but I know Operator Bane is the one who has a heart that gives. Mine only takes.

"Of course. I'm good." He shouts over the airplane's engine and harsh winds. He stands just at the edge. If he steps forward once, he's airborne. I look over his shoulder, standing beside him. We can't see shit, just clouds. "Just never been a fan of jumping, bro." He shrugs.

Time is running fast, and we can't waste any more time. The mission has begun.

I roll my eyes.

"Get the fuck out." I snarl.

He arches a brow, confused. His eyebrows are narrowing, as always when I talk. I grab him by the arm, "You're not jumping; you're *flying*."

"Creature, don't you fucking dare, don't you–" He tenses over my hold. I know he's infuriated.

I push him out of the plane, forcing him to shut his mouth. His attempt to escape my execution fails. A roar of dark laughter floods my ears as I prepare to jump with my equipment and rifle.

"Asshole!" He screams into the mic as he descends. I can barely decipher his yelling anymore; now it's my turn to fly.

PRETEND

After we landed, I took out a target on the most wanted list. Anyone who's a high-value target has committed tragically evil crimes. Another successful secret mission has been completed. Now, we were sent to assist in Overwatch.

That's what most of my missions consist of as a Navy SEAL sniper.

Thunder erupts, striking the earth's core and reverberating through my body.

I can feel the lightning strike in my bones, vibrating as it shields the sound of my sniper going off, and another bad guy falls to the floor.

I hum the same tune as I look through my crosshairs to verify the target has been eliminated. He's dead. Half of his head has fallen off, and an RPG falls to the street. Ten marines were saved tonight because I don't miss...ever. I see everything. Sniping has always come naturally to me. I passed Sniper School with flying colors, graduating at the top of my class.

Rain patters my masked face, lightning bolt after lightning bolt, and the world thunders like a damn celebration. Death is happy. Another soul he gets to guide to hell.

My black mask has half of a smile and sharp teeth engraved as a design. It covers the scars on my face. There are more scars on my body that my uniform disguises.

It's late at night, and Marines are on their way out of a dangerous village that should have been evacuated months ago. I'm not surprised there are still threats that linger, waiting to take them out.

"Hey, Creature."

Slaughter calls out from behind me. He's my spotter, making sure no one comes up from behind me as I look for threats, scouring and watching these men vacate safely. I'm their eyes in the sky.

I turn my head for a second, giving him a bored expression through my eyes, unamused to carry on conversation.

"Look, man, I know you probably don't like me. Everyone's been giving me the cold shoulder since I kind of overstepped with Ari. But—"

I cut him off, scoffing.

"You did overstep with the girl. You crossed a line, loverboy. You're lucky Grim granted you mercy because I wouldn't have." I spit, readjusting my sniper rifle and looking into the scope.

He grows quiet and shifts in his spot in the corner of the rooftop.

Entering the military did something to me. Like it does to all of us who make it through, even more so making a SEAL team, we're all bonded in a brotherhood of blood, sweat, and tears. We fight for our fucking lives together, creating unbreakable bonds. We always have each other's back, no matter what, even when it comes to who we share our private lives with.

You just don't cross lines when it comes to wives or girlfriends. And Slaughter did.

"Look, I don't give a shit about drama. I could care less where any of you guys put your dicks. All I'm saying is, learn what loyalty means." I scold him.

"I do know what loyalty means." He spits back with rage. His tone is rising, and he's on the defensive end. "It's complicated with Ari. I've been there since Paul passed away. I shared my condolences to her and her mother on the day Paul Alvarez was buried when Grim couldn't even face them. I kept the promise we all made since day one. And I don't fault Grim for that. *I'm just saying.* He couldn't look them in the eyes, and I understood why. Someone had to face them, *and I did*. And that's when I met her. I love Ari. I always will. I made the same promise Grim did. Paul's team and our team promised to watch over his family." He pauses after inhaling a sharp breath. "But I'm moving on even if it hurts. It's not an excuse for my actions this past year, but I've apologized to both of them. Grim hasn't talked to me since the military ball, really, and I know I fucked up." He pauses, choking up. "I— I know I did." He stutters. I can tell he's fighting the urge to spill his emotions over his raspy voice.

I roll my eyes.

It's getting too emotional on this rooftop.

"No need to get all sappy on me, Bane. I truly don't give a shit. You'll learn sooner or later that love doesn't exist." I tell him as I watch Marines make their last rounds, vacating the village, that it's about time for Kane and I to leave as well.

"Slaughter." I address him over my shoulder, clearing my throat. "Your mistakes don't define who you are. It is what you do after you make them that matters."

I can't see Slaughter anymore, but I know he's having a moment. Because of this, I don't involve myself with getting attached to any girl. Grim is good at his job for a reason, and so am I. Emotionless creatures, strong-willed and dedicated to our careers.

But he gave in to his now wife and the life of a family man.

I will not. *Not ever.*

"Fuck, it's raining hard," Clark chimes in from my side, changing the tone of the conversation. Clark is a Navy SEAL on Zeke Akana's team. He's assisting Kane in giving me cover and joining the overwatch.

Chills prick at my skin, and I'm tempted to shiver. Something doesn't feel right.

Thunder strikes in the distance. The rain gets louder and more persistent. Strong winds hit my face, and I swallow the ominous dread on my shoulders.

Something is about to happen. I can feel it.

I've always had this sixth sense. I can sense if danger is about to unfold. I can tell if someone is good or bad. Just by looking at them and when they speak it just confirms this weird ability I have. And right now, alarm bells are going off, and I'm searching for it.

"How's the weather up there, boys?" Grim asks through comms.

"Sunny with clear skies." I sarcastically remark with a chuckle. Rain continues to fall harshly, and lightning strikes in the distance, flashing the village and Marines like a camera going off with a blinding flash.

"The rain isn't letting up," Lopez responds in the mic. Cobra and Texas are somewhere down there with the Marines.

Zeke and Kane engage in a conversation about the superbowl and who they think will win, and I'm tuning everyone out because I'm on high alert, looking at other streets, buildings, and trees. Anything.

I shift my scope, and my heart begins to pound, but still. I'm calm.

"Something's wrong," I whisper.

Kane and Zeke stop laughing and slowly move into silence.

"Nothing is wrong. We're almost done here, mission accompl–" Zeke begins but doesn't finish.

PRETEND

A loud pop sends my heart sinking. I know this sound too hauntingly well. A shot has been fired, and it's not from us. A Marine goes limp and falls to the ground, screaming in agony, causing chaos to spread. Everyone raises their rifles, and Kane hisses behind me, "What the fuck just happened?" Everyone covers while I clutch my sniper, trying my hardest to find the threat.

"We've got contact!" Grim shouts.

The way the Marine fell...I know what sound this is, and it's from another sniper.

"Everyone, take cover!" Zeke shouts. The marine holds onto his nearly severed leg, blood pouring out of his wound, and it leaves a bright red trail as he gets dragged to safety by Rooker.

I get to work, holding my damn breath, investigating every possible location.

"Where is this guy? He has to be far. It sounded far away." Kane asks from behind me, panic laced in his tone.

"I'll find him...I always find them." I deadpan. I'm focused, and the whole world gets tuned out. I can't hear the rain anymore. I can't hear the screams of an injured marine or the shouts of leadership.

I can't hear anything but my even-paced breathing.

As promised, I find him.

I see the enemy sniper. Yards away on another rooftop, and I grit my teeth. He's hiding underneath a built-in tent that blends in with the night and building. He has his sniper pointed at the marines below, smirking confidently, with his hand on the trigger about to take another one of the marines out, or he's going to finish the job. He's holding his breath and has his finger on the trigger, but so do I.

I send it.

The rifle recoils into my shoulder, thunder striking, and the silencer stops the ringing of what you would typically hear once a non-muzzled shot is fired into a warzone.

My eyes never leave his body. A flash of red sprays everywhere around him, and his rifle immediately falls to the ground along with his spiritless flesh and bones.

Humming the same tune, I always do when I get a kill confirmed, I whisper into the mics, "Target eliminated."

"Why do you hum the same song?" Kane asks softly, barely decipherable over the rain and thunder.

I tilt my head to the side and crack my stiff neck.

"Maybe one day, I'll share the story with you, loverboy."

"Great job tonight. I can't believe you found that sniper. You saved all those men tonight." Admiral Ravenmore crosses his fingers, intertwining them as he leans in his chair.

The mission is over. A job well done.

"Because of you, that marine who was shot gets to live another day. They all do."

I nod, not sure what to say. I'm not good at these things. I stand in a small office room in front of his wooden desk with neatly piled paperwork and one photo framed of him and his wife. We're back on base and returned safely after taking fire. I stand in my uniform, my half mask on, and my hands crossed behind my back.

Fuck, I'm tired. My uniform is still soaked from all that rain.

"Just following orders, sir…how is he doing?" I ask.

"He's stable. He might lose his leg, unfortunately."

I swallow the guilt forming in my chest. My hands turn into fists, and the demons start to scream. Even though I eliminated the threat, I failed. I failed because blood was spilled. I know shit happens, and it's out of my control.

But I like to be in control.

That's war.

Seven years in, four deployments later, I've learned and seen who the true monsters are in this world.

Humans.

They're people inflicting pain and evil on others because they can.

War is unforgiving, brutal, and, most of all, unfair.

"Grim left," He stands, walking towards a closed cabinet with a lock on it.

Damn, already? We just got back.

"I wasn't aware."

He plugs in a keycode, and the cabinet opens. A nice, tall, beautiful glass of bourbon sits there along with other whiskey bottles, sending my dry mouth-watering.

My favorite.

"Yeah, the team leader is gone. Grim is a family man now. He flew back home not too long ago after receiving word his wife was in labor, and he's rushed home. I still can't believe he married Paul Alvarez's sister." He shakes his head in disbelief. "Can you believe that shit? Danny Rider? Operator Grim Reaper, a husband and now father?"

I haven't known Danny Rider too long, but what I do know is he's the military's most lethal operator. Smart and cold, he embodies his operator name...*Death*.

After witnessing Kane get his shit kicked in at the military ball months ago, *which was one of my favorite highlights of the year*, I was unfortunately caught up on the drama that involved Paul, Ari, Danny, and Kane.

Paul was known as Operator Slayer. He was a Navy SEAL killed in action a few years ago during a mission that went wrong that Rider was in charge of. Operator Slayer's little sister, Ari, a nurse from Bloomings, has the reaper wrapped around her finger.

I take a deep breath, and my shoulders relax.

What does he want me to say?

I couldn't care less about Grim's personal life. Being married and having children has never piqued my interest.

Killing bad guys is what I live for.

I don't believe in love. I don't care for it.

Ravenmore pours himself a glass of bourbon with ice and then does the same with another one. He lifts it, offering me a drink. He clears his throat, waiting for me to take it.

"Thank you, sir,"

"It's well deserved after taking out multiple targets tonight. The sniper that never misses needs a drink." He collides his drink with mine. The glasses chime, and a smooth burn rolls down my throat in seconds. Ravenmore does the same, finishing it on two gulps.

Macallan Bourbon is my favorite.

"I called you in for a reason."

Another mission? Another evil that needs to be hunted?

I'm always game.

"What is it, sir?"

"I'm like the rest of you all. I like to keep my personal life private. Family is sacred, and as you're well aware, it's insinuated when you join special operations." He serves himself another glass of bourbon. "I have a daughter. She's in intelligence, and she's on a list. Now, Grim was my number one choice. But he's...not available. He told me to go fuck myself pretty much when I asked. He's a changed man now that he's married with twins."

"Where is this going, Ravenmore?" I retort, impatience riddled in between my words.

"She is set to deploy...and I need you on a different kind of assignment."

Shit.

I don't like this.

As Ravenmore explains what he needs from me, I know he's abusing his power by assigning me this kind of task. And because I'm a workaholic, I never say no.

2

Daegan

I'M BACK IN NORTH Carolina, where I'm stationed for the time being, to work with SEAL Team Executioners. The best of the best Navy SEALS as the head sniper on the team.

I don't like being home; the noise gets loud, but it gives me an opportunity to visit my mother's grave.

After landing in North Carolina, I went straight to her tombstone. I sat there for an hour, and instead of placing her favorite flowers, I placed her favorite chocolates.

Margaret Hannibal

Died on Valentine's Day.

Every year since I became a SEAL, I do the same thing. I visit her and tell her all about what war is like, what I've seen, and how evil the world can be.

My mother had postpartum depression after having my little sister but never sought treatment. My father discouraged it and said to seek God instead.

PRETEND

Everyone saw her in a bad light. Everyone in my mother's family treated her like she was overdramatic, ungrateful, and idiotic for feeling that way after she gave birth to my baby sister. She didn't ask for it. She didn't ask her mind to turn into a prison she couldn't escape.

She killed herself. And all my life, I resented her for it. How could she leave me? How could she be so selfish as to leave her children and husband? How could she be that cruel?

I stare at the wall in the dark.

"I think I get it now, Mom." I laugh out loud to myself with no one around but a dark room in my lonely one-story house.

No one will want me like this. A man full of scars. The scars on my skin and the ones engraved into my soul.

Ever since I was tortured, these thoughts haunt me from time to time. I don't think about it too much, but they're there.

I understand my mother better now.

I get that you can be in so much pain that you want it to end. To become so numb with zero percent chance of hope, it'll go away.

You just feel so fucked and alone.

Nobody talks about how lonely it feels when you come back home after what you've experienced at war.

Death after death.

And when you think you've seen it all, you haven't.

"You weren't alone, Mom. You had me. You had me, Mom...you had me."

You had me.

You weren't alone.

You were strong.

You weren't alone.

I wonder what she would think about.

What were the last thoughts that drove her to kill herself?

Mental illness is as real as any other illness, and it ate my mother alive...because she felt like she couldn't get help. She felt like if she sought help, she would have gotten her children taken away from her.

I wish there were more awareness and empathy for women who experience postpartum depression.

Sometimes, I do get angry at her for taking her life, but at the same time, I get it.

I fucking get it now.

She was in pain, she was lost, she was so far gone that she felt like killing herself was the only escape from the pain. She didn't mask her pain with anything. One day she said it was enough and slit her wrists.

I was five years old. Five. And I remember that day, every single detail of the day my mom was no more, from the moment I woke up until the moment I fell asleep that night. Every single detail.

I remember pouring myself cereal that morning because, for the first time, she was still in her room. I thought it was odd but didn't think much of it. So, I served myself breakfast. I imagined she was still sleeping. But then I got this weird feeling like something was wrong. I acknowledged that gut feeling when she hadn't stepped foot outside her door past noon. She hadn't checked up on me yet. When lunchtime came around, all the morning cartoons were over, and my father came home.

PRETEND

My father rushed through the front door, swinging it open with massive force, making a hole in the wall. I sat by my piano, and I stopped mid-play. He ran to their bedroom down the hall, and all I could do was listen.

I heard his erratic shouting, calling her name over and over again...and all I could do was play music and hum. My mother does that when she's sad, so I do it too.

Minutes later, lots of police officers barged in, and I still continued to play my piano.

Minutes later, my mother was carried out on a stretcher, blood falling onto the floor profusely from her wrists as someone was on top of her, performing compressions on her chest.

In those few quick seconds of getting wheeled out of the house, I saw the origin of the blood.

Slashes on her wrist, blood dripping down onto the wooden floors in a trail. Every time, the medic pushed on her chest. Her arms would jolt like she was being electrocuted, sending blood flying everywhere.

My father held his cross the entire time as he walked with the paramedics. He prayed to God, reciting a handful of prayers, begging Him to revive his wife. His pale skin was evident. He held his cross so tight that his knuckles were white and his palms bright red. I thought he was going to make himself bleed from how tight he was holding it.

He cried uncontrollably, utterly unaware that I saw everything. Unaware that his son was playing the piano, they left me alone in the living room.

I continued to play, not registering what had just happened. I was scared, confused, and, most of all, oblivious to my mother's actions as a child.

The sun had just set, and the living room began to darken with ominous shadows, but I couldn't stop playing. Something about music calmed me, even when I was all alone.

Minutes later, my neighbor came rushing in. Her blonde hair was tucked back in a ponytail. She was wearing a red kitchen apron, most likely cooking dinner for her own family.

She bent down so we were face to face. Her cheeks were damp from crying, but I could not stop playing. She grabbed my hands and forced me to stop playing, which only angered me. And with red eyes, she searched for mine.

"Are you okay?" She asked me with a shaky voice and forceful smile. Her mascara was smudged underneath her blue eyes.

"Where's my mom? Is she going to be okay?" I asked with a trembling voice. She's forcing me to ask the questions I was trying my hardest to avoid.

I wanted her to come back and tell me that my mother was coming back, that she was going to be okay, and that she was going to play the piano with me and we'd hum music together.

Mrs. Rivers held my hands in her palms and gave me a gentle squeeze. She was always kind and baked cookies for me and my best friend. She would let me go over and play with her son every weekend.

Mrs. River's fake smile fell down so fast at the mention of my mother, and I knew right then and there that my mother was gone.

I'm humming the same song my mother would to me when her episodes would come on.

I'm staring at my bedroom wall while one of my favorite movies, *The Devil's Advocate,* end credits flow down the screen.

Paint it black plays on the screen.

PRETEND

The tune I sing when I shoot and kill bad guys. If I can't hum it out loud, it's in my head because my mother would do this.

She would sing to herself in an effort to calm her anxiety. That habit has clawed into me. I don't sing, but I'll hum tunes whenever I need to deescalate the turmoil in my head.

We were sent home after another well-done mission and deployment, but I'm ready to return.

Fortunately for me. I've been placed on a special mission, and I've been doing extra homework that keeps me busy and intrigued.

My hand tenses up; there's one bullet in the chamber, and my fingertip slides onto the trigger gently. I don't know why I'm holding my gun, but I think it's a part of me always to have something on me, ready to defend myself…even when I'm home.

Like if, at any moment, someone will bust open my door and try to kill me.

The sounds of explosions, bullets spraying, bombs going off, dying kids screaming, and blood splattering echo into my mind.

"Another day, another scar."

Those words are in my head every fucking day.

The visuals and sounds of evil, the darkness, the stress. The layers of war interrupt and overload my brain like a plague without a cure.

Even with what I've experienced, I'm still addicted to multiple things.

I'm addicted to war, the adrenaline it gives me to work, to defend and protect, and take bad guys out. I'm addicted to numbing the darkness that creeps in with bourbon, cigarettes, sex, and painkillers.

But then my phone buzzes, snapping me out of the dark thoughts I always get consumed by when I return home. Exhaling the intense breath I've been holding, I look at the television, and it's gone black. It only runs black when I haven't been flipping through channels or touched the remote after thirty minutes.

Fuck.

How long have I been holding this gun, staring at the wall? I swear I blinked, and time flashed by.

I drop the gun, placing it on my thigh, turning the safety back on.

My phone chimes again, and I give in. I checked my missed notifications and was unsurprised to see Kane on the screen. I tolerate Kane. He's the one I talk to most on the team. I hardly speak, so that's saying something.

It's the group chat I'm in:

> Kane: Whispers?

Whispers is a popular strip club in downtown Bloomings. Service members tend to occupy the lounge very often. It's known for that.

Two minutes later,

> Kane: Phantom of the Opera, you there, bro?

> Me: Already miss me? I'm flattered.

> Lopez: I miss you *bebecito*. Come out to Whispers tonight. Let's celebrate another fucking job well done.

> Me: Fine, I'll come out to play. Only if we stop by El Devine first.

3
Alessia

Present Day

I SIP MY ICED coffee while I flip through my romance novel. I'm sitting at a table in front of the window at Chrome Beans. A small indie coffee shop that calls my name every time I need alone time or a break from the chaos in my head.

It's eight at night, and while I read, the smell of fresh coffee and baked pastries helps calm my nerves after another busy day at work. It's not too busy at Chrome Beans, but it's not slow by any means. I spot a few college students typing away research papers or studying hard on their laptops and groups of friends here and there chatting away.

Twenty minutes into reading, my phone pings, and my heart skips a beat. A part of me hopes it's Jack telling me he's going to cook dinner tonight or asking me why I'm not home yet. He's been acting a little more aggressive than usual, and I'm hoping this will be some type of start to change the tone of our relationship.

The distance feels like a breath of fresh air in a way.

> Unknown: Why the sad face?

Confusion sets in as I narrow my brows at my brightened phone screen. It sits on top of the table before me, and I re-read the text for a few seconds. Gripping my book tight in my hand, I study it.

What an odd thing to say from an unknown number. I grab my phone slowly, dragging it among the wood, and look around to see if it's Jack playing a weird joke on me.

But nothing is out of the ordinary in the calm scenery surrounding me. I even look outside the clear windows of Chrome Beans but see nothing but cars driving by in the darkness and people in their own bubbles as they walk the sidewalk.

This text...something about it sends a chill up my spine.

Is someone...*watching me*?

I shake myself out of that eerie thought.

Sometimes, I'll get texts that say *hi* or something random, but this feels too real. Too personal. It's too thought out because usually when I get random texts or calls, there's a number attached to it. But this is different. I hold my screen, still staring at the text with an unrecognizable number. It just says unknown.

> Me: Who is this? I think you have the wrong number.

I quickly tap my response and hit send, and I'm not sure if that was the best idea, but something inside me was urging me to reply. Usually, I ignore messages because they're just wrong numbers looking for the wrong person.

PRETEND

"Alessia!"

A familiar voice calls out for me, a voice that belongs to a Navy SEAL.

I look up to find Zeke Akana entering Chrome Beans, still in his uniform like he just got off work. He has a wide smile pulling at his lips. His dark hair is cut short, and he's clean-shaven. His dark brown eyes light up when he spots me sitting two tables away from the door. I return the smile with an awkward, shy one.

Zeke and I have been friends for years. He's been flirting with me for two of them, and recently, his persistence has a new edge to it. It might be because he hasn't seen Violet since she returned to Texas.

We became friends when Ravenmore hosted a BBQ for my high-school graduation party, and that's where I met SEAL Team Executioners Paul Alvarez and his team. Paul Alvarez died almost two years ago, but his imprint is still felt throughout the community.

My heart sinks as another dreadful familiar face follows behind Zeke.

Frankie.

Frankie is an ex-sailor who had multiple violations in his short career and was thrown out of the Navy.

We went to high school together, and somehow, he's weaseled his way into finding a friendship with Zeke.

There's a reason why I cringe whenever he's in the same vicinity as me. He's harassed me multiple times whenever we catch ourselves at El Devine at the same time.

They both stalk towards me, and my heart thumps against my rib cage. Frankie has a creepy grin on display. He's balding, with a few strands of hair left, and he is wearing a baggy jacket and jeans.

I close my book, ready to leave, wanting to get as far away from Frankie as possible. I'm sure he won't try anything publicly, especially in front of Zeke. Still, I wouldn't put it past him to try.

"Zeke. What's up?" I scoot out of my chair, grabbing my things slowly. "I was just leaving."

I startle him unintentionally. He pauses, stopping merely a meter away from me, with his hands ready to help me in any way I need.

"Leaving already?"

"Yeah..." I quip faster than my tongue can keep up. "I gotta get home. I was just stopping by for a quick coffee."

They both continue to watch me, and I take a step forward, but Zeke gets in front of me, blocking me from the doors.

"You look sad. Why the sad face? Trouble in paradise again?" His question throws me off. A whip of deja vu hits me, and a frown replaces my shy smile. Whoever this unknown person is asked me the same thing.

What a coincidence.

He knows about Jack, and he's always held a slight jealous cloud over my relationship. I've opened up to him about past arguments drunkenly at El Devine—something I regret doing.

"Oh, uh," I shrug, "I've got a lot on my mind. I'm getting deployed, but I'm sure you know that. We'll be working together the last time I checked."

"Right... We leave in just a few days. I'm looking forward to it. It's your first deployment, right?" Zeke finally moves, and I can feel Frankie's eyes burning holes in my back. Zeke holds open the door for me at Chrome Beans.

It is my first deployment. I went through multiple schools to get to this point in my career. Jumping through several challenging hoops, and I'm excited to do my job. At the same time, I'm well aware of the dangers and risks. The brutality of war has my nerves in knots, but I'm confident about what I signed myself up for.

"Yup," one foot is outside, ready to dart out to my car, but I turn to give Zeke a proper goodbye. He doesn't deserve the cold shoulder I'm giving his friend.

"Are you going to El Devine before we head out? You know one last party?" He asks as he puts his hands in his pockets. I shrug.

Gabe asked me the same thing earlier. Gabe is the owner of El Devine and used to be a Navy SEAL but medically retired two years ago. After he retired, he opened up his own business, and that's when El Devine was born. It sits about five minutes from the Navy base, and sailors and marines are about 90% of its customers.

"Maybe." I chirp, trying to hide how uncomfortable I'm feeling. Frankie's dark eyes turn into slits, and I'm internally cringing. "I gotta go, I'll see you later, Akana." I pretend Frankie is nonexistent and leave. Zeke waves me off and makes his way to the nearest barista.

My phone buzzes again, and I dare to check it as I get to my car.

> Unknown: Just a ghost on the wall.

What the hell?

When I get to my car, I look up from my phone. There's a bouquet of marvelous flowers tucked into the windshield wipers. They're all black daisies like they've been painted that way, except one bright yellow in the center, untouched and glowing against the others.

"Let's fuck." He whispers into my ear, cold liquor breath lingers into my nose, and I groan in response. I already know who it is. My eyes are still closed, and I'm annoyed he's waking me up before I have to meet with Ravenmore.

"Jack...no. Please. I have to be up in—" I glance at the clock on my nightstand, opening one eye and staring at bright white digits.

2:12 am

"I have to be up in a few hours to see Ravenmore. Please stop."

But my college sweetheart boyfriend of three years doesn't, as always. He keeps pushing my boundaries and not in the ways I desire. I'm on my stomach when I feel his hands snake into my bottoms, pulling both my underwear and shorts off all the way down to my ankles. He yanks them off aggressively from my toes, and the clothes fall to the floor. I inhale sharply, my mind still blinded by sleepy fog. His intense demands forced my senses to come alive. His moves are rooted in the fierce salacity he exhilarates.

He's never done this before, and usually, this is something I've been wanting to explore...but not tonight.

I feel his chest on my back, his hardened length on my ass, trailing it down to my entrance. He stops when he finds my pussy, and I hold onto my bedsheets, preparing for the painful intrusion. I scrunch my white blankets into my palms until my knuckles match the color of my silk bedsheets, and then I shut my eyes tight.

PRETEND

"Babe...Alessia. I have to give you a proper goodbye." He bites my earlobe, and I grind my teeth, irritated...but most of all hurt.

He knows I'm getting deployed.

"Don't, Jack. Let's just sleep. We already said 'goodbye' this afternoon," I beg. Even though I didn't want to. I don't have a sex drive these days, but either way, I gave in to him, bending me over the living room couch after dinner. The stress of work and the upcoming deployment has me wound tight, and I can't think of anything else lately but work. Either way, despite my dry mindset with sex, I gave in to him, letting him fuck me before he left for his friend's place earlier. He's just now returning home, drunk. As usual on Friday nights.

"Please, stop," I continue to plead with his drunken capacity, but my words fly over his head and into the thick night.

He doesn't stop. He ignores me, kissing my shoulder three times before his lips disappear.

"Let me say goodbye again." He growls, unable to take my rejection with patience.

I really don't want to fight with him, so I look at him over my shoulder and nod.

He grabs my waist, digging his hands onto my skin so tight, so drunkenly. I whimper from the unwanted pain. I love pain with my pleasure...just not right now, and lately, not from him. He pushes me up until I'm on my knees, bent over...still holding onto the bedsheets, and I close my eyes.

Then he pushes himself into me.

"Fuck, I'm going to miss this tight pussy," he moans.

I close my eyes tighter and let my mind drift into a different place while he abuses my body in the way he wants. Then, just like that, I'm in a different place of peace. The beach. The ocean is so blue in the summer. A warm breeze, not too hot. Not too cold. The sun shines bright, reflecting off the serene atmosphere. I smell fresh seafood and piña coladas by the water.

Yes...that's where I am right now.

I'm not being forced to have sex by my boyfriend so hard that the sound of his waist pounding against mine fills the air. My whimpers escape me with each pound of drunken lust he gives me. It all doesn't matter anymore. Just the sound of delusional waves and—

My eyes bulge, and Jack stops fucking me when the glass breaks from our bedroom window, and I scream.

The sound of glass shattering ends in seconds, and so does my stunned yelp from my lungs.

"Ah fuck! Something got my shoulder!" Jack shouts, holding onto his wound.

He gets off me, and I scramble underneath the bed sheets for cover. Jack hides on the other side of the bed, grabbing his jeans to cover himself, and tears that had formed five minutes ago roll down even harder.

"What the fuck was that?" Jack looks at his hand, and a few drops of red appear on his fingertips.

I look at my broken window and then to the floor, trying to wrap my head around our situation. Jack investigates to see if anyone is standing outside our third-floor apartment building, but...nothing. There's no way someone could be on our patio without entering our home first. There are no stairs and no ladder to our deck.

PRETEND

"Did someone throw something at our window?" Jack stands up and throws on his jeans. He runs a hand through his red hair, and I search for my clothes, dressing myself once again.

"I don't know..." I wipe my tears away and search for any object thrown inside our home, looking through the broken glass, but nothing.

Not a brick? A rock?

Then I spot a hole in the wall. My eyebrows arch, and I walk fast towards it, eyeing the destruction I'm most likely going to have to pay for someone to fucking fix because Jack will do a botch job if I let him.

I get closer, and my eyes circle.

"It's a gunshot."

But why didn't we hear it ring loud? Why didn't we hear a loud pop, like if it was fireworks on the Fourth of July during the summer?

It was quiet...*silenced.*

Whoever is held responsible for this gunshot has a silencer on their weapon.

"We have to move. Let's get out of the bedroom now." The thoughts sink into me, ringing alarm bells that this was not an accident.

"Someone shot at us?!" Jack shrieks, looking at the hole in the wall. He hovers over me shirtless, his lean frame on display in the moonlight.

Now that he's in close proximity, I notice he's still bleeding, barely. It looks like a scratch, his flesh grazed.

I decide to investigate further, digging my small fingers into the hole, and that's when I feel the culprit.

I pull out a fired bullet, my fingers shaking, unable to hold still. I twist in my palm.

"Who would do this?" I ask Jack before I take off into my living room. I grab my cell phone that was hooked, charging into the wall, and dial 911.

Jack hadn't always been this way with me, but lately, he was struggling and had been going out more with his friends, and God knows what he's up to with them that he's been coming home with liquor stained on his body.

Did he piss someone off?

I wanted to question him, but I didn't feel the need to start an argument at two in the morning.

"Fuck if I know babe." He rubs my shoulders before running his hands across his own elbows for comfort.

I relay our situation to the 911 operator and put my cell phone onto my kitchen counter, sighing frustrated. I run my hands through my long black curls, and the need for a hair tie screams at me. I rub my temples, massaging the bizarre jitters from minutes ago.

I just wanted to sleep before I was in front of Ravenmore's desk, staring into cold, vibrant green eyes...my mother's newest endeavor.

I always fall asleep early so I can at least get a minimum of six hours before bed. It's the military in me. My body has grown accustomed to early morning hours and falling asleep as soon as the sun vanishes.

"Call your dad too...Admiral Ravenmore, right? He'll know what to do." He tells me before he sits on the living room couch and texts away at his phone. Even with his girlfriend being in the military, Jack is clueless when it comes to titles, ranks, and how it works.

"It doesn't work like that. He's not a police officer."

My mother has been with her new husband for years now, but I refuse to acknowledge him as a father figure. I already have a dad.

PRETEND

"What about your mother? You can talk to her, right? I'm going to get some sleep before I have to go job hunting in the morning." Jack shuts off his phone and goes to the kitchen. He opens the first-aid kit and cuts open a broad bandage.

Oh, good. He can wake me up from my peaceful slumber and make me go back to sleep now that I'm up with adrenaline and violation.

"Okay," I give in, not wanting to argue with him. "And Ravenmore is not my dad. Please don't call him that. He's just Henry to me, and I won't worry my mother with this." I reach for my coffee and start making a fresh pot. It looks like I won't be getting any sleep, so I might as well stay up.

4

Alessia

I HEAD OVER TO Henry's building, or as the entire military likes to call him, "Admiral Ravenmore." He texted me earlier this week that it was urgent, and of course, I obliged. Ever since I joined the Navy, I have kept it professional with him. I avoid him as much as I can. So I head over, no questions asked.

Although, I thought it was weird because even though he just returned from overseas a month ago, he was also headed to Iraq with the Executioners.

Operators Grim Reaper, Bane, Cobra, and Texas were all very well known. They're Ravenmore's favorite most prized possession of a team. Wherever they went, he was right there. They were set to deploy, and if I wasn't mistaken, Grim had just taken out another most wanted high-value target. The man doesn't stop working, and rumors say his wife is well into her pregnancy.

I walk into the cold, rundown, ancient brick building, swinging the door open, and it's usually busy as hell. But not today. Sailors and marines walk in and out, but it's a Saturday, and everyone is at home—except me, except the Admiral.

I take off my cover because I'm in uniform. When you're in uniform, you're required to take it off when indoors. So I hold it in my hands, taking long strides toward the elevator in the center of the lobby. I reach for the black button, my finger an inch away, but someone beats me to it. Someone else's long masculine fingers press it before me.

I raise my eyebrows, and my mouth falls slightly open. I look to my left and see a man in a uniform, wearing a mask—an Executioner's mask—but I don't recognize him.

To my knowledge, they only wear masks on missions, so why is this man still wearing his?

It's not Grim. It's not Slaughter. It's not Rooker, and it's not that mischievous Texas cowboy, Lopez.

The button turns bright yellow, and I take a step back, creating space between the SEAL and me. I retract my finger and clear my throat nervously.

His frame looks familiar, but I can't pinpoint why. He's so tall he has to be the same size as Grim. But his eyes...his eyes make me question where I've seen him before, and then I realize I'm staring.

They're grey...almost white with hints of ice blue. It's hard not to notice the scars on his left eye. Marks that start at the top. It's above his eyebrow and goes down to his lower lash. Maybe even down to his cheek. But I can't tell behind the black fabric.

"Are you going up?" His deep voice asks me, and I hadn't realized the elevator doors had opened for us. His voice sends a quiver to my heart from how husky and unique it is.

I shake my head, tearing my gawking expression away from him like ripping off a band-aid embarrassingly.

"Uh—yeah."

He bows his hand so I can walk further in the elevator. My teeth sink into my bottom lip. I'm already acting like I don't get any social interaction and have my foot in my mouth.

He follows me into the metallic silver room with horrible dull yellow lighting and brown walls. Standing in front of the buttons, I wait for him to walk in before I press the fifth-floor button.

He enters, holding his hands behind his back, and walks to the back of the elevator.

The door closes, and I rest my hands at my side, still clutching my cap. I watch the number switch from one to two...then to three.

I blink, and the next thing I know, my body jolts with a forceful pull of gravity; the elevator sways vigorously for a split second, my balance getting thrown off. I fall right into the arms of the masked Navy SEAL. I was going to fall face-first into the doors before he grabbed my hand, pulling me into his chest. His right hand is on the railing of the elevator, and his other is securing me around my waist...almost protectively.

I let him hold me for a second longer as I try to catch my shaken breath. He smells...good. That's when I realized our unfortunate situation: The elevator stopped moving and won't open.

Oh, no.

Oh, hell, no.

"No, don't tell me we're trapped!" I start to panic frantically.

PRETEND

I let go of the stranger's hands and smooth my uniform down with my palms, collecting myself. I pick up my hat, that I dropped accidently, and walk closer to the doors.

"You're welcome, by the way." He says nonchalantly.

I hadn't thanked him for the impending doom of a bump on my face.

"Sorry, that was very rude of me. Thank you so much for saving my forehead." I breathe out jokingly, with a welcoming smile.

After pressing the emergency button several times, he walks backward into the corner, but no one is in this building besides Henry. There may be a few officers, but I doubt they'll answer the emergency button.

A short husky chuckle reverberates out of his throat, and it's so warm yet mysterious…and—

I have a boyfriend.

I have a boyfriend.

I. Have. A. Boyfriend.

"I don't do well with small spaces." This isn't good. Nausea slithers into my senses, and I can feel myself turn green at the thought of being stuck here for hours.

I get anxious with small rooms and spaces, even at doctors' offices or MRI machines. Having to be still in tight medical machinery always makes me nervous. Don't even get me started on planes.

"Don't worry, Valentine. They'll find us." The stranger reassures me.

My heart sinks, and my eyebrows crease inwards. I tear my eyes away from the elevator buttons and look at him leaning on the wall, one leg over the other and crossing his arms. I only see two light eyes piercing through my brown ones.

"How'd you know my name?"

I'm on edge after my apartment was shot at. The police didn't find any leads but advised us to stay at someone else's for the night. But with my busy deployment schedule, I'm hopeful the police will find out who it is so Jack can sleep in our bedroom peacefully.

He doesn't say anything in return. He doesn't have to. His eyes say it all when they dip down to my chest and then up to my lips...

The way he studied my chest and lips sent a wave of unfamiliar heat I hadn't felt in a long time from a man who hides behind a black mask. So, I do what I do best when I get overwhelmed by something that's out of my routine: I hide. I pretend like it's not happening.

I look down at my chest and realize how stupid I am.

My name tag sits below my collarbone on my uniform.

Valentín

"Oh, duh. It's...Valentín by the way."

"Sure." He nods, and the skin around his lashes creases, indicating a sinful smile that creeps into his features. I just know it.

"Ms. Valentine." He finishes darkly.

5
Alessia

After sending Henry a few texts letting him know I was stuck in the elevator, he rounded up a team to get the elevator working again.

It would just take an hour or two.

This is excruciating.

I didn't know what to say or do to the stranger next to me, so I started reading an E-Book to pass the time. As I finished another chapter, it dawned on me.

I'm reminded I'm trapped in a small space.

I am trapped in an elevator with vaguely mysterious eyes that look like I was transported into a frozen winter wonderland.

He hasn't said a word to me since calling me Valentine. We both chose opposite corners and settled into our own bubbles of seclusion while we waited for our rescuers.

My mind drifted to Iraq and how I would be getting space from Jack and his drunken nights.

Thank God.

I love him—I do—but I know something is wrong. Maybe we can salvage it. Perhaps he'll change. I've been with him since I was eighteen, and I'm afraid of losing him entirely. A part of me wants to give it more time, and maybe our relationship will grow stronger with space.

I realize I'm no longer concentrating on my phone or the story about a small-town romance. So, I dare to take a peek at the SEAL in the corner.

The first thing I see is his combat boots trailing up to his pants and his thick, muscled thighs.

Then I see his hands. They're big hands, with veins that make their presence well known all over. He fiddles with a bullet. Tracing it in between his fingers, still standing in the corner.

That's weird.

Then I tip my head slightly up, and immediate heat flashes across my cheeks like I was just caught with my hands in a cookie jar on a Christmas night.

He's staring straight at me. I can't see his face, but his eyes tell me everything. He's watching me like I'm something to study.

I blink fast, pretending I wasn't staring back at him, and I purse my lips, returning to the E-book on my phone.

"Why so red, Valentine?"

Shit.

I swallow as if that will hinder me from what I truly feel inside.

"It's hot in here," I lie. My response came out faster than I intended it to. "And it's Valentín." I correct him once again.

I readjust my position, sitting crisscross.

PRETEND

But am I really lying? There's no AC in here, and something about the stranger next to me has me wanting to fan myself.

Then my eyes circle when I see his name tag.

Hannibal

Hannibal is also the name of the operator who escaped when he was a prisoner of war. The one that hasn't taken off his mask since his capture.

Operator Creature.

The sniper with the longest distance shot ever recorded. The operator that never misses when he shoots. He hasn't missed one shot since joining the Navy...*maybe ever*.

"Are you Daegan Hannibal? Like *THE* Hannibal. Operator Creature?"

"I don't know Valentine. Am I? Do I look like a creature to you?"

He says it wickedly, and I can't tell if he's testing me or if I genuinely mistook him for another Navy SEAL. "Technically, we are all creatures by definition," he finishes.

"Oh, I'm sorry. I just thought..." I shrug, looking away from those silver eyes, and I go back to my phone, typing my passcode in promptly.

A few minutes pass by with silence as our only companion. Before I know it, he sits next to me, intruding into my space.

I look at him incredulously, taken aback by his boldness. He's invading my haven of a boundary, and I don't know what to say or do.

A small voice in my head tells me I like it. Another voice tells me to throat-punch him.

"Umm?" Is the one word I can muster out of my nervous lips.

Then he pulls out a knife, and my breath hitches in my chest. He holds it in his big hand, and I see the shiny blade glimmer across the poor elevator lighting.

My chest heaves up and down, my pulse thundering in my neck at the thought of this man stabbing me.

Is he going to kill me? What the fuck?

"What the hell are you doing?" I ask him, frightened, but for some reason, I can't move. Because even though I don't know him, the goodness in my heart believes he wouldn't do something so stupid, like murder the Admiral's stepdaughter on a Naval base. In a fucking elevator.

Then again, it's perfect for him because I have nowhere to go in between these four walls.

But then he moves his knife closer to my neck, and I regret not releasing the scream in my throat that bangs against my vocal cords. Then he leans in closer so we're now face to face. I can feel his cold, icy breath on my lips, his cologne so sharp it makes the pulsation in between my thighs come alive.

The way he's moving…it's dangerous. But not fatal.

He smells of cigarettes, cologne, leather, and more, but maybe it's just him. I'm flustered, scolding myself to stay still…but the sudden proximity draws me in more, making it hard not to shutter.

He stares at me the entire time, shades of grey-blue dilating as he moves the blade slowly through my hair strands like he's savoring every single second of being close to me. And it's so quiet I can hear my heavy breathing and the blade slithering through my hair. I didn't know a blade could be so loud.

Then, with a flick of his blade and his hands on a patch on my shoulder, he whispers darkly, "Irish Pennant."

He slices off the leftover linen on my uniform, and crimson flaming red erupts in my cheeks like a volcano at the sound of his deep voice.

His voice…it's enticing.

PRETEND

Damn him.

"Oh, uh, thanks." Finally gaining a blip of courage, I scoot away from him, looking down at my shoulder just as the elevator pings and starts to move to the same floor he chose.

Our destination.

I guess personnel managed to fix the elevator and get it moving. Perfect timing.

We both stand up, and I clear my throat, readjusting my hair back into a tight bun. After fixing my hair, I walk in front of him so I can look more presentable for the Admiral. Meanwhile, the masked man puts his knife back into his uniform and puts his hands behind his back.

Not creepy at all.

The elevator doors open a few seconds later, and I expect to walk alone to Ravenmore's office, but no...the creepy stranger in the elevator follows me.

He keeps a distance behind me, and I peek at him. He's watching me so intensely that I feel I'll disappear.

"Are you following me?" I ask him, not bothering to keep my gaze on him as I get closer to Ravenmore's office.

"Maybe you're following me."

I flinch at his response. Pursing my lips, my eyebrows pinched together, I shake my head dubiously.

"Why don't you answer questions with yes or no's?! Like a normal person?!"

There's a pause of silence, and I think I won at getting him to open up to me with an average answer, but then he says.

"Maybe I'm not normal."

Finally, I'm outside Ravenmore's office and take a deep breath before entering. I hate being around him. Just the thought of being around Henry Ravenmore makes my skin crawl.

I'm about to reach for the silver doorknob when the masked man twists it open, pushing the door and motioning for me to enter.

I look at him and give him a polite nod. "Thank you."

I walk into Henry's office and see his nose deep in paperwork. I know better than to call him by his first name when we're in uniform. We're both good at turning our personal relationships on and off when it comes to work and family.

One wall has bookshelves, and it smells like old wood and must. Photos and awards are framed all over, and one picture of my mother is on the wall. This man is completely dedicated to his military career. The last time I checked, he's been well in over twenty years. I don't know why he hasn't retired already.

"Valentín, how's my stepdaughter? Hopefully, you didn't go too crazy in that box." He takes off his reading glasses and slumps in the chair.

"I'm good, sir...just—" I turn my head, catching Hannibal in the corner of the room, looking at the admiral, with his hands behind his back, still. Looking professional, like he's listening in on a meeting or ready to take orders.

"What's going on? Why did you call me here? Why is...he here?" I arch a brow in Hannibal's direction.

"Yeah, about that...That's Daegan Hannibal. I'm sure you met him when you were stuck in the elevator." Ravenmore looks at Daegan in the corner. "Operator Creature. The newest asset to the Executioners."

So I was right!

Jerk didn't want to confess.

"Okay?" I murmur out slowly. "That still doesn't explain anything."

PRETEND

He shifts in his seat, both elbows now on the arms of the chair. He is looking like he's trying hard to bite his tongue and force out words.

"Your name popped up on a list." He says simply.

"What list?"

"Military intelligence. They found a list with names of people that Omar's army wanted to find...*to kill*. There was a mission not too long ago. Where we found HVTs in Georgia; while conducting this mission, we also stumbled across human traffickers. We've pissed a lot of people off lately. And to my surprise, there's an investigation surrounding the base. There might be service members that are involving themselves in human trafficking."

"And I'm on that list of people they want to traffic or kill?" I gasp.

He nods.

"What? How? Why?"

"I don't know, to be honest. My guess is that my name is on that list, and you are my stepdaughter. My step-daughter who wears a uniform. So, by association, they want you dead or taken as well. For some odd reason, you hold a high bounty. We're still trying to figure out why."

"What the hell?" My eyes circle when I realize I cursed in front of the Admiral. "Sorry, sir, won't happen again. But is this because of the stateside mission that the Executioners did?"

"Maybe. We don't know why evil people do evil things. At the end of the day, all we can do is try and save lives. *Your* life."

"But I have to be on a plane on the way to Iraq soon!"

"I know that. And you're going but...with Creature. He has been tasked with keeping you safe in terms of a personal security detail. Your mother wouldn't have it any other way."

"What?! Why? I'm not a politician. I'm not a general...or a high-ranking officer?" I stutter over my words, waving my hand in the air defensively, trying to point out all the reasons why this is a bad idea and he needs to rethink this.

"No, but you're a target, dammit!" Ravenmore loses his cool and slams his fist on the desk, and my mouth shuts closed. He's always had a bad temper.

"Someone has to watch over you while you do your job over there. And it's going to be him."

"But!" I continue to protest, shifting uncomfortably.

"It's done." He snarls. "Operator Creature will be watching over you until your deployment is over. It's not just the list, Alessia." He slips up when he addresses me by my name. "It wasn't just a coincidence that Operator Grim Reaper was ambushed and Operator Slayer's little sister was kidnapped."

"What are you talking about?" I cross my arms.

"Someone on *our side* betrayed us for that bounty's reward of money. I don't know who. It could be someone from Delta. Someone from the SEAL teams or someone who works in intelligence. It's under investigation. And if this person was able to turn in Ari and get Grim almost killed, they know what they're doing and how to do it. They're good. So," he knocks on the wood two times, "Operator Creature and Operator Bane have been placed on PSD for you, with Creature taking the lead."

PSD. Personal Security Detail.

This is all so much information, and I'm trying to wrap my head around it. You mean the man who held a knife to my neck just a few minutes ago? *Great*.

"Is all of this really necessary? Is all this because of what happened to my window last night?" My voice rises.

He flinches, and his head tilts to the side, confused.

PRETEND

"What happened to your window?"

Does he know? Should I tell him what happened? If I do, my mother will only worry about me more, and I don't want that.

I change the subject. I look down at my boots and fiddle with my fingers, swallowing nervously.

"Nothing..." I mumbled under my seething breath. "It's a six-month deployment," I counter, reminding him of my orders. "Surely, Daegan's qualifications are needed elsewhere."

Ravenmore opens his mouth, but the deep, crisp, masked stranger replaces his voice.

"I'm aware," Daegan mumbles behind me, bored. I'm glad our family quarrel is keeping him very entertained.

"It'll be fine. You won't even know he's there. He has a reputation for acting like a shadow and his stealth of silence." He gives me a sarcastic smile, his green eyes flashing anything but comfort. "I would have had Grim babysit you but—sorry, not babysit, bodyguard you. But Grim is on leave for God knows how long, and I only want the best for you...someone I can trust. And I don't trust that vexatious cowboy. He has a reputation with...never mind, it's not important. So I'm assigning Creature."

I raise my hand, my index finger pointing up like I'm about to list about a hundred reasons why I don't need a babysitter, before Ravenmore quirks a brow, daring me to resist and disobey.

I snap my jaw closed.

"When does this start?"

Ravenmore studies me, then glances at the corner of the room, throws his glasses on the bridge of his nose again, and gives Hannibal a nod. "I'll send you a text with Creature's contact information since the deployment is coming up."

I pout, turning my lips into one flex to the left side.

"Am I dismissed?"

He nods, not looking at me, and I pivot my foot and head for the door. But then he stops me again.

"Oh yeah, cancel your initial travel plans. You're going on a plane to Iraq with the Executioners instead."

He says it so casually like it's not a big deal. It's like he's making this already so weird. But I guess I have to trust him. Maybe he feels like it's safer to be with them on the ride there.

Still, I don't like the idea of someone intruding on my privacy and whereabouts for six months.

"Now you're dismissed." Admiral barks out his order through a clenched jaw.

I bite my lip and walk toward the exit.

Creature salutes the admiral and holds open the door for me right after in one swift movement.

I glare at the ice-cold eyes before I stomp into the hallway, making my defiance known.

I decide to take the stairs this time, wanting to avoid being trapped in a small enclosed space again, not bothering to see if my 'bodyguard' is close.

As I descend the stairs, heat runs into my cheeks at the thought of people wanting me dead. On top of that, I'm being babysat like a child.

PRETEND

Are those the people that shot at my fucking window last night? Missing me completely? Was it an assassination attempt to send a message? Well, they have shit aim. They completely missed Jack and I.

What is my life right now?

"You couldn't even last ten minutes in an elevator with me without getting antsy. I want to see how scared you'll be on a plane ride that travels across the world," Hannibal coos behind me mockingly.

6

Alessia

THE WHOLE STUCK-IN-THE-ELEVATOR SITUATION and the conversation with my mother's husband about requiring a bodyguard made me livid.

Now, I'm taking a flight with a masked operator who doesn't say much, and when he does, it's sarcasm. He's always playing with a bullet or watching my every move. It'll just be the two of us on a flight, and I'm not looking forward to it.

The rebellious part of me wants to give him a hard time and test his patience because I would really be testing Ravenmore's patience. I can frustrate him through Daegan...

A light bulb turns on in my head, and my lips curve mischievously.

This airplane flight will be fun.

"Your flight is soon. I have orders to drive you there. You're mine starting the day of our plane ride."

PRETEND

I roll my eyes at him.

"I'm yours?" I spit mockingly. "Look, I don't need a babysitter. I'm good. In fact, more than good. I'm not a child. I can defend myself. We get mandatory training. I know how to keep myself safe. I can't believe I'm getting dragged into your guys' mess by getting put on that list." I point to my chest. "So to make these next six months run by more smoothly..." I pause, contemplating if I'm really going to offer him a proposition. "I won't tell him anything." I shrug. "You're free to do whatever the hell you do when we land in Iraq, and I'll be out of your hair. I'm giving you an out, Creature. Take it or...you'll regret it." I arch a brow, daring him to take the bait. I wait for him to give in even though he doesn't look the type. He has to want out of this assignment. I don't know any special operator who enjoys being away from their team.

"Are you giving me an ultimatum? Are you threatening me?"

I nod, smiling ear to ear. We're in the middle of the parking lot. I stopped walking to plead my case and offer him an option...so far, he's not taking the bait. The sunset shines directly in his ice eyes, and a flicker of unknown emotions flashes through them.

"I don't take kindly to threats," his voice is threatening.

I smirk, placing my hands on my hips. I lick my lips, followed by my teeth. He makes it so easy.

"What are you going to do about it? Punish me? Tell my step-dad?" I throw air quotes around, 'Dad.'

He stiffens, his eyes darkening.

I'm pushing him. I know I am.

He doesn't say anything.

I turn around on my heels, unlocking my car with my keys, and the car responds with two beeps.

He walks me to my Honda Sedan in just a few steps. He picks up his pace, steps in front of me, beats me to the door handle, and opens it for me.

"Thank you," I mumble through a locked jaw. I slide into my car, sitting down in the driver's seat. I reach for the handle to close it, eager to speed my way home from this forsaken building. Away from Ravenmore, who just placed Creature on an unnecessary assignment. Like if I'm a rebellious teenager throwing a tantrum. If he thinks this will win him points with my mother, he's dead wrong. If he thinks this will make up for whatever distress he's caused in their relationship, he's got another thing coming.

"Sorry Valentine. But you're my newest assignment. I never break the rules. I never question the Admiral. I always follow orders, no questions asked. Those orders tell me that Alessia Valentine, age 24, will be mine for six months starting the day of her deployment. Get used to it," He snarls, his eyes flash with anger.

He slams the door on me, and my mouth falls open. I pout the entire time, crossing my arms over my chest. I watch his massive frame stalk away from me. He reaches into his pocket and walks away. Something in the way he moves has me entranced. God, even the way he walks should be illegal. He pulls out a pack of cigarettes, disappearing deeper into the parking lot, and I no longer have sights on him.

I'm seething.

My first deployment shouldn't go like this. I know it's for my safety, but I don't want it to look like I'm getting special treatment. I worked hard to get to the position that I'm in today.

PRETEND

Screw Ravenmore and screw Creature even more because although I can't truly see him, just his eyes have a magnetic effect on me, drawing me in and deterring my anger. The way his eyes say more than his mouth, taunting me to unravel him one layer at a time, like a challenge I can't say no to.

My car engine rumbles on, and Lana Del Rey plays throughout the speakers. I drive out of the parking lot, thinking of all the ways I'm going to annoy Creature.

As I drive home, my phone rings.

Ella Winters pops on the screen, and I quickly tap the green button. She works with me in military intelligence, and we're both on the same orders. I can't wait to tell her what orders Creature fell under. I wonder if she knows about him.

"What's up, Winters?"

"Happy birthday, Alessia!" She exclaims with giddiness. I roll my eyes, and I smile. "I was wondering if you're going to El Devine tonight. Bailey wants to see us before we deploy." She gets straight to the point. Music blasts in the background as she mentions our other best friend, who bartends at the country bar. "A whole bunch of people from work are headed there tonight for one last night of fun before we deploy. What do you say? Pick you up at nine?"

I smile, "Sounds like fun. Count me in. I need a drink after this morning." I shake my head, gripping the steering wheel tighter than usual.

"Oh, no, what happened?" She lowers the music in the background.

I turn onto my street, and seconds later, I'm parking in the driveway. Jack's home, surprisingly. His jeep sits on his side of the driveway. My stomach growls, aching for some food. I skipped breakfast this morning.

"I'll fill you in tonight," I sigh, turning off my car. We say our goodbyes as I pull the keys out of the ignition.

My phone pings, and it's Ravenmore. As promised, Daegan's and Kane's contact information stares back at me. I quickly add them to my contacts and get out.

I walk into my home; the TV is on, and the volume is unnecessarily loud. Jack doesn't acknowledge me. I frown as I make my way toward our bedroom. Jack is on his back on the couch, his legs crossed over. A movie plays across the screen, but his attention is on his phone screen. He types away, and there's a giddy smile on his face. His brown eyes were fixated with joy.

"I'm home," I announce.

"Oh, hey, babe!" He shuts his phone off. Still not acknowledging me, he turns his head to the side towards the TV. "Can you make me lunch? I'm starving."

He doesn't bother asking me about what Ravenmore wanted. I want to tell him everything. I need to tell him.

It's like I'm a ghost in my own home...and lately, I feel like one, too. I feel unseen by my boyfriend.

"Sure thing."

I walk into my bedroom and go straight for the laces on my boots. I sit down on my white bedsheets, but something unfamiliar catches my eye.

In the center of the bed sits a bouquet of flowers. They look just like the ones in my car. Maybe two dozen peonies and one bright pink one in the center.

PRETEND

I drop my phone just as fast as my heart falls to the pit of my stomach. Am I being watched? Can whoever this sick person is...*see me*?

I turn around, looking at my surroundings. The broken window is boarded up with wood. There's no way he can see me. It must be another wrong number or text message.

"Jack?" I rush out of the bedroom, tripping over my foot. I stumble, but I manage to regain my balance. I stomp toward him and get in front of the TV, blocking his vision.

"Are these from you?" I jolt the flowers in my hand.

"No?" he responds, clearly thrown off by how his brows pinch together and his tone laces with questions.

"I found these on our bed. How did you not know these were there? Weren't you home all day?"

"Yes, I—I mean no," he stutters. "I left for a bit to take the jeep for an oil change. Who is leaving you flowers? And how the fuck did it get in our house?"

Sweat coats my skin. Is this unknown person a problem?

"I don't know, but I'll find out."

7

Alessia

THE CLOSER I GET to those black entrance doors of El Devine, my boots hit the pavement with anticipation. I can almost hear the glass windows vibrate from the music and drunken chatter. It is a Saturday night after all.

As soon as I swing the door open to El Devine, I'm met with the usual bright neon cattle skull in the center of the bar. The TV in the corner shows a sports game, and country music is playing loud as cowboy hats and boots galore fill the small yet wide space.

One last night of fun with my friends before I'm on my way overseas.

I filled in Ella Winters on my stepfather, who ordered two SEALS on a "personal security detail" for me. She knows we need drinks.

I look around to spot Jack since he left the house before me. He told me he would meet me here because he was meeting his friends. He was too impatient to wait for me.

PRETEND

I walk forward, and a loud uproar of cheers and sounds is coming from the bar area. With Winters at my side, I can hear the scoff she spills as her pink lips form a smile. I follow her gaze, and my mouth drops open in disbelief as I soak in what's in front of me.

Slaughter and Hannibal have their shirts off.

Operator Bane and Operator Creature *have their shirts off.*

Daegan has a massive dragon tattoo that covers his entire back. Its wings spread out, and its mouth is open like it's about to breathe fire with about a hundred pointed sharp teeth. A pile of skulls on his lower back. It's a work of art. His back muscles are...captivating, to say the least. He's muscular but not too muscular, and— I need to look away.

I *must look away. But I can't.*

My eyes trail down, and I spot more tattoos.

He has another mythical creature on his ribs that starts from his chest. A Kraken with tentacles all over, holding onto an anchor. His left arm has a sleeve tattoo. I squint, trying to decipher what the symbols are, and it becomes clear when I spot a Cheshire Cat with a big, creepy, sharp-toothed grin on a tree branch.

'We're all mad here' in a smoke cloud in a funky font, just like the movie Alice in Wonderland. A Saint Michael, the archangel tattoo just below the Cat all over his arm to his wrist. His other arm is covered in spider and snake tattoos.

This man is defined all over, with a mass of muscles that clearly says he takes his physical fitness very seriously. I quickly examine Kane for a second, and it's not surprising he's extremely fit.

My lord, it's hot in here.

And then *Take My Breath Away* by Berlin starts to play, making the temperature skyrocket, and I want to throw my hat at it.

When they both turn to their side, I can see their faces. They lock hands, and it becomes clear what mischief they're up to tonight. It's an arm wrestling match.

Rider, Rooker, Lopez, and Zeke crowd around them with beer bottles in their hands. More men I don't recognize chant 'Creature', and others chant 'Bane.' Daegan and Kane both have aviator sunglasses on, and their skin is kissed deeply by the sun. This time...I can see part of Daegan's face.

This time, only half of his face is covered. A black half-mask that hides a layer of mystery.

My heart stops when I realize I get to see more of him.

He has a head full of thick strands. But not just any hair. Beautiful dark hair that's long but not too long. Their dark, wavy locks go down just past his ears. A dark beard that follows his jawline, surrounding his full lips and a face that has my legs screeching apart, wanting to welcome this flutter of lust that sparks.

Damn him because holy shit.

He's fucking hot.

I just dared this man earlier, saying the words like *punish me* in a parking lot during my short fit of rage.

And then he has the audacity to smile when he sees me—his enchanting lips curve, revealing straight white teeth with sharp canines.

He blinks, ripping his vision away from me, and goddamn, when he does that...an unfamiliar firestorm and butterflies swarm together around me like an unforgiving wave that's rolling through my chest. I thought these lost emotions were long gone.

But no.

They're here.

And it's like a part of me I thought had died, coming back to life. In that split second, I was hit with a shot of adrenaline stabbed straight through my chest.

I swing my gaze away from his overconfident wink and clear my throat. The loud music I tuned out regains its strength, and I unglue myself from that corner.

"Let's go find Jack," I plead, hooking my arm into hers and trying to pull her with me. But Winters doesn't budge; she keeps her brown cowboy boots planted onto the wooden floors.

"Wait, I want to see who wins." She grins, crossing her arms against her chest, and her eyes brighten. She's smiling a little too hard, but her eyes are stuck on Daegan.

I sigh, slumping in defeat, and I watch with her. I place my hands on my hips, my ring digging into my skin as I clutch my hips tight. We stand close together, and I'm trying to force myself not to care...but for some reason, the masked operator has me intrigued.

Daegan grins. His sharp incisors curve against his bottom lip and his biceps bulge as he flexes them. His veins stick out against his muscles as Kane applies pressure.

Kane's forehead is coated with sweat, his jaw twitches with stress, and he pushes down hard. His body shakes, and it's working. Daegan looks relaxed despite losing the match. His hand is slowly going down.

Kane is going to win.

Wow.

Daegan's knuckles are about to touch the wood, and the crowd pounds the counter, egging them both on. Kane's name is being chanted into the thick, humid air like he's already won. Daegan's knuckles are just a dime away from losing. But suddenly, there's a shift in Daegan.

He lifts his unscarred brow and smirks sinfully.

Cocky. As. Hell.

"My turn, Bane," he smirks like a devil. He fooled him...he fooled everyone.

Kane's dark blue eyes bulge in panic.

Out of nowhere, Daegan retracts like he was saving all his energy for this moment and pushes against Kane's force. In the blink of an eye, Kane's hand goes down with a hard bang against the wood. Kane's whole body drops in defeat, while Daegan jolts in victory. They both must be so drunk. He pushes Kane's shoulder hard in celebration; meanwhile, everyone's tune changes.

"Ohhhh!"

"Creature! Creature! Creature!" All the Special Operators chant drunkenly.

"Drink up, Bane." He pushes three shots of hard liquor towards Kane. It glides against the wood, the liquid almost jumping out of the shot glasses.

Kane sighs. Placing both his palms on the counter, he grips it tight, causing his triceps to flex. He shakes his head in disbelief, smoothing his hair back. He grabs the first shot and grits his teeth.

"Mother fucker hustled me." Kane spits like a sore loser.

He shrugs before drinking them all one by one, accepting his fate. Lopez laughs while he holds his phone as he records Kane. Daegan grabs a shot for himself when Gabe finishes preparing it. He joins Kane in his torture and downs the poison like it's water. He drops the empty glass just as Kane drops a hundred-dollar bill, sliding it toward him.

"Grown men acting like children, what's new," I roll my eyes as I try to hide the fact that it was kind of funny. I pass Winters, hoping she follows.

"I know, I know...what do you expect though? This is their last night for months or even a year. You gotta admit that was hot." She hits me with her hip playfully. "Bane and Creature can arm wrestle me any day, and I'd gladly let them win."

I walk away, rolling my eyes.

"Girl. Stop. You know you can't get involved with them romantically. You'll put your job and theirs at risk."

"I'm only joking..." She walks into the dancing crowd, and I follow right behind her. "Half-joking," she admits in her lustful confession.

"Now...where's Jack?"

"Thank you for the beer, Bailey," Jack thanks Bailey behind the bar counter. He takes a long swig of his beer before slamming it down on the counter. It chimes with a layer of emptiness. He wipes his wet lips with the side of his hand, watching the dancing crowd, his brown eyes anywhere but me.

Jack stopped by for free drinks an hour ago, and I was hoping I would see him with a smile on his face and his hands over my body.

But alas, he shows up distant, only seeking free beer from my close friend.

"You're welcome, Jack," she chirps before she attends to another customer. Her beautiful blue hair sways over her shoulder as she walks away from the three of us.

Bailey is tall, beautiful, sociable, and has the most welcoming aura about her. She has quotes and nature elements tattooed on her fair skin on both arms. We met at El Devine years ago and hit it off over time. We've been friends for three years and have never swayed. After hanging out consistently, she knows me, Winters, and Jack very well.

I sit in between Winters and Jack, sipping on a beer, as Bailey comes back with shots for all of us. We all cheer our glasses and swallow down the burning sensation, and I accept it without making a grimace.

I'm limiting myself tonight. I leave for deployment tomorrow. It's also the day I'm turning twenty-five, and I'll be spending it on an airplane.

Jack's attention gets pulled away as someone taps his shoulder. I don't have to turn around to know who it is. The air takes a turn, growing thick with dark vibes.

Frankie Blanchard.

He makes advances on me every time we're around him. I don't understand how my boyfriend keeps his friendship with him knowing these things.

He's a regular here, so I'm not surprised. He still wears his football varsity jacket like he's still the cool kid senior who refused to give up his social status once he graduated.

I've vented to Jack about Frankie many times, but he tells me just to ignore him and cover up with more layers of clothing whenever I'm around him...like that'll help.

Completely dismissive.

PRETEND

SEAL Team Executioners still stand in the far right of the bar, near the television and restrooms, drinking like we're not on orders for a deployment tomorrow.

"I'll see you back at home, okay?" Jack looks at his phone, typing away, and curiosity gnaws at me. I slump on the barstool, the tips of my boots hitting the floor.

"What? You're leaving already?" A frown transforms onto my disappointed face, eager for him to stay.

"Yeah, babe. I'm tired."

I look at my watch. Despite the numbers on it, the night still feels young. Either way, I don't stop him.

"I would just think you'd want to spend more time together on my last night out." My biceps tense as I lean on the counter, trying to get a peak at his phone screen, "Who's texting you so late?" I take a swig from my beer.

I feel like he's hiding something from me, and I can't help it. But guilt immediately replaces my assumptions, and I try to bite back my tongue and retract my question, but I fail.

He's never given me a reason not to trust him.

"Huh?" He pockets his phone and pretends he can't hear me. His body goes rigid like he's afraid I'm reading his brain.

"Your phone...what's going on?" I place one hand on my hip and lean on it.

"Oh, it's nothing. It's just my sister. Goodnight, babe...love you." He cuts our conversation short in a distasteful manner. He's defensive, and I want to poke and pry, but it's not the right time.

It's midnight, and he still hasn't wished me a happy birthday. Instead, he came in for free beers with his friends, talked to anyone else but me, and is leaving without noticing the damage he's done to me.

"Night." My tone rolls with an obvious irritation at his oblivious behavior.

"Alessia, babe, are you really mad at me right now?" He rolls his eyes. "I came to El Devine for you." There he goes again—his gaslighting and manipulation, which he's mastered so well over the course of our relationship.

I don't want to argue in public. El Devine's bar owner, Gabe, walks back and forth behind us, attending to customers. Drink after drink, shot after shot. Winters by my side, watching us.

"Of course not." A fake smile lights up on my face. "Look, I'm fine. Just go, please. Get home safe."

His eyes soften, and for a second, I think he realizes what he's doing to me...the night before I leave for months. It's my birthday, and I'm still hoping for some type of affection.

It hurts when you put so much into a relationship and then feel like you're the only thing keeping it afloat.

"Okay, night." He turns around on his heels and heads for the exit without doing any sort of double-take. There is no kiss on the cheek—nothing but a numb farewell.

He probably doesn't remember that today is my birthday, or maybe he has a surprise for me at home.

He reaches the doors in no time. He walks out, picking up his phone again, but this time, he holds it to his ear like he's making a phone call.

I want to go after him. I want to ask him why he's been such an ass lately. But then Winter's calls my name, snapping me out of my thoughts.

PRETEND

"Alessia, Bailey is gonna bring us some nachos on the house."

I'm still upset about the whole PSD situation. I turn around, and she places her hand on my shoulder and squeezes in a comforting gesture.

My eyes search for Daegan down the counter, and he's nowhere to be seen anymore. All I see is Danny Rider and Enzo Rooker chatting away.

Maybe he left.

It'll be my first deployment, and I have a babysitter.

With a SEAL that wears a mask.

Cody Jinks plays loud, and I tap my fingers to the music. The bar will keep its doors open until three in the morning, and then I get to go home and make sure I have everything ready to go and packed for my upcoming deployment.

I have to ensure I have all the proper uniforms and equipment accounted for.

My phone buzzes in the back pocket of my jeans, vibrating against the bar stool.

> Unknown: How's your boyfriend doing? Did he get a band-aid for his little flesh wound?

8
Alessia

I CLUTCH MY PHONE as my blood drains from my shocked face. But then it falls to the ground in a second as my vision blurs and spins. Bile rises in my throat, causing a soft burning sensation. I swallow it down as my body slowly grows cold.

This person is texting me again.

Does this person mean what I think they mean?

I reach for my phone with trembling hands, staring at it like it's going to come alive and bite me. I look around the bar...searching for a shadow.

This terrible feeling gnaws at me like someone is in here.

Like someone is watching me.

My vision swings to the left and the right, but all I see is a very confused and concerned Winters and strangers drinking and dancing the night away—nothing and no one out of the ordinary.

PRETEND

Country music continues to blaze loudly and vibrate through the walls in a muffled manner. I gather my strength and move my fingers.

> Me: You must have the wrong number. Please stop texting me, or I'll report this to the police.

It has to be a wrong number. I hold it tight, awaiting their response in suspense. I chew on the insides of my cheek before I flutter my lashes rapidly. My jaw tightens as the seconds go by, and sure enough, a response pops up.

> Unknown: Report what? A concerned citizen? I'll do something worse than a little flesh wound if he forces himself on you again, Alessia.

They know my name.

They know my freaking name.

This person shot at us?

I'm taking this to the police. I have to. I can't take this anymore. I don't know why I keep giving in to this sick game this person is playing.

> Me: It was you? You're stalking me? Watching me? Why are you doing this?

As I type vigorously, every press on my phone makes a small thud of aggression.

> Unknown: But why? It's so much fun to see the raw moments of a person when they don't know they're being watched. The secrets they keep are interesting. You really get to know who someone is when they don't know they're being watched.

I grit my teeth, my blood boiling with more wrath than fear. The two emotions mixing with each other finally come to a head, and I decide to dare the bastard.

> Me: Reveal yourself, you coward.

> Unknown: You should be thanking me. I'll see you soon…don't worry.

I roll my eyes, exhaling an exhausted breath. My mind begins to race with every scenario, debating with myself.

Who is this person?

Do I know them?

Is this some kind of sick prank?

Should I tell Winters or Jack what's going on?

Should I call the police?

The thought of having policemen swarm El Devine to take my report weighs heavily like dread.

Policemen who know my "step-father" very well.

You know what…no. I won't do this right now. I refuse to deal with this bullshit.

I'll call the cops tomorrow and make a report before I have to deploy. He won't be able to stalk me on a military base in Iraq, that's for sure.

I turn off my phone, and all the chills that dance upon my skin fade to nothing as I get back into party mode.

Bailey comes back with nachos and drops it in front of us. The smell of cheese makes its way into my senses, and my mouth waters.

I grab a chip full of cheese and pop into my mouth.

PRETEND

"Thank you, Bailey."

"Of course, anything for the birthday girl." She winks at me and wipes her hands with a towel. "I'm off early tonight, ladies, but good luck with the deployment, Alessia. I'll miss you too much!" Her red lips pout. "Please remember to text and call me." She pleads, batting her long lashes.

"Of course, I will, bestie. See you in six months."

She gives me a small smile before offering her arms in front of me for a hug. I lean over the counter, and we embrace. Winters hugs her after me. It's a short and sweet, see you later, farewell.

A large group of female college students stand vacating the bar with drunken giggles and stumbles. That's when I spot SEAL Team Executioners talking to Gabe to my right. There is no longer a border between me and the special operators.

I can't help it, but something like quicksand is pulling my attention in that direction. And it rhymes with cannibal.

Danny Rider sits in his chair with a black glistening ring on his wedding finger. I haven't seen him in a long time, but he used to come here frequently. He would always order his favorite whiskey to drink alone or with a random girl on his arm or his team. I can't deny noticing Rider every time he walks into a room. He has that magnetic pull on everyone, not just me.

Enzo Rooker sits beside him. His peppered hair is clean-shaven at the sides, and his eyes are fixated on Danny's phone like he's showing him something important.

Kane Slaughter sits at the end next to Lopez, fully clothed again. And at the end…Mr. Daegan Hannibal, Operator Creature. Or, Operator pain in my butt for the next six months.

This time, he wears a white shirt that hugs his mass of muscles. The shirt is still unable to hide his well-structured and curved back.

My heart jumps in a split second like a shock to the system when he notices Winters and me gawking.

Shit.

Thankfully, it only lasted half a second, even though it felt like hours. Lopez pulls Daegan's attention away, giving me a chance to breathe the air he stole from me. I put a chip into my mouth, my lame attempt at playing it cool, and crunch on it inconspicuously.

They engage in a conversation with Slaughter, quickly replacing the indecipherable moment.

A moment of peaceful bliss settles in like home, and my world is okay for a couple of seconds the entire time Daegan has his cold eyes on mine.

It's a weird feeling. I'm almost excited he's here.

They're all frequent visitors here…except Daegan. This is the first time he's made an appearance. I'm assuming it's because he's new to the SEAL teams.

Gabe places the basket of food in front of the Executioners, and they attack it like prey.

"Girl. Why did Jack leave? It's your birthday?" She grabs a chip.

A frown quickly replaces my flat lips.

"I don't know," I shrug, focusing on the basket in front of me. "Said he was tired."

She studies me, picking up on my energy.

I don't want to talk about how my boyfriend literally forgot his girlfriend's birthday, even though we've been together since college.

He's just tired. I lie to myself.

PRETEND

He's just tired.

"Don't you think it's weird?"

"What's weird?" I ask, tapping my fingers on the wood.

"The rumors about Hannibal."

I roll my eyes at her. "Oh gosh, there's rumors? There's actual drama surrounding him?"

"It's not necessarily drama, but people talk. You know how there was a leak from the inside?" she whispers, closing the distance between us.

I nod.

"Well, there's a few of us that think it's a little weird that once Creature showed up, things started to go wrong. It makes perfect sense. He was captured, remember? Maybe he befr-"

"Girl, please don't. What you're saying is so wrong." I interject, backing away from her.

I want to steal a glance at Daegan, but I refrain. I'm thinking hard about the rumor, refusing to let rumors taint how I view him. I mean, I don't like him already, solely because of our situation. I don't know the man personally, but I'm the type of person to get to know someone before I make my own judgment. I don't let others tell me why I shouldn't like them or not.

"Ravenmore wouldn't have assigned him as my personal security if he had doubts."

I can't believe I'm defending him, but this is a silly rumor. I can't imagine being tortured and having numerous people question it.

"Sorry, let's change the subject, shall we? I'm going to introduce myself to that cowboy next to me. Be my wingwoman, please." She hooks her arms into mine like a fish hook, yanking me towards the surface of the Navy SEALS.

"Well, hello there, *senorita*." Lopez tilts his cowboy hat at Winters before he pops a fry in his mouth just as she slides in next to him. She's on a mission tonight, and it looks like her eyes are set on Vicente Lopez, Operator Texas. He grabs a toothpick and chews on it. His eyes flicker as he flirts with my friend.

Daegan doesn't eat. Instead, he stands, walks behind me, and plops on the bar stool beside me...closing the gap.

What does he want?

It takes everything in me not to let myself go rigid like stone. I don't know how or why, but he has this foreign power over me...and I don't like it.

"How's your boyfriend doing?" His deep voice asks a familiar question, sending cautious alarm bells to chime. He raises the glass back to his lips. Heat pours like lava into my senses, and my eyes widen. My breathing hitches ruggedly, and Daegan's tone is so serious, so tense, forcing a cold shiver to run up my spine.

The text message from the unknown number asked me that same question.

"What...what do you mean?" I turn to him with my brows pinched together.

Did the police tell Ravenmore about the shooting?

Suspiciousness and suspense claw at me. How does he know I have a boyfriend? We just met earlier today. The way his tone shifts into something dark sends shivers down my spine, but the way his sarcastic smile reflects across his beautiful, sinful face relaxes me.

It's a weird combination of emotions.

Daegan smirks, and a devilish grin forms on his cheeks. He crosses his arms, his biceps tensing, grinning devilishly like he's enjoying how I'm tensing up fearfully.

"How is he doing with the news of his girlfriend deploying? Your father told me you have a boyfriend when he assigned you to me," he tells me nonchalantly.

Oh. Right.

Of course. Gosh, my paranoia is getting the best of me.

"He's handling it well, I guess. It's the best anyone can handle when their spouse is deploying."

He holds the glass, his eyes never wavering from mine. A low, deep hum subtly joins the bar's music.

God...even the sounds he makes are entrancing.

"Of course," he finishes his drink, placing it down softly on the counter. "Didn't know the Admiral's daughter likes to frequent El Devine."

I scoff.

"Step-daughter," I snap at him quickly, like I'll bite his head off if he ever refers to me as his daughter again. "He's just Admiral Ravenmore to me, Hannibal. And yes, I like to come here. Tonight is my last night out."

"Yeah, I'm going to miss this gremlin. She's the sweetest customer." Gabe ruffles my curls in a playful manner, and I politely shoo him away, biting my lip. Gabe knows me well after countless girl's nights.

"Where's Graves at? I haven't seen him here in a while. I haven't seen you both...since Dario—" Gabe lowers his voice as if he regrets his question. Daegan's hauntingly dashing smirk fades, and he stiffens.

His eyes widen, but then they slowly turn into a soft glare. "He's busy. Always busy...as am I."

So he has been here before. I've just never seen him.

Daegan lifts a glass full of amber liquid, taking a long swig, but something flashes behind those eyes when Gabe mentions Dario's name, almost as if it's painful for him to talk about.

I watch his Adam's Apple bob up and down as he swallows, and I'm not sure why, but he even makes drinking so captivatingly hot.

I assume he's drinking whiskey. That's all that they tend to order when they come in.

"Who is Dario?" I lift an eyebrow.

"Uh—" Gabe starts but gets cut off.

"Alessia, cutie pie. Why did Jack leave so suddenly? Why would he leave his girl in a bar full of men?" A drunken, slurred, high-pitched voice interrupts our conversation, sending a ripple of discomfort and the hair on the back of my neck to stand.

Frankie.

I grit my teeth, and my body tenses when he says my name. I grip the counter tight with my fingers until my knuckles turn white. I can't believe Jack is friends with this guy.

But Frankie isn't alone. Zeke stands behind him, grabs a chair from a nearby table, and sits on it.

"He's tired," My voice pitches with a forced friendly tone as I turn to Frankie, and he palms his heart like he's hurt.

Daegan turns to his right, just enough so that he studies him for a second with a tightened jaw. He flexes it twice before his eyes are on me again. Frankie is so drunk that he doesn't notice Daegan glaring daggers at him.

9
Alessia

"**W**HAT CAN I DO for you, Frank?" Gabe asks, clearly aware of his history.

The way Frankie looks at me makes me want to crawl out of my skin.

"I'll take some wings, man," Frankie tells him innocently, the smell of alcohol already seeping out of his pores and into my nose.

"Coming up." Gabe smacks the counter and disappears.

Daegan continues to look at Frankie like gum under his shoe.

"It's a little crowded here, don't you think?" Zeke pulls Frankie away from Daegan and me. Frankie's cocky wicked grin lingers as he licks his bottom lip. He blows me a kiss, and I immediately cringe, contorting my face.

Thank God Zeke gets the hint and pulls Frankie away.

The aura of dread melts away, and I sigh in relief. My shoulders relax.

"Why do I get the feeling you don't like Ravenmore?" Daegan probes.

Another bartender stops in front of us and serves Daegan another cold drink with ice.

"Bourbon." A tall, beautiful, dark-haired woman tells him. She's gorgeous. Her hair is flattened so straight, and it glistens under the neon lights. She winks and brushes her hand over his, letting her fingers linger longer than usual. I pretend not to notice the way she flirts, but I do.

He doesn't react. He deadpans, and I'm unsure if he's welcoming her overly friendly demeanor or despises it. She blushes, biting her lip seductively as she walks away with more sway in her hips than before.

I scoff and press my lips together, unimpressed.

Watching this woman throw herself at him is not something I enjoy. I don't like seeing this in general. Daegan isn't special.

He takes a sip, and his lips turn into slits.

He is a whiskey man, after all—no surprise there. It's hard and smooth. I've had it before, and it's like drinking straight fire.

"Again, I take it you're not a fan of Ravenmore?"

"It's that obvious, huh?" I rub my lips like I want to keep them locked. If I tell him anything, I'm afraid it'll get back to Ravenmore, and who knows what'll happen.

As if he could read my mind, he tells me, "Look, whatever you tell me tonight, it doesn't get back to him. Your secrets are safe with me." He holds out his pinky, and a half smile forms on my face.

A small, cute gesture, and I force my smile away.

I hook my finger in his, and we intertwine them. The touch of our skin, his finger swallowing mine whole, the veins on his big hand are evident, and God, those hands have me swooning.

PRETEND

What is it about big hands?

This is innocent. It was an innocent gesture, the beginning of getting to know the man who will watch over me for the next few months.

"He's my mother's husband. We've never gotten along, and I don't want to after the things I've seen. I'm uninterested in holding any sort of relationship with him that isn't required. That's all I'll say."

I let go of his finger when it's the last thing I want to do, but I have to. The more I feel his skin on mine, the more I'm sure there's a slight burning pink hue forming on my cheeks.

"He's not so bad, is he?"

"You only know him as the Admiral. I know him as Henry. My relationship with my mother and him has always been complicated."

"Fair enough." He concedes that he won't push me for more, and I'm grateful for that.

"Alright, men, I'm going home. I promised Ari I'd be home to our babies before two in the morning, and I intend to keep that promise. I'll see you assholes soon anyway with the next deployment." Danny Rider gets out of his seat and slides Gabe cash. "Have a good night, boys, and stay out of trouble. I'm looking at you, Lopez." He points at the cowboy from Texas, and Lopez throws his hands up innocently as if he knows nothing.

Then Mr. Rider gives me a soft, gentlemanly smile, his beard fully grown out. He wears a backward ball cap, and all I can see are the tips of his dark blonde hair shaggy over his ears.

"Alessia." He throws me a nod of farewell.

"Rider." I bow my head and wave him goodbye.

Rooker follows suit, and they all give each other brotherly hugs and handshakes goodbye. Two Navy SEALS are now gone, and there are just three left.

"Alessia."

A deep voice calls me. I know that deep voice anywhere now. After just a few interactions, it's become engraved into my ears.

"Yes?"

"The Admiral just wants to see you safe. I'm not happy about this babysitting gig either." He swallows the rest of his bourbon.

Of course, he's not happy about this. He's a special operator. I don't know one who isn't obsessed with his job and taking out bad guys.

"Wait. You've been placed on PSD?" Gabe interrupts.

"Yeah."

Gabe shakes a drink and slides it to Lopez. "Damn, dude, I know you'd rather be on missions and the team, saving people like you did for me."

"Wait, you two know each other?" I ask, my eyes widening.

"Hell yeah. I would never let a man walk in here with a mask; Creature is the only one who gets a pass. Because if anyone else walked in with one, they would go straight to jail *immediately*. Hannibal and I go way back. We deployed to Africa once. Fucker saved my buddy's life. I didn't know who did it at first. All I know is the guy behind me, holding an RPG to him, got sniped. I found out later it was Creature." Gabe raises his hand, turning them into fists, and they knuckle touch. "This was before he joined Grim's team."

Suddenly, glass shatters a few feet away from us and interrupts the trip down memory lane. It's loud but recognizable. It sounds like someone dropped their big glass pitcher of beer on the floor.

PRETEND

While I'm unphased, Daegan gets startled and stiffens. His eyes quickly search for the origin of the sound, like he's ready to fight someone. His hands clench, and his knee starts to bounce fast and hard.

He stares down the men that caused the ruckus. Customers on the other side of the bar are the culprits. They're yelling at each over God knows what, poking and daring each other to make the first punch. Gabe shakes his head like he's used to these things happening all the time. I assume he is, being the owner of El Devine. He throws a white towel over his shoulder and whistles to security, leaving Daegan and me alone to confront the drunken men.

I expect Daegan to continue to pry about Ravenmore, but he hasn't moved. I do a double take, watching him, concerned. His knee continues to shake, and he's reaching into his pocket. He pulls out a bullet, spins it between his fingers, and hums a tune.

It's like I'm not even here anymore, and Daegan is somewhere else.

His eyebrows narrow inward, still watching, and another glass breaks, causing him to spin the bullet faster like he's pissed off. His shoulders tense, and his skin begins to shine like he's in a cold sweat.

I open my mouth to say something, but nothing comes out. I want to tap his shoulder, but someone beats me to it.

Kane pats his shoulder three times, and Daegan stops humming a tune and fidgeting. He pockets the bullet and lifts his face to Kane.

"Let's go burn one real quick." He holds a pack of Marlboros in the air, shaking it.

Without another word, Daegan gets up from his chair and leaves with Kane. They go towards a patio outdoors where there's tables and a smoking area.

I retreat to Winters only to find her gone, her seat empty with no Lopez in sight. I check my watch, and realize it's nearing closing time. People are starting to leave for the night.

Deciding to venture deeper into the bar to look for my friend, I check my phone, sneaking it on my walk through the dancing crowd to the bar for any missed messages from Jack.

But nothing.

"I'm going to eat this ass one day." A drunken, slurred raspy voice snarls into my ear.

Frankie's slap on my ass has me stumbling over my feet. A burning sensation floods my skin, the pain intruding every boundary I have, and I yelp once his fingers dig in more over my jeans, hard like he's trying to take my clothes off literally.

"Frankie! Stop!" I brush him off, push him away with my hands, and he takes one step back. As I walk away, he tries to get a hold of me again. Thankfully, my reflexes are fast, and he misses. He aimed for my hand like he wanted to pull me into his chest, but I snaked it away just in time. He stares at me with lustful, drunken, glossy brown eyes as I walk away.

"Leave me alone!"

He giggles, letting out a loud burp in between his humiliating laughs.

"We're just getting started, Alessia! Jack isn't here." He shouts over my shoulder as I pick up my pace and make my way towards the El Devine restrooms to let the tears fall.

No one has violated me like that before in public. Frankie pushed his limits tonight. His terrible flirtatious ways changing into physical assault have me fuming.

PRETEND

I want to tell Jack about Frankie. I want to call him and tell him his friend just groped me, but then I'm reminded that Jack probably won't do anything to comfort me.

He'll tell me it's my fault that Frankie touched me this way.

Hoping he'll prove me wrong, I send Jack a text.

> Me: Frankie just groped my ass. I'm not okay. Will you come pick me up tonight?

I stare at my phone as I walk faster, and thankfully, Jack reads it. Typing bubbles reflect, and I'm anticipating him to say,

Of course, babe.

I'll come to get you.

Punch him in his throat.

Anything.

But then the typing bubbles disappear, and that hope is gone.

He doesn't reply.

Fury implodes even further, and all I see is a black hole that I keep digging myself more into. This is supposed to be a fun night before I leave, and this?

I walk into the dark hallway, and my throat tightens, and pain pierces my eyes as I try to force myself not to cry.

Before I can reach the door handle, my wrist is being pulled in the other direction, and I grow fearful of my life.

Did Frankie chase after me? Is he here to push me even further?

Oh, no.

My other hand balls into a fist, ready to make contact with Frankie and show him I'm not one to fuck with.

I will fight back.

But I'm met with those same mysterious, ice-blue eyes that look like a winter wonderland full of snow.

"Why are you crying?"

Daegan. Hannibal.

I hadn't noticed until he pointed it out. The bathroom hallway is dark, and we're alone. The music switches from country to slow.

"I–uh," I take a deep, shaky breath, wiping it with one hand, and look down at my fingers that are now wet with my tears.

"What happened?"

Taken aback by his presence, my thoughts scramble, not knowing what to say.

"Someone, uh," I sniffle, doing everything I can to gather my thoughts.

No. I can fight my own battles.

He squeezes my wrist tighter in a protective, urgent manner that doesn't hurt.

"Who, Alessia? Give me a name." Daegan spits, clenching his jaw once more. To my surprise, his eyes aren't glossy. He doesn't seem to be inebriated. His tone is stern and demanding. His eyebrows wilt together angrily.

I shake my head.

"It's nothing, Mr. Hannibal. I'm okay. I'm not your assignment just yet. You don't have to protect me." I pull away again, and he lets me go.

The last thing I see is his nostrils flaring, his tightened jaw, and his menacing eyes that hold limitless threats.

Even though I told him to leave me alone, he watched me enter the restroom like he was making sure no one else followed.

10

Alessia

"**S**O WHEN WILL YOU say yes?"

I gave up trying to find Winters. She texted me while I was gathering myself in the women's restroom. She's dancing with Lopez and made sure to mention he's a great kisser.

Lopez and Danny have reputations for being womanizers. Well...Danny *used to* have that reputation. Now he's married to his best friend's little sister.

I watch Gabe slide Miller Lite beer to Zeke. It glides across the counter smoothly. He takes it into his hand and downs a swallow.

"Yes to what?" Zeke never gives up on asking me out.

"To a date with me? Maybe the military ball that's coming up after the deployment?"

I dislike going to military balls. Something wild always happens. Men act like they're in college again or like it's their first time at a college party, getting wasted and fighting. I try not to attend when I don't have to.

"Zeke. Really? You know I'm with Jack. *And* you know I don't like going to those." I tell him, drinking my water.

"I've been trying to go on a date with Alessia since she first came in for her 21st birthday. Get in line, buddy." Gabe says over his shoulder as he walks by, serving another customer a beer.

Daegan slides in next to Zeke, not bothering to introduce himself, and my heart quickens.

"Ahh, Creature, what can I do for you, buddy?"

"I'm just wondering why you're talking to the Admiral's daughter when she clearly has told you no." He takes a sip of his bourbon; his eyes scream a murderous gaze. The way he stares at Zeke is sharper than a knife.

"Step-daughter." I correct him. "Mr. Hannibal, it's okay. Zeke and I have been friends for a while."

Why do I feel like these two know each other? I don't remember Zeke being a part of the executioners. How would they know each other?

"Friends for now," Zeke winks at me, and I throw a forceful, uncomfortable smile. He was in a friends-with-benefits thing with a girl named Violet, and that still hasn't changed how he feels about me.

I tighten my grip on the counter, cringing at his flirty attempts and attitude.

My eyes fall on Daegan, and he's tense like a rock.

"It looks like Alessia here is just too nice and letting you down easy. If any of us would take her to the military ball, it would be with me. Wouldn't it?" Daegan teases.

My jaw drops open, and my immediate reaction is to protest. Tell him he's insane; deny it. My tongue goes to a standstill, and a smirk unfolds on him. This is my way out. He knows it. We both know it.

PRETEND

So I fall silent.

"Does the Admiral know about this?" Zeke's tone changes to jealousy.

"Of course he does. He was the one who assigned Alessia to me. He trusts me. I'm her personal security, remember? I don't know if he can say the same about you."

"But not as her date, Hannibal." Zeke snarls, "Mind your business."

Daegan grins with humor like he's enjoying purposefully getting under Zeke's skin, refusing to back down.

They're both glaring, none of them wanting to wean. Finally, Zeke looks at me, his brown eyes pleading with me to say Daegan is wrong. When he digests my silence, he realizes I'm not going to. Zeke clenches his jaw, and an awkward silence fills the tension. He takes his beer, watching Daegan.

Frankie decides this is the perfect moment to butt in. He gets in the middle of the men, palming the bar counter for support.

"Creature, there are rumors."

Daegan folds his arms across his chest. "Ah, what kind of rumors?"

The entire section of where we are standing changes. The air thickens with red and rage, and I can feel a bar fight coming along. Then, as if on cue, Kane Slaughter enters the chat, standing behind Daegan with a pointed chin on his right and my left.

"That you're blind as fuck."

He did not just fucking go there. That's a low blow. I've heard the rumors that Daegan lost his vision in one eye while he was captured.

If it's true, how he's still a sniper is beyond me.

Kane's eyes widen with disgust and so do mine. I'm about to shout at Frankie to get the hell away from us, but Daegan doesn't get angry. Doesn't get defensive. Instead, he lets his head fall down, his chin almost touching his chest as he chuckles deep and slow.

Zeke pats Frankie's shoulder like he's trying to de-escalate his demeanor.

"Do you want to see how blind I am, Frankie? Do you want to test this theory? Do you want to see if those rumors are true, Zeke?" Daegan smiles, his canines digging into his bottom lip.

Frankie's drunk, and instead of shutting his mouth, he tests Daegan further.

"Whatever you have in mind, Creature. Let's see 'Mr. Best Sniper in the military'." Frankie throws air quotes with his fingers above his head. "I'm game. Can you even see me?" Frankie laughs, but no one else chimes in, with the exception of another guy in Frankie's circle. He's short and wears a beanie with tattoos all around his neck.

"Are you sure you're game?" Then Daegan pulls out his knife. A sharp, thick, shiny blade glints across the neon cattle lights of El Devine, and I feel like I'm the only one strong enough to say something.

"Zeke, stop this! Gabe!" I turn around, desperate for help, my chest heaving. Where the hell is Winters?

I'm hoping Gabe has already called security on Frankie.

"Let them be," Gabe orders from behind me.

Daegan is smiling ear to ear, his eyes crinkling with excitement and adrenaline.

"I'm not a coward," Frankie shrugs, getting into Daegan's face.

"Slaughter," he orders, and as if Kane can read his mind, he hovers over Frankie, pushing him towards the counter and making him face my direction. He tightens his hold on him, locking him into the chair so he can't run. He holds his wrist, forcing him to plant his palm down on the bar hard.

PRETEND

Daegan grabs Frankie's wrists, and he grits out, his throat hoarse and dry, "What the fuck! Let me go!" He wiggles, but Kane overpowers him easily.

"You said you were game, Frankie...and I love to play." Daegan smirks, "Try not to move...or do. *Please, do.*"

He starts stabbing the spaces in between his fingers fast and hard. I gasp, holding my hand over my mouth. Gabe chuckles behind me, shaking his head.

Frankie starts wailing like a baby, realizing he can't escape his current fate. He doesn't struggle, like he's fearful if he moves an inch, Daegan will miss. Zeke has his mouth dropped open, as is mine.

Everyone is stunned with shock. No one dares to try and de-escalate the situation anymore.

Then Daegan doesn't bother looking at Frankie's hand anymore, not bothering to see if he'll stab him or miss. Instead, he looks straight into Frankie's watery eyes and laughs wickedly.

"Do you think the rumors are true still, Frankie? Huh?"

"No! Please! Stop! You're fucking insane!" Frankie's eyes circle with desperation.

"Aww, you flatter me," he continues, but this time, he increases his speed, the counter taking every blow. The only thing everyone can hear is Frankie's pleas and dark snickering coming from Daegan's throat.

Frankie struggles to claw out of Kane's tight grip, but Kane holds him down and smirks.

Suddenly, Daegan stops but holds the blade in between his index and middle fingers. The blade is still stuck into the wood. He managed to do all of that without nicking Frankie's skin.

"This will be the last time you come into El Devine. Do you hear me, Frankie?" Frankie nods erratically, sweat forming and dripping down his face. "Apologize to Alessia for touching her." Daegan tilts his head in my direction.

My chest rises and falls with each intense breath.

Frankie looks at me, blinking fast and nervously. He's flushed and embarrassed. A crowd of sailors and marines circle them, laughing.

Frankie reads the room, and then he lets out a hard, breathy scoff. He doesn't want to back down.

"Fuck no, I'm not apologizing. She's begging to be touched and slapped with the outfit she wears!" Zeke turns away from Frankie, shaking his head like he wants nothing to do with him.

Wow. I have no words.

"Thank you." Daegan spits with glee. He takes out the blade from the wood in one swift pull, but Kane doesn't let him go. He still holds him down, restraining him despite Frankie's desperate wiggling. Everyone in the bar is confused, including me.

My palms are still pressed to my lips.

"For what? I didn't apologize to that slut." Frankie spits, his saliva flying out of his face as he fights Kane's hold.

Daegan roars with a burst of accomplished laughter. He leans in, licking his teeth, and whispers into his ear, barely loud enough for me to hear.

"Thank you for giving me a fucking reason to see my favorite color."

Daegan raises the blade, slamming it into Frankie's hand. The sound thunders as the knife pierces through flesh and bone until it's pinned into the wood. Blood pours out along with Frankie's screams. Everyone in the bar gasps with awe.

PRETEND

Red. His favorite color is red.

Daegan sucks in a breath like he would a cigarette, his cheeks hollowed, furrowing his brows, "Ooo, I love the sound of bones breaking!" He exclaims with ominous glee. A hellish, sinful grin draws on his face, and he shakes his head once like he's having the best time of his life. He licks the bottom of his straight white teeth. His tongue grazes his sharp canines, and the sight pulls me into him like he's magnetic.

11

Alessia

He just stabbed someone. He just fucking stabbed someone. Because he wouldn't apologize to me.

Holy shit.

Everyone in the bar yelped with bewildered gasps. My body subconsciously jumped in fright, my ass in the air for a millisecond, when the blade pierced through his hand and into the wood.

I cover my eyes with my hands, my heart twitching with astonishment.

He's unhinged. Now I know why Admiral Ravenmore placed him as my personal security.

Daegan Hannibal, Operator Creature, the man in a mask.

Daegan pulls the knife out of Frankie's hand and looks at his knife, twisting it in his hand, looking at the blood coating the silver Damascus blade.

He laughs dark and sinisterly. "There's just something about the color red that really brings out the beauty in my knife. Don't you think, Frankie? I made this knife from scratch, you know." He talks to Frankie like he's a good friend of his and not like he just drilled a hole into his hand, probably crushing his bones in the process. Daegan looks like he's having fun. Pure pleasure radiates from him. His smile reaches ear to ear.

"You're fucking psychotic over this fucking bitch!" He wails, clutching his bloody hand.

Oh, no.

I narrow my eyes at a sweaty Frankie, shaking my head.

I turn to Gabe, and he just shrugs like it's another normal Saturday night.

"I let security leave early," he drawls.

Great. So there's nobody here to stop this storm of a fight that's brewing.

Frankie stands straight up once Kane lets him go, still holding onto his very open wound. His blood profusely drops down his forearm, splattering everywhere. On the counter, the floor, even on his own clothes.

Daegan got him good.

Daegan licks his lips, smirking like a determined devil. Frankie slowly backs away as if trying to retreat into Zeke's safety, but Zeke doesn't offer him anything. He walks backward towards the exit, keeping his eyes on Daegan. It's like he's afraid he'll stab him again. With the way Daegan's crazed mind works, I think he just might.

"Since you don't know how to talk about Alessia respectfully, your tongue is next." Daegan grips the blade and stands fast like he just made a promise he intends to keep.

I need to do something.

I grab his shoulder over the chairs, and I'm touching a fucking mass of muscles underneath his sleeve. I squeeze gently but urgently. My fingers dig into his white shirt. Daegan turns away from Frankie, and his eyes, once filled with unforgiving fury, soften after a few seconds with my hand on his bicep.

"Please," I beg. "He isn't worth anything more." I plead with him, not wanting him to risk his job further.

Winters finally emerges and stands beside me. Her lipstick is smeared all over—evidence of her making out with Lopez present.

"Bro, shut the fuck up!" Zeke scolds him, flicking the back of Frankie's head. "Get out of here!"

Zeke rushes him out of the bar and closes the door on him.

All the while, Daegan chuckles.

"And with that," Gabe throws a white towel over his shoulder. "I'm closing the bar early. Everyone, go home!" He motions everyone out. His two fingers pinch his lips, and a loud whistle pitches into the air. He points to the door, and everyone groans but descends towards the exit anyway. Body after body disappears out the door as Gabe holds it open.

The music is cut off, and all of El Devine's lights turn back on.

Daegan pulls out his cigarettes and sits back down in front of me.

"*You are insane.* He's going to call the police." I choke out with a shaky tone. "Aren't you worried about your career?"

"No, he won't, Alessia." Kane chimes in, almost condescendingly, like I have much to learn about how their minds work. He pats Daegan's shoulder and leaves.

Mr. Slaughter and Mr. Cowboy Lopez have always been handsome to me. Everyone on SEAL Team executioners is tall, handsome, and just built with a mass of muscles. But Daegan...something about Mr. Hannibal has me feeling some type of way.

PRETEND

Just this magnetic force I can't untie myself from.

"*Pinche loco*," Lopez pats the masked man's shoulder too. He tilts his cowboy hat at me and follows Kane. "*Adios, senorita.*" He tilts his hat at Winters.

I turn to her, shaking my head in disapproval. "Incredible." I scold her, and she blushes.

"What? Don't judge me! I'm going to the ladies' room before we go," she tells me quickly. Then she turns on her heels and leaves Daegan and me alone.

"You didn't have to do that, Mr. Hannibal. I'm not a damsel in distress. I can fight my own battles." I cross my arms over my chest.

He lights his cigarette, not bothering to look at me. I continue when I realize he isn't going to say anything.

"I'm not going to the ball with anyone. One, I have a boyfriend. And two, I'm pretty sure Ravenmore will have a fit if I ever date one of the special operators he's in charge of. He would kill you or fire you if I went with you. I wouldn't doubt it if he were to write you up and get you kicked out of the Navy. Plus, risking my own car—"

He doesn't let me finish my ramble.

"You're breaking my heart, Valentine." He inhales, bright sparks at the end reflecting red. I don't bother telling him to smoke outside. I'm pretty sure Gabe would let any of the executioners smoke inside.

"You think I care what anyone thinks?" He asks me confidently.

That's a good point. He doesn't seem like the type to give a crap about anyone's thoughts or feelings.

I roll my eyes and check my watch. I'm getting home earlier than expected.

Daegan stood up for me. All be it, he really went overboard, but...he didn't have to. He did something that Jack could never do for me in our entire relationship. And then those dang butterflies swarm again. I do my best to make the heat die down, but this mysterious man makes it hard.

Is this what lust feels like?

"Alessia." Daegan's voice pulls my attention away from my watch.

"Mr. Hannibal," I turn around, exhaling.

He flexes his jaw, grabbing a napkin and wiping off the blood from Frankie's stab wound.

"Sorry about the mess, sweetheart." He wipes it twice with the napkin until there's no more blood, cleaning the mess. "I'm going to head out too. Slaughter's my ride." He stands and heads towards a trash can, keeping his cigarette between his teeth the entire time.

I take that as his farewell and decide to meet Winters at her car.

Gabe heads into the kitchen, probably to let everyone know that he decided to close early tonight.

This is one hell of a weird night.

I grab my personal belongings that I kept underneath the bar and swing them over my shoulders. I need to go home, shower, and sleep.

I don't see Daegan anywhere anymore...he's probably already down the street with Kane and Lopez. We have a big day tomorrow.

I send Winters a text saying I'm meeting her outside.

The walk from the bar to the front doors of El Devine isn't long. El Devine went from blasting music and crowd chatter to silence. My shoes click on the floor with each step I take.

I reach for the door, but a large hand pulls it open first.

PRETEND

Dark hair, silver eyes, and a voice that has my thighs rubbing against each other. My god, Ravenmore wasn't kidding about me not even noticing him. He really is like a quiet shadow.

"I got it."

"Thank you," I say, giving Mr. Hannibal a shy smile. At 5'3, this man towers over me easily. I walk outside, and I'm greeted with fresh air. Stars twinkle in the sky, and a fresh breeze makes me wish I had brought a light jacket tonight. I continue my journey to Winter's SUV when I hear his voice again.

"Happy birthday, Valentine."

I'm halfway down the pavement at the edge of El Devine when I stop in my tracks. I squeeze my bag tight, and my brows pinch together.

How does he know?

I pivot my foot, slowly turning around.

"How did you—?"

"You're my assignment. I know a lot of factual things about you. I've done the homework that's required of me when your father...I mean, *the Admiral*, assigned you to me." He takes a deep hit from his cigarette and blows into the dark night. It lingers into the sky, and I smile.

"Thank you...umm, seriously, thank you. You're the first person to say it." I brush a curl back behind my ear nervously, my chest tingling from being unable to breathe. He does this to me.

"How are you going to celebrate?" He inquires.

I shrug, "It's just another day," I tell him, kicking a small rock off the sidewalk. He stiffens, clenching his jaw. He looks like he's upset I said that.

"It's a shame you think that." He puts one hand in his pocket, staring into my soul, and then says something with a charming tone I'll never forget: "The day a girl named Alessia Sahara Valentine entered this world isn't just any other day." He takes another hit of his cigarette. "Doesn't your boyfriend tell you that?"

I can't feel this.

"Another year of life should always be a celebration. You never know when Death will come to collect."

I chew the inside of my lip.

"Fair point..." I giggle. He inhales another hit, and I let my curiosity get the best of me as I stare at his half-mask.

"Why do you wear a mask? Is it because of what happened to you?"

He flicks his cigarette once, ashes falling to the ground, and his face intensifies.

"We all have broken pieces, love. We all have scars we hide underneath a mask. What's that saying again? Show me yours, and I'll show you mine?" he dares me.

Smirking like a devil, I chew the inside of my lip.

I start walking backward, "Night, Mr. Hannibal." I give him a polite nod, doing my best to hide the flustered wave brewing on my face.

"Goodnight, Valentine."

Something about the way he says goodbye has me enchanted. I turn around, biting my lip, trying to force the giddy curve of my lips away, refusing to let him see the effects he has on my body.

12
Alessia

THE EVENTS OF TONIGHT gave me a whiplash.
The only thing that made me smile weirdly was the mention of the happy birthday. Daegan showed me that I'm not numb like I thought I was. He protected me, although he did take that to the next level when he pulled out his knife, and even more so when it sank into Frankie's skin.

I close my front door softly, not wanting to wake Jack up. I lock the door, pulling on my hair tie. I take it off, freeing my curls. It falls down my back, onto my behind.

I have long, thick, black, curly hair, and I probably should have cut off an inch or two before the deployment to trim off the ends, but I haven't found the time.

I massage my scalp as I bend over to take off my boots, but a loud feminine moan shrieks into the quietness of my apartment.

I feel as though I was hit in the chest hard by a baseball bat. My heart pounds, and a cold sweat takes over my body. I stop breathing, forcing my body to be still and frozen while I listen. My whole world comes into slow motion, and I wait. I'm hoping and praying to God that this is all in my head...*it has to be.*

I'm desperately praying for more silence, but no. More moans follow, and my skin cripples with shivers. I grit my teeth and no longer know what I'm doing. I have no control over my actions; I begin to black out as I follow the cringe-worthy sounds that I wish would stop.

Please stop.

They're coming from my fucking bedroom.

Please be a movie. Please let it be that I'm catching Jack with porn on our bedroom television and that the volume is too loud...but no.

With my luck, it's one of my worst nightmares coming to life when I push open the door hard and fast. It hits the wall with a loud thud, marking it and probably drilling a hole into it. My eyes widen with disgust. I find Bailey riding my boyfriend. Her hands are in her own blue waves of hair, and her head is tilted forward. He has a hold on her waist as she continues to move.

Fucking sick.

I'm going to be sick.

Jack immediately sees me. He lets go of biting his lip, and his sensual expression quickly forms into a mixture of shock and guilt. He pats her thighs to stop, looking straight at me. He swallows, and she halts her movements, watching his gaze on me. She turns over her shoulder and gasps, grabbing the blanket to cover up, but doesn't get off him.

She's still on him.

Betrayal.

PRETEND

Betrayal is written on both of their cowardly faces. There's no masking that.

"I always had my suspicions. But I was the crazy one, right?" I cry out, my heart breaking. Two people who are major components of my support system. Two people I used to trust in my life.

"I was the crazy one for thinking that one of my *best friends* would sleep with my boyfriend. I was the crazy one to think that you guys could be so fucking cliche and do this. Every time I asked you, Jack...you made me feel crazy."

He doesn't say anything but pats Bailey's thigh again. She doesn't move; she's in shock, and her eyes turn glassy.

"Bailey?" I ask her. I want to throw questions at her and insults, but this hurts more coming from her.

One of my best fucking friends. This is another level of pain I never thought I'd go through. A breakup with a friend you saw as a sister is more heart-wrenching than you'd think.

Bailey cowers at my words. She doesn't try to defend her actions. Neither does he.

She looks around the room, anywhere but my eyes. Of course, she can't face me.

She's too much of a selfish coward.

"You guys are perfect for each other. You can have him. Happy fucking birthday to me."

I storm out of the bedroom without another word. I turn my head one more time before walking away from the snakes that finally shed their skin and got caught.

"Alessia. Wait, please. You weren't supposed to be here for another hour!" Jack pushes Bailey off of him. She flops on the side of the bed, taking the blankets with her. *My blankets*. She can have my fucking blankets, too, at this point. There's no way in hell I want anything from this apartment anymore.

I don't stop. I keep walking, grabbing my bag off the kitchen counter, ready to hop into my car and head to an unknown destination.

I can't go to Winter's place. She's probably dead asleep. I don't want to worry her. And I definitely don't want to wake up my mother or Ravenmore.

What is my luck lately?

"Babe, stop!" Jack pleads again.

"Fuck you!" I spit.

"Alessia!" He trips over the couch, falling on the floor.

Serves him right.

He gets on his feet again. He managed to pull on his white underwear from the bedroom, too.

I grab the lock on the doorknob and turn it but then stop. The door slams again with a loud thud.

"Damn it. Stop it, now!" He yells, grabbing my arm tight and pulling me back. I inhale sharply, hissing from his forceful yank.

"Let me go!" I snap, trying to get away.

"What do you expect, huh?" His brown eyes are shades of manipulation. "You've been a shitty girlfriend. You're never home." He tightens his grip on my arm, and I wince in pain. "And now you're going to deploy?"

"Asshole!" I break free from his grasp. "You know what's going on! I can't do anything about falling on orders, you insensitive jerk. I've given everything to this relationship, and you've only taken. I've taken care of you! Even when you're out of a job, I'm the one taking care of everything, making sure you're always okay. That my friends are okay, my mother is okay, *my sister is okay*.

PRETEND

Everyone before me!" My throat tightens, and my eyes start to water. I refuse to cry in front of him. I won't let him win. "We're over, Jack. Don't ever come near me again. Get your shit out of my apartment by the time I come back home in the morning."

He grabs my arm again, holding it so tight I feel another sharp sting.

"I'm not leaving this place. Bailey and I are happy. I'm sorry you had to find out this way, but then again, I'm not. This makes us even. You have a man buying you flowers. I don't think any guy would just do that if he's not getting pussy in return. Bailey rides me good. She lets me fuck every part of her body, and she blows me better than you ever fucking could. Good job on paying the bills, but I'm tired of your insecurity issues." He's emotionless—a full-on narcissist. Nothing is ever his fault.

Jack claws his hand harder into my skin like he's the one mad at me for busting the affair open. One tear falls out of my eye, and I scrunch my nose full of rage.

He's hurting me. I'm tired of men thinking they can touch me without consent and there won't be consequences.

The next thing I know, my leg swings forward, full of wrath, and I kick him in the balls. Hard. He finally lets go of me as his eyes widen full of pain, and he immediately stops breathing. Holding his breath, he falls to the floor in agony, turning red as a tomato.

"I warned you. Don't ever touch me again. Both of you need to leave my home, and all of your stuff better be gone by the time I come back in the morning." I repeat myself, making sure he gets it through his head. "Goodbye, Jack." I slam the door on a teary-eyed Jack cradling himself on the floor.

I don't know where I'm going. It's been two hours, and I don't have a destination in sight. All I know is I just need to keep driving until the ache in my chest is gone, but the more I speed, the more miles down, and my path to nowhere gets clearer, the more tears fall down my cheeks.

I clutch the steering wheel so hard that my blood circulation halts, and my skin rubs against the leather harshly until it burns.

I haven't blinked, and I'm holding the storm inside me at bay. The chaotic storm of betrayal and the unknown brew, and I haven't been able to let it out. I refuse to let it escape.

I guess I'm stubborn that way.

Even though I'm alone, I refuse to let myself fall apart over them.

Bailey and Jack are happy…while I'm crying?

Each second that passes, I look at the amount of gas, and it's all the way down to E, but my Sedan keeps pushing forward. I was so distracted by catching my boyfriend in the act that I didn't notice I'm almost out of gas.

Come on, just a couple of more miles, and we'll be at the next gas station.

Rain hits my windshield hard, lightning lights up the sky, and my eyes are so tired that I swear I'm starting to see things.

Every time I blink, the swelling around my eyes greets me with pain.

Then my car starts to slow.

Oh, no.

PRETEND

This can't be my life right now. I'm going to get stranded. It's dark, with no street lights around. The windshield wipers go to a standstill. I pull to the side of the road, and I barely make it on the flooded grass.

I safely managed to park it before it stopped running.

I'm surrounded by tall trees and forests on both sides of the road. The storm is just getting stronger. The wind thrashes against my car, howling through the windows.

I sit there in silence as my car sways to the left and right from the strong winds. The rain hits the window and the hood of my car, and I'm just sitting there...with frustration, sadness, stress, and betrayal simmering in my veins.

Finally, I let my emotions wreak havoc on me. I rest my forehead on the steering wheel and let it all out.

I'm crying hard, gasping for air, as my whimpers join the natural sounds of rain. My mouth gapes wide open as I bawl the last bit of energy I have out. Shutting my eyes tight, I feel like everything is coming down on my shoulders hard.

A part of my support system feels obliterated, and the world becomes quiet and lonely. All the good memories of my relationship with Jack flash in my brain while my eyes are closed tight, and I let my panic attack run wild.

All of the good times of us falling asleep in each other's arms, every holiday, our college graduation, and how he was there when my baby sister got in a car accident that left her with permanent damage to her arm.

How could Bailey do this to me? How could she hurt me like this? How could I be so stupid to trust people?

At this exact moment, I would call my best friend Bailey. Or Jack.

But that's dead and gone, taken away by their selfish needs and cliche betrayal.

I refuse to worry anyone. I won't do it. I don't care how bad the situation is; I won't have anyone get out of their beds at three in the morning for me.

I decide to call my mom. I hate asking her for anything, but I have no choice.

Screw it. I need someone.

My heart drops when I see my phone battery life.

Shit, I'm at one percent, and I don't have a car charger on me.

Of course.

My mom doesn't answer, unsurprisingly. She's probably asleep.

I can call an Uber. But I don't feel like going back and forth right now, waiting on an app.

Opening the car door, I take one last breath of air before I face the storm outside.

I'm immediately drenched by thick water drops. Fast and harsh winds hit me, making my hair slap around. They patter my skin roughly as I started my long walk to the gas station.

It's five miles up the road. I'm going to get soaked, but at least I can get to another phone in case mine dies or to a charger.

As soon as I open my Uber app, shielding it with my hand, I get a text.

It's a photo.

Of the person who's stalking me.

There's a picture of a gloved hand holding a piece of my hair on his palm over a sleeping body.

My sleeping body.

I'm on my side wearing my Jack Skellington pajamas.

> Unknown: Where's the birthday girl tonight?

He's been watching me sleep, too?

What in the actual hell?

Is that my hair? Did he cut off my hair?!

I stop walking for a second, and I panic. Blood rushes to my ears, and I lose my balance when a rush of strong winds hits me.

My phone is about to die.

He's stalking me.

I act quickly, typing in three numbers, and hold the phone to my ear.

"911, what's your emergency?" a female operator asks me, but the voice sounds choppy with static.

"Ma'am, someone has been texting me weird things. I think I'm being sta-"

"Hello? Ma'am, I can't hear you. The line is weak."

"I said, someone is watchi-"

The line goes dead.

Shit!

Damn it. I should have called the police when I had the chance earlier.

I panic at the realization that every second is precious. I look around again, but all I see are trees swaying.

Think Alessia.

Think.

I call the first person that pops into my head. It's the only one that makes me feel safe recently yet scared at the same time. I don't know why I do. I should be dialing 911 again, but instead, it's Daegan's number that is reflected on the screen. It rings once before he answers, and I'm met with a deep, chiseled voice that's been seared into my brain. His voice sends chills all over my body.

"Valentine." He says my name like he's surprised. I'm sure he is. I can only assume what he's thinking.

The Admiral's daughter is a mess.

Why is she calling me so late at night?

Doesn't she have a boyfriend to bother?

I would be lying if I said I hate it when he calls me Valentine, but I don't.

"Mr. Hannibal. My phone is about to die any second, so I'm going to make this short." I rush out with a shaky tone. "I uh...I'm stranded. I'm on Lockdown Road, near the Fast and Speed gas station. I'm around five miles away from it. I need help. I know we don't know each other well, and I'm sorry to bother you, I really am, but—"

My phone dies.

"Shit," I curse to myself. I stop shielding my dead phone and hold it tight in my hand. I look around to see if I can see anything out of the ordinary, but nothing.

What a hell of a start to my birthday.

13
Daegan

One Month Earlier

I PUT ON MY full mask this time. The only thing it doesn't cover is my eyes. It has a smile design on it: sharp teeth curved into a U-shape smile over where my mouth goes, so it looks like I'm smiling big. The teeth are like sharp triangles.

Fifteen minutes later, I'm outside her window.

She's sleeping.

She sleeps so beautifully.

I look at her through the crosshairs of my rifle and instantly feel the blood rush down to my groin. I'm getting so hard that I have to rub myself over my jeans.

Jesus. If I let myself, she could be the ruin of me.

I followed her home, having been following her since the day the Admiral assigned her to me. I always go above and beyond the task, so I decided to look into her extensively.

Maybe I wasn't supposed to go this far, but that's just who I am.

I always cross lines with a smile on my scarred face.

I know where she was born. The hospital and doctor's name who delivered her. When she was born, her birth weight, the time. Who she spends her time with, who her friends are, and who her parents are—her ethnicity, hobbies, and where she lives.

That's what my research told me about her.

But then I laid eyes on her through my crosshairs...and my whole world stopped. The earth stopped spinning, gravity stopped pulling, and I felt my tainted soul come alive as I watched her.

I know all of these factual things about her...*but I wanted to know her.*

I want to know how she takes her coffee in the mornings, even though I know where she buys it from. I want to know if she snores and what she dreams about, even though I know what bed she sleeps in. I want to know what kind of music she listens to, even though I watch her dance when she thinks she's alone. I want to know what her future plans are. What drives her to meet her ambitions, even though I know her contract in the military lasts until the end of this year, and I know that she loves the rain because she opens the window and falls asleep to the sound of it whenever a storm rolls in.

I know the longevity of her life...but I crave all the beautiful details that make up the in-between.

What the fuck is going on with me?

I'm acting like this is my first time seeing a beautiful woman. But she's more than just beautiful. She's majestic, unreal, heavenly, and I need a taste.

But it's forbidden. Her blood I desperately want to see on my tongue...is forbidden because the Admiral is my boss, and she's his stepdaughter.

PRETEND

If I cross him, it's my job. My life. I would no longer be accepted on the special team of Executioners, and I'd be kissing my unblemished career goodbye. He warned us all before assigning her to me.

They're like family to me. The team is the air I breathe. The missions I take on are my adrenaline.

"Watch over my wife's daughter. Protect her at all costs, Daegan. And to the rest of you, she's off limits. You hear me, Texas? If I find out any of you assholes has laid a finger on her or tried anything past professionalism, you can kiss your spot on this team and, most importantly, your career goodbye."

I have to remind myself of this conversation over and over again like a broken record player whenever my sinful desires take over. Because what I want to do to her is anything but good.

I want to make her bleed because I want to see if she does it pretty. I want to see how she looks with my come filling her mouth as my cock is deep inside her throat. I want to see just how far I can break her until she's crying my name, begging me to stop because it's a sweet tune I desire to force out of her, and when she begs me to stop, I'll keep going.

So I'll take what I can get.

I fist myself as I watch her sleep, stroking slowly at first from the crown to my shaft.

I want to fuck her. But I can't.

It's a fantasy, I know. But maybe, just maybe, in another life, she's my good girl.

And I know all about that little boyfriend of hers. I was the one who shot him when I realized what the asshole was up to. I was going to stop watching her, but then I saw the way he was forcing himself upon her...*and she let him*. I couldn't just watch; my job was to safeguard her, after all. I know my assignment isn't due for another couple of weeks, but the covetousness runs rampant to harbor her from everything. It possesses me like a plague I don't want a cure for.

And that's what I'm doing.

She's just so beautiful. Fucking perfection. She could look at me, and I'll come undone inside my pants.

Goddamn.

Control yourself, Creature.

Control.

I'm in my car, watching her serene body through a scope. I stroke myself, and then I see her shift in her bed, her curls across her lips, begging just to be pulled on, and I'm done.

Thick white ropes explode from my cock, and I grunt, grinding my teeth, when I imagine myself pulling her hair like a leash as I wreck her from behind.

Fuck.

How am I supposed to babysit her these next few months when all I'm going to be thinking about is how I want to mold her cunt to my cock?

I have to touch her.

Control, Creature, control yourself.

But the next thing I know, I'm doing something I've never done for a woman.

I break into her house. Fifteen minutes after I cleaned myself up, I unlocked the doors to her apartment.

Her little boyfriend isn't home, as always. He's either out fucking her best friend or out fucking off her hard-earned money. A part of me wants to kill him, get rid of him from her life permanently. But he'll do that all on his own when the truth comes to light. The guy is a sorry excuse of a human being.

PRETEND

I'm standing over her now, watching her take slow, even-paced divine breaths, and I want to steal them, breathe them in my own lungs.

She's in cute black and grey Jack Skellington pajamas—an oversized shirt with matching pajama shorts.

So, she has a thing for the Pumpkin King. So do I.

Her curls not only look soft, they feel it. I trail one knuckle over her black strands, and my index finger glides alongside her hair like she was designed for me.

I hum, sucking in a breath, and smell her. I close my eyes as I inhale her scent. My nose is just one millimeter from getting lost in her hair.

She smells so clean, warm, and sweet—light and airy.

I pull my knife and take a piece of her with me before I make my clean, stealthy, silent exit out of her bedroom.

There are multiple reasons why I'm stalking her, and it's not just because she's my assignment, and it's not just because she's outrageously beautiful. Maybe I'm stalking her because it's the only way I know how to lust. I'm fucked up for it, but I can't seem to stay away.

After all, I don't believe in love.

PRESENT

I knew everything. I knew when and what Frankie said to her as he assaulted her. I just wanted to hear it from her mouth. I wanted to break both of his hands right then and there, but I decided a more public humiliation would send a message.

I don't know why I care so much.

I don't. I don't care.

I'm just watching over her like Ravenmore wants me to. Yeah...that's my excuse.

She's a devastating distraction, taking me by storm with no remorse, and I've let her consume every part of my tainted soul.

I'm saving any part of me that's still capable of feeling human emotion for my job. Not for her...right?

No one will touch her the way Frankie did ever again. I won't allow it. Frankie will know not to fuck with Valentine again, or anyone for that matter.

I sit in one of my good friend Graves' 'dirty work' buildings, laughing the entire time I partake in something I used to do before I joined the Navy.

Torture.

"Aaand, that's the last one." I yank the last tooth out of Frankie's mouth with metal pliers. I plop them on the wooden table next to me, placing the last molar he had in a bowl.

Every time Frankie screams, I smile harder.

"Try to fucking eat now."

I heard what he said about eating her ass. I heard every fucking word. And I'm making him regret it.

Her ass, her cunt, her mouth, *and her soul* are elements that no one on this earth is deserving of...including me.

I found the local Emergency Room, followed, and waited until he was discharged to make him pay for touching my little valentine.

Nobody touches her; nobody will bring her pain, and if someone with a beating heart would dare do such things, it'll be me.

Wishful thinking.

I grin sadistically, satisfied that I always follow through with my promises. All of his teeth sit in a bowl.

Frankie's mouth is a bloody mess. He's strapped tight on a chair as he wails and screams until, finally, he passes out.

Thank fuck.

Graves looked into him, and unsurprisingly, this imbecile has a history—two DUIs. Multiple domestic violence charges, and then Graves hit the jackpot while he conducted his investigation.

He's a drug trafficker.

"Fuck, man. What did this one do to piss you off? You didn't even let me interrogate him for information. I know multiple people looking for him." Graves has one arm on his hip, pulling Frankie's head up by the ends of his brown hair.

I shrug.

"He was...*annoying*. That should be sufficient enough." I stand, the chair I was sitting on screeches backward.

"True," he nods, slapping Frankie's cheek to see if he's really unconscious, and he doesn't flinch from the deep slumber I put him in. Letting Frankie's unconscious head fall back down, it flops, and his whole body slumps over.

His yellow shirt is now a permanently stained waterfall mess of red.

Graves slaps his gloved hands over his palms like he's trying to get rid of Frankie's germs. He's wearing a black suit and tie, with a Rolex on his wrist. He always likes to dress up in fancy suits as he works. I prefer comfort over flashy suits and jewelry. Right now, I'm wearing a dark sweater and sweatpants.

"But there's more you're not telling me." He walks over to me, crosses his arms, and leans against a wall.

The room is dark, with little to no light. Lit candles surround it, along with torture toys to get anyone to sing loud.

"He was touching a girl."

He raises a brow at me, pressing me for more information. I don't like talking about my personal life. In fact, I don't like talking at all. But for some reason, when I'm around the Admiral's step-daughter, I can't shut the fuck up.

Graves, being Graves, my step-brother, I tell him everything. He owns a security company. He also offers other services, including torture, which I sometimes partake in when I'm not on deployments or missions. He's also in the mafia.

"Spit it out, Creature." He throws one of Frankie's teeth at me, but I dodge it in time.

"Her name is Alessia."

"Jackpot! And you care about this girl." He grins, crossing his arms like he's entertained.

"I do...I guess. But I don't want to care. Our situation makes it hard."

"Ah, did you ask this one out on a date like a normal dude would or...?"

"Graves, I can't, but I've been stalking her," I look at the pliers soaked in blood. "I've been watching her from a distance. We go on long romantic walks together, except she doesn't know about it. She's caught my attention, to say the least."

"What's stopping you?"

PRETEND

"She's my boss's stepdaughter. I can get fired if I cross any lines. You know that." I remind him of my position. I know my place, but her existence makes me question how much my career truly means to me.

"I think you already have crossed lines." He points to Frankie. "It makes sense. I know how much being a SEAL means to you. You can just keep it hidden. You're already doing a good job at that."

"Secrets always come to light, one way or another. I need to stay away from her, but I can't. I've been placed on PSD."

Graves bursts into laughter while my face deflates at his reaction. Of course, he thinks it's humorous. "PSD? Personal security detail? Operator Creature is placed on babysitting duty. Good fucking luck with that. At least you're getting paid to follow and stalk her."

I lift an eyebrow, and a mischievous smirk unfolds. I never thought of it that way. I can't complain too much.

"It's whatever...plus my intentions aren't good anyways. I don't commit. I don't put my career at risk, ever. Still, she's very..." I rub my beard with my fingers, "Tempting."

I take out a cigarette, lighting it in seconds. Burning one helps out when I'm stressed. Graves takes his job very seriously.

We're around the same age, and to my surprise, we're very much alike.

Workaholics. In our thirties. Single, with no interest in marriage in sight. Although, he likes material things like overpriced suits and luxurious cars and mansions.

I'm simple. I have no interest in owning the most expensive clothing, houses, or cars. I like music, food, whiskey, the outdoors, and a good fuck when the desires get too much.

"How have you been?"

His question makes my stomach sour, and I inhale deeply to prevent the horrid memories of The Surgeon from resurfacing...and Dario.

I know what he means. I know why he's truly asking.

Of course, he's asking me this. I've been avoiding everyone lately.

"I'm fine." I lie with bitterness laced in my tone. This is my cue to leave. I don't like to talk about it.

"You know, you can't control everything. Sometimes, shit happens, and—"

"Graves. I like you. And I don't like too many people. But keep pushing me, and you'll end up like my good friend Frankie here." I pat Frankie's unconscious shoulder, smiling at Graves.

Graves snaps his mouth shut and purses his lips. He grips the table and tilts his head to the side, avoiding me further.

"I'll take care of this, and you get outta here. I'm sure it won't be long before you're called out on a mission."

He's right.

"I heard about these traffickers teaming up with special operators on post." Graves opens up about the current crimes plaguing the base. He knows everything.

I sit there, twirling the bullet in my hands, as he spills out information he's learned. I can't concentrate on Graves. The obsession to explore what Alessia's insides feel like possesses my every thought. After he finishes, I step off the chair and walk towards my victim.

"Well, this was so much fun...we should definitely do this again sometime!" I exclaim to an unconscious Frankie in his ear before patting his shoulder twice. I give Graves a brotherly hug before heading towards the elevator.

PRETEND

"Hey. Your father has been asking about you. He wants to see you soon since you're back home." He starts texting on his phone, probably reaching out to his other business partner. They are always on standby for him, twenty-four-seven.

"You told him I'm home from deployment?" Anxiety twists inside my chest.

"Yeah. He is like a father to me. He misses you. He wants to talk." He keeps typing away on his phone screen, and I exhale heavily, feeling a wave of guilt surrounding the rift between my father and me. I rub my beard in deep thought.

"I've gotta go. It's getting late." I drawl, avoiding the subject of my Catholic father. Graves gets the message and leaves me alone.

I already miss my little Valentine.

Time to play.

14

Daegan

I DID NOT EXPECT her to call me, but I'm finding the little games I play with her are paying off. Graves is making sure any calls to 911 from her phone are being screwed with.

I find my little valentine one mile away from her car. She's on the side of the road, trying to wave down a truck that's in front of me by a couple of feet.

If that truck driver wants to live longer than tonight, he'll keep on driving. Alessia keeps waving at them and mouthing something like "Please stop," and to my satisfaction, he ignores her.

What a shame.

Her shoulders slump, and she removes her wet curls from her face, unblocking her vision. She's still around three miles away from the closest gas station, her clothes stuck to her skin, hugging her like glue. I slightly pass her, parking my challenger a couple of feet in front of her. The roaring engine slows down, and all I hear is harsh rain pattering my window. It's almost as brutal as hail.

PRETEND

She halts, pausing like she's afraid. Perhaps she doesn't know I drive a challenger. She bites her lip nervously when I don't get out right away. Her chest heaves up and down, and she turns on one foot like she's going to run.

I would love to play a game of hide and seek.

God, I would love to chase her.

But not tonight...what am I saying? Not ever.

Not with the Admiral's stepdaughter.

I grab the umbrella I always keep in my car in case of weather like this and get out. Quickly spreading the all-black umbrella open so I have cover, I stand tall and wave her down. She squints through the rain, trying to evade the raindrops in her eyes. Even through the storm, she gives me a shy smile that has my heart twitching and chest tightening.

"Mr. Hannibal?!" She shouts over the thunder.

"Valentine. Get inside, let's go." I command.

She gives me a frantic nod and walks faster to my car.

Sliding back into the driver's seat, I tuck my umbrella away in the back seat. Before she can get a chance to get in, I close my door. I race to the other side and wait for her to catch up. I hold the passenger door open and close it once she slides in.

Seconds later, I'm back in the driver's seat, wondering what the hell I'm going to do with Alessia and questioning my decision to pick her up.

"Thank you for coming. You were here so fast. How were you able—"

"I live ten minutes away." I cut her off, deadpanning.

She's all wet. Her white t-shirt is completely soaked. She's wearing a very thin pink-laced bra. I know this because I can see her hard nude brown luscious nipples poking through the wet fabric.

Jesus.

God, give me strength and stop me from not ripping that off her body right now.

I silently pray to myself, hoping it's enough not to act on my impulsive desires, flooding my senses and nerves.

The urge to put them in my mouth is overwhelming. I want to suck and bite on them.

She doesn't realize I can see more than just her wet shirt...until I tear my gaze away from her so quickly. It was so quick but long enough for her to notice. I furrow my brows and clear my throat, putting my car into drive and lightly pressing on the gas.

She catches onto her little pointed situation. "Oh..." she crosses her arms over her chest, hiding her nakedness, like she's embarrassed.

Yeah. *Oh. Oh is right,* but it's nothing to be embarrassed of.

A red hue paints her cheeks. Her skin is almost pale from the cold rain, and her olive-toned skin is textured with harsh goosebumps. She reaches for the button to turn on the heated seats, adding to her urgency to get warm.

"You don't mind, do you?" Her teeth chatter, and it's taking all of me not to just pull her into me so that I can warm her up with my own body heat. I've never been so jealous of my damn passenger-heated seats. Her ass should be on my face.

Shit.

Control yourself, Creature.

"Of course not—" I'm close to the gas station when I see a red, slightly light, bruised handprint on her bicep, and that stops me from saying anything more. I press the brakes, making the car come to a full stop in two seconds. Her body jolts forward, but she is smart enough to buckle herself in.

Who the fuck put their hands on her so hard that it left bruises?

Who the fuck caused her pain that didn't come from me? From the day she was assigned to me, I've dreamt about giving her marks. Marks that she asks for, *begs for*. I want her to be mine so I can do all those things to her. Only me. And God, how I want to mark every part of her with my teeth.

Fuck, it's been a while since I've fucked a woman. Too long. Maybe I need to get it over with. Maybe it'll help the fatal temptation to devour the lovely divine soul next to me.

"Alessia, what happened to your arm?" I growl, softly pulling her bicep to me so I can examine it further. I make sure to hold her gently but stern enough for her to know how desperate I am to know everything.

There's clear fingerprint bruising like someone had her pinned with their hand tight. It's fresh and new. She didn't have this earlier at El Devine. It couldn't have been Frankie because I had eyes on him all night.

"It's n-nothing..." she stutters, whispering softly. The windshield wipers are disguising my heavy, rage-filled breathing. That's when the red and puffy eyes come into view.

She's been crying.

Now I'm fucking livid.

Control, Creature...*control.*

She frowns, retracting her arm back to her side, and looks out the window. She rubs her triceps to keep warm. I take off my leather jacket without another thought and place it on her lap like a blanket.

Still, she doesn't move, and I don't know why, but it bothers me. I want her to let me in.

What could have happened from El Devine to now? Did she find out about Jack?

I was too busy with Frankie to keep tabs on her. I stopped by her home earlier to find her place empty.

I need to know who did this.

"I'm not driving until you tell me what happened to you," I demand, my voice joining the sounds of harsh rain hitting the windshield. I'm cold, my tone emotionless.

She shakes her head, still unable to look at me. I don't know what gets a hold of me, but I reach out to touch her. I'm on the side of the road again. Seconds later, I'm unbuckling my seat belt, letting the cold parts of my heart warm up because her presence does this to me. She taints me, and I do everything I can to fight it. At the end of the day, I'm only a man capable of human errors. I just hope this isn't an error to let myself indulge. I can't cross the lines that have been in place since I found out who she was. A devastating error that could wreck both of our careers.

I lean over the center console and push her hair off her shoulder. Long green trees sway in the wind in the back of her, darkness floods the scenery, and lightning strikes the sky again.

"Valentine," I call out again.

She finally turns to me, and with the most heartbroken voice, she tells me. "Can we just pretend for this one moment?"

I don't say anything. My eyebrows pinch together, confused by her request.

"Can we pretend that Ravenmore is not your boss's boss for tonight and that you're not my bodyguard and maybe just..." she hesitantly asks. A solace pauses between us. "Please, hold me?"

PRETEND

The ends of my mouth tilt upwards comfortingly, "I can pretend."

"I know you're not happy about being assigned to me, and—"

I put my thumb to her mouth, hushing her.

She wants to pretend with me? *Well, I can pretend all fucking night if she wants me to.*

She's doe-eyed, blushing, as I brush her soft, pink bottom lip back and forth, with my thumb. She blushes bright red, clenching her thighs together, and grips my leather jacket hard underneath her hands.

She parts her lips after a second or two...and I see the wetness of her tongue as she sucks in a breath.

I will not fuck the admiral's stepdaughter in the passenger seat of my car.

I will not gag and choke her with my fingers and dick.

I.

Will.

Not.

Then she throws her arms around me, hugging me tight like she's begging someone to tell her it's going to be okay. Not knowing what's wrong is killing me.

I stiffen for a split second, enjoying her touch, not caring if she's getting me all wet. Her hard nipples graze against my chest...

Goddamn.

I hold her back, caressing her in small circles with my fingers.

She sniffles and hiccups into my neck so softly I can feel her nose graze my skin.

She smells so sweet, as always.

And for about three minutes that feel like seconds, I hold her until she's ready to make her next move.

"I caught my boyfriend cheating on me tonight," she sobs into my shoulder. Heavy, warm breaths follow from her mouth.

I don't know what to say because a sick part of me is happy she finally found out.

"With my best friend. How cliche is that, Mr. Hannibal?" She doesn't let me go. She continues to hold me tight as her body heaves up and down from her cries.

There's something about the way she says 'Mr. Hannibal' that enlightens the obsession to claim her even more.

Fuck.

"The ones closest to you are the ones who hold the most power to hurt you." I sigh. "The ones closest do the most damage. Please remember that the next time you decide to let someone in," I tell her.

I keep my circle small, and even then, I think it's not small enough.

"Why does this always happen to me? I try to take care of everyone. I always try to do what's right. I care deeply, and it's like it always bites me in the ass to be kind? Why does the world work like that? Why does the world bite your arm off when you give it a helping hand?"

And that's why I hate people. I've been watching her for a while. This girl gives and gives; when she thinks she has nothing left to give, she'll find it.

I want to rip any being's heart from their fucking chest that has made her feel any less than worthy. All I need is a fucking name. Or a face.

"My car has no gas. I'm sorry for bothering you...and then..." she whispers, fear evident in every syllable. She pauses like she's trying to choose her words carefully. "I keep getting these weird text messages. Someone is...*watching me*. I didn't want to tell Ravenmore. It would only justify the assignment, taking you away from your time on the team and missions to watch over me. I didn't want to tell him he was right for having me under personal security. But I'm scared now. I don't have anywhere to go right now. Can you take me to a hotel?"

"No," I growl, low and husky. She stops holding me, slowly retracting her hands from my body and sitting back in her seat. She wipes the tears off her cheeks, fidgeting with her fingers.

"I'll be okay. I promise." She reassures me, but her words are not convincing enough.

"I can't take that risk. I can take you to your mother's place. Ravenmore wouldn't have it any other way, he-"

"Do not take me to their place!" She insists. "The relationship between my mother and I is complicated." She mumbles, protesting, waving her hands in front of her.

"Fine. Then where? And don't say a hotel," I snarl.

She ponders, looking out the window again.

"Do you think I can crash on your couch then?"

My heart skips a beat. That's not a good idea. As much as I want to take her there, I can't.

"I'm not sure Ravenmore would approve of that. It doesn't look good if anyone finds out you slept over at my house."

It's the truth. The thought of people gossiping about Alessia staying over at my place makes me nauseous. I cannot risk losing my spot on the team over her. My secret obsession needs to stay just that.

A secret.

"Please. I won't say anything, Mr. Hannibal; it's just for tonight." Her hand slides on my knee, gripping it in an innocent way. My eyes flicker to her small palm on my sweatpants for a second. It sends a shockwave of pure fucking flames throughout my body. Flames I thought I couldn't feel anymore.

A low growl reverberates through my chest.

How am I supposed to say no to her? Ever?

"When did this start?" I ask.

"The text messages?"

"No, the rain," I remark sarcastically. "Yes, the text messages, Valentine."

"Oh, right, of course," she chuckles.

Her laughter could be my new national anthem.

I take the car out of parking mode and put it into drive.

"A week ago."

"You're not safe. I guess you'd be safer staying with someone you know tonight. Until we figure out who the fuck is texting you. What about Winters? We need to charge your phone and report this to the police. Why haven't you done it already?"

I'm being manipulative, I know...but I don't care.

"I've had a lot going on. Between my job and falling on orders and my boyfriend—I mean ex-boyfriend—it's all too much. A part of me thinks this person is playing a sick game, and I hoped he or she would just leave me alone. Winters...well, I'm pretty sure she's riding Lopez tonight."

I wouldn't put it past Vicente to hook up with someone from work before deployment.

We pass the gas station, and Metallica plays through my car on low volume.

PRETEND

"I know it sounds like I'm making excuses, and this is something I should have taken seriously."

"Do you have any idea who this stalker problem of yours could be?" I try to change the subject.

I can feel her brown honey eyes on me as I concentrate on getting to my place through the harsh rain. She stays quiet, an eerie silence I don't like. With a somber tone, she tells me, "No, but we're leaving on deployment soon. I just hope it's not the people that created that list," she squeaks out.

I tighten my grip on the steering wheel and bounce my knee.

"I'll take care of it for you," I promise her.

"W-what?" She murmurs.

"I'll find this person..." I turn left, eight minutes away from my place now. She lifts an eyebrow at me. "I always find them."

15

Alessia

WHEN AN ALL-BLACK CHALLENGER pulled to the side of the road and didn't get out, I feared it was my stalker problem standing before me, ready to meet and seal my fate finally. I don't know what this person's agenda is. I don't know if this person gets off on scaring people, but they're winning.

Maybe they're the people involved with human trafficking.

But then, a tall, familiar masked man got out with an umbrella, and I saw those vibrant ice-grey eyes.

Daegan is wearing his full mask again. It looks like he changed outfits from El Devine to now. He's wearing dark grey sweatpants, a black sweater, and black and white Converse.

I squinted through the rain, seeing those eyes I've come to know so well, and a wave of relaxation hit me, washing up the apprehension and hesitation.

PRETEND

He's massive, tall, and mysterious. I asked how tall Danny was one day, and he told me he was 6'6. So when they both stood up at El Devine, I realized they were the same height.

Daegan waved me over, ordering me to get in his car. I complied immediately, and I had to do whatever I could to stop my eyes from bulging when I saw the outline of his cock through his sweatpants.

If my eyes didn't deceive me, he's huge.

When he brushed his finger over my bottom lip, I couldn't help but enjoy it too much. I wish he had pushed it into my mouth, and for a moment there, I thought he was going to. When his finger was on my mouth, it sent a pulsating strike straight in between my thighs, and my dirty thoughts went rampant. I wonder what his lips would feel like on mine. I wonder what his entire face looks like.

The energy in his car shifted into something hot and forbidden.

God, what is wrong with me?

I know I just broke up with Jack a few hours ago. Maybe I'm sad, maybe I'm depressed, and maybe I'm angry, but why does a night with him intrigue me so much?

It's been so long since I've felt this heated attraction with someone. Even though I've been with Jack since college, I feel so inexperienced when it comes to pleasure and different kinks that I'm curious to explore.

The break-up with Jack was long overdue. I lost feelings for him a long time ago. Our relationship turned into contentment. But then he started to become aggressive and distant, and our connection dwindled.

And now, the betrayal I didn't want or see coming came true.

Bailey's friendship is gone with it.

Our proximity in the car sends my thighs clenching tight together. His cologne hit me hard, mixed with smoke and his leather seats. Those smells combined created an aroma I could get lost in forever.

Call me crazy, but I fucking love it.

I want to know more about Daegan. I want him to let me in. I can only imagine he wears the mask because he doesn't want people to ask questions about how he got his scars or tell the tale of what it was like being a prisoner of war. Maybe he doesn't want to open up about what he went through, but if he ever did, I'd be all ears.

I hate myself for asking him why he wears his mask. Maybe I overstepped, but his response tells me he didn't mind it.

As we sit in silence listening to Metallica, we turn into a neighborhood.

His house is one story but very spacious. It's in a neighborhood on the outskirts of Bloomings where everyone has one—to two-acre lots. All the houses look like newly built ones.

He really does live around ten minutes away from where he found me.

The storm gets dangerously louder with thunder, and the rain doesn't let up.

He shields me from the rain with his umbrella as we make our rapid walk to the front of his house. He opens the black-painted door fast, motioning for me to get in, and I practically jump inside.

As soon as he shuts and locks the door behind me, we're met with darkness and a smell that's familiar. His home smells like Daegan in all the right ways. I'm still shivering from the cold and wet. He flicks on a switch, illuminating an entryway.

"There is a shower in the hallway, but you can use the shower in my bathroom. There's shampoo in there since I live alone, and I'll let you borrow some of my clothes, so you have something dry to sleep in." He walks in front of me, guiding me inside a hallway. His Converse makes low thuds as he walks. Before I make a turn, I see an all-black couch that wraps around the entire living room and a TV mounted to his light grey colored wall. An all-black colored kitchen with minimal to no decorations but whiskey bottles and sprinkles of military awards on scattered modern pieces of furniture.

A decorated hero.

We turn into the hallway, where there are photos framed alongside it.

There's a photo of two other men, and it looks like they're at a bar that's not El Devine. They're holding up pizza and beer and look happy, like they're cheering for a celebration. Another one follows, and it looks like a deployment photo somewhere overseas. They're in their uniforms, holding rifles, alongside a SEAL team. I see Mr. Rider and Enzo Rooker, which means it has to be SEAL Team executioners.

The last photo I see before entering his bedroom is of a beautiful woman with long black hair holding a baby boy wrapped in a blanket. She's in a long white dress with sleeves and blue eyeshadow painted beautifully across her eyelids. She has the same ice eyes as Daegan. There's such a peaceful essence in the way she's holding him while sitting on a couch.

"Is that you as a baby with your mother?" I point to the photo on the wall, and he looks over his shoulders.

"Yes," he whispers coldly.

We continue to walk through his dark bedroom and get to his bathroom in seconds.

"I will be taking the couch tonight, and you can take my bedroom." He holds the door open like he's already ready to close it. I step in, examining the black and white shower curtains that mimic mountains and snow scenery. I turn around and immediately open my mouth to argue.

"I will not! Let me sleep on the couch. I-"

"I'm not asking Alessia. *I'm telling you*. I'm taking the couch." He barks.

My teeth jam shut when he says my first name.

I like the way he says my name.

God, he can order me around, and I'll gladly obey.

Shit.

I'm already acting like Winters with Lopez.

"Your boyfriend did that to you." He lifts an eyebrow and points to the marks on my arm.

My head falls down to the red and purple marks. I hold where Jack gripped me with my palm, rubbing it up and down as if it'll erase it. Erase the betrayal. Erase the bruises. The memory of my best friend screwing me over, quite literally with my boyfriend, comes back, and I'm tempted to start bawling my eyes out until I ache.

This hurts so damn much. She was my best friend. They both were.

And now?

I feel like I have no one.

A lump starts to form in my throat, but my somber thoughts slowly fade when my attention gets pulled toward a deep, husky voice once more.

"Didn't he?" He growls, trying to pry the answer out of me again.

I nod, my lips turn into white slits, and I'm silent. I don't know why, but I feel ashamed, even though I have nothing to be ashamed of.

Or maybe I feel shame for staying with Jack this long.

PRETEND

His eyes scream disgust. The same type of gaze he had when he stabbed Frankie. He grips the doorknob tight, his knuckles turning white. The anger radiates off of him, thickening the energy in the room. He shakes his head violently, like he's doing whatever he can to hold back his fury.

"I was trying to leave the apartment when I found him and my best friend together. I was at the door to my place when he tried to stop me." I murmur, unable to look at him anymore.

"I'm going to kill him."

My eyes bulge out of my skull, and I launch forward to stop him before he can dart out of the bathroom. Before he can take another step forward, I squeeze his hand desperately, and I cry out.

"Mr. Hannibal, no, stop! You can't!" I plead with him. After seeing what he did to Frankie, I can't imagine what he would do to someone who left bruises on me.

Why does he care so much anyway?

"I kicked him in the balls," I scoff, remembering Jack's red face. "He's probably still on the floor crying about it, honestly." I grab his hand gently, gripping it, hoping I can stop him, just like I did at El Devine.

His eyebrows narrow intensely at my palm like he's fighting an internal battle. I can't tell if I've overstepped. Either way, it's not enough to stop me.

His chest rises and falls fast as he takes in heavy, fiery breaths. We're both still watching each other like we're watching a horrible accident before our eyes, and we can't stop it. There's a connection between us. He knows it. I know it. An indecipherable connection that only time will unravel. We both take in this moment of our skin touching, savoring the intimate silence I don't want to break.

He must feel what I am, too.

He has to be. I watch him...watch my hand, and my lips part.

"They are meant for each other. I might be a little angry and a little upset, but it's the betrayal that still has me in disbelief."

I swallow the rock in my throat, refusing to cry in front of him. I don't want to cry anymore. He senses what I must be holding in because he returns the comforting gesture.

My heart jumps when he starts to trace his thumb over my wrist in circles, and a low hum slips from my mouth.

"Are you this protective over all your assignments? Why do you care so much?" I ask, daring him to answer. Is he a womanizer? Is he like Lopez and Rider? Bailey would tell me about their constant trips to El Devine with different ladies in their arms every weekend.

I take a step forward, not caring if he can see my very hard nipples through my wet shirt. I hope he can see them, and I hope he can feel what this sudden, unexpected attraction is doing to me.

I don't know what's come over me. I'm a mess right now. Figuratively and physically. Why not make more of a mess with a very attractive Navy SEAL?

His eyes move from my hand to my arm and finally stop at my chest. I take another step forward, placing my other hand on his in a way that says *thank you*.

He clears his throat, rips his hand away, and mutters, "Towels are underneath the sink." He vanishes from the bathroom and shuts the door with a slam like he's trying to escape me like I'm a plague.

I stand there, startled with mixed emotions.

Lust, astonishment, curiosity, but most of all aroused, and I'm questioning every rational part of my mind.

After my shower, the stubborn part of me yearned for Daegan. As the water rained on my hair, I kept replaying the moments at El Devine, his car, and the elevator over and over again. When my time in the shower was over, and I was cleaned up, I found myself searching for him.

His aura was one I wanted to match.

He's just so...*unapologetic* about how he portrays himself. He doesn't care what anyone thinks about him or his decisions.

I wish I could be like that. It's not in my nature, but maybe with time, I can be.

No one has ever looked at me like Mr. Hannibal. No one.

I want to know him. Every single part of him. He's a captivating mystery in my life I want to explore. Even if those depths are deep and dark, I want to dive into them blindly, not caring if I get stuck in what I think is his madness. He has made me feel seen and heard. I want to be near him like a month to a flame, mesmerized by his scent, his voice, and those eyes.

Cold, grey pools of ice.

With my tiptoes, I creep into the other side of his house through the dark living room. With each step, my feet and drops of water from my hair hit the cold floor. There's an hourglass lamp in the corner that's on with a cream lampshade. He must have left it on by accident. I reach for the string, switching it off before

I coat myself with bravery to wake him up. I bite my lip, thinking twice before I do.

I look around hesitantly and spot the kitchen island to my left. A tall glass of Makers Mark Whiskey sits with an empty shot glass.

Did he drink before bed?

I peek at his all-black couch and see his massive sleeping figure with white socks on.

He's still wearing his mask.

Is it because I'm here? Does he always sleep with a mask on?

He should never be ashamed of having scars if that's why he covers himself up.

He's still in the clothes he picked me up in—dark grey sweatpants and a black top. I walk slowly, gripping my towel tight around my breasts.

I don't want to be more of a burden than I already am. I'll sleep in my panties and a towel, refusing to wear his clothes. I won't take more from him than I already am.

He's breathing heavily on his back. Shouldn't he be taking slow, steady breaths if he's asleep? He seems the opposite of relaxed, with his finger muscles slightly twitching around his veiny hands, and his chest rises and falls like he's trying hard to breathe.

Is he having a nightmare?

A frown curves downwards onto my face. I reach for his shoulder, finally taking a leap of faith. He's probably not used to sleeping on the couch. He needs his bed. Maybe that's why he's having a nightmare because he's out of his familiar element.

Which is why I'm here.

"Mr. Hannibal," I whisper while pushing against his bicep with my fingers. Two fast movements have me waiting for a reaction. But nothing follows. I suck in another breath and attempt to wake him up again. He's probably a deep sleeper.

"Daegan," I mumble his first name softly as I get closer to his masked ear, my wet curls falling forward, and they slightly graze his chest.

Faster than I can blink or register what I've done, I'm on the floor in seconds with a knife held to my throat.

16
Daegan

"**H**AVE YOU BEEN PRAYING, Hannibal?" *Dario Marchetti, my step-brother, asks me. We're walking through a village in Iraq, patrolling, sweat on our foreheads, sand all over our uniforms, dragging our feet.*

Dario became my best friend when our parents married. We've been inseparable. Always up to no good. Daring and pushing each other to do stupid shit to get us in trouble.

When my mother passed away, my father remarried a woman he met in church years later when I was in high school. He felt guilty for moving on until finally, I pushed him to. I hated seeing my father alone all those years.

He went into a deep depression when my mother killed herself. He carried her death on his shoulders...and probably still does. He blames himself for her suicide because instead of pushing her to get help from doctors, he encouraged faith over medicine.

PRETEND

A part of me holds that against him now as an adult. As a child, it was harder for me to grasp the magnitude of my parent's choices.

"Of course." I spit out the tobacco I've been chewing onto the floor next to me. I tower over Dario as always, our shadows reflecting the drastic height difference. He's lean, while I am not so much.

It's hot and dry, and the heat is scorching upon us with no mercy. My beard is fully grown out, and my long hair is tucked behind my ears, covered in sweat. My uniform and gear make it harder to breathe, but we keep pushing forward like we've been trained to do.

"Is Mrs. Marchetti finally taking your calls?" I ask. *His mom didn't take my father's last name even after her first husband passed away and she remarried my father.*

His mother hasn't spoken to either of us since we joined the Navy together. He was on a different path. He was going to be a doctor. But instead, he dropped out of medical school, followed in my footsteps, and joined the SEALS. It's a miracle we graduated together.

It's rare.

He went on to become a SEAL with a focus on medicine, and I went on to sniper school.

"Nope, Mom is still not taking my calls. But your Dad says she'll come around. I'm going to see her when we come back from deployment."

"She doesn't talk to me either. She blames me for your decision to follow me into the Navy. So thanks a lot for that, asshole." I nudge his shoulder with my hand; he stumbles a foot or two and spits out his tobacco in front of us. Barely missing my boot by an inch.

He laughs dryly. He and his mother have a very close relationship. He's a mama's boy, I guess you could say. His brown curly hair is cut short, hidden underneath his cap. He is his mother's twin. They share the same features, but his face is the opposite.

She tells him all the time that she sees his father every time she looks at him.

When my father looks at me, he sees my mother's eyes. He can't look me in the eyes since my mother passed away...ever.

"She'll come around for both of us soon, I hope." He grunts while readjusting his rifle and takes in a sharpened breath.

Dario's mother and I have a cordial, respectful relationship. She's always treated my older brother, little sister, and me well and respected the boundaries my father set in place.

He's told me time and time again that his new wife will not substitute my mother's shoes.

We've reached another building we need to clear, and our teammate is about to knock down the door. He positions himself, ready to breach, but our mics go off. Chaos from the teams shout into our ears manically, their voices colored with urgency.

Fuck.

I know we've made one wrong move, and my heart anchors down into the pit of my stomach. In the blink of an eye, our lives have changed forever. It all happened too fast, almost to the point it wasn't registerable. We don't get a fucking chance to change paths, to change into a defensive position. Our fate has been stamped permanently without our say-so.

A loud explosion follows. The beginning of the worst time of my life hits me. Everything goes black, and the only thing that makes sense...is the pain.

PRETEND

Everything was black until I found myself in color again. I'm pinning the Admiral's stepdaughter to the floor, my knife to her throat, and my other hand cuts off her airway, choking her. The color of her skin turns reddish purple.

Her hair is wet, and her face is completely natural without any makeup. The smell of my shampoo wafts into my nose, but it isn't enough for me to snap out of my haunted thoughts. I'm scanning her head to toe like she's a threat. Watching her every move like my life depends on it because for a second there...I thought I was in Iraq. I thought she was one of my captors trying to kill me, and I was merely a centimeter from cutting into her throat and taking her life.

I look around, doing a quick evaluation of my surroundings like I'm expecting The Surgeon to slice my face again. The lamp has been turned off, sending me further into ominous terror. The day I was kidnapped, the same dream I dream of every night haunting me, and tonight is no different. The torture that lasted days still hazing my mind with no end in sight.

I glance back down to a scared, confused Alessia. I'm pinning her down, my knife grazing her neck, and the blade is now painted with crimson. She's bleeding. I've cut her good, but not deep enough to concern me.

Shit.

I should remove the blade from her neck, but something about the way she's bleeding so majestically beautiful in front of me has me wanting to see more of it.

Her brown eyes widen with obvious fear for her life. Her wet lashes flutter open and closed rapidly as she tries to find her words. I can't find any of my own. Blood rushes down, and I can't move.

"Mr. Hannibal, it's—" she struggles to suck in a breath, a vein presently bulging on her forehead. "It's just me, let me go." Tears fall down the side of her face.

I huff out a frustrated breath and let her neck go, granting her the air that was forced out of her.

Chokes follow suit, and she whimpers.

"Why? Why did you do that to me?" She coughs out hoarsely, turning her head to the side.

"It doesn't matter," I scold her.

"I came here to tell you I'd be taking the couch, and you can go back to your bedroom!" She shouts, attempting to turn on her side like she's trying to escape me, but my waist still pins her down, my blade resting on the side of her face against the wooden floors.

"Don't you ever wake me up like that," I snarl, getting into her face. My mask is still on. Our body heat becomes one, and I swallow the lust that wants to spill over.

Fuck I'm so hard.

Seeing her bleed little tears for me, my hands around her neck, and she's in nothing but a towel. I want to rip it off her. Tempting...so tempting.

"I'm sorry! I didn't know," she bites out, her lips shaking.

My cock is hardening the more she cries, I know she can feel it.

We stare at each other, holding each other's gaze, getting lost in the moment. She doesn't try to fight or shove me off her anymore.

I took two shots of tequila before I went to bed. I needed to do something to stop myself from taking her. Some type of outlet that stopped me before I lost control and went into that shower, and let my desires take over with no mercy.

PRETEND

I wanted to avoid a moment like this, but here she is, wiggling underneath me, trying to get away, and it only makes me crave the screams I want to force out of her throat.

"Why aren't you in bed? Is that the only reason why you're waking me up?" I groan in frustration.

Why are you making yourself that more tempting, Alessia?

"Because I..." she stutters, blush creeps into her full cheeks, and she arches her back, one of her legs going in between mine. I'm harder than a fucking rock, and she's making it worse.

"Spit it out, Valentine."

"No, Mr. Hannibal, I...I never thanked you for standing up for me," she says slowly like she's afraid someone will hear us. It's almost like she's ashamed....but why?

My eyebrows raise.

"Something happened to me when I saw you stab Frankie. Something that scares me." She confesses calmly. Her tone is the opposite of fear.

"What happened?" I ask.

"It turned me on..." She reaches for my knife slowly, and I let her. She takes it from my hand, looks at the blade that's covered in her blood, and does something that has me questioning my sanity. Or what's left of it anyway.

Her pink tongue licks her blood off the Damascus blade clean.

Fuck.

Is she drunk?

"Is it wrong, Daegan?" She breathes out like she's enchanted. This is another side of her I've been *dying* to see. And now I'm aching to experience more now that I have her right where I want her. "Is it wrong to find what you did for me has me wanting to show you just how thankful I am?" She bites her lip, daring me.

Fucking hell. She's not as shy as I thought she was.

My obsession needs to stay a secret. The toxic addiction needs to stay in the dark. If I fuck her, I'm tainting my career...and her soul.

"Is it wrong that I want to *pretend* a little longer tonight?"

"Stop it, Alessia. You're just angry." I whisper, my breath swishing through the curls on the side of her face as I bare my teeth underneath my mask. My voice is pained with impenetrable lust and slight anger. "You're upset, and you think fucking me will make you feel better? This is not the way. You're just doing this to get back at your ex." I snarl.

I'm giving her an out. I'm giving her one chance to escape me before I unleash what I've been holding on to since the day the Admiral assigned her to me.

"You're not my bodyguard...not yet anyways." She taunts, and I'm about to take the bait like a starved shark.

17
Alessia

HE TAKES THE KNIFE from my hand like he's surrendering a vulnerable part of himself. His breathing darts in and out of the mask, brushing against my flushed face.

"I can't do this. *We cannot do this.* You are Ravenmore's stepdaughter. He will get me kicked off the team if he finds out we did anything together. Hell, I'm already risking it by you spending the night. You can lose your job as well for sleeping with someone of a higher rank. We cannot."

"I won't say anything. Again. We're pretending. Just for one night. And your hard cock against my thigh tells me you want to pretend longer tonight, too." I reach for his mask. His eyes pierce through me like a hungry beast that could devour me in seconds if I just said the words.

My fingertips graze where his neck meets the mask, and he stops me. My wrist is in instant agony as he grips me tighter.

"What do you say, Daegan? I want you, and I know you want me to." I'm convincing him. I need him to believe I truly want this, not just because of what happened with Jack but because my attraction to him is something I've never felt before.

I grind my hips into the hard, thick bulge that sits in between my thighs. Daegan responds with a low grunt and drops his forehead against mine.

He's hesitant, but he's easily a boiling volcano ready to erupt.

"Are you afraid I won't want you after I see the scars?"

He's silent, but his silence says a thousand words.

He is afraid.

This is a big moment for him. I'm not sure anyone has seen him without his mask since he was captured. Then again, I don't think anyone knows too much about him. He's a mystery to everyone.

He lets me go, granting me access to pull it off him. His breathing picks up, and mine does too. Our bodies are still pressed tight together, but he's careful not to crush me with his mass of body weight. I can feel his muscles trembling on top of me.

My heart thrashes against my chest so hard it's almost painful, and I can feel my entire world burst into flames. I start to sweat as I slowly pull it off.

At first, his beard and full lips are revealed. His chin is coated in dark hair around his jawline and his mouth. I pull it up a centimeter more and see the first few scars he always keeps hidden at the bottom of his face.

Peeling off his mask, one second at a time that feels like hours, more and more deep carved mutilations are unveiled...until finally, the mask is off. I gently let it rest on the floor, indicating to him that I'm not going anywhere.

From what I can decipher, someone cut his face over and over again on one side. They start at his temple, go over his eye, and finally down to his chin. Slashes.

How could someone do this to him?

I've been exposed to war before, and often because of my job, so I shouldn't be surprised, but seeing it right now feels like a slap in the face of the reality of the world we live in.

Masculine charm staring back at me. His ice-grey eyes are dilated, but I can't tell if he's angry, scared, sad, or full of lust. Maybe all and more. His cock is still very much presently hard, stabbing the inside of my thighs.

I brush my fingertips lightly against his scars, and he closes his eyes, relishing my touch like a dream. I run my fingers through each of them. They're soft and smooth, a pale pink tone insinuating they're mostly healed.

"You're...beautiful, Mr. Hannibal." His breathing slows down, and his shoulders relax when my lips utter complete candor. He registers my words and lets me run my hands through his dark waves of hair. I just want to feel him...every part of him. Suddenly, his eyes pop open like he's in a frenzy, and I'm about to be devoured.

"Fuck it."

When he says those two words, my heart jumps, my whole body coils into him, and I melt into his arms.

Daegan doesn't waste any more time. He kisses me, not letting me say another word. His beard pokes into my skin, and there's an immediate intrusion of his tongue. Both of our mouths open wide, tasting each other, getting lost in each other's ruthless passion. Hints of whiskey and liquor are still going strong with a bit of cigarettes.

"I'm not going to fuck you, Alessia." He growls against my mouth in between kisses. My heart drops, and my brows pinch together in disappointment. He bites my lip, sucking on it. Tugging it from my bottom teeth so hard, a moan slips into the thick sexual tension that swallows us. "If I don't," he pauses, which sends me searching frantically for the reason why. We're grinding our hips against each other desperately. My throbbing sex searches for relief, but he halts his pace. I open my eyes to see him holding the knife in front of me.

"If I don't bury my cock deep inside my assignment's pussy, I'm not breaking the rules, right?" He arches a brow, and a sinful smile spreads across his face like wildfire. His eyes darken, and they scream bad intentions. Bad intentions are a new era I'm eager to dive into, and I'll do it headfirst with this stranger.

"I guess not, Mr. Hannibal," I breathe out, panting for the air the devilish man in front of me has stolen. Hesitation laced in my tone as he waves his knife in front of me manically.

Why is the knife coming into play?

"Since my knife turned you on at El Devine, I need you to show me just how turned on it makes you while it's inside your cunt." His deep voice demands, low and husky, against the shell of my ear like he doesn't want anyone else to hear.

He elicits a squeak from my throat. My eyes bulge, my breathing screeching to a halt as I contemplate his request. Does he mean what I think he means?

He starts kissing my neck, his fingers reaching for my towel, pulling it below my breasts, exposing my hard nipples.

"Fucking hell, Valentine." His eyes are glued to my naked chest. His palm goes straight to touch me, and he squeezes one breast while holding the knife in the other. The blade is now back at my throat, moving down my chest slowly like he wants to cut me but doesn't. He's soaking up my nakedness with his feral eyes, and I watch one wavy strand of dark hair fall over his forehead.

The cold steel continues to trail in the middle of my breasts, down to my core, stopping right above my belly button. He slaps one of them, causing them to bounce, and he growls.

"Oh," I moan harshly, practically begging him to fuck me. I'm melting into downright despair for his cock. I want to feel him so badly. This night feels like the longest one of my life, but I'm not complaining.

He moves forward, and I stop breathing when his mouth is a centimeter away from touching me. "You. Are. Magnificent," he breathes against my nipple right before he puts me in his mouth and sucks hard.

"I want to cut the eyeballs out of any man that has looked at you the way I am right now." He murmurs in between his mouthfuls.

"Mmm," I purr, biting my lip so hard the pain ricochets back as he continues to tongue my nipple. My gaze jumps from the ceiling to the top of his head. He sucks on them, nibbling on my points, and I arch further into his bulge—the urge to pull down his pants infecting me.

"Do you have any limits, Alessia?" His question catches me off guard.

"I...uh..."

He pulls down my towel entirely, leaving me in my laced pink thong.

"I'm not a virgin, but...I've never been kissed down there. I've only ever been with Jack, since college, he—"

His blade is at my mouth, hushing me as he presses it against my lips. His eyes narrow like I've struck a nerve.

He tsks, before his husky voice fills my ears. "Don't ever breathe that asshole's name again, Alessia."

Why am I so scared yet so fucking turned on by his primal need? The way he's claiming me right now has me in a chokehold.

"It won't happen again, Daegan."

"Good girl." He praises me as he kisses my neck. His tongue licks the bottom of my collarbone, trailing it all the way to my jaw like I'm a dessert.

"I just...I don't know my limits because they've never been tested or pushed," I confess, with embarrassment colored all over my face.

"What?" He growls. "You're telling me you don't know whether you like to be fucked hard? Fast or slow? Or choked until there's tears rolling down these pretty little cheeks?"

"No, I—"

He interrupts me like he's infuriated.

"You're telling me your ex hasn't made you come with his fingers, or with tongue?"

Fingers? Tongue? Can you come with your fingers? You can finish with a tongue?

Jack was a missionary, or bend me over type of guy. I can't remember the last time I had an orgasm.

Limits...do I have limits?

I pause, trying to recount every sexual encounter I've had with Jack, but then he intrudes my thoughts like he can read my mind.

"You're safe with me. I would never hurt a woman...unless they want me to. I can promise you that." His seducing tone softens.

Hurt me? Why would I want him to hurt me?

"Why would I want you to hurt me?"

He snickers, rubbing his chin, and a devilish grin paints across his face.

"Oh darling, the things I would love to teach you."

Jesus. Say fucking less.

"Teach me." I dare him. I hold onto him, hooking my arms around his neck, and kiss his lips. I nibble against him. God, his lips are so soft.

"Teach you?"

"Teach me, and give me all your darkest depraved desires. I can take it. I have no boundaries, and if I do, I *want* you to fracture them."

He shakes his head in disbelief.

He pulls down my panties slowly like he's enjoying every second. I bite my lip, my teeth sinking into it so hard that pain strikes back. A small sensual whimper escapes my throat as his fingers glide down my legs. My thighs are already damp from being wet. I haven't gotten wet like this for Jack...ever.

I look down, and I watch a maskless Daegan take my soaked panties, scrunching them in his palm. He places them under his nose and smells them.

"Fuck, you smell good." My underwear falls to the floor with my morals. My nipples pointed, goosebumps derived from salacity all over.

"Your pussy is already weeping, baby?" His fingers start at the bottom of my slit, coating himself in my wetness, and when he reaches my clit, flicking it in one swift gesture, a moan slips out from the intense sensitive pleasure. He puts his finger in his mouth and sucks it clean.

I tilt my head to the side, and he grins sadistically.

"Just a fucking taste," he groans.

God, it's been so long. So long since I've had an orgasm. It feels like it's been years.

"I can take whatever you give me."

He hums dark and sweet with satisfaction. "You can take it, huh? Well, now you're going to have to prove it to me."

18
Daegan

"I MAY FEEL BROKEN, but please know I want this. I want you. I want tonight. Don't hold back. No hesitations." Her nails glide through my back, and she scratches my shoulders.

She's sad. She's broken. If she were mine, I would break her again, this time into even more pieces, marking her like she belonged to me. If anyone will break her, it'll be me, and then I'll force her to know that those broken pieces are what make her so devastatingly rare.

"Can you fix me...just for tonight?" She asks me with watery eyes.

I shake my head.

"I want to rewrite the way you see your broken pieces, Alessia. I want you to embrace the shattered parts of you. You don't need to be fixed." I grip her jaw tight, and she winces. I brush my lips against the shell of her ear. "You need to learn how to embrace those dark parts of your soul. It's what makes you so divine, so addicting, and so powerful. That's what I truly desire to *teach* you. If we had more time...and if things were different, I would."

She pauses, digesting my outpour. Ever since I was tortured, I don't like people. I especially don't like them in my space, my home, *my life*.

The electrifying pull she has on me breaks my boundaries and has me cutting off her thought process with a fatal kiss.

I kiss her. I kiss her so fucking hard, like my life depends on it, and I'm the one seeing the stars. But there's only one star that stands out, one star that shines bright in my dark world, and it's her.

I move my lips against her like I'm hungry to eat her until she's nothing but bones, and I take advantage of this one moment we have together. At first, she freezes but quickly opens her mouth, granting me access to taste her and feel her tongue dance with mine. I grab her hips, pushing her against my chest and my hands up in her hair, trying to get deeper into her mouth as humanly possible.

My veins implode with pure fucking madness. I'm losing myself in her, letting our bodies intertwine into one, and then...something inside breaks and shatters into irretrievable pieces.

This is wrong. She is forbidden. I shouldn't.

I fucking can't.

My job. My team. If anyone finds out, I'm finished. The Admiral is like another father figure...*but*...I did promise I would keep her safe and I am doing that. I'm doing it in my own fucked up way, but nonetheless, I'm doing it.

It's just one night. My cock won't be buried deep in her like I've been craving to do since the first time I saw her.

Now, this is torture.

PRETEND

"I'm starving, little Valentine. I need to taste more of you," I squeeze her ass tight with my hand feeling her silky soft skin underneath my palms. "I'm not breaking the rules, right? If my cock is not buried so deep inside my assignments pussy, it's still okay?" I repeat my question as I slap her ass and grip it tight once again. A handful of her ass is the best thing I've felt in a long time.

"Right, Hannibal." She agrees, breathing hard.

"I need more, I want more, crave more of your taste. I want to eat you." I slide down further.

"You want to eat me out?" She quirks a brow, breathless. Her cheeks are rosy, and her eyes never leave mine. Excitement pulls at my chest.

"Yes. But before I do, you're going to come all over my knife."

"Wh-what? You were serious?" She stutters in disbelief.

"This is the first lesson I'm going to teach you. My threats are always promises," I lean over her, breathing over her neck, and I sink my teeth into her skin. She wiggles and scratches my back over my shirt. She moans, and it only makes my dick jump inside my pants. Fuck, I might come in my pants, just like this...just from the sounds she's making.

I flip the blade over, so now I'm grabbing the sharp steel instead. I kiss her neck, trailing kisses down to her nipples and sucking on her breasts. Taking them one by one, and I can't fucking get enough.

I want to fuck her tits. I want to fuck her mouth, her ass, her cunt.

I find her opening and slowly push forward, the handle entering her. It's not a sharp handle. It's a soft one, so it shouldn't be too uncomfortable.

"Oh fuck," she chants into my ear.

I start with slow thrusts with the knife, fucking her with it slowly, seeing if she can really take it like she said she could.

My focus is jumping back and forth between her cunt, and her beautiful face that's lit up with pure adoration and lust. Her mouth gapes open, and she tugs at the bottom of her lip.

I want to fuck that tight throat of hers as tears fall down her cheeks.

"Do you want me to stop? Is this too much for you, Valentine?" I coo in her ear, circling her clit faster. She's fucking dripping.

She doesn't say anything. Instead, she hooks her legs into my waist like she's pressuring me to give her the real thing, pulling me closer to her naked body.

"Faster!" She screams.

So I do. I fuck her with my knife, wishing, praying to God it was my dick instead, as we kiss each other in a fever-like dream. She's moaning, practically screaming against my lips when I start to finger her clit while the knife fucks her in a dangerously carnal manner. My hand grips the blade so tight because of the frustration that's boiling inside me. An ache that's thundering from not being able to feel her insides has me stricken with anger. I want to feel her soft walls clench down on my dick, and I've never hated my knife more than I do now.

The blade pierces through my palm like I knew it would, and I look down to see my hand covered in blood while I fuck her with it. Crimson is pouring down my palm onto my wrist, and droplets hit the wooden floor, creating a small puddle of red.

Eh, I'll be fine. I'm having way too much fun with my little Valentine to stop now.

I laugh, dark and slow, as I continue to play with her cute swollen clit that should be in between my teeth.

I don't know how I'm holding it together, but I do.

PRETEND

"Oh God, I'm going to come Daegan!" She shouts, breathing harshly, clawing my shoulders harder. Her hand pulls on my hair, and she brings her mouth to mine once more. We kiss each other, and I dominate the inside of her mouth with my tongue, over and over again, our tongues in an endless passionate dance.

God, she tastes so good, just like how I knew she fucking would.

I can't get attached to her. I can't grow feelings for this forbidden woman, but everything about her calls my name like she's haunting me.

I tighten my hold on the blade fucking her like I would with my cock, and then she screams inside my mouth. The knife jerks as her pussy clenches all over the handle. I continue to thrust, but this time, I slow the movements as she shakes from finishing so hard, and I kiss her forehead softly.

She wraps her legs around my waist tighter as I let her fall into her euphoric orgasm.

"You did so fucking well..." I drop my knife, and it lands on the floor with a loud thud. My bloody hand goes to her throat, holding her in place so I can kiss her lips gently without her continuing to convulse.

She breaks the kiss with a gasp and looks down at her chest as the blood gets smeared all over her neck, down to the middle of her collarbone.

"I thought about giving you a pearl necklace, but I think ruby ones are better," I smirk at the red covering her neck.

"You're bleeding? You cut yourself?" She pants worriedly. She grabs my hand to examine it.

I retract my hand from hers. She's just too cute, expressing how concerned she is for me.

"It's nothing," I reassure her, kissing her forehead.

"It is not nothing!" She intercepts my calmness with a frantic tone. "You're bleeding. You're hurt. This was supposed to be fun."

"But this is fun, don't you get it Valentine? This is just a fraction of how deep my desires go, baby girl. What's that saying? It's all fun and games until someone gets hurt. Well, it's the opposite for me. It's only fun if someone *does* get hurt. I like the pain, Alessia, and I think a part of you likes it, too."

She turns away from me like she's ashamed.

"Can I tuck you back into bed now? I think that's enough pretending for tonight. There's only so much I can fucking take," I cup the side of her head, forcing her to look back at me. I need her to understand the severity of our situation.

"I just crossed a line I will never be able to take back." I softly tell her, narrowing my eyes. Regret is evident in every breath I take.

"No." She denies me.

"No?" I question her, a low growl reverberating in my chest.

"I want more. *I need you to come.* I want to see it. I want to see you lose control. Let me see you lose control," she softly begs, lifting her head off the ground, kissing the scarred side of my face over and over again, and I'm losing it. Pure warmth fills my chest.

When I let her see this side of my face, she looked at the most vulnerable part of my body and accepted it. Not a lot of people have done that when I returned home.

But Alessia?

My little valentine has a heart of pure gold, warmth, and compassion. She didn't run, cringe, or worse, *pity me.*

PRETEND

She's worshiping my scars I hate to look at. I hate them because they remind me not only of what I endured but also of Dario.

"I'm not fucking you, Alessia," I remind her.

"No, but let me fuck you."

She gets up, pushing me so that I flip over to my back. She straddles me. Her wet curls, and her chest coated in my blood, are all the things I see, and it's making me fucking feral.

"I want to see you. Let me *see you break*." She reaches for my sweatpants, but I stop her by wrapping my hands around her wrist. Her fingers are frozen at the waistband.

"I will not be held responsible for what happens after you take my pants off. Do you get that? Can you process that? The things I want to do to you are unholy, sinful, and downright fucking cruel." I whisper darkly, but most of all, depraved, and Creature takes over.

19

Alessia

If we only have one night to pretend we're not breaking any rules, I'm taking full advantage of every hour the sun stays hidden.

I nod frantically and reach for his waistband, grabbing them, and my heart palpitates with excitement. I pull it down an inch, exposing his hair, wondering and begging to let this man give me more. This is already one hell of a night I won't ever forget.

He just made me come so hard with a damn knife.

What else does he have planned?

The V of his torso is sculptured like a God. His veins protrude above his groin. I pull the waistband lower, each millisecond in slow motion, until finally, the pink of his shaft unveils.

He grabs my hair, pulling it from the base as he manhandles me roughly. I hiss from the pain, but I don't pull away. I continue my mission to see him, *fully see him.* Then, he whispers, pushing my head down as he growls into my ear, "Suck." He orders.

One word has me dripping and already waiting for him to fill the void between my legs.

I oblige and continue to pull his pants down.

I gulp, hoping that my nervous swallows will lift my body's self-coiling...*but* his phone ringing on full blast does it for me. It snaps us out of the bubble we secluded ourselves in tonight. We were in our world for what felt like hours, and everything came crashing down like a violent, unforgiving tsunami into my spirit. The serene, secretive orb we immersed ourselves in depleted into the disastrous self-awareness of our cruel reality.

He groans, stiffening, and so do I. We lock eyes with each other, desperately breathing the thick tension of oxygen like we're drowning...*drowning in each other.*

My hands are still holding his pants, but he forces me to let go, and my hopes drop with my hands.

"That's my alarm system. Something is not right," he looks around his home like he's about to kill someone. It's the same anxious expression he had at El Devine. Darkness sharpens his words and voice.

He grabs my wrist, "I'm sorry, Alessia." He apologizes, but his words have a strange, vivid edge. And it hits me. I know that whatever we just shared is over and probably never going to happen again. I deflate like a balloon being popped, and his vibes rub off on me. Anxiety cripples underneath my skin like a fever.

Why would his alarm system go off in the middle of the night?

Is it...*my stalker*?

Is this just a coincidence, or does this happen all the time?

"Is something wrong? Is someone trying to break in?" I ask, shivers running up and down my spine.

I slowly get off him and sit on the couch, brushing my hair with my fingers. I cup my breasts with my forearms as he hands me the same towel I walked in with.

The intense, blissful moment slowly seeps away, like the night when it meets the sun. He reaches for his phone, which lies on the couch. He looks at the screen, his face falling into a stone-cold expression.

"It's the cameras. There was motion detected." He scours the screen up and down like he doesn't want to deal with it, and his brows narrow like he's upset...almost guilty.

"Oh, no. Daegan, what if it's the human traffickers? What if it's the people with *that list*?" I can't even finish my sentence. The fear of my stalker following me to Daegans place is paralyzing. Daegan stills while my eyes round. He frowns at me like I said something impossible.

Maybe I'm overthinking. Or maybe I'm not.

He walks out of the living room, his bloody hand still dripping all over the place, his hair disheveled from my constant tugging.

"I'll take care of this. It could've just been a random animal walking by, and the sensors picked that up."

He looks at his phone again, studying it until he finally exits, leaving me with my spiraling thoughts. His phone rings this time. Someone is calling him.

He heads for the door to his backyard, and I watch him, unable to move. I feel like I'm floating on clouds, struggling to come back down to the ground.

One moment, I was in my own world with him. All the pain and emptiness were filled and voided. I hold onto my towel tighter, wanting to go back in time.

PRETEND

I glance over at him, in a discreet manner, through the window that's built into the back door, and the moonlight is enough to illuminate his frame. Thankfully, he doesn't notice my gawking.

I'm still on a high.

I touch my lips as I watch him, and I reminisce about his tongue. It felt nice to forget about my problems, even if it was for only a few minutes.

Daegan lights his cigarette while he's on the phone with someone. He inhales as the tip of the cigarette sparkles with fire, and something about the way he lights it has me swooning. He blows the smoke into the air, pacing around his patio. He stands still for a moment, then nods as the call continues.

If he's getting a call in the middle of the night, it can only mean one thing.

There's a mission. A task that needs to be done. Or maybe something happened at work, and they need him to know. Maybe it's Ravenmore canceling his assignment to watch over me.

Wishful thinking.

After all, this is the life of a Special Operator. A life I don't want to be around. This is why I only asked for one night. It'll be easier that way. No strings are attached, no one gets hurt, and no one has expectations. But the way he resisted me has me questioning if he truly is interested in me. I almost had no self-control while he had it all. I just want to continue to pretend until the sun comes up.

I tear my eyes away from him and start chewing the inside of my lip. I get up from the couch and head towards the bedroom again.

Stupid, stupid, stupid girl.

He's right, we can't do this.

I'm about to run into his bedroom when my bladder demands my attention. I look to my right and see that there are two more doors deep into the hallway. I remember him saying there was another restroom in the hallway. It must be in one of those.

I play a guessing game and turn one doorknob, but it doesn't budge. It's...locked.

Huh? Weird.

Why would he lock one of his doors inside his house? I'm sure there's a valid reason, but that doesn't stop an uncanny sensation to ripple through the dark parts of my mind, causing the hairs on the back of my neck to stand up.

"What are you doing, Valentine?"

I jump like a scared cat. I'm on my toes, palming the wall to stop myself from stumbling over. My other hand goes to my mouth, and a loud squeak disappears into the air, my towel almost dropping to the floor.

"Daegan! You scared me," I pant, trying to recover from the jump scare. I can hear my heart eradicate through my ears as I try to calm myself down.

His eyes darken like he's trying to figure me out. Like I was caught looking through his diary. It's almost like I did something wrong.

"I'm sorry, I was looking for the restroom."

He points to the other door, still as a statue.

I swallow nervously, brushing curls behind my ear. The hallway light is off, but the light from his kitchen barely makes a dent in the hallway. It's dim enough to see him still.

"What's going on? Is everything okay?" I ask innocently, dreading the answer.

Then, his shadow moves. He doesn't say anything as he stalks forward. The darkness matches the silence, and I wait until he's ready to talk.

Finally, he stops. His chest is one inch from mine.

"Grim is on paternity leave, and I have to go in. I guess they want to go over something with me before my assignment and the deployment that starts tomorrow." He bites out with no emotion.

"Right this second? You have to leave right now?"

"Yes," he sighs.

"Oh," I look down at our feet.

He takes a deep breath like he has the weight of the world on his shoulders.

I'm not a stranger to what SEALS go through. I may not know all the little details about their missions, but I know enough. And I know the outcomes may cost them their lives. I don't know him…I don't know Daegan, but the thought of never seeing him again scares me.

"Don't worry, Valentine. I looked at the video footage. It was just a racoon. You'll be safe here tonight until I get back, and then we'll be on your little PSD assignment." He snaps in a soft voice, combing his hair with his hand. And that's when I notice it's bandaged with white medical fabric.

I know this must bother him. A personal security detail isn't something he asked for, which is why I did my best to plead my case with Ravenmore. And yet, every time he says PSD, there's a hint of disgust in his tone. It's the way he frowns to stop himself from grimacing. I try not to take it personally, but after tonight…it's hard not to.

"I know this assignment isn't what you strive for. You must not want it…or me." I admit, pinning my vision to the floor instead of facing his reaction.

He groans like he's frustrated.

"Is that what you think? You think I don't want you?" He says in a cold tone.

"Yes, I mean, you did say something along those lines tonight. Several times, actually." I whisper.

He spins me around faster than I can register what he's doing. He pushes my face against the wall, his hand cups a handful of my hair, and he places his chest on my back desperately. His waist on mine, his bulge on my ass. Then his lips are on my neck, and the smell of his cigarettes gets stronger.

"Can you feel that? Can you feel how fucking hard you make me? Just being next to you does this to me. I'm filled with so much fire I feel like I'll burn the entire world down if I don't get my fill of you." He presses his cock deeper into my ass like he's about to fuck it. "Do you feel how badly I want to bury myself so deep inside you until your cunt is molded to mine and mine only? Just thinking about being inside you makes me crazy." He pushes his hard length again against my ass, in between my cheeks, like he's ready to push it in again. I moan against the wall. "Can you feel what you do to me? My cock is aching, Alessia," he snarls into my ear, "and it's aching for you." He pulls my hair again.

Daegan brushes his knuckles on my face gently. "And I can't have you."

He lets go of my face, taking a step back and letting me breathe again.

"Don't ever question if I want you again. Now, be a good girl and go to sleep. It's your birthday."

I turn around to face him. "Whatever this was stays here and doesn't follow us after tonight, right Daegan?"

He pauses, his jaw tightening over and over again, his gaze piercing mine.

"Right," he murmurs softly. "I'll report this stalker problem of yours to the police. I have close friends in the department. Now, please, Alessia. Have mercy on me and go back into my bedroom. Lock the fucking door before I—"

He stops himself from going further. Palming the wall behind me, I take one step back. He's caging me into the door frame, and my shoulder blade hits the front of the door.

PRETEND

"Before what?" I rasp, daring him for more excitedly.

He towers over me, and I'm forced to tilt my head upwards. His finger tilts my chin up, and he grins.

"Before I tie you up to my headboard, gag you with your own thong, and do all the things I've been craving to do to you since I first met you in that elevator. So, no matter how loud you try to scream, no matter how bad you want to run, you're forced to just lie there like a good little nasty whore I want to turn you into and *take it*."

I gasp, my heart thundering and the sensation pooling in between my thighs. No one has ever talked to me like this before. It's degrading, but it's so hot.

"So, bedroom...now." He orders. "I hope I'll be back soon."

"I have to take another shower. I still have *this* all over my neck." I motion towards the dried blood all over my neck.

"Leave it on. I like seeing you covered in red."

20
Alessia

THE NEXT MORNING, I woke up alone, the haze of the night's memories slowly coming into my mind. Recollecting every detail sent a fire to scorch my core. Memories of his knife...getting pushed against the wall made my heart flutter, heat fueling my every pulse, just like it did when he kissed me.

He trusted me to take off his mask, and even though I haven't asked him about it, a part of me feels like he's never done that with anyone before. But it was just one night...

And in that one night, he ignited a storm—a storm I want to ride through and risk, take all of those strong winds, and go through them with him.

After Daegan and I interacted in the hallway, I escaped into his bedroom, did as I was told, and locked the door. God, I was praying that he would kick the door down and do all those things he said he would. But with my luck, he disappeared from the house in less than twenty minutes after receiving that call.

His eyes, his scars...*his knife*.

PRETEND

I'll never be able to look at his knife the same again. Not only because he made me have the best orgasm in my entire life all over it, but because of Frankie.

He stabbed a man for assaulting me and then fucked me with the same weapon all in one night. This man was making me question my own sanity. I shockingly slept like a baby last night despite the fear of Daegan's house alarm system going off and being alone for who knows how long.

Crying over Jack and Bailey's betrayal drained my energy, and my eyes were heavy ever since. It only makes sense that I fell into a deep slumber, even when my worries ran rampant.

I took a quick shower in the morning—our flight overseas is not until late in the afternoon. I watched Daegan's dried blood run down the drain, my mind clouding with work. My first deployment in Iraq will start, and the unknown claws at me.

It's only six months long…but in a weird way, I think this will give me time to heal. I'll be away from my home, away from this military town. I can't look at my room without getting hit with good and bad memories.

I make a mental note to throw out my bed and get a new one.

When I unlock my door and head towards the living room, I'm in Daegan's clothes. His clothing swallows my frame, and his shirt and sweatpants are loose at the ends. The fabric is smooth and soft against my skin.

The smell of coffee hits me, and my mouth waters. Daegan stands tall in his kitchen, the bright golden rays shining through his windows, illuminating his beautiful body.

Of course, the person tasked with my life for the next few months has to be devastatingly handsome, twisted with masculinity, and quiet and mysterious.

"Coffee?" he asks, pouring it into a mug. The fumes from the hot, black coffee seep above the mug. He isn't wearing a mask anymore.

"Sure." I politely tell him, sitting across from him on a bar stool. The mug glides across the counter, slow and soft, like he's afraid to touch me.

We sit in an eerie, awkward silence, drinking coffee. I look at him, wanting him to say something...anything. He's unpredictable. One minute, he's quiet, and the next, a ghost.

I hold the mug above my lips, tempted to break the silence and address last night's activities.

I open my mouth, sucking in a breath, but he beats me to it like he can read my mind. Maybe my emotions are written all over my face. I've never been good at hiding them.

"What I did...crossed the line. You are the Admiral's daughter."

Anger seeps into my veins.

"Stepdaughter," I interrupt him like a stubborn child.

"Nonetheless, you're related to the man. He is my boss. I love my job. I love being a part of this team. I won't ever touch you again." His tone is cold and distant. It's like he's miles away, but in reality, it's only inches. His kitchen counter is the only thing that separates us.

"Daegan, stop. We're adults. We knew the consequences of our actions, and I would do it again. I wouldn't change a thing about last night. No one needs to know what we do behind closed doors. It doesn't interfere with our work or our professionalism. We can—"

"Alessia Sahara Valentin. You don't know me. I'm not a good man. If you let me in, you'll regret it. I won't hold your hand, I won't sweet talk your ear off, and I won't invest my time into a relationship with you or anyone for that matter. I'm committed to my work." He palms the counter with both hands, his fingers gripping it hard. His scars around one eye twitch with stipulation as he stares into me.

I can't hold his gaze. It's too much. He's just too much, and I'm in over my head.

My heart sinks with the hope we can continue to get to know each other. He's ending whatever chemistry we shared last night. What did I expect? We agreed to only one night. I'm the one that's pushing for more. He's a man of his word, I guess.

I blink rapidly, looking at the hot liquid instead of his grey entrapping eyes. What does he want me to say to that? It's for the best, anyway. I just got out of a relationship. I just got cheated on. It's...for the best.

"Last night didn't exist. It was pretend, remember?" I remind him. I place my mug down as my appetite disappears. I force my confused feelings away, locking them far into my mind. I get off the bar counter, and head for the front door. Even through my peripheral vision, he stiffens, but he's still stone-cold and unreadable.

I slip on my cowgirl boots. "I need to get my stuff, and then I'm stopping by my mother's place." I give him a cold shoulder and open the door to his house. I'm going to call an Uber now that my phone is fully charged. Walking into the sunlight, I close his door softly.

I need to focus—Daegan's right. Our careers come first, and he's a distraction. I have a job to do. I have to prove that I belong there overseas with them. I didn't get to where I was because of Ravenmore or because of the imprint my mother left while she was in the Navy.

If he wants to be cold towards me, I can respect that and move on. Maybe the chemistry we shared, the stolen glances, and the soul-consuming kisses were all in my head. Either way, it doesn't matter—not anymore.

I'm on my way back to my apartment around nine in the morning. Daegan insisted he drive me back to my place, but I refused, begging him to respect my decision to go home and recollect my things alone after last night. I told him I would be okay. But he wouldn't let up. We stood there arguing on his front porch, back and forth, until finally, he had no choice but to let me go once the Uber arrived.

That night was...euphoric. And it's now over, back to reality where I just found out my best friend and boyfriend had been fucking each other behind my back. I knew our relationship was coming to an end. I knew it was. A part of me had a thread of hope, and that thread would hang on because Jack and I have been friends since high school. Then, together throughout college. But he's no longer that dorky guy who made me laugh and picked me flowers from the courtyard on campus.

No.

He's the guy who betrayed me and had the nerve to tell me I was a lousy girlfriend.

When I get to my doorstep, I find Bailey hugging her knees, cradling herself with worried lines under her dark eyes.

PRETEND

I roll my eyes when the Uber parks the car in the driveway.

She's crying? Really?

I thank the Uber driver, getting my bag and hooking it over my shoulder as I try my hardest not to run up to her and rip her to shreds. Instead, I remind myself not to sink to her level and pretend she's not sitting there sulking in her guilt I want no part of.

As soon as I stand before her, she gets up, brushes off her knees, and wipes her wet cheeks.

"Alessia, please forgive me. I'm sorry, I've just been lonely, and your friendship means the world to me."

"Meant." I correct her, fighting back tears of my own. I open the door, taking my key out of the hole. "Our friendship *meant* the world to you. Now we're strangers. It's funny how this world works, right? It's funny how you go from sleepovers, jokes, and thinking you had someone you can lean on until you realize everyone is on their own chasing their own selfish goals, no matter who gets hurt, right?" I step inside and slam the door in her face. Letting my back hit the door, I slide down until I'm sitting, finally succumbing to the hurt I hid last night.

"Please don't do this. Please don't drop me from your life," Bailey begs through the door with muffled pleas.

"No, Bailey! *You* dropped me from your life the moment you decided that our friendship wasn't worth keeping over a guy," I bellow out, crying. "I told you about him. I told you the things we would go through, how I thought he was lying to me when I had my suspicions, and you were behind it all? Fucking my boyfriend? You can have him, Bailey. I don't need this."

"Fine, Alessia! Fine! Drop me! Jack is right. You are stubborn and don't listen to anyone. No wonder he came crawling to me."

Oh, God. I'm not going to entertain this any longer. I meant it when I said they're meant for each other. I don't need this right now. I'm leaving tonight, and I need to get dressed.

I scoff, licking my teeth and rubbing the tears away. I get up from the floor and head for my bedroom. I promise myself that this will be the last time I'll ever cry over them.

I open the door, swinging it open, ready to go straight to the bathroom. I tuck my fingers underneath Daegan's all-black shirt, but a bouquet of black colored sunflowers sits in the center of my kitchen table, wrapped in brown paper with one single bright yellow in the center of them all.

Who? What?

How?

Is this Jack's lame attempt to apologize? He's never bought me flowers before, so why start now? If he thinks flowers will get me to crawl back to him, he's got it all wrong. I no longer want anything from him. I've never been so sure of a decision in my life.

I grab the bouquet of flowers, and my phone buzzes.

> Unknown: Happy birthday.

It's my stalker again.

21
Alessia

A S I SEARCH FOR fresh clothes, I notice all of Jack's things are gone. Good. There's not an ounce of me that wants him to still loiter in my home.

I hold a frame of us together at our college graduation and shove it deep into my nightstand drawer, closing it like I'm closing a book, ending the last chapter as Jack and Alessia.

If I can't have Daegan, I do want to try this thing people call 'dating.' I've been with the same person since I was in college. I won't let myself sulk in this heartache I didn't ask for. I think it's time for me to evolve and try something new. I won't make any apologies for the way I choose to grow.

I walk outside to check my mail but find my car sitting in the driveway and a mysterious man in an all-black suit. He has aviator sunglasses on, not one facial hair on his chiseled jaw, dark hair gelled perfectly back, no strand out of place, as he sits on the hood of my car, lighting a cigarette.

How? What the hell is going on? Who does he think he is, and how the hell did my car get here?

"Umm? Excuse me? Who are you, and how the hell did you get my car?"

He doesn't acknowledge my presence. Instead, he blows the smoke into the air.

"I'm a friend of Creature's. He asked me to take care of this sorry excuse of a car you have *for you*."

My mouth gawks open.

"Excuse me?"

He's unbothered by my sudden inability to hold a sentence. He radiates dark and mystery, just like Daegan. He slides his cuff down to view the time on his luxurious Rolex, and I scoff when he doesn't respond.

"I would love to stay and chit-chat with Ravenmore's daughter, but I've got some business to take care of. You can thank Creature for having me fetch your car. I filled the tank up with gas as well and had it deep-cleaned. All your personal belongings are in the trunk."

"Step-daughter," I correct him, doing my best to mask my seething tone. "How do you know him? You expect me to say thank you? You just said my car is trash." I cross my arms over my chest. "You're friends with Daegan?"

Unbothered to hold a conversation or acknowledge me, he replies. "We're *brothers*. Don't thank me, thank Creature."

He takes out his car keys and presses a button, and a beep follows. I trail the sound, and my eyes bulge when I see a luxurious Pagani sitting just a few feet away.

"By the way, some piece of advice?" The car door lifts open, and he leans in, one boot into the driver's seat. "Pretty girls shouldn't be walking the streets alone at night. You're lucky Daegan came by and snatched you."

He closes the door, the engine roaring, and speeds out of my driveway.

What a rude jerk of a handsome guy.

I finished packing, but there are still four hours before my flight. I still have time to visit my mother before I go. I throw everything in my trunk and close it with a careful slam. A shadow that isn't my own appears on the back window of my car. It's a man behind me.

"Alessia."

I jump, fisting my hands, ready to defend myself.

Oh, no.

If it's my stalker, he's caught me off guard. Blood rushes to my cheeks, and my heart palpates. I turn around with harsh purpose, but then my eyes soften when I realize I'm safe, but it doesn't stop the adrenaline from running through my veins.

I roll my eyes at a very pleased Daegan. He loves to scare me, doesn't he?

I palm my chest as if that'll help my heart rate go back to normal.

"Hannibal!" I screech loudly, brushing the long, dark curls out of my face. He smirks devilishly. "You scared me. What are you doing here?" I snarl.

"I'm driving you to the airport, remember? Per Ravenmore's request." He fiddles with a bullet between his fingers like he's already bored. He's wearing his uniform; his half-mask is back on.

"I can drive myself, Hannibal." I defy him, crossing my arms.

He scoffs, laughing. His eyes darken, and then he licks his lips. "Little Valentine, keep playing games with me, and you'll find out why I have that nickname." He stalks forward, his large boot thudding over the rocks, sending shivers up my neck. He closes the distance, and the scent of cigarettes swirls amongst his cologne into our tensioned bubble. "It isn't just because I've never missed…" He leans in, his forehead resting on the side of my head as he whispers into my ear, sending goosebumps and hairs to erupt all over my skin and a flicker of pulsation between my legs. "I never lose, and I *always* get what I want." His voice deepens like a hungry snarl. He pushes the button to open the trunk and grabs my bags like feathers. He walks away without another word and heads towards his challenger. "Get in my car, Alessia. I'm driving."

Gathering my emotions again, I shake myself out of his chokehold.

"I need to say bye to my mother first!" I shout after him. There's no way I'm leaving without saying goodbye to her.

"We will, don't worry." He calls back over my shoulder.

22

Alessia

D AEGAN KEPT HIS PROMISE and took me to my mother's place. He stayed in the car, and I promised I would make sure to say, *see you soon*, quick.

I enter her two-story home after two knocks.

"*Esta abierta*!" She calls back to me.

I walk in but don't see her on her gray couch by her floral frames, which are hung on every wall in her living room. The TV is off, and she's not watching her usual medical drama TV shows or novellas, with a glass of wine to destress from work.

I pass by the kitchen to see it spotless and clean, but there's no food roaming around.

"*Ma, donde estas? Ya me voy!*" I look for her down the halls, practically jogging through the halls. I pass by photo frames of me and her growing up—one with us together at a Halloween party as a single mom. At least, she pretended to be a single mom. I didn't meet Ravenmore until after a few years. She wanted to make sure they were solid before she introduced us.

The photo stops me for a split second as I stare at myself as a child. I was dressed as Sally from the Nightmare Before Christmas. I scoff with a minimal laugh. A swift, warm emotion pulls at my heartstrings. I don't remember that day at all, but I'm grateful for photos like these.

"I'm in my office." My mother's muffled voice peaks through the corner, and I follow.

"What're you doing here? It's late." I sit down on a chair, letting my butt fall into the soft cushion. I purse my lips with curiosity when I notice my mother is still in her work detective attire.

She was an ex-Navy sailor who inspired me to join and follow in her footsteps. After she was honorably discharged after serving eight years, she used her experience to go back to college to further her education and became a detective. She loves her job and has always been an extreme workaholic.

She holds a glass of wine in her hands, twirling the dark red liquid.

"I'm stressed out about work. There have been human and drug traffickers growing here in town, and it's an operation bigger than I thought it would be. The more I try to break it, the more we piss them off, and it's becoming dangerous. One of the leader's nicknames is 'Smiley,' he's number one on our list, and we're going above and beyond to catch him. If we catch him, the entire operation will unfold. I'm trying to get to the hornet's nest. It's been hard, to say the least. It's been shocking to learn that there are service members working with them…it's all so exhausting."

She rubs her brows with her fingers, her hazel eyes hidden beneath her tightly shut lids. She pulls back her blonde hair behind her ear and opens her eyes.

PRETEND

"I'm sorry, Mom. I hope everything turns out okay. Please stay safe." I look at my watch, and I'm shy of five minutes late. "I just wanted to say goodbye. Your husband has one of his team members on personal security detail to watch over me, by the way. It's so unnecessary." I roll my eyes as I sigh.

She forces a smile on her glossy lips, "I should be telling you to stay safe. You're going on your first deployment as military intelligence to work closely with Navy SEALS and other special operators. That's amazing, and I'm so proud of you." Her tired voice softens, and her eyes glimmer with pride. She palms her red wooden desk, and I nod in acknowledgment. "Make me proud!"

She stands up from her chair and walks over to me. Her arms are spread out, ready to hug me. "Go easy on my husband. I requested it." She embraces me, and I immediately smell her signature Chanel perfume as we hold each other for a short moment before I pull away in shock.

"Mom," I complain as I retreat from my hug.

How could she do that?

"What?"

"Why? I don't want it to be seen as me having special treatment."

"Because I have a bad feeling that one of these bad guys will be over there. I'm unsure if it's just one bad guy or an entire group. And do I have to remind you of that list? You're a target, and—"

Shit, she does have a point. I let go of her and turn toward the door in a rush as she explains herself. I promised Daegan I would make this goodbye quick. I don't like being late...I don't know any service member that likes to be late.

"Someone shot at my window the other night," I blurt out as I grip the doorknob, ready to escape before she bombards me with a trillion questions.

"What?" She reaches for me, but I'm already out the door and down the hall.

"Alessia Sahara Valentin." She scolds me as I walk into the living room.

"It's okay. I have a bodyguard now, remember?" I tell her sarcastically, almost like an insult, and she seethes, resenting my remark. She folds her arms across her black cardigan with pinched brows. She shakes her head.

"Why didn't you report it?"

"Of course, I reported it." I raise my voice in defiance, but then I calm myself down. "I'm sorry. I didn't mean to be rude, but I've gotta go..." I tell her slowly, reaching for her arms and kissing her cheek goodbye. "Okay? I love you too."

"*Te quiero mucho, que Dios te bendiga, hija.* Make me proud."

The plane ride to Iraq was long, too long. But every now and then, Daegan and I would sneak glances. Each time, we locked eyes for a split second, and it would send that same electrifying blip in my heart, and butterflies would swarm.

We sat next to each other, but he kept his distance. The space between us is thick with tension, but I kept busy with a thriller novel. SEAL Team Executioners were sitting just across from us. Kane sat next to Daegan and the rest of the team in front of us. Operator Grim Reaper stayed home with his wife and newborn twins, just like Ravenmore said he would.

I had to use the restroom during the first flight over the Atlantic. There was a long line, but thankfully, I could hold my pee. I lean against the wall, crossing my arms as I wait.

"God, I hate planes."

PRETEND

A woman to my right says. Her brown hair is slicked back perfectly. She has brown eyes and fair skin. We're both in uniform. She has a friendly smile with tired eyes.

I scoff with a warm smile. "Me too."

"What's your name and rate?" She asks.

"Alessia Valentin. Intelligence." I tell her proudly and confidently, just as the person in front of me exits the restroom, and it's my turn to use it.

"Ah, Ravenmore's daughter." She tells me, giggling at her feet.

I make room for the man who just used the restroom to return to his seat in the tight-space walkway of the plane. I hold the restroom door open and reach for her hand to shake with a smile on my face.

"What's your name? You look familiar." I tell her, trying to remember where I've seen her before. Was it at El Devine? Boot camp?

She takes my hand and shakes it with an edge. She meets my eyes directly with a smile of cruel intentions.

"Oh, I'm Mary Solis. The woman who didn't make Intel because my daddy isn't someone important like Admiral Ravenmore and ex-intel mommy." She lets go of my hand and smiles harder, and mine falls.

Is she really doing this? Right now?

I had a feeling people were saying this behind my back, but I just never thought someone would say it to my face.

Props to her, I guess.

"I didn't get to where I am because of them."

"Keep telling yourself that." She looks at her phone, peeling away from me unbothered. I stand there, still appalled.

I feel defeated. It doesn't matter what I say. The PSD that Operator Bane and Creature were placed on doesn't help my argument.

I close the door.

As soon as we landed, he helped gather our luggage, and we arrived in Iraq late at night. The first thing on my to-do list was to visit my stepfather. He informed me that Kane, Operator Bane, and Daegan would rotate shifts at night. It was a short meeting, which we kept professional, and short given the time of night. They escorted me everywhere.

I have my own private room with a lounge area. My room is small, with one bed, a desk, a nightstand, and a bathroom. It reminds me of my college days. I was so young when I joined. It feels like ages ago.

Rooker will be in charge of their schedule to watch over me for the most part. He appointed Slaughter to take the first night, which sent a wave of sadness to pulse through me.

It's for the best.

The temptation is too potent and frightening. The more I'm surrounded by him, the more I want to give into our chemistry.

"Lights out, Valentín." Kane opens the door to my bedroom, and I walk in, clutching my bag.

PRETEND

I twirl around on my heel to tell him goodbye. He stands there in the dark, the only light from my lamp. He's in his uniform, his hand on the doorknob, waiting for me to say something.

I want to break the ice with Kane since he will also be on my ass along with Daegan, making a note of my every movement to keep me safe. My intrusive thoughts take over, and my mouth opens before I can stop it.

"What did you do to get your ass kicked at the military ball the other year?" My blunt question catches him off guard, but he doesn't miss the endearment entwined in my tone. I cross my arms as he lets his head fall, and he chuckles deeply, clearly unoffended by my inability to prevent my outburst.

Kane is...beautiful.

What a man.

He runs a hand through his dark waves and smiles like he's proud of himself. "I crossed a line and kissed Grim's girl."

So Ari Alvarez had the pleasure of having two handsome SEALS after her? What a problem to have.

What a shame.

"Yeah, that explains it," I scoff with a slight smile, placing a hand on my hip as my own lips tilt into a comforting smile.

"I was....very in love with her, *madly* in love with Ari. I overstepped and hurt many people in the process. And I did a stupid thing." His smile fades and is replaced by a somber scoff. He licks his lips and looks away from me like he's upset with himself. Losing himself in the memories of the fight...or maybe it's just his journey with Ari. "But I guess love can sometimes do that to someone, right? Love makes you crazy?" He shrugs, putting his hands in his pockets nervously.

I look at Kane, and I mean really look at him, and this man is drop-dead handsome. But in a way that's warm and radiates cheer. His dark hair matches Daegan's, but Kane is slightly shorter by an inch or so and leaner in his body frame. He's still well over six feet. His dark blue eyes are welcoming, in contrast to Daegan's.

When I look at Daegan, it's a mystery, and the unknown makes it even more tempting.

"I'm sorry. I wouldn't know what love is. Lately...I don't believe it's meant for me."

"Well, it exists alright, and it's real. I have scars on my face to prove it." He points to a scar on his jaw, probably from when Operator Grim Reaper punched him. "Even though it didn't work out the way I wanted, it was still a period in time I will always cherish in my life. Even if it ended in my ass getting kicked." He pauses while his eyes brighten like they're lost in Ari's. "Being in love with her was like chasing a sunset. She was always out of reach but still the most beautiful thing to experience."

He scoffs, smiling. He glances at his feet like I've hit a nerve. When his tone changes to sadness and his voice softens, I know Ari is still probably someone he will always care about.

"I'm sorry for bringing it up." I squeeze his hand in an innocent gesture.

"It's fine." He straightens his posture and takes a step back, squeezing my hand once before letting go. His rough, calloused hand slithers out slowly. "I'm talking to someone else right now, and she makes me very happy. She's made me the happiest I've been in a long time, actually."

"I guess that's a good thing?" My voice pitches high with hope. "I get it. It sucks to make a mistake, and everyone wants to basically ruin your life for it and make you feel like the biggest piece of shit to walk the Earth, but you're not a bad person Kane. I don't know you too well, even though over these next few months, I probably will know you better than my own parents..." My voice crescendos into a murmur, sarcastically referencing his assignment to watch over me. "You're not a bad person, Slaughter. Don't let the world make you feel that way. Yes, you fucked up, but don't stay there."

He looks at me like I've struck numerous nerves inside him.

"I guess it's a good thing you didn't stay there and found this new woman in your life, right?"

"It's a blessing, Valentín. When I talk to her, I forget where I am in the world."

"Why is that?"

He brushes his beard with his hand, and a smile follows suit.

"She's the type of person that makes a dark day disappear...like it never happened in the first place."

"Alright, sir, you need to stop with all this cutesy stuff. I think you're a romantic and you fall fast, like me. We can't help it." I wiggle my finger at him teasingly. "But I'm trying not to be like that."

"Well, good luck with that. I'll get out of your hair...but one more thing."

The door swings almost closed, but his head pokes out.

"What?"

He smirks, "I see the way you look at Creature...it's the way I used to look at Ari."

My mouth falls open, and I start to stutter. I immediately go into a defensive mode, but no words come out, only indescribable sounds because I'm having difficulty choosing them.

How? Is it that obvious? We've been careful. Our stolen glances have to have been just that.

"Kane..."

What can I say?

I can explain?

It isn't true that I have some type of feelings for my so-called bodyguard?

One of the only people on this Earth I cannot date because, one, it'll taint his career, and two, he might be emotionally unavailable. But maybe that's just what I need.

He raises his hand to hush me politely and smirks mischievously.

"Secret is safe with me." He finishes with a cheerful smile.

My mouth is still dropped open like a fish with a hook in its mouth, dumbfounded.

He closes the door, leaving me with my thoughts...and forbidden grey eyes that are tattooed into my brain.

23
Alessia

MY FIRST DAY ON the job was a whirlwind of stress. I digested a lot of information. I sat down and was briefed on all recent events and targets. Learning about our next high-priority target was sickening. They call him the Surgeon. He is an evil man who worked under Omar. He's the same man who kidnapped Violet Redd and Damon Hawk. He was one of his right-hand men. He did dirty work for him, killing and kidnapping innocents, and still does even after Omar is no longer here.

He has carried on to do more evil things. Winters filled me in, and today is the day we give SEAL Team Hellhounds their next mission. It's a conference-looking room, a big screen with a PowerPoint on all of the target's known information and whereabouts and maps that hold highly confidential information that only needs to know personnel can decipher.

Slaughter and Hannibal sit in the back of the room, watching me like a hawk, with their hands behind their back in the corner behind about forty special operators that include Army Special Forces, SEALS, etc.

Daegan twirls a bullet in his hand out of boredom, I presume. But his grey eyes are pinned on me, watching me like his life depends on it. He makes me nervous, and all I want to do is prove that I belong here. I thought I already did with the numerous tests and schools I had to get through. Winters told me that some people think I got to my position because the Admiral is my stepfather. Kane gives me a warm, comforting smile like he's encouraging me. His eyes say I'm doing a good job for my first day.

The room is quiet, full of men who are ready to hunt down their next target.

"The Surgeon kidnapped a family working closely with us to catch him. We've been informed by intelligence of his coordinates. SEAL Team Hellhounds will run this one since Grim isn't here. Creature and Bane are on babysitting duty, and Texas...well, he works best with Grim and Bane together." Enzo Rooker, Operator Cobra, informs the room with a southern accent voice that's riddled with years of wisdom and experience.

He's a handsome man. Tall, masculine, and built all around. 6'4, with colored eyes, but I can't tell if they're emerald hazel, light brown, or even blue. I've never been close enough to get the details. He has a blonde beard peppered with a few white strands, and his peppered curly hair is grown over his ears. From what I know, he's the oldest on SEAL Team Executioners, happily married to his wife with twin daughters.

Winters and I received the crucial information this morning, so the Teams need to act fast to capture 'The Surgeon' before he kills and tortures more innocent people. He's a criminal, murderer, rapist, and extremist—pure evil with no redemption in sight for his heinous actions.

"We're going to need Creature for this mission. You know we need him. If he's not going to make the shot to take HVT's out, we need him as overwatch. We don't have Grim, and now our best Sniper?" Lopez sits up in his seat, throwing a tantrum. He looks around the room, and other operators nod in agreement. All the special operators look and turn to each other, and a ruckus of chatter ensues. I grow uncomfortable knowing that I may be the reason Hannibal and Bane can't do the job they truly desire.

I look down at my feet, placing my hands in my pocket. My teeth pinch my bottom lip nervously, and I start to pop my fingers while my entire body boils into nerves. I want to leave the room now. But I don't want to do that to Slaughter. Kane asked me if we could sit here when the information was being delivered. He still wanted to attend the meeting, even though his assignment is to watch over *me*.

"Stop feeling sorry for yourself..." Hannibal's voice whispers into my ear over the loud commotion. His comment is high enough for me to hear but low enough so no one else can. I look up to my right, trailing my vision from his big arms, his last name patch, and finally, his mask, which has a creepy smile where his mouth is. Sharp teeth, like triangles, slither all the way into his cheeks. I immediately get glued in, locking and getting lost in shades of ice. "I'm not sorry about this assignment, so don't you dare be sorry," Daegan orders me in a grumpy tone as he keeps playing with the bullet. It dances in every single one of his fingers until, finally, he stops and stares at me with so much intensity that I could melt into this wall.

He can't look at me like this. I'm afraid that our entire night of "pretending" will be revealed with just one look.

"I may be one of the newer guys on the teams, but—" Rooker interrupts Lopez.

Vicente Lopez, Operator Texas. He's the youngest in the group, maybe even in the entire room. He's very good at his job and dedicated, but he has a reputation for being a flirt and goofball. He's beautifully tanned with black hair that always looks combed back perfectly. He has a big Texas flag with a cow skull tatted on his arm.

"I understand your concerns, but we got this. Creature is needed somewhere else right now. Stand by and take your orders, Tex. Don't argue." Rooker demands and the entire room grows quiet. Everyone in the room straightens their back and is attentive to Rooker. "A job needs to get done. So, let's get it done."

Rooker's eyes narrow in a fatherly manner. He's straightforward and yet cold and curt. He gets his point across without having to raise his voice, show an ugly side of himself, or throw in words of humiliation to lead.

He reminds me of Danny Rider.

It's lunchtime, and I sit next to Winters and Guerra, eating a Caesar salad in the dining facility. Kane and Daegan sit with their team across from me. Even though this assignment is unnecessary, they can catch up and watch over me. I'm sure whoever this person who's doing bad things isn't here in Iraq.

PRETEND

"Alessia, you're here. I'm so surprised to see my crush here at the same time as me."

I turn to a cheeky, handsome Zeke. He throws his arm around my shoulder and gently squeezes me as he settles in the seat next to me. He drops his arm and scoots closer until our thighs touch.

"Zeke. How are you?" I ask as I stuff my mouth with my lunch. Winters blushes, and Guerra gives me those flirty eyes.

"The real question is, how are you? I heard about Jack and Bailey." My welcoming smile falls, and I start to chew my food slower as the memories of me catching him in the act come back to haunt me in public. Flashes of Bailey riding my ex-boyfriend make bile rise in the back of my throat, and the pain comes back distastefully.

I look to see if Guerra or Winters heard that, and I shrink in my seat. My shoulders slump, and I play with the lettuce, poking it with my fork over the slices of avocado.

"We're going to get some dessert and be right back. Right, Guerra?" Guerra looks at Winters perplexed with food still in her mouth, but then quickly agrees and stands up, nodding. Winters tilts her head at Guerra to follow her to the kitchen, and they both leave Zeke and me alone.

"You didn't deserve that. He didn't deserve you in the first place." Zeke points out, giving me a playful nudge with his knuckles.

"I really don't want to talk about Jack." I swallow my food and wipe my mouth with a napkin after.

"Good. Neither do I." Zeke takes out his wallet, and I watch him pull out a small piece of paper. He gives it to me as my cheeks warm into a mixture of emotions. I open it up and realize it's his number.

"Zeke..." I hold the paper in my hand, unsure of what to say. I stare at the numbers and then place the note into the pocket of my jeans.

I just got out of a relationship, and I'm not sure of what I want, but I know for a fact that it's not dwelling in the past and letting my trauma hold me back from being happy. Maybe I need to see what it's like to date around. I've only been with one person, and the thought of being vulnerable again is...nerve-racking but so tempting.

I'm attracted to Zeke; *there is something there*. But I'm not sure if it's enough to explore the feeling. When it comes to Zeke, I'm unsure. Meanwhile, there's no hesitation when it comes to a certain masked, scarred man. When it comes to Daegan, it's just a straight road I want to drive down with no bumps to make me swerve or change my mind.

Zeke holds my hand over the table, his grey eyes searching for a chance in mine. "Let me take you out. I have some time here before we head out on the next mission. I want to show you the firepit. We can talk and watch a movie. Maybe even—"

A tall shadow casts over Zeke and me. Zeke pauses mid-sentence and watches whoever interrupted him settle in before us. I follow his gaze and realize it's Daegan. He's masked with that same creepy, sharp teeth smile over his mouth.

"So we're going on a date?" Daegan chirps sarcastically. "Where are you taking us, Zeke?"

Zeke scoffs, pissed off. "What do you mean, 'us,' Creature?" He retorts and lets go of my hand, balling his own into fists on his lap.

Daegan hums.

"Well, you know, since watching over Alessia is my assignment, Bane and I have to follow wherever she goes. So, I'm going to ask you again..." he says

PRETEND

sinisterly, his humor painting each syllable. His eyes crease like he's smiling big, and the scars on his one side twitch with excitement like he's daring him to say the wrong thing. "Where are you taking us?" He repeats his questions and leans his chin on one palm as if intrigued to know the answer. He taps his fingers on his chin like he's impatient.

"You know I haven't heard you talk this much. In fact, I've never heard you say much *ever* since you joined the teams. And yet, Every. Single. Time. I'm near Valentin...you can't seem to shut up." Zeke points out something that I haven't even thought of. He smiles, which provokes Daegan harder.

Is he asking for a Death wish? Because of the way Daegan is looking at Zeke right now...it's the same way he looked at Frankie right before he stabbed him.

Daegan straightens his back, staring blankly at a taunting Zeke. He widens his planted feet as he twirls the bullet in his finger faster and harder until finally he stops it, palming it on the table with a loud smack.

His grey eyes can freeze the room with how piercingly wrathful they look. In a deep, monstrous tone, Daegan says, "Careful."

One word. One threat. One sentence is enough to have Zeke cowering in his seat.

24

Alessia

THE THICK TENSION MAKES me wonder if these two have some past because every single interaction they have when I'm around is volatile. It's like one wrong move and a punch will be thrown.

"I'm not taking her anywhere if you'll be there. You know she'll be fine with me." Zeke insists, huffing out his chest.

"I don't know shit. " Creature argues back.

Why is he acting like this?

I stare at the two men sitting in front of me. Both of them are tensed up, clearly wanting to go at each other's throats. I look around, with shivers running through my bones, hoping someone will pull me out of this situation. But Kane is deep into his lunch, and Rooker converses deeply with Lopez.

Saved by the bell, my watch pings, signaling that lunchtime is over and it's time to go back to work.

PRETEND

I scrunch up my napkin and tap my watch as the men have a dick-size contest in front of me.

"Well...I'm going back to work now..." I stand up, grabbing my tray from the table, and Zeke locks in his hateful stare, keeping his narrowed eyes on Creature. Creature stands at the same time as I do, like he's prepared to walk me back to my job.

A wave of tenderness washes over me as my previous relationship reminds me that I don't have to feel guilty about moving on. Jack sure as hell didn't feel guilty about it with Bailey. And if Daegan doesn't want to explore, I want to give Zeke a chance.

I bend down and enter Zeke's space, leaning into his ear so Daegan can't hear.

"I'll text you. See you later." I murmur warm heartedly, doing my best not to taint my tone with something that's more than just friendly. I walk away from a smiling Zeke, and he stands. Before I turn around, I catch him walking back to his team of co-workers with a chip on his shoulder. They all cheer him on, like a bunch of jocks at a football game.

"You really have to work on your whispering skills." Daegan pushes the door open to the cafeteria and holds it, waiting for me to walk outside. I roll my eyes, not caring if he heard what I said. I shuffle past him, my feet walking against rocks, and my skin gets blasted with beaming sun rays. Warm winds greet my hair, making my curls fly with them.

"And you really have to work on your people skills," I bite back over my shoulder. I walk back into my office building. Surprisingly, the hallway is empty, which makes me feel like people are still out at lunch, and I have more time to kill than I thought. I make a mental note of that to start extending my lunches longer.

"I don't like people. Therefore, I don't need to work on something that doesn't need to be fixed." He cheerfully states as he follows me, so close I can feel his gaze on my back, sending those lustful flames to burn me from his proximity.

His shadow is something I don't think I'll ever get used to.

"Daegan," I hiss under my breath, warning him to quit getting on my nerves as I continue to walk, passing my other offices and supply closets.

"Valentine." He quips back.

My heart skips a beat at the nickname.

I turn around on my heels to face him, making him come to an abrupt stop. He catches himself before he crashes into me, saving me from the impending doom of his massive body weight.

"Please, stop. People are talking. People are saying that I'm getting personal security just because I'm Ravenmore's—"

"Daughter." He finishes in a dark antagonizing manner.

"*Step-daughter*." I correct, forcing it through clenched teeth. I brush my curls back and suck in a deep breath to calm my nerves before a very stone-cold Hannibal.

"I don't need this. I don't need you or Kane watching over me. I'm safe, everything is okay, and you should be fighting this with me by talking to Ravenmore and getting this called off. You should—"

He looks around me. His beautiful, light eyes wander around, checking our surroundings behind me, like he's disengaging from the conversation.

"I don't take kindly to people telling me what to do, especially when they can't even reach the height requirement at carnival rides."

My mouth drops open. I place my hands on my hips as his eyes crinkle with a devilish smirk. I know it's there under his ominous mask.

PRETEND

"You did not just insult my height, you jerk."

"How many times do we have to have the same conversation before you understand that you're under orders just like I am? You have to follow *my orders* until your deployment is over. You're not safe. And I don't like Zeke, isn't he with a girl named Violet? I refuse to babysit you while you hang out with him. You can do better."

"One, what makes you think I can do better? And two, I'm pretty sure he's single. And three, I am safe. We're safe! I won't let you interfere with—"

A loud explosion interrupts my seething. The walls and ground vibrate like an earthquake hit the Earth, and my heart sinks to the pit of my stomach. Faint screams are heard from a distance, and people start scrambling around us in a panic. Doors start exploding open and closed as our entire environments continue to shake.

I freeze, trying to get a grip on the situation, wondering what the hell is happening, but before I can blink or swallow nervously, I'm being dragged into a dark closet by Daegan. He grabs my arm, pushing me into it, and I let him.

I'm grateful he's taking initiative when I can't seem to think for myself. Flashes of my stalker and my reality hit me hard. I'm reminding myself that I am in a zone during a time when war is ongoing. Fear paralyzes every single muscle inside me until I'm almost cramping from tensing up so hard. If it weren't for Daegan, I'd still be frozen in the hallway.

"Oh my gosh, Daegan, what was that?" I grab at my chest, finally gathering my thoughts, and pull on my seashell necklace, trying to calm myself down.

He locks the door and pulls out his phone. He ignores me as he sends messages, and I pace in a circle as another explosion rattles the building. I hang on to the shelves like a lifeline, feeling it rattle underneath my tight grip. The sound is closer and louder, causing my ears to ring. I hold up my palms to my ears and close my eyes.

"You were saying, Valentine? Please do finish your sentence...something about being safe?" He crowds my space until my back hits a shelf of paper supplies. He palms both sides of the shelves, locking me in as I still cover my ears with my hands. His voice is still muffled, but I can still hear his words clearly.

Our faces are about three inches apart. His hypnotizing scent fills every single part of me, making me forget where I am and what our mysterious situation is.

"How are you so calm right now? It sounded like a bomb!" I ask him with my brows pinched inwards, furiously.

He ignores me again and takes out a bullet when a considerable part of me wants him to hold me and tell me that everything will be okay and under control. But then again, I feel like I would get that from Kane...not from Daegan. I'm with the cold bodyguard, not the nice one.

"Do you always twirl a bullet in your fingers?" I place my hands down as he stands by the door again with his phone out. It's a dark room with no windows, so we can't see anything in the hallway or outside.

He turns around with a depraved look in his eyes. "Oh, baby girl, there are more places I'd like to twirl this bullet."

Did he?

Did he just imply?

Butterflies kick in, and I'm trying to process what he means by that, but all that leaves my lips is a snarky remark.

"Don't call me that."

"What? You're not a girl?"

"You know exactly what I mean."

"Nope, no idea."

"Stop it."

He invades my space, "I'll call you whatever I want, whenever I want." Cigarettes and his cologne hit me hard, and I want to slap him...and then kiss him because I know how his lips feel. I know how hot he is underneath that mask, and I miss it. I miss him being vulnerable around me, even if it was just for one night.

The fear that once filled my veins is now replaced with temptation.

And as if he can read my thoughts, he leans down, our height difference forcing him to bend his knees, and I catch a glimpse of his Adam's Apple bobbing up and down like he wants to match my thoughts of desire. "And you're not going anywhere alone with Zeke." He snarls, reminding me of our earlier argument. My eyes squint in defiance.

Even though there's chaos happening all around us, it doesn't compare to what this man does to my heart, and I decide to act on it, bracing myself to make a move since he won't.

The dim lights flicker, flashing against my hand as I reach for his mask.

I want to see him.

Daegan stops breathing, and so do I. But I don't get to execute.

"You're obsessed with me," I whisper, our mouths so close to each other. I can smell the hint of cigarettes and his scent.

"Obsessed and following orders are two different things." He growls low.

I smirk, taunting him further, as the throbbing in between my thighs gets louder. "You always want to know where I'm going, what I'm doing. Who I'm with...are you sure you're not obsessed?" I arch a brow, biting my lip, hoping it'll stop me from reaching in for a kiss.

"I'm sure."

I look down, and there's a tent in his pants...a very large tent.

"Your hard cock says otherwise."

Daegan hums, and his eyes crease with determination. "Don't start something you can't finish, Valentine. Because when I start something, I *always* finish."

Fuck.

Daegan takes a step toward me, my back hitting the shelves again. A stack of papers falls to the ground from it, and I'm about to make the first move.

But then it's ruined.

Our phones ping, and a loud alarm screeches through the building. Daegan grabs my hand, puts it back to my side, and walks away from me.

> Kane: There's a drone attack. Get the Admiral's step-daughter somewhere safe. You know the protocol, Creature.

"The alarms are going off, and an attack is happening. Let's get you somewhere safe." He repeats the text from our group chat and opens the door. He motions his hand forward, guiding me toward the exit I don't want to take. I want to stay here and wait it out in private until we know what's happening.

"What? Being alone with my so-called babysitter in a room isn't safe?"

I walk past him and into the hallway. I don't make it far before he grabs my arm. Instead of leading me past a crowd of frantic civilians, he growls against the side of my head, his masked nose grazing against my head, "It's fucking dangerous."

25
Alessia

By the time we walked into the shelter-like room, the attack was over, and everyone was safe. No one was hurt or injured by the mortar attack that landed outside my office building. The war is intensifying, and more people are getting sent home with injuries...and in caskets. Luck was on our side that day when the bombings went off on the base, while the devil kept trying to sabotage any type of fun I sought, especially if it was with Zeke.

I texted Zeke one night before I fell asleep, and we've been talking. It's mostly innocent, with the occasional flirty messages he sends me.

It's nearing the weekend, and after a few weeks of routine work days, it's time to go to the shooting range and brush up on my shooting skills.

> Unknown: Pretty girls shouldn't put their noses in businesses where the big sharks swim. That masked bodyguard of yours fits the perfect description of someone who would be involved in such things.

What the hell?

It's my stalker...and this time, it's scarier than I thought. How did he get into my WhatsApp? How does he know about my job, *where I am*, and who Daegan is?

"What's the matter, Valentine? It looks like you've seen a ghost." He walks next to me, matching my pace, and I quickly shield my phone, digging the screen into my hips. I don't want him to know what this weirdo has been texting me.

"Nothing." A high-pitched squeal leaves my lips. "I was wondering if your friend has found the person who's been texting me. Or shot at my window?" I arch a brow, hoping for an answer. I forgot to ask him if there's an update.

He changes his death stare and looks at the sandy shooting range before us.

"No."

We get to the range in no time, and I walk away, heading toward my group of friends. Daegan stops following me and stands next to Staff Sergeant Julian.

"Operator fucking Creature. Well, I'll be damned. If it isn't the sniper that never misses. What are you doing here in a place like this?" Julian looks at Daegan with so much respect. It radiates off his bright hazel eyes.

"Orders," Daegan spits out with no emotion. He looks up and down the range, inspecting our surroundings. He watches the enlisted shoot their targets while I finally catch up with my co-workers.

"Huh...well, we're fucking honored. Would you mind showing everyone why you hold the title of the best sniper in the world? I could use a little help teaching these kids how to shoot today."

"Sure." He replies nonchalantly. His muscles beneath his top tighten as he walks.

PRETEND

"Oh my god...he's your bodyguard. Stop it right now." Henderson says to my left.

"I can't even see his face, and I'd let that man destroy me in all three of my holes," Guerra says to my right, tugging on her bottom lip hard.

"He's a tall drink of yummy. Masked McHottie?!" Henderson says, pushing Guerra out of the way so she can get a better view of him.

"What do I have to do to get on that list so I can have him as my bodyguard, too?" Guerra wiggles her brows up and down.

"Right? Why couldn't I be the Admiral's stepdaughter?" Henderson complains, frowning. She elbows me in my ribs frivolously.

"Y'all stop. He's a pain in my ass. I'm not allowed to do anything without him knowing about it." I roll my eyes as they admire him. They're making it so obvious as they blush and flutter their lashes at him. They have giddy smiles plastered on display without a care in the world. But Daegan still has his back turned to us as he talks to Julian.

"There are rumors about him," Henderson softly whispers loud enough for us girls to hear, and we crowd in a circle.

"Like what?" My own curiosity is getting the best of me. I hate gossip. I despise it. But if there are rumors about Daegan, I need to know. He invades my personal space every day.

"I have friends of friends in intelligence and CID. Many tips are pouring in with Hannibal's name in their mouths. A lot of people think he had something to do with Operator Grim Reaper and his wife's capture."

"No! Not my masked McHottie!" Guerra complains with a pout. She peeks over to Daegan, but he's still deep in conversation with Julian.

"Yup. Supposedly, everything went to shit when he showed up on the teams." Henderson continues.

"Wow...that's crazy." Winters makes her input, shaking her head like she's disappointed.

"I've looked him up and can't find anything on him. There's no social media under Daegan Hannibal. No Instagram, no TikTok, no Facebook." Guerra counts the social media apps one by one, and I furrow my brows.

"Enough!" I wave my hands in a stop motion. I'm so tired of people gossiping about Daegan as if they know him. "Henderson, don't talk about Hannibal like this. These rumors could be damaging to his reputation and career, and..."

All three girls stare at me like they're stunned by my defensive tone. I shrink down in size and try to gather my heightened emotions. "I'm just saying there's no evidence to back up those claims. I've seen people's lives get ruined over baseless accusations just because someone wants to destroy someone's life maliciously. My stepfather would not have allowed him to watch over me so closely like this. He wouldn't have let my life fall into his hands if there were allegations like this against him. Leave it be, Henderson." I tell her with a cold stare.

They all grow quiet. I watch them disperse, shrug my shoulders, and go to my station to shoot.

After about ten minutes, I grow frustrated. I'm out of practice, and I keep missing my target.

"Great." I miss my target again and sigh, frustrated. Looking away from my crosshairs and instead at the floor.

"You're too tense, Valentine." I almost drop my damn rifle at that voice.

"Mr. Hannibal."

PRETEND

My heart jolts when I realize he's right next to me. Hovering over my ear, whispering. He kicks my feet apart with his boots, spreading my legs apart. His body heat immediately fires me up, or is it the lust that's fuming?

I try to keep my eyes forward when I can feel his stare eating me alive from behind.

"Bend over." He orders.

I start to sweat.

"Umm, what?"

"Bend forward slightly at the waist." His hand palms my hip, tight and hard, making my stomach turn into knots. I follow through, letting him put me in a new position. My heart beats out of my chest practically.

Can he hear it?

He runs his arms around my arms, adjusting the rifle into my shoulder. His cool, icy breath kisses my skin, sending a shiver down my spine and into my core. He only feeds the need to touch him, memories hitting me hard as his lips brush against my ear.

"Roll your shoulders and shoot." He demands, low and husky.

Is he teasing me? Or is this all in my head?

I clear my throat and hiss at him. "Daegan."

"Close that mouth of yours before I do it for you, *and shoot*, damn it." He scolds me.

I look into the scope and pull the trigger.

The metal pings, signaling a target hit. I look through the scope and see a hole in the center. "Bullseye," I murmur. I've never been able to hit a target that perfectly before.

"Good girl," he praises darkly into my ear, and I grow weak when I look into his grey eyes. He towers over me as I clutch my rifle tight. I can tell he's smirking underneath the obsidian mask because of the way his eyes crease and brighten.

"Mr. Hannibal, I think I need help. My rifle might be jammed." Guerra calls out for him two stations down, and I know she's lying.

I'm internally laughing at her attempt to flirt with him, and he gives me one last stare, and I swallow. The tension between us is so thick, so deep, I break first when I realize I'm throbbing in between my thighs. I blink a few times, tearing my gaze away forcefully.

He walks away without another word and walks toward Guerra. She's looking at him with doe-eyes and a flirty expression.

I go back to shooting while trying hard to suppress a jealous feeling in the pit of my stomach.

Winters pops up beside me as I pull the trigger, hitting my target with Daegan's advice. Another bullseye brings me satisfaction. My aim is getting better because of him.

"You know the HVT we've been trying to find? The Surgeon?" Winters gets close to me, and I stop shooting, arching a brow at her.

Why is she bringing that up, and why now?

"Yeah," I reply as I readjust the gun on my shoulder.

"He was the one that did that to Daegan's face...his body." I go from holding my gun tight to letting my hand relax, and my eyes widen. A strong wave of sympathy washes over me, and my gaze softens when I see Daegan. I look for him through the crowd of other service members, and he towers over a blushing, cheerful Guerra with his combat boots planted in the ground, wearing his navy blue shirt on top of his camo pants. His arms are crossed over his chest, his sleeve tattoo on display, and his sweat glistens from the sun's rays.

This must frustrate him, being assigned to me while the others search for the one who tortured him.

"Show me more tomorrow. I want to know more." I clear my throat, and Winter shrugs her shoulders. I spot Daegan again, and this time, he takes out a cigarette as a group of soldiers and sailors surround him like he's some sort of celebrity. Bellowing questions at him, he lifts his mask up just enough to place it between his lips and take a hit.

"I have to keep you on track, anyways. I'm in charge of you, and more information has rolled in. They go out on another mission soon, and you get to be the one that informs Rooker."

Great.

"Hey, I have to ask for a favor," I whisper.

Winter's eyes light up in curiosity. She takes a can of tobacco out and opens it. She lifts a chunk of it and places it in her mouth. "What's up, my padawan?" She taps my head playfully with her fingers. Winters is taller than me at 5'11.

I roll my eyes and giggle softly at her Star Wars reference.

"You're more experienced, right? You have connections with people that do top-secret squirrel stuff and people that have access to programs that we don't, right?" I ask, hoping I'm not stepping over any boundaries.

"Like what? Where are you going with this?" She arches her dark brows, concerned.

I look around to make sure no one can hear me. But with the sounds of rifles being shot and chatter, I grow more comfortable opening up about my stalker.

"I need you to take a look at my phone. I've been receiving weird texts. Is there any way you can get into contact with someone who can find the trace?"

"What kind of texts?"

"I'll fill you in later."

She smiles in a way that makes me feel warm. She brushes the sweat off her forehead and nods.

"I know someone that may be able to help." She admits before returning to her station. I take one glance at Daegan, and he's still surrounded by a lot of people.

I put the rifle back into place against my shoulder and readjust myself into the same position Daegan taught me to be in when I shoot. I relax my body, and the last thing I see before I look into my scope is Daegan winking at me.

26
Alessia

I T TOOK EVERYTHING IN me. It took every single cell in my body not to react to such gruesome videos, photos, and texts detailing why these high-value targets were being pursued.

There was a video of Damon Hawk's video being burnt alive through Akana's and Lopez's bodycams.

There were photos of Violet's injuries.

And then...there were videos of beheadings.

I could feel Daegans eyes behind me burning holes through my back as he watched on without a word as I was filled in.

"I'm going to excuse myself, sir," I tell my superior, holding back tears, bile, and a boil of emotions in my throat.

I rush out of the conference room, walking fast, and Daegan swings the door open for me before I can get a chance to touch it. I nod at him, and our eyes lock once more. His face deadpans completely like stone. But his eyes soften like a cloud.

He knows me, even when I don't want him to. He knows I'm not okay and rushes after me as I run towards the women's restrooms.

I push the door open fast, and it hits the wall with a thud.

"Don't," I glare at him over my shoulder, ordering him away from me, and he halts his movements. I don't bother to see if my cold shoulder bothered him.

I run to the nearest stall, swinging the dull grey-colored metal door open, and let the vomit spill out of me. After seeing those images and stories, something unwelcoming settles into my spirit. Fear I didn't know I had comes full circle in my head.

I'm on my knees, cleaning my mouth with toilet paper. It's a quick release, and my sickness is over in a minute. The nausea still lingers even though I flushed it all away until my stomach had nothing more to give. The loud noise of the small toilet flushing swallows my trembling sobs. I slump down on the heel of my toes and cry into my forearms.

It feels like hours go by as I cry thinking about the children, victims of war, and the gruesome details of horror and evil combined into one.

"Valentine."

I open my swollen, aching red eyes, and through blurry vision, I see him standing at the restroom stall door with a softened gaze.

"Stop it, Hannibal, stop saying my name like that!"

"I'm sorry."

My harsh words come out like venom, and I take a deep breath in as guilt settles.

"I didn't mean it like that…I," I stop myself because I can feel the layers of my shell I hide behind become transparent. I'm vulnerable, and this time…I want to be.

"I like it when you call me Valentine. The way you say it, though… it feels good." I confess as I lift off my arms and watch his response.

He swallows, and his jaw twitches. His Adam's apple bobs as he soaks in my words.

"How do you do this job, Daegan? How do you *all* keep doing this job without breaking? I feel helpless." I confess as I remember all the images and videos.

He doesn't answer. I continue to cry into my hands as the darkness of war cracks my spirit. The sounds of my sobs are the only thing in between us.

"I want to show you something, Alessia." He calls me by my first name, and for the first time since that rainy night at his house, his guard is down, the walls are cracked, and his cloak of a shield evaporates.

"Come with me." He holds his hand out, and I stare at it longer than I should, debating with myself. This is unprofessional of both of us, but I think we crossed that line months ago.

I grab his hand, and he immediately reacts. He pulls me to my feet, helps me stand, and brings me in for a hug straight into his chest. And like a moth to a flame, I melt into his arms and sob harder. He plants his chin on the top of my head as he holds me deep into his uniform. I get lost in his scent as my tears fall into his clothing fabric.

He holds me, but the way he's holding me is like he's letting me know that I'm safe with him. He doesn't have to say it; the way his body moves around me warms me, and the way he wraps me tightly with his arms, my sobs dissipate into shorter and softer whimpers.

"Let me show you a place," he murmurs into my hair. I sniffle into his chest, not wanting to let go, but give in with a nod seconds later.

He pushes open the door to the rooftop of the building. It's a tall building, five stories high. We walked in silence as I followed him through the staircase.

I trust him. Wherever he's taking me, we'll be safe.

As soon as he opens the door, the sounds of the airfield roar and the night takes over us like shadows.

It's late at night, and the stars twinkle loudly in the dark sky. The moon is a crescent, and the winds are cool against my naked arms and face.

Daegan steps forward, but my heels stay planted with hesitation. He stops walking when he realizes I haven't moved. He turns, and his eyes crease like he's smiling. He comes back and grabs my hand, gently pulling me through the door.

We walk for a few seconds until we reach the center of the rooftop.

He lets go of my hand.

"Wait here for a sec," He bends down slightly and mutters into my ear. Tingles run down my spine as his deep voice takes its usual effect on me. He disappears, going in the corner's direction.

PRETEND

"What are we doing here? Where are you going?" I whisper harshly. Crossing my arms against my chest for warmth, I look around, making sure no one sees us.

"I'm pretty sure we can't be here!" I scold him, murmuring under my jarring breath.

A minute later, he emerges with a rucksack under the bright moonlight. And no mask.

His dark waves of hair sway in the wind, and the temptation to run my hands through it gets stronger.

"Wh—what? You just have a rucksack up here at all times?"

"Valentine, you ask way too many questions." He shakes his hand, smirking handsomely.

Damn him.

Damn him and the way he smirks.

He unzips the rucksack just as he drops it by my feet and pulls out a folded blanket. It's a soft, fluffy black blanket decorated with Jack Skellington and a giant pillow.

"I love this movie..." I tell him as he unfolds the blanket and places it on the floor. It mimics a bed or a picnic on the beach...but we're in a warzone on a military base.

"Stop distracting me and tell me what we're doing up here."

He doesn't face me as he makes up a bed.

"Sometimes, when the noise, or when the stress, and darkness gets too much, I escape through nature...this is the closest thing I can get to that right now."

He lays down on the floor, throwing his hands behind him like a pillow.

"Sometimes, I watch the sky and the stars and appreciate the Earth. With our daily routine of busy work days, I think we forget that the Earth itself has a lot to offer our minds, and sometimes, we just need to sit and listen to what it has to say. Get lost in its beauty. Even if it's just for a few moments, it helps me relax when shit gets too fucking much."

I place my hands on my hips and do a double take at the door. I'm scared someone will come bursting through and start asking questions.

As my heart pounds, Daegan pats down next to him.

"Come on, Valentine, I don't bite."

After a few deep breaths, I give in to his request.

Daegan doesn't take his eyes off the sky as I settle beside him.

We lay there in comfortable silence as we watch military aircraft land and take off for exercises or missions.

"Look, it's a shooting star. Make a wish, little Valentine." He points to an airplane taking off.

There it is again. Valentine.

"That's a C17 Hannibal," I scoff, and my lips curve slightly. I do my best not to laugh and shake my head at his silly remark.

"Close enough...now make a wish."

"No," my voice comes out high-pitched, and a giggle follows.

Suddenly, I feel his big hand coil around mine, and he squeezes.

"Pretend," he turns his head towards me. I can see his movements from the corner of my eye, daring me.

I don't want to face him...I can't. An overwhelming urge to squeeze his hand back consumes me, and I have to fight it. But my body betrays me, and before I know it, I'm squeezing his hand back.

PRETEND

I twist my face, and regret immediately smacks me in the face when I see the way he sparkles...enchanting me. He's so close I can feel his breath on my lips.

"Pretend," he repeats, and his tone changes into something sultry and familiar, striking me hard. "Pretend it's a shooting star."

The memories of his house, me waking him with a knife to my throat, and the craziest way I've ever finished play in my head again.

The night I think about before I fall asleep every night replays, and it also flashes in his grey eyes. I know it. He's let his wall down for the night, and I can read him so easily. I know he's thinking the same thing. The night he made me feel so alive when my heart was so numb from betrayal.

The night we played pretend.

It feels like it's become some type of secret code.

Our secret code.

It can't be.

I hold my breath, and so does he. His thumb brushes against my wrist, back and forth. My mouth is just a mere torturous inch from his. A forbidden moment full of heat. I feel like I'm going to melt into nothing with the way his intimidating stare scorches me.

Blood rushes to my ears, something euphoric slithers into my core, and the sound of the C17 grows faint.

Daegan blinks slowly, his chest moving up and down rapidly, and his eyebrows narrow angrily with intensity.

Just when I think he's going to make a move, I snap out of it.

I close my eyes and make a wish.

With my eyes still closed, I try to pry the best sniper in the military.

"Is there another reason why you look up at the sky when you're stressed?"

He sighs, and I open my eyes to find him looking at the stars again. He lets go of my wrist, and my heart sinks. I internally tell my heart to shut up.

He tucks his hands behind his head and licks his lips.

"My mother," he replies.

The beautiful woman in the picture, holding him as a child.

"Tell me about her."

"She's dead, Alessia." He snaps.

Oh, shit.

Oh, no.

How stupid of me.

"I'm sorry."

There's an awkward silence, and I'm full of regret. I shouldn't have asked something so personal. I shake my head, trying to fight the urge to get up and run away, but he speaks before I can make an impulsive decision to escape.

"She killed herself because she had postpartum depression."

I swallow the lump in my throat before it can grow bigger, making me more stiff.

"I was five years old, but when she gave birth to my little sister, she developed postpartum depression, and it never got better. Until one day she took her life...on Valentine's Day."

Silence.

"I'm so sorry."

"You know I used to fucking hate Valentine's Day. I used to hate when February would come around because I resented my mother for taking her own life and leaving me so selfishly for so long."

Silence.

PRETEND

"Then I got a taste of that. Taste of that alienating pain. My days of being tortured made me want to fucking kill myself. I just wanted to die because I was in so much fucking pain. I'd rather end the pain than for it to be dragged out. I wanted to put an end to my misery. But in a weird, sick way, I learned a lesson because that's when it hit me. My mother felt the same as I did. Of course, it was different circumstances, but still...her pain was dismissed because people couldn't physically see what was scarring her up on the inside, but her pain was as real as any other pain."

He turns to me.

"And she killed herself."

His eyes have a sharp edge, and I'm tempted to wrap my arms around him. I ache to hold him like he held me in the bathroom. I want to return the sweet gesture so severely, but I don't wish to overstep. And alas, I stay frozen, being the ears he needs, and I listen to him unravel a part of himself I'm not sure anyone else knows.

"I hate that she felt that alone. To feel alone in a world full of people...that's the worst kind of alienation. She was in so much pain after she had my sister. Maybe there were more factors involved, but my father doesn't talk about it...and I don't ask. I wish she knew there was hope. *There's always hope.*"

And for some reason, I feel like he's reminding himself of that message.

There's always hope. There's always love. There's always someone.

A Black Hawk helicopter enters the airfield and descends slowly onto the pad. The sound of the aircraft's wings whipping the air and the engine roaring accompanies us.

"Love isn't for me but...if I were to become a father, I would worship the ground the mother of my child walks on. I will make sure she is okay every day and support her. I will make sure if she does get postpartum depression, I inform her that there are resources...and I will constantly remind her that she is loved and not alone in a language she needs me to speak. I refuse to let history repeat itself. If I ever get the privilege of finding someone who just doesn't see my scars."

He doesn't look at me. He keeps his eyes on the sky, and I ponder. An image of Daegan with a baby in his large hands sends me swooning. I do want to be a mom one day. But with the right person.

We stay silent, and curiosity gnaws at me. I have the sudden urge to take advantage of this open window he's creaked open into his world.

"Used to hate?" I ask, wanting clarification.

He lifts his scarred brow. "What?"

"You said you used to hate Valentine's Day. What made you change your mind about that holiday?" I quirk a brow.

I want to know more about my 'bodyguard.' He's holding back so much, and I crave to know more.

He rips his eyes from the sky and turns to me. He studies me, his eyes moving vehemently from my eyes to my lips back and forth until, finally, a dire smirk appears.

"What if I say you had to do something to do with it?"

I scoff. A hot blush simmers into my cheeks, threatening to expose how he makes me feel.

"I would say you're giving me too much credit, Mr. Hannibal."

He smiles, the corner of his eye creases, and the moonlight reflects among his scars. But the way he smiles, it's like he's smiling for the first time. There is something so genuine about how he does it, unlike how he usually portrays himself to others. Then he turns to his side, and I become frozen with angst.

His face hovers over mine, and it's as if he's trying to hold onto this moment for life.

I know I am.

So, I wait.

I wait for him to make the move I've been dying for him to make since we landed in Iraq. I want to taste him again. I want to feel his tongue on mine, his hands everywhere on my skin. I want to feel *him*.

Just when I think he's going to lean in, my phone chimes.

I don't know how I found the strength to do it, but I grab my phone, breaking our intensity, and look at the cockblock culprit.

Kane.

> Kane: Where are you?

"Oh? It's Kane. Is he taking over tonight?" I ask Daegan. It's Thursday. Usually, Kane takes over on the weekends, and Daegan is assigned on weekdays.

So, why is he texting me?

I turn around to find Daegan standing over me, packing up his rucksack like he's ready to leave. Our quiet, intimate moment of stargazing is slipping away, and I'm not ready.

This cannot happen. I cannot form a crush. I have to remind myself that our careers come first.

But why does it feel like maybe it wouldn't be such a bad thing to break the rules?

"Yes, Valentine. We're trying something different. He's taking over tonight on guard."

I want to protest. I want to ask him why. Is this personal? Or is it a purely professional decision? But the question never leaves my lips.

Even as we leave the rooftop and descend the stairs, there's a change in his tone, his movements, and the way the broken walls are now sealed all the way up.

Daegan is gone, and Operator Creature is back.

27

Daegan

*I*T'S COLD AND DARK. *The pain feels fresh, and I keep thinking about Dario...and God.*

The last time I saw him, he was standing on his two feet, and we were talking about how he wants to run the next marathon whenever he gets a chance to do it and how we were going to stop by the tattoo shop that sits outside of the base that everyone goes to.

And now the last image I had of him when I was going in and out of consciousness, still unable to breathe right or hear, was blood coming out of his knees because his shins and feet were no longer attached to him.

My brother, even though we share different birth moms, needed me, and I felt helpless. I tried to overcome the blast wound and check on him, but I was consumed by black shadows and woke up in a basement surrounded by HVTs, and I knew I was fucked. I knew that I should have died during that blast because what they had planned for me was worse than death.

I stare at The Surgeon as he laughs with his friends. He's cutting me open, stabbing me with the goal to make me scream...but I never give him the satisfaction of hearing it.

"So I'm going to ask you again. What's your fucking name?"

"*It's Creature, you asshole.*"

He stabbed me in my gut. The knife went through my skin and pierced my flesh. My body was starting to become numb to it all. A mercy I was grateful for.

"*I'm sure your mom wanted to name you something different.*"

"*She's dead, but yeah...no, thank you. Creature fits my smile, don't you think?*"

The last thing I see is his dark brown eyes and wicked smile after I spat my blood in his face. I'll never forget that moment. Because that was when I knew he had more ideas of torment up his sleeves.

I bolt up from my sleep and clutch my knife tight in my hand, and I swing in front of me, stabbing the eerie silent air.

I'm breathing heavily as I growl. I pull at my hair in anguish.

Fuck these nightmares.

I look around, clutching the knife so tight it stings. My chest and lungs tighten, and I'm breathing harshly as blood rushes to my head. I realized I had put my palm on my blade, cutting myself open when I grabbed it. I drop it to my nightstand, carefully placing the knife I made from scratch back by the lamp and my cell phone. I'm sweating again, and my entire body is covered in it. My bedsheets and my boxers are drenched. I'm trying to tone down my breathing because I'm not in that basement anymore. I'm in a barracks room.

On babysitting duty.

Nothing scares me, and I thrive on that. I love pain, and I love to inflict fear onto people even more. I love to work, I love to shoot, and I love to protect my brothers when we're fighting alongside each other. I love to be their eyes on the sky, taking that stress off their shoulders, knowing I never fucking miss.

I look at the bottles of beer in the corner of my room. My lamp is on, and the fan is off—it's just how I like to sleep.

I get up from the bed and head towards the beer. I snap the top off and drink it fast. It glides down, and I gulp it like water in the middle of the desert.

I haven't had a nightmare in a while. I used to dream of my time in the basement every single night, but the nightmares died down. They went from daily to weekly until finally, it's rare when I wake up like I'm fighting for my life. And it all started when I saw Alessia for the first time.

I need to change this. I can't get attached. I shouldn't want to fuck her. But I do, and I want to fuck her all the time, and show her how depraved I can get when I claim someone as mine.

TWO MONTHS LATER

28
Alessia

MONTHS CAME AND WENT, and the entire time, no more texts from my stalker since the day at the range. I guess being across the world helped and worked out in my favor. Of course, Jack still harassed my phone number, not taking the hint that I wanted nothing from him anymore.

Daegan was distant, cold, emotionless, and quiet. He treats me like a stranger, and yet the tension in the air is constant. I refuse to forget about that night…but maybe I should start pretending it never happened. I don't know how I will, but I need to. I must forget about the best orgasm I've ever had. My mind is still blown that it was done with his knife and fingers. I can't imagine how it would feel with his cock.

If he wants to forget it, then I will, too.

As I sit in my office, typing away documents that need to be completed, Daegan waits outside the room, guarding it.

PRETEND

It's Valentine's Day, and all I want to do is cuddle in blankets, read a book, and eat snacks, but I am overseas, far away from North Carolina's winter weather—miles away from home in a Warzone.

It's past work hours, and I'm about done finishing a document I need to send to the higher-ups. I type away on the keyboard, finishing the last few sentences.

"Alright, girl, I'm heading out," Winters announces her departure. She scooches her rolling chair away from her computer and stands after a few clicks of her mouse.

"I'll see you Monday," I wave to her over my screen and continue to fidget with my mouse.

Five minutes later and I'm in need of a neck massage. It's stiff and aching, and I'm already falling asleep. But then a pair of hands grip my shoulders, and I shriek.

"Sshh, it's just me," Daegan hushes me.

"Oh my gosh, I didn't even hear you come in," I relax, releasing my grip on the rolling chair.

"I'm known for silence, Valentine,"

"Why haven't you been on guard this entire week at night?" I frown, not caring if I'm coming off as needy.

"It's been arranged that way on purpose," he says nonchalantly. I keep my focus on typing the last sentence on the screen as he massages my neck.

"So you're avoiding me? Ever since the rooftop, you haven't wanted to talk to me."

"You know it has to be this way," his voice deepening, almost like a scolding.

I sigh heavily, close out my task, and turn off the computer so fast that even Daegan is taken aback. He picks up on my mood change and steps away.

I swing around him, grab my bag, and head for the door. As soon as I open it slightly, Daegan closes it. I furrow my brows, ready to protest, but he hushes me with a finger, simultaneously locking the office door like he's on a mission.

"This is fucking torture for me, okay? But I need four minutes and twenty-nine seconds before we have to exit this building, or people will start asking questions, and I want to spend them doing something I've been wanting to do since I saw you at El Devine."

My heart skips a beat. Is he implying what I think he's implying?

"Daegan, I'm not...we're not going to fu—"

He takes out his phone and puts on a song.

"Yellow by Coldplay" starts to play through the speaker on his phone.

"It's Valentine's Day. Dance with me."

"Daegan, I don't dance." My chest heaves as the song goes on.

"Neither do I, but I want to try it out with you." He grabs my hand and pulls me into his chest. I'm met with his sexy cologne mixed with cigarettes.

"Pretend with me," he lifts his finger below my chin. "Pretend we're at El Devine, and you have that same sexy outfit on that night with your cowgirl boots and dance with me."

"Daegan, what has gotten into you? You've treated me like a stranger these past few months." Warmth fills my cheeks, and I intertwine his rough hands with mine and start to move with him. Like, I have a choice.

"Maybe I like dancing with strangers," he states as we move side to side.

My entire body is wound tight, and as the seconds go by, I rest the side of my face on his chest, and he holds me back. We sit there, treading a fine line, and I want *more*.

PRETEND

We soak up this forbidden moment like it's been forever without each other, and I'm secretly praying this song will last longer than just three minutes.

"You know music is a part of me? I play the piano," he mutters softly.

"Really?"

He nods.

"That sounds nice. I don't know how to play any instruments. I wish I did."

"I would love to teach you,"

"Daegan..." the song stops, and I'm overcome by those butterflies that start to swarm.

He hums. His hands slide from my back to my hips.

"Yes, little Valentine?"

I look up, and I'm practically begging for his lips.

"I want you to kiss me."

He goes rigid. Like my request is too much for him, and he's fighting the devil on his shoulder. I reach for his mask, pulling it slightly up so it unveils his scars, beard, and full lips I have missed since that stormy night.

"Kiss me," I whisper, pressing my chest against him. My heartbeat picks up, and all the consequences fade away when he leans down. Instead of kissing me, he picks me up by my thighs and lifts me in one swift movement.

I suck in a breath, feeling like I'm floating on a cloud, looking into his dilated grey eyes. We stay like that for a good three seconds, like we're both accepting that being together means trouble and our ending is uncertain.

He crashes his lips against mine, his familiar taste erupting in my mouth, and I feel like I'm going to vanish into euphoria. His soft lips move against mine like he's hungry, feral, and begging to do more.

He walks forward, dropping me down on my desk. A sharp, high-pitched moan colors the thick mood we're soaking in. I'm clawing at his back over his uniform like that'll help relieve the ache that pulses in between my thighs. To my surprise, it doesn't; it only deepens and begs for him to take it away.

My ass hits a pile of paperwork, rearranging them into a clutter. I palm them before they fall off the desk as we continue to make out like it's our last day on this earth. Our bodies are grinding against each other like we're both burning with desire.

He cups my face with both of his hands aggressively as his tongue travels deeper, marking the inside of my mouth with his, and I'm enjoying every bit of it. I palm his very hard cock desperately, rubbing it up and down his shaft, over his pants, and he groans into my mouth. He changes the rhythm. He's faster and rougher. He's an unstoppable beast, dominating me kiss after kiss, and I'm gladly submitting.

His hand snakes underneath my top. He slips underneath my bra and squeezes my breast.

"I want to do more than just kiss you," he breathes against my lips.

"Show me," I reach for his pants, and a feral growl slips out of his throat.

"If I'm going to show you, it won't be in a building full of people that will hear the way my girl sounds when she's getting fucked. I can't." He blinks rapidly, "I won't." He breaks away, and I'm left confused by the sudden change.

"My girl?" I repeat.

I wait for him to confirm if I heard him correctly...but he doesn't.

I'm panting hard, trying to figure him out, but he gives me nothing. He turns around, pulls down his mask, and unlocks the door. I jump off the desk, hitting the floor with my boots, and we're left pretending like the last five minutes didn't happen.

He pockets his phone while I readjust my top and try to calm myself down.

"I'll wait for you outside the building. Kane is taking over anyways," he opens the door, breaking my heart as he pulls away from me once more.

"But it's your night."

He looks at me with a cold expression, his hand tightening over the knob until his fingers are red and his knuckles are white.

"Not anymore."

29
Alessia

I WAS FURIOUS. THE teasing had me frustrated...and even worse. Sexually frustrated. So when Zeke asked to take me to the firepit, I said yes without hesitation.

Zeke isn't scared to ask me on a date or pursue me. He's been persistent, and I think I'm ready to explore more. I sit next to Zeke while holding a Shiner Bock in one hand, staring at the fire while rock music plays. There's a movie playing on a projector pinned to a white wall.

It's nearing midnight, and I'm not the least bit tired. My mind is fully awake, and I keep thinking about my stalker, my job, and Daegan.

I'm going back home soon, and there's still so much left unfinished between him and me.

Guerra's laugh snaps me out of my self-pity moment, and my eyebrows raise at the familiar tune. My heart cracks because of that laugh. Oh, it's that silly, *give me all your undivided attention, your are so funny laugh*, it's so familiar to me.

PRETEND

She's flirting...but with who?

I search the crowd, and when I see her toss her head back and then forward against someone's broad shoulder...my heart drops. She's holding him by the bicep as she laughs, blushing even.

It's Daegan.

He wears his mask, a full one this time. He's not in uniform, like everyone else, for once. He's in civilians. A black sweater, black jeans, and boots. His scarred eyes look in her direction, and a pang of jealousy hits me like a train.

It was only two seconds. Two seconds to watch my friend flirt with my bodyguard, and I hope he didn't see me.

So, is this why he switched shifts tonight? To be with Guerra? My friend?

The trauma of Jack's betrayal pierces through me, and I feel like I'm drowning. This man had his lips on mine, moving against me on my own desk, and now? He's with my friend?

I know we're not together, but I didn't expect him to do that.

I shift in my seat and glance at Kane behind me. He looks at Daegan and then at me. His dark blue eyes harden, but he doesn't say anything.

He knows. He knows exactly what I'm feeling. His eyes soften as if he's apologizing to me on Daegan's behalf.

I purse my lips in acknowledgment and turn back around. I'm going to enjoy my date. If he can...so will I.

"Who do you think is the one who gave up Ari and Grim for the bounty? It has to be someone in intelligence. And they better not be here in Iraq with us." Operator Doom speaks from Zeke's right, tapping his fingers on the bench to the beat of the music.

He's a dog handler for the SEAL team, Hellhounds. His brown eyes flick between Zeke and me. I don't like to comment on things like this, so I keep myself busy this time and go on my phone to scroll.

"I don't know, man. I have suspicions, and I think it's a special operator. Someone who popped up on the teams at the same time those targets made their way into Georgia. SEAL Team Executioners got mixed up with human traffickers." Zeke replies, taking a swig of his beer.

"Are you thinking what I'm thinking?" Doom furrows his brows, waiting for Zeke to respond.

Zeke brings his beer to his lips again and nods.

"Creature seemed to have shown up just when everything went to shit. What a hell of a coincidence that once Ravenmore added him to Grim's team, he was almost killed, and Ari was taken for money." Zeke states with no remorse.

"He's weird, man. There's something clearly off about him." Doom shrugs, grabbing a beer of his own. "I've never seen him take a day off of work or engage in a normal conversation about anything. He doesn't talk to anyone. The dude hums when he shoots."

Even though I'm angry with him, maybe even a little jealous, I can't stand when people gossip. We're all on the same team here. We all want to find out who did this to Grim and Ari, but to point fingers at someone just because he's new and may seem off to other people. I won't stand for it.

"Look, I don't know too much about Hannibal, but he takes his job very seriously. There's no way he had a part in that." I interrupt their theories and surprise myself when I catch myself defending Daegan. I didn't mean to add any fire to this conversation, but it feels wrong for them to accuse Daegan just because he's the new guy.

PRETEND

The man doesn't want to touch me because he doesn't want to risk his spot on the team. Being a Navy SEAL means a lot to him, I can tell. My job means everything to me. I can relate to Daegan in that way.

Doom gets the sharpened tone in my voice as I give him a blank stare. "Sorry. Maybe you're right."

Zeke turns to me and smiles as Doom focuses on the movie playing.

A part of me hopes and wishes that his smile does something to me, but I'm only left with disappointment. Especially when my stomach twists and turns uncomfortably, when his hand reaches the inside of my thigh and gives it a gentle squeeze.

"Want to get out of here?" Zeke leans into my ear and kisses my cheek.

He moves towards the shell of my ear seductively. His mustache brushes against my skin, and it takes me back to the night Daegan kissed my breasts. I'm begging my body to want Zeke's deep voice and his touch, but it's not his voice that turns my world upside down. It's someone else's. Someone in a mask.

"Actually, I want to stay for one more drink, and then you can take me back to my room."

I subtly remove his hand from my thigh.

"Or I can take you back to my room." He counters, the smell of alcohol seeping into my nose. "We can keep it a secret."

His mouth brushes over my neck, and I giggle from the ticklish sensation it gives me. Maybe I should give in? Zeke isn't all bad and is on a SEAL Team Hellhounds. That's the only reason why Ravenmore hasn't lost his mind on the whole situation of showing up here tonight on Zeke's arm.

Zeke's phone pings loudly, and he coils back in his seat. He holds the phone in his palm, waiting for me to give him an answer.

But I'm quiet.

"I'll let you think about it, Alessia. I have to take this," he flashes me his white teeth as he smiles and stands, giving Doom a knuckle touch before he walks away. I'm left alone, and I'm tempted to wave Kane over and tell him I'm headed to bed. I don't dare to look in Daegan's direction any longer.

I lift the beer to my lips and notice that it's empty. I tell Kane I'm headed for more in the USO room, and he doesn't follow me. His phone rings and his girlfriend's picture reflects on his screen saver. His eyes light up and sparkle with anticipation. The man is so in love.

"Just take it. I'll be fine. It's just the USO room." I encourage him, pointing to the empty small building behind him. Everyone is either sleeping or at the firepit.

"It's a clear sky tonight, with twinkling vivid stars. It's a perfect night for you to video call this mystery woman of yours." I gently nudge his shoulder with my knuckle. "Talk to her. I won't say anything, and I'll be back in a few seconds."

"You're the best." Kane towers over and nods. With his big hand, he reaches over my head and ruffles my curls in a brotherly fashion. I slap and push his chest away playfully as he slides the button to answer, already walking away from me.

I walk into the empty, cold building that sits across the hangar where helicopters are stored. I grab the beer out of the ice chest and turn into a fucking wall.

30

Alessia

It turns out the wall I ran into was of the human type.

"What are you doing here with Zeke?" A familiar voice interrupts my isolated moment. I drop the beer, but Daegan catches it before it hits the ground.

"Oh my fucking gosh!" I almost stumble and fall. "I could ask you the same thing." I rip my gaze from his shadow on the floor to his massive frame towering over me. His grey eyes aren't welcoming. They're lethal, and his mask is gone. His dark waves are carefully brushed back on both sides, and it's enticing.

"Why are you here with him?" He drawls, stipulation evident in his rugged voice. "And what the hell are you doing drinking? The alcohol is only for SEALS. This is your third beer. Don't you think you should slow down?"

I straighten my back, astonished.

He's been watching me? Tracking how much I'm drinking?

"I–uh. Yes, I'm drinking, and yes, I'm with Zeke tonight. He's providing the alcohol for me. I don't owe you an explanation. Nice to see you too, grumpy." I take my beer from his hand, and he steps forward, closing the distance.

"I don't like to repeat myself, Valentine. Why are you with him?"

I land on my two feet, my hair tied back in a bun, with a few loose curls in the front.

"What do you mean, why? The deployment is almost over, and this is my last night out for a while. I could ask you the same question."

He raises his brows like he's amused by the witty response. He smirks, his sharp canines brushing his bottom lip.

"So you broke up with your boyfriend and tried to get laid right after *with me, and now with Zeke*?" He hardens his voice, scolding me like a child. I stare down layers of grey as he wrathfully burns holes through me.

"Oh, so what are you saying? That I'm a slut? Is that what you're implying?"

He narrows his brows, his pointed nose scrunching, and then relaxes as I argue back.

I won't stand for this.

"Why are you so upset, anyway? You're with Guerra right now, aren't you? You were the one who said we couldn't do this. We can't be together in any form, remember? I can lose my job. *You* can lose your job," I point to his chest, stepping forward. "You can get thrown off the team. I am free to do whatever I want." I poke his massive chest. "*You are free to do whatever you want*. You can't just show up out of nowhere and hover over me like I'm...like I'm..." I stutter, trying to find the words.

"Like you're what?" He steps closer to me as I stare up at him like he's challenging me to overstep and push my limits and get off on it.

PRETEND

"Like I'm your problem." My voice is lethal.

"You are my fucking problem." He argues back, his breathing elevates.

"What?" I shake my head, confused, taking a step back, creating some distance between us because I'm scared of what I'm feeling. Something about him is messing with my brain chemistry.

"I don't like what I see. Your stepfather knows about your stalker problem. He wants you back in your room before 0100 hours. I'm sorry, but it's past curfew. Kane knows about it, but he's being nice. But me? I have no fucking problem being the bad guy." He snarls, closing the distance again, taking my breath away.

"He put a fucking curfew on me? You told him about my stalker?" I shout, my voice high-pitched.

Oh, now I'm pissed.

"I'm not a fucking child Hannibal. I don't listen to Ravenmore."

"Your mother told him, actually. If I have to throw you over my shoulders and carry you out of this building, then that's what I'll do." He hisses under his breath, the music outside getting louder and louder.

There's a hint of beer in his breath, mixed with cigarettes.

Minty. Masculine. Woodsy. Completely hypnotizing.

Still, I hold my ground even though his presence always sends me into a daze.

"Why? I'm having a good time with Zeke, and we're on a date." My eyes narrow in defiance.

His grey eyes darken, and the scars on his eyebrows flinch when he hears me defy him.

"You call this a date?" His tone is envious, and he smiles, but it's anything but happy.

"Yes...it's what we got, and I'll take it over staying in my bedroom trapped alone for the night. What would you know about dates anyway? You told me you don't believe love exists, remember?"

"You don't need to love someone to take them on a date." He breathes slowly. His body goes rigid as his vision pinballs from my eyes, my lips, and then my chest.

"Really? Why is that?" I challenge back, daring him to open up to me and daring my so-called bodyguard to talk more than just a few sentences and give me a piece of his personal life. "Tell me why being out tonight with Zeke isn't a date," I argue.

His eyes crinkle with a sinful, dark smile. He takes one more step, hovering over me, and I lick my lips nervously. He laughs deep and low, slowly, like he's ready to do something I'm unsure of. It's like he's about to snap me in half.

He leans into my ear, rubbing his chin, his lips grazing my ear as he whispers, "Because a date with me usually ends with the girl screaming my name, my hands in her hair, her ass cheeks raw from spanking her so hard. Her jaw and throat sore and bruised from gagging on my cock all night long...until she's crying pretty little tears for me and I lick them away as I'm filling her insides." He whispers darkly into my ear, and it's seducing. My narrowed brows relax, and my eyes widen instead. A sensation in between my legs goes haywire. Then he retracts from my ear. Getting so close to my mouth, teasing me. It's like he's about to kiss me but doesn't. "Because I'm addicted to the art that is making women come, Alessia. There are so many ways to do it. I desire to break women until they're screaming my name, women that beg me to—making women come hard over and over again. I like to make them bleed for me. It makes me so fucking hard to see my come drip off their chin after I finish on their face, and I push it back into

PRETEND

their mouths, making them choke on it. I like making their cunts weep until they're dripping down their thighs, begging for me to fuck their ass too."

I flush red hot with his admission.

"That's what my dates consist of, baby girl. It has nothing to do with love and everything to do with lust. I love to fuck, and lust to come."

I'm tired of this push-and-pull game with him. I won't let him win. I will show him that two can play this game.

So I challenge him, smirking innocently as the dare leaves my tongue. "Then I guess I need to explore what Zeke's version of a date is at the end of tonight...maybe it'll match up with yours."

He stiffens like he's in utter shock. He pauses, as do I, but it's short-lived just as I watch his nostrils tick and his jaw setting so tight, I can hear his teeth grind. He goes quiet. No words come out of him, and I know I just won the argument.

I cross my arms in victory, pushing my breasts together unintentionally, and his death stare changes direction from my soul to my breasts. I grab the beer from his hands and start to walk past him. I don't make it one more inch.

He shakes his head with a sinful smirk, and faster than I can register or protest, Daegan grabs my arm, lifting me into the air, throwing me over his shoulder, and thunders out of the corner we're in.

"No way in fucking hell." He stalks forward, kicking a door open.

"You can't do this to me, Hannibal! Why are you sabotaging my night out?"

"It's not safe. You're not safe."

"Bullshit!" I protest. Thank God no one notices I'm getting taken away like this. It's embarrassing. "I'm in an area full of service members!"

"Do you forget they still haven't caught the traitor responsible for Grim's bounty?"

I ignore his valid retort and continue to try and scramble out of his grasp, but he's too massive and too strong for me. Through my scrambled curls, I see someone who can get me out of his arms and won't ask questions.

We stalk past Kane, who clearly is in shock. He looks up from his phone, startled.

"Kane! Don't just stand there. Help me!" I wave my hands, trying to pry out of his grasp.

Daegan stops walking, and Kane's eyes are saucers as he holds his phone, unsure of what to do. He stares at me and then back at Daegan, who clearly doesn't care if he knows anymore.

"Don't you fucking dare try and stop me, loverboy, or I'll cut your tongue out so you can never tell a tale again." He threatens Kane sinisterly like it's a game. Kane throws his hands up, surrendering as I still struggle in his grasp.

"I think I've learned my lesson with Grim. I've already got my nose broken once. I don't need that to happen again. I'm getting too old for this shit." He groans, annoyed. "Just please don't kill her, is all I ask. I'm going to bed." He concedes with a heavy slumber sigh.

He turns around and walks away, and I glare at his back as my mouth falls open.

"Really Kane?! After all we've been through?" I whisper yell at him, but he doesn't care. He keeps walking away from us. Daegan continues to hold my ass in place. His hand snakes around my hips and squeezes tight. So hard, pain makes its presence known.

"Shut the hell up, Valentine, or I'll use my cock to gag you."

He sprints down into another empty building, opening the doors to an empty hallway.

PRETEND

"Are you jealous?" I hiss.

"Jealous?" He roars with disdain.

I nod against his shoulder. He drops me to my feet, making me stumble, and I almost fall. I suck in a breath, taken aback by his strength. He doesn't help me regain my balance. He almost threw me to the ground. This man picks me up and throws me like I'm a damn feather.

Jesus, *he really is upset with me.*

He gets into my face, and his scent makes me want to smother myself in his arms again, despite the fact he's manhandling the crap out of me.

"Jealous doesn't begin to describe how I feel right now. I want to fucking chop off Akana's hands and take his eyes out of his skull and make him eat them for just looking at what's mine. Anyone that gets to hold your hand is a dead man walking. Let alone..."

He doesn't finish; the way his voice trails off makes me believe he *doesn't want* to finish his sentence.

"Let alone what? Fuck me?" I'm poking a bear, but I don't care.

He towers over me, grabs my jaw with his fingers, squeezing my bones hard, and I hiss in pain.

"Careful, baby girl. You won't like it when Creature comes out to play."

"And what if I want him to come out and play?" I taunt.

He chuckles, letting his head fall, and he rubs his chin like he's planning something.

Something bad.

I dare him to. "Show me what you would do to me if I were your date."

"Trust me. There's nothing I've ever wanted more in this world, and that's you. But I won't allow myself to cross this line. If I take you, the admiral will fire me, probably making up a reason to throw an Article on my career. I was a prisoner of war. I have endured days of brutality. But you? Not being able to devour you the way I've been thinking about since you were assigned to me has been the worst form of torture I've ever had to go through." He softens his words with a pained pinch of his brows. "Walk away from me. Walk away, and go to your bedroom, and fucking lock it."

"No." I defy him, walking closer to him. I haven't felt so alive in a long time. Daegan sees me when I can't even see myself, even when I'm staring at my own reflection in a mirror. The way he looks at me, especially right now, with dilated eyes and a clenched jaw. I feel wanted when I don't even want to be in my own meat suit some days. "I've never felt so hot and so cold at the same time, Daegan. You're the only one who has been able to do that to me. Not Jack, not Zeke. *You*. I know you're upset. Show me how upset you are. Don't tell me." I tease.

"You *really* want me to show you just how fucking mad I am, huh?" He questions me like he's trying to convince me to second-guess my request.

"Yes," I take one step forward, touching his chest. My heart is thundering as hard as it is in between my legs, starving for his taste, wanting him to give into our desires. As soon as my hand touches his all-black sweater, he spins me around, pushes his chest against my back, and grips my hips tight over my pants. I whimper in pain, and at the same time, my skin bursts into sensual flames. He brings his waist, colliding it with mine in a primal way. His hard size digging into my ass like that one night in his hallway. His palm reaches the center of my neck, squeezing it, but this time he's not letting me fucking breathe.

His chokehold has me clawing at his palms, scratching his skin, as horror floods my senses. He's suffocating me with his calloused, rough palms. My brows knit together, and I'm scowling at him.

PRETEND

"Are you sure you want to see just how beyond *jealousy* I am, my little Valentine?"

I nod, licking my lips, and a depraved smirk crosses his face.

I don't want it to be safe. I don't want normal. I want tragic, unremorseful, shattering, lustful, painful sex, and I want it from him. Jack was boring, slow, and very predictable. I always saw what was coming next. Missionary or I was bent over until he chased his own finish line.

"I don't want you to treat me like I'm fragile. I want you to use me because I want to love sex too...I want you to test my limits that I have never gotten the chance to explore. I want all of those things you told me, but I want the fear you inflict upon me. I want the pain. *I want to be your whore.*" I admit, and I'm surprised by my own candor.

Will I regret this?

"Fuck... You really don't know what you're asking for."

I push my ass further into his waist, and he's already huge and hard. "Show me. Teach me. *Break me.* I want it all." I counter.

I reach for his pants from behind me, but he stops my wrists. He goes for my throat, squeezing it tactically, fast, and precisely to cut off my air supply without actually hurting me. He pins me against the wall by my throat, my back bangs, and I grin ear to ear.

Something's come over me. Like a soul being born. A new one.

And it's because of him.

Pinning me against the wall so I can't move, he bends down, reaching for my throat, and then I feel his tongue trail the bottom of my neck all the way to my earlobe.

Oh my god.

"On one condition." I choke out; he stops and instead brushes his nose against me. He leans his forehead on the side of my head.

"No falling in love." I grit out.

His breathing comes to a stop.

"You want just sex?" He asks.

I nod since he's making it hard to talk.

"You just want to be my little whore behind closed doors so your step-daddy doesn't find out how much of a slut you are? You don't want Admiral Ravenmore finding out that she's begging one of the team guys to fuck her so hard until she can't remember her own name? You want to be used, Valentine, is that it?" He coos devilishly into the shell of my ear, sending a cold shiver up my spine.

I nod, trying so hard to suck in a breath.

"Yes. But no—" he tightens his grip, and I swallow. "Falling in love."

He clenches his jaw...like he's pissed about the condition. He can't be...right? Is this all in my head? This should push him even more to take me the way we both desire.

"Promise me." I pry again.

"I don't believe in love, little Valentine. You don't have to worry about that. I don't want to make love to you. I want to fuck you so hard that every time you sit down, every time you feel that soreness between your thighs, and the bruises on your ass, you'll know who you belong to. Your ass, your cunt, this tongue, are all mine."

"Yes, please."

"I don't think you know what you're asking for. I'm possessive and depraved. I want to punish you for coming here with another man tonight. I want to tear off your pants, take off my belt and choke you with it as I fuck every single one of your openings, marking you vindictively. Ever since I licked your wetness off my knife, you are all I fucking think about. You are in my head all the time, you've imprinted yourself there without my fucking permission. Don't you see? If we do this, there's no going back. You are mine until *I say this is over*," he growls, pulling my hair hard, and I hiss in pain. "Do you understand, little Valentine? Do you still want to go through with this little down-low relationship proposal of yours?"

"I know what I'm asking for," I retort. "I want all of that...but you scare me. And I think I like that even more."

"You shouldn't."

He leans into my neck so that every time he exhales on my skin, it sends shivers down my spine. "Run, little Valentine. Run away from me. I'll give you a headstart, but you better run fast because if I catch you, you will regret asking Creature to come out to play, and I'll show you just how mad you've driven me." I can feel the sadism through his fingers.

"We're on a military base. There is nowhere to run." I barely choke out as I feel the blood pounding in my head from the circulation getting cut out, and I swear I'm about to pass out. Darkness clouds the edges of my vision, color fading in and out. I glance at Daegan, and for the first time, his ice eyes beam black with anger. I blink slowly, trying to beg him to stop, but I've grown weak, and my lips are paralyzed. I'm trying to let him know I've found a boundary I might want him to break.

I can't fucking breathe anymore. Wetness flows down my cheeks, like a rainstorm, when I realize this is exactly what he wants. And that makes everything so much hotter. The fucked up side of me is smiling, and my clit throbs with need.

My feet grow weak, and alas, my hearing goes silent as he continues to choke me. He tightens his grip one last time just before everything goes full obsidian.

He lets me go, and like the earth needs the sun, I gasp for air over and over again, coughing as I recover. I fall to my knees, and pain strikes back hard as I hit the floor. I desperately inhale the air that was stolen by the devil in front of me, like it's my last day on Earth.

This man is going to kill me...and my dumbass would say thank you.

"That's your problem, Alessia. Your headstart starts now. You better run to your barracks room for the night because I swear to God, if I see you with Zeke again, a bodybag will be filled tonight."

"You're an arrogant, self-centered asshole. Let me live my life. You're supposed to watch over me. Not control me." I argue.

"Watch me."

"Fuck you." I massage my neck, yet I'm so turned on by his unforgiving hand necklace.

"By the time I'm done with you, you'll be begging me too, baby girl." He stares me down like he's starving.

31
Alessia

I WANT TO TICK him off even more, I whip around fast, my hair whirls around to my other shoulder, as I head for the exit.

"I'm going to finish my date with Zeke."

"Alessia," He growls as I throw the door open, "Don't." He finishes his stark warning from behind me, and I take off running.

I hear a feral groan over his indignant steps, like I'm being chased by a monster.

I can't believe I'm doing this.

I zip out of the building as fast as my feet let me. I run into the night's dry air, passing the fire pit. I sneak a glance at everyone surrounding it, and Zeke looks confused as he sits next to Doom, texting vigorously on his phone. He's oblivious to what's going on behind him.

"To your room, Valentine." Daegan barks out from behind me.

A vast shadow is catching up to me, and I smirk, taunting my bodyguard further.

Where I go, he has to follow.

"No," I murmur.

His eyes darken under the moonlight, and his head tilts to the side. "You want me to chase you?"

I walk backward, biting my lip until I taste iron.

He keeps stalking toward me as his ice-grey eyes light up. His scars tweak with madness.

"You want me to break you?"

I take another step back, inhaling sharply.

"You want me to lose control and take you?"

My cheeks are on fire, and my panties are soaked.

"You want me to tear off my dog tags right now, and wrap them around your throat for disobeying my orders?"

I don't answer. I hope my silence grants him the permission he seeks because, my lord, I want all of those things and more.

I turn around before he can grab my hand. His skin grazes mine for a split second. I'm running in between buildings. The music and movie from the firepit die down the further I get away, and I end up running into a hangar.

I turn inside the dark, off-limits space. Pushing the doors open, surprised that it isn't locked. No one is allowed in here, especially if there isn't work to be done. It's pretty much empty, and everyone is either at the firepit or sleeping.

Two Black Hawks are parked here. The government machinery is most likely here for maintenance since it's not out on the field, ready to fly with the others.

My chest rises and falls chaotically. The thrill of him after me is breaking my morals. It's even a little bit toxic. Seeing him so angry and out of touch with the calm and composed Daegan I once knew is shocking.

I look left and right before he can enter the hangar. I try to find another exit but fail miserably as the seconds tick by loudly like a clock in my head, mimicking my fear. The sound of a door slamming open jumps my bones, and I look at the black hawk.

It's open, so I jolt forward just as I hear the door close again, and I jump in. I want him, and I hope he wants me to. Even though deep down, I have a feeling this is the start of a journey that shouldn't have begun in the first place. I should go back to my room or give Zeke a chance. Either way...Daegan is only giving me one choice tonight, and I need him to make his.

32

Daegan

SHE'S GOING TO REGRET coming here tonight with Zeke. I thought I could stay away from my assignment, but I can't. She's forcing this out of me, and I'm succumbing to her taunts. I haven't felt this way in a long time, and I want to hold on to something that feels good in a world that seems so wrong. I see her disappear into the black hawk, and I swear under my breath about twenty times every swear word in the book.

I'm already on her heels; it's fucking cute the way she thinks she can outrun me. She runs fast, and I'll give her that, but it's still not good enough. There's nowhere she could go where I wouldn't follow. She could jump off a cliff, and I'll be right there.

She climbs in just to try and climb out of the helicopter. Her hands barely make it to the cold metal before I snatch her by her hair and pull her back inside. I shut it closed before she can escape me. My jealousy is getting the better of me. It's so thick it's almost palpable in the air.

Good.

"You wanted this, remember?" I snarl at her depraved.

I force her to look at me.

"What are you going to do, Daegan?"

I snicker devilishly, not missing one beat, shaking my head with a grin that radiates pure sin.

"I'm going to fuck the Admiral's daughter in a helicopter."

I pull on her hair again, and she squeals.

"You're such a pain in my ass, baby girl. So, now I'm going to physically take yours until your pussy is screaming for me to stop."

"Do it." She taunts. God, her mouth is so fucking filthy. Just the way I like them to be.

"Oh, I'm going to have to cleanse this back talking mouth of yours." She stops fighting me, letting me devour her, spreading herself open on the Black Hawk seat as she sits with those brown eyes that glimmer so beautifully. She admires me, every part of me that I've shown her, even the horrid marks on my face, and it makes me feel weak.

I grip her jaw until my fingers are digging into the hollows of her soft, red cheeks. Sweat beads on her forehead as our body heat clashes together in this tight space. I'm too tall for this. My hands alone can break her. They almost swallow her face.

"Opening your mouth and legs already because you're so needy for my cock?" I mock and degrade her excitement to feel me even more. My dick throbs with so much blood, *too much blood*. My pants are tighter, and my balls are so damn full of come just waiting for her pussy so I can combust inside it.

I'm really going to do this.

I really want to fucking do this.

If there's one thing I love more in this world than erasing the evil from it, it's to fuck. I'm not going to lie to myself anymore, the fact that her pussy is so off-limits to me makes this so much more thrilling.

"I'm going to make you regret pissing me off by making you choke on my dick."

Her brown eyes light up, and she licks her lips.

"Pretend, remember? You want to keep pretending because one night with me wasn't enough for a slut like you?" I degrade her. "You want to pretend? Pretend this Valentine." I grab her, hooking my fingers in her shirt, and pull it down until the thin fabric tears. Her beautiful tan skin glistens with a thin layer of sweat, her breasts bounce underneath her bra, and my mouth waters for her brown nude nipples that are slightly exposed over her green bra. I push the bra down more until her luscious tits fall over the velvet cups. They're perfectly pointed, just begging to get sucked on and bit.

She moans out a sensual gasp as I expose her, making my dick jerk in response. I want more of those sounds. I need more. Fuck, her moans are a heavenly tune I want on a continuous loop. But only because of me.

"Hell, yes, I want to pretend." She opens her mouth wider, sticking out her tongue. She obeys my command and opens wide. I smirk, and a scoff of satisfaction leaves my lips.

I grab the beer from earlier, take a quick swig, and spit in her mouth. It touches the back of her tongue that runs over her bottom lip. I close her jaw rough, and she swallows.

PRETEND

"You're gonna have to pretend like you're safe with me because I'm about to fuck you like I want to kill the both of us. Just remember you wanted this, and I never quit."

ALESSIA

I honestly don't know this version of me, but I'm not complaining. Daegan loosens his grip on my jaw and lets me take off his belt. I pull it through every loop until it's out and on the floor. I'm desperate to taste him, craving to please him like a fool after all this built-up tension.

He sits next to me on the black hawk, his hips touching mine. The side of his scarred face by mine.

When I pull his pants down, I'm met with black boxers, and that's when it hits me. Finally, the intimidation of being with another man catches up to me. I hesitate, and the doubts of being able to pleasure him rack in my brain, making my confidence fall to an all-time low.

"Mr. Hannibal...I've only been with one man, and—"

"Sh, baby girl, I know I'm not your first, but I will be your last." He caresses my cheek and leans in. A soft side of him exposes for a split second, and I take advantage. I lean in for a kiss, but he pulls back, leaving my lips unaccompanied and begging for his.

"I'm not a nice man, and lucky for you, I'm still mad."

He reaches for his neck and tugs off his dog tags. They break off, and then he holds them in front of me. I watch them dangle and collide with each other.

"Listen up, baby girl. Every time you taunt me, this is what will happen." He holds up his finger. "I'm going to wrap these around your neck while you have my cock so deep down your throat that you can't breathe. Every time you try and sneak in a breath, I'm going to pull on it."

Oh fuck, he wasn't kidding.

He grins sadistically, and I swallow nervously.

What have I done?

He's scaring me, but I want him.

And I want him bad.

He wraps the chain around my neck twice and holds my head close.

He pushes his fingers inside my pants, and his hands immediately go to work on my clit in treacherous, devastatingly good circles, working my body so good and precise, like he's a professional at making women go feral for him. I moan, closing my eyes because I feel so ashamed for doing this, and out of all places, in a parked helicopter.

If we get caught…my lord, if we get caught…

I don't want to think of the consequences and overthink. I just want to get lost in something and someone that will very well be my undoing if I let myself.

"This little cunt of yours wants to get filled?" Daegan's beautiful, deep, dark voice entraps me more, dragging me down in his dark bliss.

"Yes," I breathe sensually. He withdraws his hand and fingers, my pussy already missing him. I pull down his boxers, and I expose a pierced, long and thick, massive cock.

I've never been with a man this size before, never mind a pierced one!

What am I supposed to do with that? It's going to break me just by looking at it.

He smirks happily and snakes his rough hand into my hair. With his other hand, he tilts my chin, so I look at him, wide-eyed and curious. This man is so handsome—the hottest man I've ever known.

PRETEND

"Eyes on me, baby. I want to see them roll back." He slaps my face and chin with his hand hard but not hard enough to hurt me. My eyes widen with self-realization that the man is ruthless.

Slap kink? *Unlocked*.

Mental health check? *Buffering*.

Questioning my morals because the pain and degradation coming together has me swooning so hard I'm not sure I ever want to get back up? *Triple check*.

I stroke his cock a couple of times as he pulls at my hair strands. He's massive. I'm going to choke to death.

You know what? Maybe he's right. Maybe I don't want him to come out tonight. Maybe we should put *creature* back where he belongs because it did not come out to play; it came out to destroy me.

How the hell is that going to fit in my mouth?

"Nope, nope, nope. I don't feel like dying tonight."

His pre-come glistens in front of my mouth, tempting me to lick it.

Daegan laughs, deep and wickedly. He tightens his grip on my hair, making a mess of it. He runs his thumb against my bottom lip, smirking lustfully.

"Good because after tonight, you'll feel the most alive you've ever felt. Now spit on my dick." He slaps my breasts, and I moan.

"We're going to finish what I've been dying to do since the night at my house."

I lick the precome off first, tasting the saltiness. I hum in satisfaction. He tastes so fucking good. Before I put him in my mouth, I lick his entire shaft. Starting from his balls and I trail my tongue all the way up to his crown. He growls and tilts his head with closed eyes. And then I swallow him. I take him in deep until he's down my throat, and then I give a strong suck before releasing him.

"Good girl, just like that. Let me use this mouth of yours." He praises me, and the sound of him doing that makes me more wet and the void in between my legs bigger.

I want him inside me.

I start sucking, licking him, tasting his dick. It's thick, so enlarged it doesn't entirely fit in my mouth, but I don't stop. I'll take him down my throat. I roll my tongue against his sensitive nerves, and he groans in response.

"Fuck. This tongue of yours..." He grunts as he continuously holds me in place, getting a fistful of my hair tightly in an unforgiving, unremorseful fashion to make me gag on him. Tears prick in my eyes each time his cock gets down into my throat. My vision blurs, but he doesn't let up, and neither do I.

I want to make him feel good. I want to show him. I want him just as badly as he wants me. I push him against the cabin so he sits back. He gives me full control of the pace, so I kneel in between his legs and let him relax for a second as I continue to suck him off until tears run down my cheeks.

I'm holding my breath, practically choking on his cock, but it doesn't deter me. I want to show him how devoted I can be when I've been challenged.

Damn him, though.

Because this is a game that's tainted for me to lose, my lungs start to burn, so I breathe through my nose. He catches it quickly and yanks on his dog tags. They tighten around my neck, forcing me to gag. He shoves his cock deeper down my throat, and it only makes me wetter and ache. I look up at him with blurred, hot vision. I'm pissed off but so turned on, with tears and saliva that continue to run down my face.

33

Daegan

If I thought she was flawless before, my dick down her throat is another sight I'll never get rid of from my mind. I take a mental picture of my boss's step-daughter with my dick in her mouth, smiling as she licks and sucks, and palms my balls as I fuck her mouth. It's sloppy, messy, and cruel, but I don't give a fuck.

I'm fucking her mouth so hard saliva drips down her chin until it falls on her swollen breasts that still spill out of the cup. Her lips are already swollen and red.

"Take off your pants, let me see your needy pussy."

I need to see how needy, pink, and wet it is for me. I shudder as she gives the head a twist and a lethal suck. Her mouth pops off, and I hum, satisfied when she pulls down her pants, and there's no fucking underwear.

She drops her pants beside me with confidence; it's shaved, dripping down her thighs, and glistening with her honey.

I'm about to finish all over her face, knowing she's not wearing any. But then I remember it wasn't for me; it was for Zeke.

"You were going to fuck him, weren't you?" I taunt; a deep chuckle slips into the hot air as I grin with sinister intentions. She stiffens like she got caught doing something bad. It's because she did do something terribly bad, and now I'm going to make her regret it.

"You were going to let him take what's mine?" I grab her by the hips, lifting her into the air quickly, picking her up so easily, and I sit her ass on my lap, my concrete shaft grazing her slit, as she tightens her hold against the back of my neck, locking her fingers together.

"You were going to scream for him, drip for him?" I dig my fingers into her hips as I cup her ass, marking her with my bruises. She whimpers seductively, already trying to grind herself against me. I shake my head, denying her. I fist my cock, stroking it briefly before I slap her clit with it. Bobbing it over and over until slapping noises fill the air. My piercing flicks her swollen bud, and she shivers. Her body trembles and her mouth gapes open, pleased.

"Daegan, please." She moans and begs me as she tries to keep herself up and steady.

"Well, now, you're going to take your punishment and bleed for me." I reach for her lips, and my teeth sink into her skin, drawing blood gently.

I kiss her lips, hard and ferocious. Mixing her blood with my tongue and I lift her up by her ass until my cock enters her. As soon as her velvet insides collide with me, my soul fucking shatters into oblivion.

Dammit, I already want to come. No, no, no, I will not finish just yet. I want to make this last forever.

"Alessia, you're so fucking tight." I hiss at her, brushing my lips against the shell of her ear as she sits down on my cock and gasps for air.

"Oh my God!" She screams in my ear, her forehead rests on mine, like she's in pain, having a hard time fitting my cock inside her. She doesn't back down. Instead, she clenches her pussy on my crown, and I groan with greed.

"I am no God but don't get me mistaken, baby. You will be on your knees praying for me to fuck you harder."

"Daegan, fuck, it hurts, don't stop." She heaves and starts to ride me. I let her chase her euphoric orgasm because I'm already so fucking close to mine. She pushes her breasts into my face, and I get lost in her full tear drops. I take a nipple into my mouth, and I suck. I slap her ass over and over again as she bounces on my cock, her wetness dripping more and more all over my dick and balls. Her ass cheeks are red and raw, but I don't stop. She's so fucking tight and good.

"Give me all of your come." She tugs at my hair strands, vehemently like she's searching for me to give her her spirit back. I arch a brow with the deadly temptation.

"I want to, God, I want to see my come drip out of you, but—"

"I'm on birth control." She admits as she clenches down on me even harder, milking my dick and balls.

"And why does that piss me off even more?" I growl, grinding my teeth at her admission, and pull on her hair. She opens her mouth, pinches her brows together painfully, and ruins me with that look on her face. With tightly closed eyes, she tilts her head back as she bounces, getting lost in our flames that may as well burn us both to ashes if our dirty little secret gets out.

"Daegan!" She moans perfectly as she climaxes, her pussy squeezing my cock, making this the best fuck I've ever had.

I combust, break, and pulsate my come inside her. Shooting my liquids, and she orgasms at the same time as I do. Our grunts and moans mix like a song in a duet made for each other. The desire that overwhelms is hypnotizing. I let go of her hair and let her ride out her paradise high, relaxing my hands on her hips as I come down from a place I don't want to.

Shit.

Fucking hell.

I want to keep fucking her until I die.

She reaches down and kisses my scarred face, touching the ones on my chest, and I know I'm well and truly fucked, physically and metaphorically.

34

Alessia

D AEGAN HAS ME AGAINST the wall in a second as soon as we close his door. Apparently, me riding him in a hangar was not enough for him. Hell, it wasn't enough for me. It'll never be enough after I've felt what he's like. After I've unmasked his ways of desire to take me.

He can take me wherever, whenever, he'd like. I'd never deny him or myself.

He picks me up by my thighs after he locked the doors, grabbing ahold of my hot flesh so tight the pain flares back. I know there will be marks in the morning. He forces my back to hit the wall, and I reach for his shoulders to hang on. His pants hang around his thighs, and mine are all torn to the floor.

He was so impatient that he didn't bother de-clothing himself.

"I'm going to ruin you for anyone else tonight." He growls, watching my tits jump up and down as he pounds inside me. My head tilts back and rests on the wall, and my cheeks flush into a fire at his declaration. My pussy can't bare it,

I feel so fucking full. It should be illegal to have a dick like that; it's stretching me...*breaking me*. But it feels so heavenly with the devil inside me.

Breathing hard, I tear off his mask and let it fall to the floor. His scars stare back at me, deep and contoured on his beautiful face. I am internally grateful that this man is still here and still alive, thriving after what he's been through. I trail my hand among them, and he lets me. "Or maybe I'll ruin you." I kiss him hard after my words pierce him sharply, not giving him a chance to interpret them. His body stiffens, but his lips burn me alive. His tongue dances with mine with twists and turns as my pussy throbs. Something inside my core swirls hotter than fire, and I'm practically begging to chase this feeling, hoping there's not an end.

My phone pings loudly with a familiar ring tone, and Daegan grunts, pissed off when he spots the caller ID on the floor with my clothes. "It's Zeke! This is the fifth time he's called me." I breathe hard in between our kisses. He cups my face with his hands and sucks on my bottom lip.

"Zeke can never take a fucking hint, can he?" He snarls angrily as he moves with me. Daegan reaches for my phone easily and hooks it with his fingers. He pushes it into my hand, and I blink up at him, confused. I'm still pinned against the wall with his pierced, thick and long dick inside me.

"Answer."

"I'm not going to answer, crazy!"

"Answer," he growls.

"You want me to answer while you're ten inches deep inside me right now?!"

He doesn't talk. Instead, he presses the green button, and as soon as Zeke says, "Hello? Alessia?" Daegan rams himself inside me more, going so deep it hurts.

He palms my lips, suffocating the scream I almost let out when his dick touches that one sensitive spot inside me. I'm on the verge of my second orgasm tonight.

Yeah, I was wrong; make that twelve inches.

"What's going on? Where did you go? I went to make a call, and you were gone?" Zeke's voice pours out with panic and maybe even a little hurt.

He thrusts again while he mouths, "Answer." His hand still muffling my moans. I narrow my brows at him as sweat drops down my cheek. I shake my head, but Daegan devilishly grins and lets go of my mouth, granting me permission to answer him. I grip the phone tighter in my hand as he continues to rail me against the wall ruthlessly.

"I—uh. I wasn't feeling too well. The beer got to me, and I'm in bed for the night." I bite my tongue, grinding my teeth as blood pressure rushes to my head and ears.

I shake my head at a very well-pleased Daegan, disapprovingly. He sucks my neck harder, leaving purple marks in their wake.

Don't moan.

Don't scream.

"Want me to check on you?" Zeke offers kindly while shuffling around his phone.

My eyes widen, and a low growl vibrates against my tits as Daegan stops sucking on my hard nipple. "Mine." He snarls quietly against my sensitive skin. He squeezes it with his palm hard and rough, and I'm about to finish again.

"No, I'm fine." I do my best to keep my voice regular and leveled despite getting fucked so hard against a wall.

"What's that noise? It sounds like—"

"I gotta go, it's the TV. Goodnight, Zeke!" I turn off the phone just as Daegan pulls me up even higher against the wall; his massive dick pulls out, and my back grazes upwards. He lifts me so quickly until my calves are over his shoulder. I claw at his hair and back, and my mouth opens with pleasure. The thing he's doing to me...

He has his mouth on my pussy in no time, takes me off the wall, and walks while holding me over his shoulders as he eats me out and sucks and bites on my clit.

I'm trembling with salacity as he throws me onto the bed, and my back hits his all-black comforter unforgivingly. A man that can throw me around and devour my pussy while walking to his bed is a keeper.

We love a multitasker.

He goes down on me, licking and sucking, nibbling on my clit, and I pull on his hair. He's letting me drown him in our built-up lust, and I want to scream. I lose myself. I toss my head back and forth as my thighs tremble against his cheeks. I moan out, "Daegan, oh my gosh, I'm gonna—"

"Say it again, baby."

Then I feel a finger enter my ass, my eyes shoot open, and then I'm closing them again. I'm about to come. I grab at my breasts, squeezing them, and he slaps my ass when I don't answer. Stroking his finger into my ass, my curiosity piques. Jack never touched me there...and I like it.

"Say, my name again, Alessia. Use your words."

"Daegan!" I whisper-yell full of seduction.

"Good girl, such a fucking needy slut just for me." He growls against my clit, and I come undone at his degradation.

"You'll never ride anyone's tongue but mine again, Alessia. That thought alone drives me crazy."

I trail my fingers against his chest. His pecs are covered in slices like scars. My eyes threaten to tear up, thinking about what he went through. I can't imagine going through days of torture and pain, knowing that his life was out of his control and into the hands of evil people. Torturing him. Probably wishing they would kill him, grant him a quick death instead of a long, torturous one.

I refuse to fall in love with him. After how Jack treated me and then lied and cheated on me? With one of my close friends?

I'm scared.

I'm scared to fall in love. I fell for Jack. I was very close to Bailey. I opened up to her about things that made me vulnerable because she was there when I didn't have anyone else to go to. We were friends for years and they did those things to me. I've lost faith in people.

I need to go back to my room. This was only sex.

I get off of Daegan and reach for my clothes. My feet dangle from his bed, but then the blankets shift.

Daegan stirs, stopping me in my tracks. I freeze and turn toward him, hoping I was careful enough that he stayed asleep. But no, he's wide awake, in a cold sweat. He grabs my arm and squeezes my wrist so tight that his fingers wrap around it easily, the pain instantly brewing underneath his fiery touch. A bruise will reflect shortly. I know it by the force he's inflicting. His power is strong.

I hiss, my eyes turning into slits, and I pull away from him. I hope he'll let go with each pull, but he only tightens his grip.

"Where the fuck are you going?" His question catches me off guard. This isn't Daegan. He would never actually hurt me. He has to be still asleep, or at the very least groggy.

"Daegan, you're hurting me." I stare at his large hand around mine. His dark hair falls in front of his scarred side.

"Why is the light off? Why is the fan on? *Why am I here*?" He interrogates me like he's a prisoner. The darkness isn't enough to shadow his sad expressions.

He's angry, even a little scared. The way his deep voice vibrates with desperation tells me everything. He was having a nightmare. A whirlwind of emotions flickers in his grey eyes.

I raise my brows, patience filling every part of me. With my free hand, I caress his cheek, the scarred parts, and my thumb brushes up and down in a soothing way.

"Hey...it's okay. *You're okay*. It's safe." I bow my head to meet his beautiful eyes. My knees skid across the mattress to get closer. "I'm not going to hurt you. You're safe." I kiss his lips once making sure it's fast and stern. I need him to wake up. I need him to realize where he is without sending him into a panic.

It's a quick kiss, but long enough to make me feel like I'm in a cloud of bliss. Daegan makes me forget anything and everything. The first man to have this effect on me, and it scares me. My heart rate is racing, and now it's becoming more peaceful with each touch.

PRETEND

Daegan stiffens, his body turning to stone like he wants to fall apart or push me away. I open my eyes, and his other hand holds his knife. The moon shines against the Damascus blade, and my eyes widen.

Was he going to stab me?

He lets go of the knife, replacing his weapon with the back of my head instead. He crashes his lips against mine, rough and needy. Sexy and full of lustrous growls between each kiss. His tongue travels between my teeth, and he kisses me over and over again. Fast and messy. His beard pokes against my skin with each collision.

God, I love it when it does that.

His body weight pushes me down until he's on top, and my back is back in the bed. He makes his way in between my legs, and I can feel the tip of his cock, begging for my entrance. He's hard, but his face is harder.

I dare to open my eyes. He's kissing me like he's determined to forget whatever he was thinking about. It's like he's trying to forget what he was dreaming about and get lost inside me instead.

I break away from his soft lips. "Do you want to talk about it?" I hold his face with my hands, my soft attempt to stop him. Has he had anyone to talk to about the things he went through?

He shakes his head, "no."

And with one detrimental thrust of his hips, he's inside me again. His entire length enters me, and I moan into his shoulders. He grips my hips hard, pulling me into him like he's greedy to go deeper. I claw at his back as his disheveled hair falls over his forehead. He hits that spot again inside me, my climax already wanting to finish me as he thrusts deeply, in and out.

"I don't want to talk. I want to fuck until I can't think anymore. Let me drown in you."

His eyes are the most comforting essence when they're on mine. My whole body crumbles into peace when I lose myself in those ice eyes. The stress deteriorates into nothing, and the calmness in my spirit thrives when I'm around him.

He is the silence to the havoc I self-inflict.

35

Daegan

We're in a room full of military intelligence, SEAL Team Scarred Executioners, and Zeke's team. I stand in the dark corner, my half mask is on.

I listen to Alessia inform us of the execution plan, followed by overwatch. Rooker and the Admiral stand beside her in front of us all.

The Admiral has no clue I was deep inside her, making her come all over my cock, making her scream my name, and her tits in my mouth just a few hours ago last night and this morning.

I already want to do it again.

She wants to be used, and I'll gladly be the one to do it.

> Me: How does it feel?

I take in a deep breath from the corner of the room as I watch her. She's in work mode; the way she moves and the way she speaks, she's passionate about doing this job just like I am with mine, and it's so fascinating to see. Her hair is tied back perfectly in a tight bun that I'm tempted to make a mess of. Her uniform hugs her body, and she looks confident.

She tenses as she feels her phone buzz.

"Excuse me." She pardons herself and pulls out her phone. She shakes her head. She's doing everything she can not to flush. But before she can turn off her phone, I don't give her a chance to ignore me.

> Me: How does it feel to be up there while my come drips out of your well-fucked pussy in front of everyone?

She clears her throat and shuts off her phone. I can't help but chuckle.

There's a map, and she explains what she's found to help us execute our plan, the orders that need to be followed through, and the top-secret missions that no one knows about except the very few people who will be working on them.

Alessia finishes her first speech and begins her next one, and Kane follows her behind as she grabs another folder. My heart skips a beat, and I track their movements. My eyes follow her ass as she walks. Blood rushes down, and I blink rapidly.

I take a deep breath, and it clears my head.

She looks so fucking sexy when she's in her uniform. She looks even better when she's underneath me.

Fuck, I can't concentrate.

I whip out my bullet and start twirling it. I grind my teeth and start going back and forth myself. Should I stop this relationship, we agreed on before it gets too much?

"The families that The Surgeon captured...they were killed." Alessia's once hardened administrative voice turns into something fragile and breakable. The

PRETEND

news shocks everyone. Wrath begins to fill my soul. I straighten my posture, and I ball my fists. She exchanges glances with the multiple SEAL Teams in front of her, then with Delta and other special operators to her left. Everyone grows quiet as she continues. "He recently captured a group of soldiers and..."

Then she pins her brown eyes onto me in the back of the room. They're not sparkling or shimmering like they always do. Usually, I love the way her honey iris' glow when she sees me, but, instead, they're full of something I don't like. I don't like what I'm seeing at all.

They're full of pity...and I resent it.

You've never looked at me like this.

I stop twirling the bullet and look down at my scarred hand.

I'm seeing red. Complete darkness consumes me as I listen to her give the details of the next mission regarding plans to get to him. Memories of being tortured are back in full swing with demons that swarm my broken soul.

They're going out on missions. And I'm fucking stuck here. My initial anger when Alessia was first assigned to me howls over my mind.

I can feel the phantom pain in my face...and it wreaks havoc on my spirit. All of a sudden, the room is smaller, the air is thin, and my body grows taut because I know what he did to them before he killed them all.

I tune Alessia out as my body grows cold and painful. Suddenly, her voice is replaced with the Admiral's and Rooker's, and then a hurricane of chatter thrives.

Work is done for the day, and we're escorting her back to her room, but Rooker's voice stops me. Kane continues to walk Alessia out.

"You're taking the reins, Creature."

I shift on my feet, my heart racing at the thought of leaving Alessia alone.

"What about Valentin?"

"Bane and Texas will take over. We need your skills on the forefront this time, keeping us safe while we do our job."

I will never fail a mission, especially if I take out bad guys. It's been a while since I've looked an evil soul in the eyes as I eliminated them. That sounds like a good plan.

"Lopez doesn't know his head from his ass. Are you sure he can protect her?" I ask Rooker.

"Really, asshole? I'm standing right next to you." Lopez mutters with offense.

"I'm just saying...I know you like to mess with women who are off limits, cowboy."

Rooker and Lopez stand puzzled at my threat. I don't like to talk or voice my opinions on anything, but this is different.

His eyes turn into slits. He knows exactly who I'm talking about. Alessia's co-workers and nurses are from the on-base hospital. The man has a long sheet of women he's fucked in the workplace. If he wanted to shoot his shot with my girl, I wouldn't put it past him.

"The last time I checked, Valentín was single." His eyes narrow at me suspiciously.

I might be making it obvious that I care for this girl...and yet. There's not a single part of me that gives a fuck.

I arch a brow at his comment.

No one can know this girl is mine. No one. It'll be my job, my career...my new family, I've found. But why does she feel like my new home?

"She's the Admiral's daughter, Texas. Don't go there." Rooker shakes his head, eyeing the both of us as he did at Kane and Grim at the military ball.

PRETEND

"Creature, get your shit ready and report to the airfield tomorrow. We're leaving tomorrow night," he says, walking away from me. His southern accent is thick, cold, and curt.

When it's just Lopez and I in the room, I see black and don't know what comes over me. The dragon, the invincible creature, is waiting to burn him alive. I can't control my emotions.

I'm always in control, but when it comes to her. I break, I shatter, I burn for her. She does this to me, and I will do everything and anything for this whole fucking world to know she is not one to fuck with. Not when she has me taking care of her.

She doesn't need me. But I want her to need me. However, I'm pissed off at everything right now. I'm mad at the world, knowing that people are getting tortured right now. And I'm angry that Alessia looked at me like she feels sorry for me.

Still, I lose control. I always lose control for her.

I push Lopez up against the wall, my blade at his throat.

"What the fuck!" His brown eyes glare at me with shock. He tries to push my forearms off his chest. I'm taller, stronger, and bigger; no matter how much he tries to struggle in my hold, I keep him where I want him to be.

Under my knife while I make my statement.

"The Admiral's daughter is already shaken from everything that's going on right now. She's overwhelmed with this being her first deployment. If I find out you've touched her in any way or even breathed the same air as her, this blade will not graze your skin; instead, it'll be underneath it, in your heart."

36

Alessia

DAEGAN WAS SUPPOSED TO be here tonight, but he's not, and it's making me question everything. Kane is not the one who's supposed to be watching me right now, but he stands outside my door, awake and on the job.

I've sent him multiple text messages, but he hasn't responded. I may be coming off as needy, but all I want is transparency. Is he already going back on what we agreed on? Does he regret it?

I close the book I'm reading and get dressed in civilian clothing. I put on leggings and a black tank top. My dog tags are still on, along with my seashell necklace, which I got as a gift from my biological father when I was in college. I love the beach. It's always been a place where I can relax, no matter how bad things are.

I replay the way his eyes looked painful in the conference room. We found another high-value target that works under 'The Surgeon.' It must be triggering for Daegan, knowing we're so close to catching him. It's personal for him,

I know it. How can it not be after what he's been through? He's witnessed firsthand the brutality this person holds.

After putting my shoes on, I swing open my room door, and Kane looks up at me.

He puts his phone away and stands. "Umm, hi? Where are we going?" Kane asks while putting his hands in his pocket.

I give him a contemplative look and purse my lips together.

"Where's Hannibal?" I ask, trying to keep my tone calm.

He sighs, readjusts his posture, and then stands straight again. Then he places his hands behind his back.

"I don't know. All I know is that he's not in his room, and he asked me to take over."

My shoulders sink down, and I look around the hallway, thinking of all the places he could be at this time of night.

"I need to ask him something, and he's not answering me."

"He likes to be alone, Alessia...for the most part. Let him be."

Frustration and worry build, forcing me to crumble. I don't care if he knows about us. I don't want him to be alone. It's like these men don't want to show that they're human, as if it's so weak to feel pain.

"No one should be alone after hearing what I said earlier in the conference room. I'm going to find him, and you're going to let me."

He places his hands on his hips over his belt. He sighs deeply, rubbing the temples of his forehead.

"Look...*fine*." He huffs out. His dark blue eyes soften just a bit. "I'll help you."

"No, let me do this alone." I bite my lip as a memory floods my scrambled mind. Kane stops moving and stares at me like I asked him to do something crazy.

"I can't let you do that, Valentin. Your step-father—"

"Just please. Let me do this alone." I quip, urgently grabbing his arm and begging him to understand me. Kane ponders my request with vivid creases near his brows.

"I'll be careful. Plus...I think I know where he is."

I push open the door to the rooftop of the building alone. Kane stayed behind, guarding my room as if I were still there. The dry air immediately greets me, and I soak it in as I walk forward. A helicopter can be heard from a distance. Its blades whip the air as the moon shines bright over it.

I turn to my right, and sure enough, there's an ominous dragon on a scarred back facing me. Daegan's shirtless with only black sweatpants on. His back muscles tighten and untighten as he leans on a railing in front of him.

He's staring at the sky, smoking a cigarette, like he's lost in thought. I watch a cloud of smoke swirl into the air as he blows it out. Finally, he puts it out. Then he lets his head fall, and he stares at the ground. He grips the railing tight, his mask tucked under his palm.

I want to help. I want him to open up to me...but only if he wants to. It must be frustrating, dark, and painful in his head. I can't even imagine the things he's had to go through and experience firsthand. I only get videos and photos of evidence. He had to live through it.

I stroll toward him and palm the railing when I'm side by side with him. He doesn't move or acknowledge my presence, and I'm trying not to let it affect me.

Maybe I should leave him alone.

But I'm a bleeding heart, and I can't help it sometimes.

No one should be alone when they're going through something. At least, that's how I feel when I'm going through it.

"Daegan?" I arch a brow, longing to hear his deep voice.

He doesn't answer me. It's rare when he doesn't wear his mask. His scars are on full display, and his waves fall over his face as he continues to ignore me.

"Daegan? Why did you switch with Kane tonight?"

Still…nothing. He won't talk to me. The side of Daegan that's familiar to everyone else but me. He's known for not saying much to everyone in the military, and now he's doing it to me. But why? What did I do for him to change his demeanor?

"Did I do something, Daegan? Are you…?" I choke up, unsure of my ability to finish that question.

Crap, why am I acting so immature? Why can't I be honest with him and just ask him if he regrets our secret agreement of just sex?

"Are you having regrets? Do you regret that night?" I whisper softly, making sure no one can hear me. My paranoia gets to me, and I look around the rooftop to make sure we're truly alone. After doing a 360 glance, we're in the clear. It's empty, except for his rucksack.

"Daegan, talk to me. Please?"

Silence.

Daegan locks his jaw over and over again, unbothered. His triceps tighten, and his archangel tattoo catches my attention on his arm. I reach for it slowly and rub my thumb over his scars. They're soft like it's still fresh to the touch.

"We're going to get him, Daegan."

Nothing.

"He did this to you? Didn't he? All of these scars are from him?"

He looks at me like I hit a nerve, and then he retracts his arm. I frown when he pulls away from me. I look up at him; his grey eyes are ice-cold, capable of making me freeze so hard I can't even think.

But I don't take offense. I keep trying. So he understands that no matter what, I'm not going anywhere.

"You could have walked away from all of this...and got out of the Navy. Why didn't you?"

He doesn't want to talk about it.

I take a few steps back from him with patience. Tears are already threatening to fall. I must go back, anyway. I promised Kane I would be quick...and now that I know he's okay, I can go to sleep.

"I'm sorry if I did something wrong. I don't know what I did, but I hope you can forgive me. You don't have to. We can call off whatever we agreed on. I can see you have a lot on your mind already, and I won't—"

Daegan grabs my arms and puts me against the railing until I'm facing the ground below. He has me by both of my wrists with one hand. The edge digs into my ribs, and Daegan is quick to palm my screams.

"Daegan, what the hell?!" I muffle against his hand.

Still, he doesn't say anything. He's manhandling me, throwing me like I'm a doll. He pulls down my tank top until my breasts fall out, and I'm heating up.

Oh my god. He's not going to do what I think, is he?!

He lets go of my hand as if he trusts me to stay quiet. He hums behind me when he finds my nipple. My heart flutters as he roams my body. My breast fills his hand, and he squeezes it hard until it's painful. Making me moan from the agonizing pleasure. He's being rough and angry. My curls fall forward in my face, and all I can do is let him do what he wants to me.

I want whatever is about to happen.

My pussy throbs and I can feel myself getting wet.

Still...he doesn't say anything. My hands are still tied together. Both of my wrists are crushed together, and he pulls down his sweats until they're at his thick thighs.

"Daegan," I murmur.

He growls as I call out for him. He pulls down my leggings until I'm bare and exposed. He starts circling my swollen clit, causing me to drip more and more.

I can't take it.

"Daegan, talk to me!" I whisper-yell. But he ignores me. He puts his fingers into my mouth, making me warm his flesh as he pulls out his cock. I feel like a fish on a hook as I taste myself on his fingers. He won't remove his hand.

I feel his piercings at my entrance.

"Fuck me, Daegan, please."

He doesn't hesitate any longer.

He pushes into me, and my wetness lets him glide easily. With one hand on my breast and the other in my mouth. He forces me to tip-toe so he can fuck me while we're standing.

Then, he pulls backward so the crown of his dick is almost out, and just when he's going to pull out, he rails into me hard and fast.

He begins to fuck me deep and cruelly, making it so hard not to scream. My body jolts from colliding with his waist, and every time I think I'm going to fall over from the power he inflicts, he pulls me back into him like he wants to break me. So, I suck on his finger harder to stop the incoherent sounds from coming out of my tightening lungs. I stare down at the ground below from stories above, doing everything I can not to moan.

If he wanted to, he could lift me up by a few inches, and I'd fall off.

What in the world has gotten into him?

Still, it's driving me crazy because I want him to keep fucking me like this. Then his cock hits that one spot inside me, making me squeeze my eyes shut tight. He hits it over and over again, making the pleasure fucking blinding, and I'm seeing golden sparkles. Finally, I'm orgasming, coming all over his cock as he pounds me. But he doesn't let me ride my orgasm out like he's done before. He's fucking me like I'm nothing to him. He keeps thrusting in and out until I'm biting my lip.

He feels so good.

My pussy tightens as euphoria spreads into my core and throughout my veins. I'm imploding from his massive cock that makes me full. So. Goddamn. Full.

Finally, he pulls my hair back so that our cheeks are side by side. He grips it so tight that I'm hissing. Then he grunts into the shell of my ear. His cock twitches and jabs into me hard and slow as he fills me with his come.

He's emptying himself inside me, and I'm happily taking it. He rests his nose on my cheek as he evens out his breaths. We're both panting, hot, and soaking in this weird moment for a few more seconds.

He pulls out of me and readjusts himself. I push myself off the railing, used and abused in all the best ways...like I wanted. *Like he wanted.*

PRETEND

I'm breathless, my leg muscles quaking from how rough he gave it to me. I brush my curls out of my face as sweat forms on my chest and forehead.

I still want more.

What is wrong with me?

He walks away from me after he picks up my leggings with my underwear and dresses me so I'm not exposed anymore. He tucks my breasts back into my top, and I help him. I turn to him, but he's already looking the other way. This time, I'm speechless, and all I can do is watch him leave the rooftop without one word. I'm left dazed, confused, and used.

37
Daegan

I'T'S BEEN A FEW weeks after a mission was well done and executed. And it's been a few hellish weeks since I fucked Alessia on the rooftop. Her absence has affected me more than it should.

Before we go back to base, we're assigned to do last-minute overwatch with Marines.

"Don't fucking touch me," I snarl at Zeke's pat on my shoulder. I fight the urge to let go of my rifle and cringe from his touch. I don't let anyone touch me but Alessia. And it's not because I was kidnapped once. Or tortured, burned, or sliced. I'm not used to another human touching me. I don't like it. I don't like people...but I like her.

"Hey man, I'm just trying to congratulate you on a shot well done. You just saved those marines." He flinches and walks away from my prone position. I can't see him, but the tension grows thicker with each second.

PRETEND

I scout more land and keep my Overwatch on full send. I'd rather have Loverboy up here than Zeke. I don't like that he's close friends with my little Valentine. Some people may call it jealousy. I call it like I see it. I don't like the way he looks at her. Because the way he looks at her is how I look at her. And no man will live to tell the tale of what it's like to be the reason for her smile but me.

I reload my sniper and keep my eyes out.

"I'm gonna take a piss. You don't mind, do you, Creature? I can go right here in this corner, so I still got your six."

"Get the fuck out of here if you're going to pull your dick out and stink this rooftop with your piss. We still got a few more hours on Overwatch, and I will not spend it like that," I snap, arching a brow, and he stiffens. I look away from my scope and stare him down. He cowers, putting his hands up and surrendering.

"Chill out, Creature. I'll just go to another room. What's with you, bro?"

I scoff, returning to my crosshairs.

"What can I say? You bring out the nice side in me, and I have a way with words."

"Yeah, no kidding, I'll be back. Might take a shit too. You sure you'll be alright if—"

"Akana, I'll give you," I look at my watch, tilting my head to the side and exhaling at the digital watch, "five seconds starting now to leave before I lose my patience."

And with that, he exits the rooftop, and I roll my eyes. Shit and piss? In the corner of this rooftop? I can endure a lot of things, but if I can avoid smelling Zeke's shit and piss, I'm taking it.

Every building looks secure. I see no threats, but I stay vigilant and alert. I'm taking slow, deep breaths and relaxing, but my mind keeps traveling to Alessia. The sun is setting, and I'm counting down the hours. It's been a while since I've felt alive like this. I look forward to waking up each day. And she has everything to do with it. Before, it was like I'd been living stagnant, the same thing every day: work, work, and more work. The team is the only sense of family I've ever had until I met her.

All I want to do is bury myself in her skin, her flesh, her bones, and drown. Obsession is an understatement.

Everything is going smoothly, and then I feel the same dark premonition on my neck.

Something is wrong.

I'm looking everywhere, but I don't see anything out of the ordinary. Then I see a dark shadow creeping in the corner of a building, making its way closer to the group of marines, and I'm ready to send it and unleash hell on anyone who dares.

With my finger on the trigger, I hold my breath, waiting to confirm a threat. The shadow grows bigger, my heart pinching my brows to reveal...a dog.

A heavy breath leaves my mouth from all the buildup of holding in my oxygen, and I sigh with relief.

I look down at my side to recover before it's back to work, but then I see a shadow towering over me.

Zeke really wants to see my bad side today. I don't think it's polite of anyone to get behind me without addressing themselves first. Everyone knows that I don't take it kindly. Before I scold Zeke and tell him off, reminding him of my ticks, I feel a sharp pain in my shoulder when I move slightly to the left. A sharp pain is an understatement because I quickly recognize the same feeling of what sharp steel feels like.

I've been stabbed.

A sharp sting melts through me, and I grunt from the surprise. A thick blade breaks through my uniform, and I know I'm in trouble. I know this feeling too well. I was tortured for weeks.

Time to have some fucking fun.

I manage to elbow whoever the fuck stabbed me in the nose, and they stumble back. I stand within seconds, dropping my sniper to face a man smaller than me, wielding a thick, long knife dressed in all black. He tries to slice me again, and I take a step back, causing him to miss. His eyes explode with pure evil hatred, and he plunges forward. His body strikes me in the stomach, and I tighten my muscles to lessen the blow. He manages to tackle us both to the edge of the rooftop, and I burst into laughter.

"If I'm falling off this roof, you're going down with me, buddy." I elbow his face as he hovers over me, his spit flying everywhere as he shouts.

He's snarling at me, and he gives me a good hard punch. My head falls to the side, and I smile. He got me good.

"What the fuck is going on?" Operator Cobra shouts into my mic, but I'm a little busy with my new friend here to give him an answer.

A wicked grin transforms the scowl on my face, and it only angers the man before me.

He tries to finish his job and raises his knife over his head. It's a big mistake if he thinks I'm going to let him take me from a world where my little valentine exists.

Even when I'm fighting for my life, even in a moment like this, she's all I fucking see. And that's when it hits me.

I'm falling for a woman who is forbidden, and I'll do whatever it takes for her to be mine. Even if we have to hide it, I want it. I want all of her.

I smash my forehead with his, causing him to lose his bearings. I take full advantage of the disorientation spell he's under, twist his hands until his bones break, and grab the knife for my safety.

It all happens within a blink of an eye. I stab him in the chest, where his heart is, and it goes through like butter. I'm chuckling the entire time, humming the same song I do when I shoot.

I throw him off me, and he falls to the side as he struggles to breathe and attempts to pull the blade out of his chest. I watch for a few seconds, my chest heaving, and I wipe the blood off my mouth as I wait until he takes his last breath.

He stops reaching for his wound, and goes still. Unfortunately for him, he's no longer holding himself up, and he falls off the roof once his body goes still.

Zeke enters from behind me a few seconds after the threat falls off.

"What the fuck happened? I go to take a shit, and this? You alright, bro?" He asks me, but I ignore him. I walk where the man falls and look down at the edge of the building. He lays there lifeless in a pool of his own blood, his knife deep into his chest next to Operator Cobra. Rooker takes a step back from the dead body and looks up at me, bewildered.

Mics go off, everyone shouting for answers, but I need a damn cigarette first.

"Umm...explain. How and why did this person fall off your roof right fucking next to me?" He orders an answer through the mic.

PRETEND

"One second." I huff out, breathing hard. I light my cigarette, the bitterness taints my tongue, and I hum, satisfied.

"What the fuck happened? You look like shit. You're bleeding," Zeke stands beside me, studying my shoulder.

I shrug nonchalantly and hollow my cheeks to take a hit.

"You should see the other guy," I nod towards the ground, smirking.

"Creature," he scolds.

"I don't fucking know. Once you left to take a shit, I got stabbed in the back. I defended myself, we wrestled, and I eliminated him, and he fell off once he took his last breath."

"That's fucking enough, Creature. Get your ass to a medic to get that wound checked out. Akana, take Creature's place, please." Cobra orders.

"Fuck no, I'm finishing the mission, then I'll get myself checked when I'm goddamn ready, Cobra," I spit back, and Rooker grows quiet.

38
Alessia

"You slut."

Winters's statement throws me off, and I immediately feel like I'm screwed. My eyes bulge, and I start coughing on my own spit. We're having our horror movie marathon in my bedroom while Kane and Lopez stand outside.

It's the weekend, and there's not much to do. So, staying in and watching movies with my closest friend sounds like a great idea. When all I want to do is be in Daegan's arms. He didn't tell me anything. He switched shifts with Kane after our explosive night of giving in to each other, and then...that was it. He's been gone for almost three weeks now, not a text or a phone call.

Kane told me he was sent out on a mission...but it bothers me that I didn't hear it from him. I'm still very new to having a relationship that's solely based on sex, so maybe I have to get used to things like this. It's normal for this to happen, though.

PRETEND

I know when they are out doing missions, they can't talk, so I have to remind myself he's out there, doing God knows what, but saving people. All I can do is hope and pray he comes back alive. This is the part where I liked being with Jack. He was a civilian and unemployed for most of our relationship, but when he worked with his dad as a paralegal for him, I didn't have to worry about him being in the warzone.

I can't say I'm in love with my bodyguard, but I do care about him. I'm not sure how deep my feelings go, but...I can say he occupies my mind more than he should.

I sit up, and the soreness between my thighs screams back at me. Daegan tore me, stretched me, fucked me so hard I still feel his imprints like he promised...and I would do it again. It was the best sex and orgasm I've ever experienced. It was life-changing, to say the least. His piercings made it even more enjoyable.

I changed positions from laying on my stomach to sitting against the wall on my bed with a mouthful of microwaveable popcorn. I shrug, doing everything I can to play it cool. I do a quick double-take around my room, ensuring there's no sign of Daegan in here, while Winters stares at me suspiciously. She pops a single popcorn into her mouth and chews slowly.

"Why am I slut?" I ask casually, but on the inside, I'm a hot mess. I place the bowl of popcorn down, but because I'm stressing from the chaos happening on my tiny TV on my desk, the distractions of the screams of Neve Campbell, and a very wary Winters, the bowl falls off the edge of the bed.

"Oh, snap." I curse under my breath, and Winters squints at me like she's caught me in a lie. I pick it up and run to my closet to grab a mini broom and dustpan. She still doesn't say anything or get up from my small couch to help me. She watches me pour the remains into the trash can, and I sit back on the edge of the bed, hugging my pillow tight into my chest.

"I thought we were closer than this. How dare you hide this from me!" She scolds me and grabs more popcorn, talking down at me like I'm a schoolgirl.

I start nibbling on my nails and let out a high-pitched giggle, hoping it'll mask my nerves. "Hide what? I have no idea what you're talking about." I switch glances to the TV, unbothered, hoping my acting skills come through for this moment.

She can't know I slept with Daegan. Kane already knows, and that's enough people. I don't care how close I am with Winters. I can't say anything. We'll both get in a shit ton of trouble. Plus, this relationship of sex will never be anything more, so what's the point of talking about it?

"Care to explain that bite mark on your chest?"

Oh, fuck.

Oh, no.

I'm wearing a tank top, no bra, and my Navy sweatpants. I'm about to go to sleep soon, so I wanted to be comfortable…and now it's biting me in the ass. I can feel my cheeks turning as red as a tomato. The heat is evident, and suddenly, I need a cold bath.

"I—I," I stutter, looking at her, studying her reaction. She doesn't look mad or upset. In fact, she seems the opposite. More amused than anything.

"Who did that? Because if you did that to yourself, I'm pretty impressed."

"Let's just watch the movie, please." I turn away from her, pursing my lips after a small smile. I wave my hand toward the TV and hug the pillow tighter.

We sit in silence for the next five minutes. I'm grateful she isn't prying further, but it's short-lived.

"I'm your friend and want to see you happy after Jack. Nobody should ever feel betrayed by their partner, never mind by one of their close friends. By the way, I still can't believe Bailey did that to you. Side note, what a bitch, but anyways, before I get off track...I'm not going to ask. Maybe it isn't my business, but whoever it is, you can get in trouble for fooling around while you're here. It's not my place to bring it up with our boss...never mind your stepfather, so you can count on me. I won't do that to you. " My heart plummets to the ground at the mention of Ravenmore. I bite my nails and suck in a deep breath as she continues. "But it is my place to remind you of the consequences."

I can't look at her. I'm scared I'll break in half at her sharp tone. But I can feel her stare digging into the side of my face, and I want to run.

"I know," I whisper softly, letting my head fall, and I stare at the mark on my chest. Fire ignites, and yet, a fleeting wave of shame hits me.

"By the way, I don't really have an update for you. Whoever is texting you is good at hiding their tracks. I've gone to the best of the best when it comes to tracing the unknown, and there's no answers."

My brows arch and hope shatters at catching this person. I look at Winters to my left, and she yawns, placing her hand in front of her face as her eyes close. She sits back down and covers herself with a purple blanket, getting cozy.

"That's unfortunate." Very unfortunate is an understatement. "Thank you for trying," I reply, looking at a sleepy Winters. She unhooks her hair tie, causing her waves to fall over the pillow.

If they could find this unknown stalker of mine, Daegan and Kane could return to their team faster. And I could stop looking over my shoulder. The last thing I would ever want is to be kidnapped.

"Yeah, no problem. You know your mom texts me often to check up on you. It's cute that her little mini-me is following in her footsteps and wants to ensure you're doing okay under my guidance." She teases playfully.

I smile and lay down on my bed, but then guilt strikes my nerves. I lay my head on the pillow, tuck my hands underneath my cheek, and Daegan crosses my mind. Maybe I should call this off. I really don't want to, but the thought of getting caught and disappointing my mother...losing my job, or even tainting Daegans hard-earned reputation sinks into me, and I'm full of remorse.

39
Daegan

S HE'S SLEEPING. ON HER stomach, her long black curls sprawled out against her naked back. My dick hardens immediately, watching my little valentine closed off to the world.

She is so innocent, but she has a fire inside her when someone pushes her buttons the wrong way. She isn't afraid to stand up for what's right or wrong.

As soon as I saw Kane outside her door, I sent him to his room. I waited until he had left entirely to enter her room. She had locked it. Clever girl, yet foolish to think a locked door could ever stop me from getting to her. The number of ways I know how to get through locked windows or doors is limitless.

I take off my mask, blood still soaked on my chest and back from where I was stabbed. I'm supposed to be in the hospital getting stitched up. But the first person I wanted to see as soon as the helicopter touched the ground was one person. My little Valentine. A short girl with beautiful tanned skin and curls I like to pull on.

I slowly take off the blanket, my heart racing as each agonizing second ticks by, and then I see my goddess, and an ache swells my dick to the point of pain. I find her mostly naked underneath with only her laced panties on. She did this on purpose.

Jesus...

Her smooth olive-toned skin aches to be touched and worshiped. Goosebumps erupt all over her back, her body already reacting to being uncovered.

I trail my finger along her spine down to her ass.

She's such a good girl...of course, she's naked.

"Mmm." She hums and groans while asleep. Fuck, I love to hear those sweet moans. She's moaning for me. I will never let her moan for another person as long as I'm alive.

"I'm back, baby," I whisper into her ear, ready to devour her like a hungry predator. God, she makes me so hard it hurts. Even when I was on the mission, every time I saw her mesmerizing face, it pained me. I had to forcefully block her out so I could fucking focus.

Is this what my secret obsession with lust has driven me to?

I need her to put me out of my goddamn misery.

She stirs in bed, a small smile pulling at her soft pink lips. She blinks slowly. Her lashes flutter as she wakes up.

"Daegan?" Her sleepy voice calls for me. The blue moonlight from her window leaks through, making it barely visible.

"I'm here, Valentine," I say.

She turns onto her back, her nipples pointed onto her perfect full breasts, and I'm tempted to suck on them.

She smiles, and I can see that because the light she left on in her closet leaks through the cracked open door. She left it on like that because she knows that's how I sleep. Did she know I was coming back tonight? Or has she kept it on like this every night?

My dick pulsates with need. I want her. And I want her now.

"Daegan..." she groans when my fingers grace her clit, teasing her, circling it, not entirely giving her the sensations she craves.

"Alessia." I crave to hear her say my name on her lips for the rest of my life. She's ruined me, taken me for herself, leaving no room to think about another woman. Not that I will ever *want to* again.

"I've missed you." She breathes softly, twitching as I continue to work her body.

I chuckle, then slip a finger inside her, feeling her soft, warm insides. She's already so wet and ready for me.

"Your pussy is crying for me."

She bites her lips and nods as I stroke in and out of her with two fingers.

"Mr. Hannibal. Kane will hear us." She looks at the locked door, her eyes widening with worry.

"Good. He needs to know you belong to me." I tease.

"I won't—" She starts, but I interrupt her with my movements. I slide in a third finger, making her hips buckle and steal the air from her lungs. Her body trembles as I thrust a little faster than before.

This is wrong. This is so fucking wrong. If Ravenmore finds out what I've done with her...I can kiss my job goodbye. I've entered my "fuck it" era. I'm just going with the flow now, and that flow is Alessia Valentine. I'll gladly ride out these waves with her.

"I won't risk you losing your job. Or mine." She finishes her sentence, barely. She opens her legs wider for me, and her bare-shaven pussy is begging to be fucked.

"You worry too much, baby. He's gone already."

She relaxes, finally, as I continue to push and pull my fingers in her.

"Make love to me."

I stiffen at the mention of the word that doesn't exist. Life has proven that to me time and time again.

I grip her hair tight in my hand.

"Love doesn't exist." I snarl into her ear; my beard brushes against her as I speak. I stop finger fucking her. I'm coated in her wetness, her honey dripping all over my skin, and I force my fingers into her mouth. She gasps, clearly taken aback by how feral I've become. Her lips part, granting me access, but I don't stop on her tongue. I go deeper until I'm touching the back of her throat.

"Taste yourself, baby. Taste how fucking heavenly sweet you are. *Swallow* how addicting you are." I demand, growling from the chaos building up. She makes me crazy. She's making me feel things I thought weren't meant for a man like me.

She gags, her throat threatening to close up, but then she continues to take it well. Her beautiful honey eyes glisten because of the tears threatening to fall on her rosy cheeks. Her watery eyes are on me as I stand over her, my lips an inch from her mouth. She sucks my finger clean and swallows.

I lean over her, pulling her underwear to the side, not bothering to undress myself at this point thoroughly.

All I know is I need her before I pass the fuck out. I'm tired, I'm sore, and I may even be hurting, but it's not enough to overcome me.

PRETEND

I unzip my pants, still with my uniform on.

I enter her, gliding in her wet, soft tightness like it was made for me. Her walls clench down on my cock as soon as I push into her fully.

"Oh, fuck Daegan." She groans as she gasps for air, pulling at the back of my head. Her eyes narrow, and she bites her lip like she's in pain. She wiggles underneath me like she wants to escape my greed. My need to devour her. She thinks she can't take my length, but she can and will.

"There's no escaping me now." I grip her waist, digging into her skin, pulling her back into a place where I continue to thrust hard and fast. She grabs hold of my back, holding on like a life jacket.

Our skin slapping fills the room. The bed shakes, and I forget we are in her room beside Kane's. She does this to me. She makes me forget where I am, and I get lost in her soul.

She has a body that could make a demon feel deserving of heaven.

She is my piece of heaven.

I don't want to break her. I don't want to scare her.

I want to keep her.

I want to make sure the only time she shatters is when I'm so deep inside of her, hitting that spot that makes her come undone every single time. Fucking her into oblivion is the only exception to her screams I yearn to hear.

She throws her head back against the pillow as I bury my face into her neck, planting hungry kisses. She tastes too good. I bite down. Sucking and biting all over her neck and collarbone. I move onto her pointed tits, sucking on them as I continue to slide my dick in and out of her. I pick up my movements, one hand on her hipbone, holding her in place, grabbing her so tight that bruises will form. The other hand is full of her other tit, and I squeeze.

"I want to carve my name into your waist, baby."

With one fatal thrust, I know I'm close. I hit her spot, causing her to roll her eyes back, and her eyelids squeeze shut, shielding her hypnotizing brown eyes.

I don't have a condom, and I'm tempted to fill her up.

"Let me fill you up. I want to see my come drip out of what's mine."

"Daegan, fuck, Daegan!" She screams my name louder than I ever thought she would let herself. Letting go of her breast, I cover her mouth instead with my palm.

"Ssh, baby. If you scream loud again, I'll hurt you for it." My threat gives her a whiplash. She opens them for a split second as she continues to endure her euphoric orgasm and then closes them tight again.

She clenches her pussy, right on my sensitive crown, and I come undone. I close my eyes, grinding my teeth so hard my jaw hurts. I pull out barely in time when all I want to do is fill her with my babies. The idea of Alessia pregnant shakes my core. It takes all my strength to not empty my balls inside her soft, tight warm cunt.

That could never happen.

Thick white come spreads across her pussy, and she watches me with a blissful smile. She reaches down and massages my balls as I continue to stroke and empty myself on her. I keep rubbing myself hard and fast, riding out my high that is Alessia's insides.

"That was...amazing. Let's do it again." She reaches down with her finger and pokes my come, getting some on her fingertip and putting it in her mouth. I watch her panting like a monster. She hollows her cheeks and swallows it. She hums and smiles.

I smirk. I can't get enough.

"Letting me taint your perfect soul was a mistake, little Valentine. A mistake I'll forever be grateful for...but I need to know why."

She arches a brow through pink cheeks and clammy skin. I want to know why she kept pushing herself toward me. It's not like it's something new. Women throw themselves at me...too often. But after showing her my scars...she still wants me.

"When I look at you and see you, *the real you*, to me, you're not the deadliest sniper in a mask. Or Operator Creature." She throws air quotes with her fingers around my nickname. "Thousands of fireworks explode inside me. I want nothing but the best for you, Daegan, even if you decide that when we go back to living our normal lives in Bloomings after. You know, after I'm not your assignment anymore...I want you to be happy. Even if I'm not in your life, I need you to know that I—"

Something catches my eye. Something falls in between us. Something red drops onto her chest.

Shit.

I'm bleeding through my uniform. I thought it would have stopped by now.

"Daegan, why—? Are you? Are you bleeding?" She asks, still breathing hard. The pulse in her neck thundering. The hickies on her neck are bright and evident as she swallows. Another drop of blood splashes against her in the middle of her breasts.

When will the bleeding stop?

"And we're done here." I sigh weakly with a hint of sarcasm.

The mood has shifted, and I get off her. I zip my pants back up and fall to my side.

"I'm okay," I reassure her, swinging my feet off the bed until my feet are back on the ground, ready to stand.

"You *are* bleeding! What happened on that mission? Are you okay?" She grabs my shoulder, assessing my wound.

"I just fucked my girl. I'm more than okay." I kiss her lips, smiling. I'm hoping it's enough to mask that my energy is frail and my muscles are aching.

I am okay.

I tell myself. I'm fucking okay. It's a fucking scratch.

And yet, the contrast happens. The room starts to spin as I try to stand, but my legs give out; Alessia's worried murmurs, screeching for me like someone is lowering the volume in a car, are the last thing I hear. Her nightstand blurs like a dream. A bad dream.

Suddenly, I'm back in the dark with the same nightmares.

The Surgeon...and Dario.

40

Alessia

DAEGAN PASSED OUT ON me. How I was able to stop him from tumbling to the floor is beyond me. I laid him back down on the bed, and he went unconscious. He was pale.

As soon as I got dressed, I ran for Kane. I didn't need to explain anything, and I'm grateful Kane didn't ask. He's the only one who knows about us and hasn't told a soul.

He helped me call a medical team, and they were able to put him on a stretcher and rush him to the on-base hospital.

This is the third time I come to visit, but this time, things are different. There are restraints on his wrist, pinning him down to the bed.

They said it was because, for the first time last night, he woke up but became extremely aggressive with the nurses and doctors. They don't know how to calm him down. They don't know him like I do. They need to approach him softly, not with needles or forced sedation.

His monitor beeps peacefully. His heart rate is normal for a 6'6 mass of a man passing out after losing a lot of blood. He's been out for two days, and it's been hard not to expose our relationship. I feel like there have been whispers and eyes on me ever since he got hospitalized by the medical staff and even my co-workers.

It could just be my paranoia. Or his stubbornness just may have exposed our no-strings-attached relationship because he refused to get medical attention when he was supposed to.

If I could have it my way, I would never leave his side until he woke up. I want to be the first person he sees when he opens his eyes, but if I am, then everyone will definitely know that there's something going on between us.

So, every time I come to visit, it's with Kane by my side, escorting me since he's still on PSD for me. That hasn't changed. I stay as long as I can and then leave with Kane, hoping it won't make anything obvious. Worrying about the person who has been assigned to protect you shouldn't be a crime. Right?

"Slaughter."

"Yes, Valentin?" He props his head from his phone.

"Thank you."

"For what?"

"For not saying anything. For keeping our secret." I motion towards Daegan and me with my finger.

"Of course. Creature and Lopez are the only ones that didn't judge me or shun me off the team once shit hit the fan with Grim's girl. He doesn't say much. And when he does, it's cryptic and morbid. His dark humor is a mask. He doesn't let anyone in, but for some reason...he let you in. He did with you, and I don't want to fuck with that. We all deserve a love that's worth bleeding for...even if it's forbidden, complicated, and chaotic."

PRETEND

"Kane. I really hope you've found the one with this girl. You're too kind. and if she breaks your heart, I will hunt her down myself." I joke, nudging him with my shoulder playfully.

He laughs, and his warm smile radiates with sunshine and bliss. His dark lashes blink rapidly, and he scrolls through his phone, quickly like he wants to show me something. Finally, he lifts it so I can see the screen.

It's a selfie. A picture of Kane and his girlfriend. He holds her close as he wears a black beanie, his beard grown out, and her hand on his chest. They're in Bloomings, North Carolina. I can tell by the background on the phone. That Navy base will always be familiar to me.

Then he pulls out a ring from his pocket, and a beautiful oval-shaped, bright, glimmering diamond shines underneath the white hospital lighting. He holds it in between his fingers like it's the most delicate thing in the world, and I gasp. My vision blurs with tears.

My mouth falls open, and the tears threaten to fall down my cheeks. God, I hate myself for being a hopeless romantic. Things like engagements and weddings always pull at my heartstrings. I'm not sure if I ever want to be married after Jack, but something tells me that if I meet the right person, maybe I can. Maybe with someone who makes me forget I'm broken.

"She is the one. I knew it the first time I kissed her. When we met, she was a single mom. My girlfriend and her son are everything to me now." He swipes left, and it's another picture of the three of them together. Kane carries him in his arms while his girlfriend holds his arm in the middle of a soccer stadium. "Little man is about to be five years old. He says he wants to be a SEAL like me. He's the cutest thing."

"That poor boy wants to be a SEAL like you? Does he know you have shitty aim?" Daegan starts to twitch. His deep voice sends a shock into my system, almost paralyzing me with happiness. The muscles on his arms flicker, and a low, dry groan escapes his throat. His dark hair is messy, and the scars on one side of his face move as he frowns.

He's waking up.

"Oh my God, you're awake." I jump out of my seat and hug him. I hold him over numerous wires and his IV. He winces underneath my touch and groans harder.

I wasn't expecting him to wake up so soon. The nurses warned us he may have needed another blood transfusion, leaving me in a constant state of anxiety and distress. I pull back, apologizing as I take off his restraints. Before I can control my emotions, I kiss his cheek urgently and brush my knuckles over his scars.

He likes it when I do that. I know he does. He loves it when I touch his scars.

"Why the fuck am I wearing this dress?" He opens his eyes for a split second before he slams his vision shut and pulls on his hospital gown like he wants to tear it off.

Kane chuckles in the corner while I hold his hand excitedly.

"Alessia..." he murmurs, swallowing after he says my name in that same tone that drives me crazy and wild. His eyes are still closed as he shifts in the hospital bed.

"Daegan," tears fall down my cheek, and I try to get a hold of my emotions as I look at him. He finally regains more energy and squints in my direction. He lays his head down on the pillow, and his Adams apple rolls. A smirk crosses his handsome face, and I melt. I've missed that sinful grin of his. I missed it way too much. I almost lost him because he downplayed his injuries and Rooker's orders to get looked at.

"Rooker told Kane what happened. I'm still so upset with you for being so stubborn." I shake my head before I kiss his lips. But this time, Daegan's tired lips move against mine. I kiss him hard, needing him to know how grateful I am that he's awake, talking, and, most of all, *alive*.

"I need to be more stubborn, then." He tells me as he kisses me deeper, bringing his IV hand to my hair and stroking it like he's praising me for caring about him. I rub his arm soothingly, touching his muscled, tattooed arm, getting lost in this moment. His beard pricking against my mouth and—

"Oh, I-I'll come back later, then." Guerra's stunned, shaky voice pops our bubble of reunion, and I cringe internally.

Oh, no.

Shit.

Oh, no.

I got lost in the moment. *Kane* got lost in the moment, too, covering his eyes with his hands jokingly, and didn't warn us either.

Kane and I turn toward Guerra. She stands there like a statue in her uniform as if she were watching a crash happen before her. She runs her rigid hand over her tightly gelled brown hair in a locked bun. She blinks rapidly, skipping on her feet like she doesn't know where to escape. Finally, she turns left and leaves as I try to process the events. I try to follow after her, with my reddened cheeks to match hers, but I catch the *Get Better* long note she was going to give Daegan, which is thrown to the floor.

I grip it in my hands, doing my best not to read it, but in big letters are overly friendly comments and her number on the bottom. I didn't know she was crushing *this hard* on Daegan. I'm hoping our friendship is enough for her not to look at me any differently.

"Guerra!" I call out after her just as a doctor comes in with a very confused face. I back away from the door, watching her turn down the busy hospital hallway full of other nurses and service members, and she disappears.

One crisis at a time.

I walk back into the room and stand by Kane, cleaning my lips off with my palm and doing anything and everything to erase the evidence of our shared kiss and play it cool.

The tall man in a white coat walks in with a chart. His black pepper hair shines back, and he has dark under eyes. *Doctor Diaz* is clear as day on his name tag.

"Chief petty officer, Hannibal. I'm Doctor Diaz. I'm pleased to see that you're awake. That's a very good thing." His positive attitude paints his tone as well.

A nurse with bright eyes and tattoos on her sleeve walks in, and her lips curve into a giddy smile when she spots Daegan. She stands next to Daegan, looking at him and then his monitor. She assesses his wound and looks pleased when she covers up the bandage again.

"Ah, Lori, what a pleasant surprise. I'm so happy we get to meet again in the same conditions. Small world, don't you think?" He teases her and winks at me.

I shake my head at him. How can he be so calm right now, while I want to hide under a bed now that someone who isn't Kane caught us?

"We shouldn't be meeting under these circumstances, Hannibal. Your team needs you at work. Not in a hospital bed." She teases back.

"I can't help myself. You guys have good drugs in here." Daegan points to the IV bag above him nonchalantly.

"Now, Daegan, we need to go over some important medical stuff. They can't be in here. It's confidential." Doctor Diaz starts as his brown eyes look at me and Kane over his chart.

"We'll wait outside," Kane tells them as he hooks his hand on my bicep and escorts me out. I want to cement my feet to the ground, I don't want to go anywhere without Daegan, but we already fucked up once. I can't mess up again in front of medical staff.

Am I falling for him? My heart quickens at the thought, and hope bleeds into the once-empty space that Jack left in me. I've really fallen for Daegan when I was the one who made it a rule, *not to*. And I don't think I've just grown feelings for him. It's more than just sex; it's a connection...and it's an all-consuming one.

"Thank you," Doctor Diaz chirps as he walks closer to Daegan. Kane opens the door to the room, waiting for me to cross over, but one sentence shatters my impending actions and thoughts. I stop walking, and confusion riddles my brain when Doctor Diaz opens his mouth again.

"I've already alerted your wife since she's your emergency contact when it comes to these things. You are—"

I clear my throat and turn around, stunned, my heart pounding outside my chest. I'm sure the entire hospital can hear it.

I arch a brow at him, and Daegan stiffens with narrowed brows and darkened eyes, clenching his jaw as he holds my stare.

"His wife?" Kane asks and advocates for me when I'm too shattered to move or even breathe right now. They have to have gotten it all wrong. He doesn't wear a ring; he doesn't have a wife, and there were no pictures in his home when I stayed there.

But there was a locked door.

And I was too oblivious and such an idiot...it didn't cross my mind to ask such a basic question.

His ice-cold eyes light up, and he moves to stand, but Lori reacts quickly.

"Hannibal, sir, don't move. You are not in the clear to move, never mind being discharged. Stay in the bed." She orders him sternly and unafraid.

Daegan looks away from me, going into that same side of him that I'm not familiar with. Cold and distant, with no words to explain himself?

"You're..." *married*? I want to say it. It's on the tip of my trembling, dry tongue, stabbing me in the chest. A tear rolls down my cheek; the betrayal already settles in as I try to keep calm, but there's only one thing I can do right now to save my job. And it's going back to work. I start the treacherous sentence but don't finish as I watch Daegan's chest move up and down with edge as he takes deep breaths. His anchor tattoo jumps with deep, desperate breaths as he tries to get me to stay with pleading eyes.

He warned me.

Those haunting words he told me when he picked me up when I was stranded.

The ones closest to you are the ones who hold the most power to hurt you. The ones closest do the most damage. Please remember that the next time you decide to let someone in.

"Get her out of here, Slaughter." He pleads, but it's more like he's ordering him like he refuses to accept anything else.

PRETEND

I can't look him in the eyes; it'll only hurt more that those very eyes I've fallen hard for are more forbidden than I thought. His monitor starts to beat erratically and thunderously.

"Tell me it isn't true," I murmur softly. I tense up my throat before it can crack from agony.

I dare to look at him. The doctor and nurse look rigid. Doctor Diaz holds onto his device firmly while Lori looks around the room inconspicuously and rocks on her heels. They're uncomfortable. I don't care if they can read the room. I need to know.

But the operator, who is known for silence, is doing what he's good at.

I nod sarcastically when he doesn't deny it. Tears are blurring my vision.

Kane turns into stone and moves us out of the room before I fall apart in public. Lori and Doctor Diaz act oblivious to what is transpiring, and I'm grateful for that.

If he wants a different outcome, I need him to say, 'You're wrong, Doctor Diaz. I don't have a wife. I'm single. You're confusing me with another sailor.' But no, as Doctor Diaz continues, he just sits there, shocked and wounded.

"Your wife, Stella Hannibal? We told her and—"

"Ms. Valentin." Daegan roars behind me. He stands and tries to rip out every single wire that's attached to him. He stands up and towers over Lori, but I don't stop walking. Two security personnel rush into the room, bumping into Kane's and I's shoulders.

I can't hear anymore; I'm too far gone from the room, and I'm moving in slow motion. My body is moving, but my brain is elsewhere, lost in thought. Kane wants to put his arm around me in a friendly manner, but I push it away and rush forward, beating him to the exit of the hospital.

"Alessia, do you want to talk?" Kane calls for me, but I ignore him as I return to work. If our short affair isn't out now with Guerra, it sure is now.

Daegan once promised me he would ruin me for anyone else...and he has. But in the end...he just ruined me.

41

Daegan

IT'S BEEN A WEEK since I last saw Alessia. A week without her is worse than the nightmares I succumb to every time my mind goes to rest for the night. She left to go back to the States, as ordered by her boss, and Admiral Ravenmore made sure to stamp the final okay for her to leave her deployment early with consequences.

She knows I'm married. She doesn't need me anymore.

She doesn't want me anymore.

But I need her. I want her. Even though she's across an ocean from me, she will never be too far away. Her magnetic pull is detrimental and fatal; I will never be able to stay away from her. The overwhelming urge to make sure she's okay is an obsession I can't shake.

I tried to fight my way out of the hospital bed. It took five security officers to take me down. If it weren't for my weak health, I would have been able to break free and see Alessia again. I could have grabbed her and made her listen to me before she left.

But my blood loss was too much. I ended up fainting again after being strapped down. I tore out the IV, making blood drip everywhere, and I needed more medication and blood to be pumped back in.

Kane hasn't updated me at all. After numerous text messages, I wanted to know how she was doing. He informed me he had to take her back to the States. Her boss and my boss found out because of Guerra, and it created a significant problem.

They sent her back home, and I know she hates me for not only lying to her about being married, but now her job is at risk.

It's good that she despises me.

I deserve it.

"Close the door, Creature!" Ravenmore roars as he sits at his desk. He takes off his reading glasses and places them on his desk. He throws them, and they hit a photo frame.

I stand my ground.

"Before you say anything, Sir. Before you decide to throw questions at me or accusations, I need to say something first. Yes, yes, my relationship with your stepdaughter became romantic. I overstepped. But to be fair, she is an adult. She can make her own choices. No, I am not a good man. But for her...I've been nothing *but* good to her."

"I'm disappointed, Hannibal. I want to suspend you. I must suspend you." He stands up, pissed off. His shoulders tense underneath his clothes, and he walks away from me and stares out his window—a picture of Alessia, and he sits on a shelf to the left.

PRETEND

I'm tempted to take it and steal it from my boss's office. I want all the pictures of that gorgeous girl who wants nothing to do with me. I don't give a fuck.

There's a shift in the Admiral, and I'm prepared to take it on.

"Creature...my fucking daughter?!" He gets into my face and snarls in fury. I stand my ground and don't respond as he yells.

"Out of the entire team, you were the one I didn't have to fucking worry about!"

I stare at the wall, standing behind him as he continues to shout.

He throws a pile of books off his desk, and they hit the other side of the wall. He breathes hard, and I stay calm.

"You're married, for Christ's sake!"

I swallow as he continues to bellow out. His face reddening as he throws the facts in my face.

"I am," I tell him. My voice is as cold as my heart.

"She's my little girl!" He throws a glass at the wall, and it shatters.

He goes rigid. He stares at the broken glass and holds his breath like he's trying to talk his own demons down.

I am married.

I did fuck up.

The Admiral clears his throat and takes in another deep breath. As soon as he is more calm, he speaks.

"The team needs you. Whatever you shared with Alessia is over. I don't want your name or hers to reach my desk again, Creature." He rubs his peppered scruff over his chin, deep into his pensive thoughts. He stares outside the window, overlooking an Army formation of soldiers ready to be dismissed for the day.

I nod, and a victorious smile paints my masked face.

"I'm going to suspend you. You will not get special treatment from me." Ravenmore concedes his outburst and rubs his temples.

"Then do it. Do what you must. I broke orders. I acted unprofessionally, and for that, I am sorry. It's not like me. I always place the mission first. I promise it won't happen again." I stand my ground, placing my hands behind my back, and get lost in the memories.

Stalking her for work, stabbing Frankie for her, putting my own job at risk when that's all that's mattered to me since I joined the SEALS.

I'm not sure I want to fix this. I think Alessia and I have done enough. I haven't reached out, but seeing how pissed Ravenmore is makes me rethink everything.

Should I let her go?

Ravenmore paces back and forth for what feels like an entire minute. Work always comes first, and I can't let our relationship get in between anything anymore...maybe this is all for the best, and I won't see her anymore.

Ravenmore's co-worker enters the room, looking up at me. He's a short, older man who is wearing his uniform. It has too many medals for me to count, and he sits in a chair, staring at me like I'm a piece of shit.

Well, I guess I am. There's no denying that.

Admiral looks at his co-worker and then back at me before sitting back on his desk.

"I need you on this next mission, but then I'm sending you back home until our investigation ends. I don't know how long, but your skills are needed for this next mission that your name is already on. And then—" He sips his bourbon and sighs heavily.

And then?

I want to say it, but I feel like my soul is dead already, and the old me that doesn't like to talk overcomes my ability to do so.

"And then it's back to North Carolina, Creature." I'm about to leave, but Ravenmore's cold voice, I'm not used to hearing, stops me.

"Promise me that it's over. Whatever you were doing with my stepdaughter is over."

I hesitate. Not knowing how to answer it.

I want to tell him to fuck off.

I want to tell him that I like to lick his daughter's pussy, and there's not a damn thing he can do to stop me.

That's when it hits me.

I clench my teeth, and I'm desperate to pull out my bullet.

I'm a married man.

I shouldn't.

I can't, and I won't.

And I will put a stop to this.

My obsession is getting to me.

The truth of my established career shouts at me. Operator Grim Reaper's absence reminds me that having a family doesn't interest me.

It fucking doesn't.

Danny Rider changed.

I will not.

I've done enough.

I look back at Ravenmore.

"I promise it's over," I tell him truthfully.

42

Alessia

GUERRA OUTED DAEGAN AND me, which resulted in Kane escorting me back home. It's well deserved. He's only here for a few days for a four-day weekend and then has to report to base.

My stepfather hasn't said anything. He sent it down the chain of command, had Winters be the bad guy, and let me know that I was to return to the United States for misconduct in the workplace.

I was ashamed because it hit me...hard.

I was embarrassed not only because I tainted my career but also because I embarrassed Ravenmore...my mother—a well-respected veteran who used to work in intelligence like me. My mother and Ravenmore are a power couple, and I failed them, too.

Daegan hasn't reached out to me. He hasn't called or texted, which breaks my heart even more. No groveling or answers I deserve to know. I mean, what can he say? He most likely feels the weight of our consequences and realizes I'm not worth apologizing to. And yet, still, I want to know how he's recovering. He almost died and lost a lot of blood, and I'm still worried about him.

How could I let myself get here?

I put myself in a place where I got my heart broken twice in one year. So what am I doing? I'm going to drink and drink until I can't remember my own name tonight. I'm going to put myself first for the first time in a long time.

A knock on my door wakes me up from my sleep. I'm still heavily jet-lagged and exhausted from crying. After almost twenty-four hours of traveling halfway across the world back to North Carolina, I don't want to feel the weight of my mistakes.

I fucked someone's husband...the guilt of that eats me alive.

Sleep sounds good, and it feels good after failing myself and everyone around me.

I get up from the bed with sadness clouding my brain. I rub my eyes as the knocks keep going, and I put on my black Jack Skellington slippers before I walk out of my bedroom.

I take a glance in my hallway mirror.

Tangled, messy black curls.

Red and puffed cheeks.

Dark under eyes.

Yeah. I'm a mess.

Who could be at my door right now?

I look through the peephole and see my mother standing there with her sunglasses on, pressed lips, and folded arms that look ready to pull my hair. She's in a floral blouse and black leggings, with low-top heels.

Well...crap.

I take a deep breath in and open the door.

The sun's rays blind me momentarily, and I raise my hand to block it out.

"Mom...please, I got back from Iraq not too long ago, and I would really like to rest." I yawn and stretch my arms over my head.

"I'm coming inside. We need to talk." She quips as she brushes past me and walks into my home without another word, even though I didn't invite her in. She will not leave here without giving me a piece of her mind, and I don't expect anything less from my mom, who radiates black-cat energy.

She's strong, independent, and doesn't take crap from anyone...and somehow, I came up short whenever I tried to meet her expectations.

She enters my living room and places her sunglasses on my coffee table. I trudge to the couch and let myself fall onto the other couch in front of my furniture. I sit in the corner, far away from her, preparing for her to cuss me out in Spanish.

"Look, ma, I'm a grown woman. I messed up. I know I did, and I'm sorry. I feel disgusted with myself."

She turns to me, and just when I think she's going to glare daggers at me or raise her voice, she meets me with eyes of understanding.

"Did I ever tell you the story of how I met Henry?" She asks.

I shake my head.

"No, you didn't...but honestly, I never asked because I really don't care to know anything about him. You know how I feel about the divorce from my father. My dad still loved you, and you left him for Ravenmore. At least that's Dad's side of the story." I mutter indignantly.

PRETEND

"Well, I guess that sums up most of it, but...it was more complicated than that." She finally sits down on the other side of the living room and tucks her legs into her thighs.

"Yes. To your father, I was a villain. I guess. We had ended things right before I went on my first deployment. He watched over you while I left for Afghanistan because you were only three years old. He was angry I was leaving, not at me specifically but at our situation. We were still freshly married, and my job was a whirlwind. He was forced to leave his home in Illinois. That's where we met, remember? But because I had orders to Virginia, he followed me...he didn't like that he was giving up on his plans to make our relationship work."

"Yes, I know. He did tell me that. The military lifestyle was not for him, but because he loved you and me, he stuck around longer than he wanted to...he said he tried to keep us all together, but the deployment was the last straw for him."

She nods while staring at her sunglasses. Then she flicks her hazel eyes at me.

"He left me while I was deployed. He sent me divorce papers without giving me a chance to save our marriage...but then again, I was already at a point where I knew if I tried to save it, it would have been a lie. I was heartbroken and sad about our situation because I knew our divorce would affect you. I signed them and sent them back. We were divorced within months, we worked together to reach a mutual understanding, and our divorce went smoothly and quickly. Right before my deployment ended, I found solace in Henry."

Is she trying to imply that history is repeating itself in some way? A workplace romance...like Daegan and I?

"Are you telling me you fell in love with *your boss*?"

She swallows passively. "Yes."

I remember her telling me they met when she was an Ensign and he was a Commander.

"I'm not mad, Alessia. I came here to tell you that everything will be okay. And to do better next time. Don't repeat the same mistakes."

I look away from her as a lump forms in my throat.

"He's married mom. This is different because he's married. I didn't know. Henry wasn't married, was he?"

She shakes her head. "No." She gets up from the couch and walks over to me. The tears I've been fighting fall down, and I can't look at my mother. I feel disgusted with myself. Memories of Daegan flash through my mind—our night of stargazing when he told me about his personal life.

"I'm sorry, *mija*. I can tell you to move on and to let him go because you deserve better. It's the truth. You do deserve better. But even I know it's easier said than done."

Maybe drinking isn't the solution. I know it's not the solution, but I let Kane drag me out of my house after three weeks of crying non-stop. He was supposed to return to Iraq but he was ordered to stay back home longer.

We've gotten closer lately, and I'm not mad about it. Winters is still in Iraq doing her job...where I'm supposed to be. I can't talk to her the way I want to speak to her about it. There are just some things better left said face to face rather than on the phone. And for me, this is one of those things.

PRETEND

I did want to chase my feelings with Daegan selfishly, risking both of our careers, so I can't place the entire blame on him. I can't fault him for my actions because I knew exactly what I was doing.

I'm angry at myself for being so damn stupid in every way. For risking my job and reputation. And secondly, for falling for Daegan's lies.

I was ordered to go back home by my stepfather after the rumors spread about my relationship with Daegan. I think he did it to protect me, but still, I was angry I couldn't do my job, and now I'm labeled as a slut.

"You know, Kane. You could be spending time with your girlfriend. I hate that I'm burdening you with my problems."

"Listen, Valentine." Kane starts to tease me with my freshly earned nickname, and I purse my lips, narrowing my eyes at the dark blue dots in his eyes that flicker with humor. He mouths to Gabe 'shots.' "I've been where you are before, it sucks, and I don't think being alone helps." Kane nudges me with his shoulder over his black leather jacket. "Plus, I invited my brother over to join us," he looks at his watch and then at me, "he should be here any minute now. He just joined the teams. Fresh out of graduation. We might as well celebrate his accomplishment while we're reunited."

"You have a brother?" I ask.

"I have several brothers and sisters."

"Already back home, beautiful?" Gabe leans over the counter to hug me. I'm not going to lie. I like the way Gabe smiles at me. He's always so lovely and has given me plenty of drinks on the house.

"Yeah. It's a long story…" I tell him. A hard rock in my throat forms, and I choke up. I look away from Gabe and stare at the neon cattle sign behind him instead, blinking fast.

Gabe grabs my hand and gives it a gentle squeeze.

"I've got time." Pure admiration radiates from him. He has a ball cap on, and warmth flashes in his brown eyes. "Maybe we can go for frozen yogurt. Maybe it can be a date?"

I pause, my chest tightens, and I'm actually considering it for a split second. I don't say anything at first, but then the liquor I've been drinking for the past hour starts to coat me with frustration.

I can't believe I'm one of those girls. Did I really fall for a married man?

"I would love nothing more than that. I should be free since I'm no longer deployed, but I'll let you know..." I murmur as Kane collides his shot with mine, and the glasses chime. I down the shot Gabe handed me a few seconds ago.

"One of these nights it'll be a definite yes." Gabe kisses my cheek. I sink down into my chair feeling guilty. Another customer calls him over and he leaves.

Kane raises his brows as I down my drink next.

It rolls down my throat, burning and scorching my flesh, and I wince, letting out a ragged breath. I slam the shot down, fighting the pitiful large lump in my throat.

I don't have answers from Daegan, and I'm not sure I want them anymore. I burp drunkenly.

"Alessia, want me to take you home?" Kane asks.

"Hold that thought. I'm going to the restroom." I scootch out of the chair, and the ground on my feet starts to feel like I'm on an escalator.

Yup, I think it's time I go home.

I walk to the bathrooms in El Devine. The rain grows harsher, battering the windows of the exit door at the end of the hall. Even through the blurred rain streaks, I can see the trees sway in the distance with strong winds, and the bushes hit the glass.

I stumble, and the liquor hits me even harder. I'm starting to see two of everything. I didn't drink that much to have these kinds of side effects. I palm one side of the wall before my ribs crash into it. Arching my brows, I shake my head twice to try and escape the blurs.

"Alessia?"

Someone calls my name. Someone who used to have my heart, someone who broke it.

I turn around slowly and palm the wall. I squint through the dark hallway and cringe when I see Jack. I grimace, furrowing my brows, and roll my eyes, not giving him an ounce of my attention.

I'm definitely going home now.

"Alessia, I've been calling and texting you. I'm not with Bailey anymore because I realize I fucked up."

He's quick to explain himself, as if he knows I don't want to give him the opportunity to talk to me.

I snap my teeth, rubbing my forehead as I turn my back to him. I keep walking, and I'm almost to the ladies' room. Does he really think I care about their status?

"Zeke told me what happened."

I'm about to push open the women's bathroom door, but I stop in my tracks when he finishes his sentence.

Did Zeke, your supposed friend, mention he asked me out on a date, too?

I don't say it, I want to say it, but I don't.

"Move on, Jack. I moved on...and so should you." I give him a glimpse, turning my head slightly, and I almost fall over again.

Am I a lightweight now?

"Yeah, you moved on with that freak who wears a mask." He throws out his insult with a pointed chin.

His hateful words spew out his mouth with so much resentment that it stings. His words are sharper than a knife. I'm upset with Daegan, practically broken by him, but I will never stand for bullying.

"D-don't talk about him like that. He's more of a man than you'll ever be. You'll never measure up to him." Now he has my attention. I let go of the door and look at Jack. His hands are fisted, and he looks down at me with pressed lips and narrowed dark eyes that radiate hatred.

"Frankie won't step foot at El Devine anymore," he points swiftly to the bar behind him. "He had to have his entire jaw reconstructed, and he won't tell anyone why."

"I'm not sure how that's a bad thing given the fact he always harassed me and others." I spit back, trying to keep myself still and from swaying. Jack walks to me with veins bulging from his hands, like he's angry.

"Why are you defending that blind freak?" Jack stalks toward me with aggression. "Was fucking him worth ruining your reputation and job? Getting sent home on your first deployment?"

I snap my mouth shut. I'm really never talking to Zeke again. How dare he share this information with him? I mean...I suppose after constantly rejecting him, he would see it as a way to hurt me back.

"What're you doing here anyway? Drinking your problems away, huh?" He scoffs, satisfied. "You fell for him, didn't you? Let me guess?" He has his hand

PRETEND

on his chin, sarcastically looking pensively. "He hasn't called you since you found out? You really thought that fucker loved you? You really thought he was interested in more than just fucking you? He used you, Alessia. At least I loved you."

I shake my head as my throat and eyes begin to burn.

"So you walk away from me?" Jack gets closer until he's right in front of my face. "You walk away and end our years-long relationship because I'm such a piece of shit, right? But *you* end up fucking a married man?"

The lump in my throat comes back full force, and this time, the tears fall down my cheeks with humiliation fueling them. I keep my stunned gaze on his puffed-out chest over his yellow shirt as he spills my reality back onto my face.

"I'm a piece of shit for fucking Bailey, but what does that make him?" I don't answer, but I stare at my ex-boyfriend this time. I look up at him, with tears still leaking out of my lashes, probably leaving trails of black from my mascara. I can't answer. It's too disgraceful. I flare my nostrils and sniffle as I suck in a breath, my chest tightening. Jack doesn't like my returned silence, so he grabs my shoulders, shaking them as his fingers dig into my skin, "Huh? Answer me!" He roars with disgust. He has to be drunk. Jack has never put his hands on me before like this. But then I remember that one time before I tried to leave him when I caught him in the act.

"Jack, stop it! You're hurting me!" I shriek, but for some reason, I can't scream. It's like my lungs and tongue won't work with me. Why can't I defend myself the way I want to? It's like I'm being pulled away from my senses, and my hearing goes in and out.

"If I'm such a terrible person, what does that make him?!" He repeats his question as my body jolts back and forth, my curls bouncing, getting into my eyes and face as he moves me.

A tall, dark shadow swallows us, clouding Jack and me.

"It makes me your worst fucking nightmare." A sinister, wicked, possessive tone interrupts Jack, and he stiffens for a split second as he tries to turn to the man slowly. His face reddens, and his eyes widen with fear, and I'm still as a statue.

I know that voice.

43
Alessia

A FAST, STRONG PUNCH knocks Jack to the floor, and he's out cold, almost lifeless. Daegan stands there with menacing eyes. Even though it's been weeks since I've seen him, I forget how massive this man is. He wears his full mask, his eyes colder than his heart, and the archangel tattoos on his sleeve light up when lightning strikes behind me through the glass doors.

"Damn, that was way over-fucking-due." He snickers as he looks at Jack on the floor like he's entertained and wants to keep fighting.

"D-Daegan?" I stutter, and I feel like I'm going to pass out. The aftermath of the drinks is getting to me. "What are you doing here? Please leave me alone! I don't w-want to s-see you." I turn around weakly, walking away fast, but my legs don't reciprocate—they're slow and heavy.

"Is my little Valentine drunk?" He coos behind me like he was the one responsible. Like he knows the answer to his own question.

Blackness starts to cloud my vision, and with every step I take, I feel like I'm sinking into quicksand.

"You think the deal you made with me was voided? The rules still apply. You are mine until *I say this is over*, not ink on orders, and definitely not the Admiral." Daegan's manic voice is trickled with desperation. His palm silences my scream when I realize this is a side of Daegan I don't recognize. Turmoil implodes the air, and I can't breathe.

"Daegan, please stop! Get away from me!" I claw at his hand that covers and muffles my mouth, and he laughs like he's enjoying everything. He grabs me by my stomach and waist, and I do everything I can to stop him. I slap at his chest and arms repeatedly, over and over again as I try to walk into the rain outside, but he's too strong. My vision blurs, dizziness possesses everything inside me, and I'm gone into darkness.

"Daegan, please don't do this."

"You should have thought about that before you made a deal with the boogeyman, little valentine. Goodnight." He presses his lips to my cheek, and I succumb to darkness.

My head is pounding, and my throat is dry. I'm awake, I know that much, but the bed I'm sleeping in…it's not mine. The sound of someone playing on a piano—it's a beautiful, serene, sad tune.

The sound of thunder chimes outside, joining in on the somber music, and I feel like I'm still dreaming.

I claw at the bed sheets, pushing myself out, and groan softly.

The piano keeps going.

"The day I came back home, after my time in the hospital, after multiple surgeries to reconstruct my hand and my vision..."

Daegan's voice can be heard in the dark corner of his room. A lamp illuminates the music sheet. He sits there with his shirt and mask off, and a dragon stares back at me in an ominous way. I see the back of his head, and his messy dark hair waves are longer than before—scars all over his back, like slices.

I readjust myself on the bed as the memories of me at El Devine with Kane, his girlfriend, and Jack resurfaces. And the last thing I remember is my world spinning.

"How did I get here?" I rub the side of my head and blink to escape the grogginess.

Daegan starts to play the piano more aggressively.

"After all that physical pain and suffering, I was excited to come home. My wife hadn't visited me once in the hospital. She said she was working...when in reality, she had been fucking her co-worker while I was deployed. And when I came back home, maskless..." Daegan stops playing the piano and palms the keys. His back muscles sway underneath his tattoos and scars, clearly full of tension as he remembers the past. Lightning flashes through the windows once more.

"She took one look at my face and cringed. She didn't want anything to do with me. She told me she couldn't love a man that looked like a monster." He scoffs out with a laugh and turns around to face me. He's smiling, but his eyes are watering. His abs flex in the dark with his fast breathing. "She used my injuries, my time away from home, *my trauma* to justify her cheating."

I sit up, and my heart sinks. How could she do that to him? And where is this going?

Still, I need to get the fuck out of here.

"That happens a lot, you know? When some of us get wounded in action, our spouses can't handle it, and they leave. She couldn't handle my physical scars, let alone the ones stained into my soul. The nightmares...*my face.*"

I look around and find his door, but Daegan catches my gaze and stands from his piano. Each step was a vivid warning for me not to try it. He walks toward me, his vision pinned on me, and it scares me.

"After she cheated on me and couldn't get used to the new makeover the Surgeon gave me, I ended it." He kneels in front of me, and the unknown of how I passed out at El Devine scares me.

I don't trust him.

He reaches for me, and tears start to fall out my eyes. He pushes the hair out of my face, and I tear myself away from his beautiful face. If I look at him, I'll fall apart. I need to stay strong. He caresses the side of my face with his large palm, soothing me.

"When you saw my scars, you didn't flinch or run away from me, and you didn't pity me. You're the first person who doesn't judge me by my appearance or how I am when everyone else has labeled me as a Creature who doesn't talk or act normal. I can be Daegan Hannibal with you, and you don't run away from me. Instead, you welcome me, even if I may be terrifying to others."

I chew the inside of my mouth as I listen to him. This can't be easy when you're repeatedly shunned by people who judge you with a closed-minded thought process.

"You see...in the state of North Carolina, it takes one year for any divorce to be finalized. I'm just a few weeks from my court date, and I'll legally be single."

I turn away from his headboard and lock eyes with him, searching for any hesitation.

Is he telling the truth?

"I haven't been with her since I found out she cheated on me while I was getting tortured. I'm separated but legally still married, and I'm sorry for not telling you that. I'm still in disbelief you want me...even though I look like this." He points to his scarred face. "I didn't believe anyone could love me after my mother died. After Stella called me a monster. After those moments in my life, I convinced myself in the end, it's better to trust no one. It's better to believe that love doesn't exist because *it's easier to live like that*. But then I met you."

A tear falls from my eye, and I wipe it away fast before he continues.

"I wasn't sure where we were going, and I didn't want to hurt you."

"It's a little too late for that," I reply.

"Listen, you can hate me. You can be mad and pissed off, but no one can make you feel like I can. I won't ever let anyone get a fucking chance to."

He presses me down on the bed, my back hits the sheets, and I try to push him back as the rain joins our harsh breathing.

"The way you scream and come with my name on your lips. The way your eyes dilate whenever you see me. The way you smile when I talk to you. You're in love with me, and if you're not consumed by me yet, *you will be*."

"Daegan, you're acting crazy!" I try to hit him with my knees, but he pushes them down like I'm nothing but a toy to him. The back of my knees hit the mattress and I sigh in defeat.

"You do make me fucking crazy. Fight me. It only makes your pussy wetter and my cock harder." He coos in my ear as he pushes my legs apart, and I feel his hard cock already begging to destroy me.

"I won't sleep with you, Daegan. You're still married, and I'm still mad." I seethe.

"Well, that makes two of us."

Daegan grabs his dog tags from his back pocket and ties up my wrists as fast as his waist pins me down.

What the fuck?

I'm unsure what to do, but I'm letting him. I don't fight him anymore. I don't know what that says about me.

"You're mad? Mad at what?!" I wiggle beneath, but it's no use. He's right; he does hold this power over me. I'm wet and begging for him; I already miss the way his hard length stretches me and fucks me, hitting that same spot inside me as it always does, making me climax with just half of his cock. His dog tags dig into my wrists, and I try to pull and kick, but he holds me down. He's way bigger than me.

"How are you the one that's mad right now? You drugged me, didn't you?"

He goes down in between my thighs, and I raise my foot to kick his face, but he catches it with his hand, squeezing tight until I hiss in pain.

"Because I missed a shot."

He's not making any sense! "What?"

He goes to the end of the bed and grabs a rope from his pocket, tying it to both ends of the bed.

"Daegan, let me go! I refuse to be here. You can't force me to be here; you can't drug me and then tie me up because you want me to listen to you!"

"You love being tied up. Would you have come here willingly?" He points out with an angry growl.

"Hell no."

"Exactly my point, little Valentine. I could have done worse, be thankful."

He finishes tying my ankles to his bed and then pulls out his knife. The same knife he fucked me with months ago. The Damascus blade glows and glistens against the moonlight. He grins with sadism in the tilt of his lips.

He hovers over me, and with a quick gesture, he pulls my dress up, slicing my underwear off. He grabs my underwear and holds it to his nose. My eyes bulge as I watch him sniff my torn panties. My pulse begins to race harder and thunders along with the storm outside.

"I love the way your pussy smells, and I love the way it tastes."

He's going to destroy me, and I'm going to hate every single second of it, but not because I don't want it. *I need it.* And I'll hate it because I know how I ache for him. It overpowers my morals and self-respect because of how badly I miss him.

He drugged me, and now he's tying me up, and I'm letting him?

I must need therapy because of the amount of mind-fuckery this man has me going through...I can't keep up, and what's even worse is that I'm heating up more and more.

He pulls out the bullet he constantly twirls, and I watch his lustful smile fall into a depraved one.

"Can you bite the bullet, little valentine?"

The bullet is long and thick. He hovers over me and starts to pump the bullet inside me. It's cold and glides in and out over and over again over my slick wetness. A loud whimper slithers off my tongue, and he hums with sick satisfaction. He thumbs my clit, and I begin to shudder with his precise circles as he continues to pump my pussy with his signature bullet.

"I missed a shot because of you," He growls against my naked nipple, and finally, he takes it into his mouth, biting down on it hard, like his main goal is to make me scream, and he wins because I let out a moan that comes out like a cry. I don't think I've ever made a sound like this before. The way he's making me cry out for him is insane, and I tell my body to shut the hell up.

We're supposed to be mad at him! Not begging for him!

44

Daegan

I GRAB HER BY the throat, choking her.

"I've never missed a shot. Ever. And guess what happened? When you left, there was a mission that needed me. The mission was still successful, but I couldn't fucking focus. I couldn't think straight. You know why?"

"Why?"

A growl unleashes onto her pretty silky skin on her neck. "Because you drive me to the point of madness, insanity, delirious rage. *You have corrupted me.* And the thought of anyone else experiencing such a beautiful soul like yours drives me over the edge. I won't let you ever forget who you belong to. I crave you all the time, Valentine. And right now I'm starving. You're under my skin. Imprinted in my bones. Running through my blood. You've engraved your place into my flesh more permanent than the tattoos on my skin."

I fuck her faster with my bullet while I suck on her tit. She is about to come undone. I know it by the way her muscles are tensing up. The way she rolls her eyes back into her skull as she shuts her eyes tight. The way her breathing has become faster, and more shallow, like she's gasping for air.

I smirk as she tries to free herself from her restraints. I can feel her pussy clenching on my bullet, and a feral possessive growl comes out of me. I remove my bullet and unrestrain her wrists and ankles.

"Oh, Daegan, please! Why'd you stop?" She begs me for an answer, and to hear her plead to chase her orgasm on one of my favorite bullets has me on fucking fire. She holds her sore, free wrists to her chest as she sweats. Her beautiful, tanned skin glimmers with clamminess and her full cheeks turn crimson. Her curls are everywhere, and I want to mess them up even more.

"I will never again let you come on anything but my dick, fingers, or my tongue. If your pussy is not on my flesh, *you don't get to finish. I own* all of your orgasms, your pleasure, your moans. Get on your back and clean up your mess," I demand, looking at her. Her eyes roll up, dazed and feral.

She takes the bullet into her mouth, sucking it clean.

Jesus.

She gets on top of me, straddling me, her knees digging into the bedsheets.

"I'm still mad at you. So mad at myself for wanting all of your come inside me."

"Every single drop will be inside you."

She grabs my hard cock, stroking it a few times in her hand, and she hovers over my groin. Lifting her waist, pumping it up and down slowly, "You make me so fucking crazy, baby." I throw my head back into the pillow each time she pumps my shaft.

Each stroke has me shaking with insanity. She flicks the tip of my dick right on her swollen clit, teasing herself, getting herself off and wet. Her high-pitched moans and sharpened breaths escape her throat each time she touches herself with my pierced dick.

She licks her lips, biting her bottom lip as she continues to electrocute us both.

"Filthy." The tip of my dick is already leaking pre-come, and I swear I can finish just like this.

She slowly slides the tip of my cock down her wet slit, so soft, so smooth. And all mine. She's dripping all over me.

Fuck.

"Do you want to be my good little girl tonight or my dirty little cum dumpster slut?" I slap her full breasts, sending them in a shake. I slap her rough but careful not to actually hurt her. She sucks in a breath.

"I'm tired of being a good girl all my life. I want to be your dirty whore."

She continues to flick her slit and clit with my piercings, teasing the both of us, and I'm about to throw her over my knee and spank her ass until she's red for it.

Finally, she stops at the entrance of her pussy, about to sit on the crown of my dick, but I have other plans.

I smirk, and with a depraved growl, I grab her wrist, freezing her sensual movements, squeezing her bones with my hand, and she hisses.

She arches a brow, confused.

"No. In your ass, now." I command. "You're going to ride me with my dick in your ass."

"Daegan...I've never had someone fuck me there before,"

Something comes over me, something primal, something crazy, like a starved man, and she's my only sanctuary. Her body is my only antidote to my demented addiction. I bolt up and grab her jaw, forcing her to open her mouth. She winces, still sitting on top of my rigid concrete cock. I spit into the back of her throat. Her eyes widen, swallowing right away, and she hums, licking her lips satisfied.

Nasty...so fucking filthy, and I love it.

"Not another fucking word out of you, baby. Just your moans and screams are the only things I want you to sing to me tonight."

She scratches my stomach again, and I growl, my dick surging and throbbing for her tightness. I need her, and I need all of her right the fuck now. She positions my dick further down, and now I'm at her other entrance. I get to claim her other velvet rim.

"You can take it."

She moans, her mouth gaping open as I push into her tight ass. She lets her head fall down, squeezing her eyes shut and then reopening them so she's staring at my abs. Her hands roam my stomach again, her fingertips trailing the hair above my dick, and then she's back into my abs, her nails digging into my skin, scratching me as I tighten my muscles.

Pain. Fire. Desire. Pure fucking madness is what she is.

Did she just make me bleed?

When her fingertips move, a trail of red follows.

Fuck, I'm in love.

"I'm going to fuck you so hard, you'll be begging me to stop, and when you do, I'll fuck you just a bit harder."

I grab the back of her long black hair, pulling it with my hand, and she moans. She likes the pain. My cock drives into her deeper, settling past her tight rim, and she hums a sweet high, pitched moan again. She opens her mouth, grabs my hand, and puts my fingers into her mouth, sucking on them as I push in and out of her.

"Dirty...dirty girl, *my* dirty girl."

For the next ten minutes, it's just that. The headboard bangs against the wall, and her screams of pure ecstasy drive me over the edge over and over again.

Can we just stay like this forever?

"I want all your pretty little holes dripping with my come."

"I haven't gotten my birth control shot."

My heart smiles as I reach over to my drawer and pull out my box of condoms that I'm going to empty for the night. They all have holes in them, but she doesn't need to know that. I want her, and I want her so badly that the demons smile at the thought of her carrying my child one day. I drop the box as she looks at it, without knowing my sick plans.

"Daegan, fuck. You're so big." She moves her hips up and down, rolling them slowly, taking my length a portion at a time. God, I want her forever. I will forever be sickeningly obsessed with this woman. I want her all day and night. She needs to be mine until the end of time.

Finally, she moans as I play with her clit, circling it with my finger as I take her ass. I tighten my grip on her hips as she grants me access to help her with the motions. I pick up my pace, and so does she. Her hair falls forward, clouding her face, as she continues to claw my stomach.

"It hurts, but it feels good, Daegan." She screams, and it drives me over the edge.

"That's it, baby. Just a little longer. Let me use you just a little more. I wish you could see how pretty you look riding me."

She bounces on my dick, and her screams of pleasure make me smile. Knowing that Alessia Valentín is screaming my name, pure satisfaction runs through my veins. The headboard continues to bang, and I don't give a flying fuck if the entire neighborhood can hear us.

I pump faster, harder, circling her clit until she's shaking from the pleasure. The way her ass clenches on my dick has me grunting hard. Up and down she goes, and I slap her ass, getting a handful of her soft skin. I squeeze her cheeks as she rides me with my cock in her tight ass marking her with future bruises.

"I'm going to finish! Come inside my ass, please." She begs.

"Filthy girl," I drive into her deeper, and I spank her hips again. The sound of our skin slapping against each other fills the room. She moans my name, falls over my chest, and grips the headboard. She clenches down on my cock, causing a feral growl to rip through my clenched teeth. I circle her clit faster and smoother, and finally, she's reached the finish line. She rides out her orgasm over my dick and fingers. Her legs tremble, and she screams my name over and over again.

"Daegan, oh Daegan."

I made her come with my dick in her ass, but now it's my turn.

"Turn around."

At first, she doesn't understand, but finally, she gets the idea. She's hesitant. I give her tits another suck, biting down on each teardrop gently. I'm an animal for her, a beast that needs to taste and see how she bleeds.

"I want to see if you bleed just as pretty as your smile," I kiss her right breast and let the monsters in my head take over.

I bite her skin, just below her brown nipple, and she whimpers in pain. I bit her for the purpose of drawing red. A metallic taste fills the tip of my tongue, and she claws at my hair as she still straddles my dick, still high on her orgasm.

I've marked her as mine, and this is just the start. I'm going to mark her ass cheeks next with my teeth.

I kiss her, my tongue traveling down into her mouth.

She sits reverse cowgirl on me, settling in and out, and my dick rams into her rim like it's my new permanent home where I'll always have the keys to. She's so fucking tight here too, *fuck*.

"Don't tease me again unless you're going to do something about it, little Valentine." I threaten.

"Oh yeah?" She taunts over her shoulder. She bends forward, massaging my balls as I fuck her behind. Her soft palms grip my balls, softening my darkened thrusts.

I grab her hair, pulling it hard as she bounces on my dick, and I release havoc. In and out I go, and the bed shakes, the sight of her tits and hard nipples bouncing up and down with each detrimental thrust I inflict on her divine body.

She's so sexy.

She moans, and through gritted teeth, I groan back in sweet nirvana.

"Fuck baby, use me as your chair any time." I continue to pull on her hair and fuck her as hard as she lets me. She falls forward, grabs my shins, and decides to take control of the pace I set, and I let her. I throw my head back as I grab onto her ass and hips. Her hips roll, and my cock swells, throbbing and begging to release. I never knew patience like right now because I want to do bad things to her.

I want to fuck her against the wall, the desk, the nightstand, and the shower right after this. I want to tie her up and never let her leave this room until she can't walk. Every time she takes a step, she'll feel my markings.

But the way she's moving and feels, it's like nothing I've ever experienced or known. No one has ever come close to her. No one has ever tasted as good as her or laughed and loved as sweet as her.

My little valentine.

She has me trapped under a spell, and I know I'm in trouble.

I reach over and bite her ass until she bleeds for me. She grits out a moan. "Oh fuck, Daegan."

I follow right after, letting myself drown in our forbidden lustrous affair, draining my balls inside her, my strokes deep and slow and fucking sensitive. Her mouth gapes open from her blissful high the entire time. She glides off my dick slowly, her thighs buckling over, and she almost falls over from the exhaustion. Watching the come fall out of her ass is a sight so majestic, I want to see it again.

I grab hold of her arms before she topples over the mattress, and I kiss her lips softly, my pace of action the opposite of a few moments ago.

Her lips brush against mine softly and slowly. I kiss her like I want to savor this moment for eternity...like it'll be the last time she'll ever let me touch her.

Her cheeks are flushed, sweat coating her beautiful tan skin, and I kiss her cheeks over and over again. She pants hard and holds me tight, around my neck like she doesn't want me to let go, and I don't plan to...yet.

She palms my rib tattoo, wholly exhausted with closed eyes, but a slight smile is painted on her face. Her nose digs into my neck, and our skin is damp from sweating.

I flip her over gently so she's now resting on her side, still breathing heavily from the world-shattering sex.

Her curls are wet from the sweat on her face, and I brush them away, tucking them behind her cute little ears.

"How are you feeling?"

She let me claim her ass, and now I need to make sure she's okay. I brush my knuckles on her face, pushing her hair behind her ear.

"I'm great. Can we please do that again soon?" Her shallow breathing is all I hear, along with her angelic voice. I could listen to her talk all day. She has the kind of voice that could make demons change sides, the kind of voice that makes you believe heaven is on earth too, not only in the afterlife, and a voice that could make me believe in love again.

I chuckle at her response. My girl likes rough pain, and well...so do I.

She shifts positions, placing her leg over mine. I welcome her as she reaches over me and rests her head on my scarred chest.

"Daegan. What happened to you?" Her fingers find the slashes on my face. She trails each one with her fingertips, gently, one by one. And this time, I don't freeze from the unpredictable touch. I welcome it.

She's the only one who's touched them, and it will stay that way for the rest of my life.

She doesn't have to specify her question. I know what she's asking about. Usually, I hate talking. I haven't bothered trying to get to know anyone for years, consumed by my job, but after stalking Alessia that first night, I knew I was the one in trouble. I became the prey, the one who would meet their demise if I didn't make her mine.

I'm in love with her. I'm profoundly in love, to the point that all I want to do is make her happy, make her laugh, make her feel good, and fuck her into an oblivion she never wants to escape from for the rest of her life.

"My half-brother, Dario, and I were deployed together. We were so excited. This was before I got moved to SEAL team Executioners. After my father remarried, my stepmother had two sons. Graves and Dario. I was blessed to have always had a good relationship with them. We've done everything together. Middle school, high school, the football team, and even went to boot camp together. We were placed on different teams, but as luck would have it, we got to go on a deployment together, our missions colliding."

She kisses my chest and holds me tighter.

"Long story short, he stepped on an IED, and while the blast severely injured him, taking his legs, it knocked me out. A few nights later, I woke up being tortured by The Surgeon."

"We don't have to get into this, Daegan. I'm sorry for asking. I shouldn't have,"

"Shh, it's okay." I rub her back as I continue to lose myself in the worst days of my life. I stare at the fan, watching it. It's off, but it still has that weird effect on me. I've never told anyone this story...but I'm telling her.

"He sliced my face open, stabbed me in places all over my body." She looks at the scars on my stomach. "He purposely would torture me. Make sure I wouldn't die from the wounds he inflicted on me. He *wanted* me to know why they called him the surgeon. He wanted to get as much information out of me as he could. He wanted to break me, but he never did. He would do this for hours until he got his fill and went to bed. I sat there in my blood for hours, conjuring a plan. I spent the nights alone. And so I used that to my advantage to escape."

"How did you escape?"

"I broke my own hand, crushing my bones just enough for me to slip out of the cuffs. There was a loud, chaotic thunderstorm that night, so when I broke a window, nature swallowed the sounds away, and I was able to find help after hiking a couple of miles naked."

She tenses as the story goes on.

"Well, you're here now," she murmurs lightly, pressing her lips softly on my scarred eye. The gesture elicits that unfamiliar emotion I've never felt, and I welcome it.

"Alessia,"

"Hm?" She hums sleepily, trailing her fingers over my tattoos, blood rushing down, and I'm getting hard again when she massages my balls and dick.

She feels good. She makes me feel good.

"I'm a liar,"

She freezes, divulging my awkward confession.

"What do you mean?" She tilts her head upwards, and I brush the curls out of her perfect face. Alessia's wide eyes glazed with perplexed wonder. Like I just told her, the sky is falling, or dogs have wings.

The temptation to touch her always overwhelms me, and I plant a kiss on her forehead. I would kiss her all day and night if I could.

A deep chuckle of laughter escapes me, and I might send her running for the hills after this. But I don't care. If she does end up running away from me, I'll always find her. I'll drag her back to the pits of hell I endure every day.

She might end up hating me in the end, but I just need her to know. I need her to know, at this moment, what her existence has done to me.

"I promised I wouldn't fall in love with you. But I'm a goddamn liar." I continue to run my hands through her soft hair, and her brown eyes sparkle with an emotion I can't decipher.

Is she happy? Upset? Shocked?

"It's been 152 days since we met, and there hasn't been one day that you haven't lived in my head. 152 mornings and nights where my days began with haunting thoughts and ended with you in my dreams." She stiffens, her eyes watering. But it doesn't stop me from spilling out.

"I...Daegan," she pauses and breaks her gaze away from me. My heart cracks as the tune in her eyes takes a turn. "We can't...we promised we wouldn't fall in love with each other." She murmurs low into my chest.

"I know..."

A strange, unwelcoming, and unpleasant silence is in between us, and it's driving me crazy. I was always supposed to make sure we got here...but the level of authenticity was never supposed to exist.

"Put me out of my goddam misery, baby, and tell me it's not all in my head? Tell me, I'm yours too? Because you sure as hell are mine. I'm in love with you, and if you're not in love with me, then give me my soul back by lying to me. Pretend you're in love with me until you feel it back because I've got time. I will wait for you forever, in this lifetime and the next, for you to fall in love with me like I am with you."

45

Alessia

"YOU'RE IT FOR ME, Alessia. There is no one else for me. It's not just this game of lust anymore."

I lay on Daegan's scarred chest in disbelief. Surely, a man like him could never commit to a girl like me. I want to say it back, but I can't find the words. I feel the same, his eyes begging for mercy. His light grey eyes are so bright with unwavering hope, and it kills me. Pure heat travels into my blood, exploding every broken piece and putting me back together when he looks at me like this.

"If I say it back, everything changes, Daegan. When I fall, I fall hard. I'm naive when it comes to these things, and if you hurt me, I don't think I'll recover. I've had this wall up purposefully to avoid falling in love and getting hurt again. I don't want to feel that again, and I don't want to feel it with you. *Especially with you*. Especially with a man that has made me feel and experience things I thought were dead and truant."

He looks away from me.

"So...if I honestly say those three words. Can you promise me one more thing?"

"Anything."

"No more pretending. I want honesty. I want the truth. No more secrets. No more secret relationships. I want this relationship we have behind closed doors to come to light."

He inhales long and hard, his chest rising and falling slowly, but I can't tell what's going through his head.

He nods slowly, and I can't tell, but a part of me feels like he isn't being honest—like he's hiding something.

"I'm in love with you, Daegan. Please don't break my heart. I am yours."

He climbs on top of me and grabs a condom from the nightstand. He rips the wrapper open with his teeth. His sharp canines tear it off in a second. He glides it on his massive pierced dick and strokes himself a few times, coating his tip with my wetness before entering me. His movements are slow like he's savoring every single detail of this night.

After Daegan made love to me, I felt like I was in my own world. I couldn't fall asleep, but right after he came inside me with the condom on, he kept whispering I love you in my ear, and every time he did, my heart fluttered, and my breathing stopped.

I'm so in love with this man, it's scaring me.

PRETEND

As soon as I stand up to go to the restroom, I feel fluids fall out of me. That's weird. I must be really wet...right?

But when I turn on the lights, more slips out, and I panic. He wore a condom. Why is his come falling out of me?

Did it fucking break?

Shit. It must have broken. Before my mind spirals out of control, I can go into town and find Plan B somewhere. It'll be okay.

After I'm done using the restroom, I'm staring at the door in front of me. The one he keeps locked at all times. I know I shouldn't do it, but something is screaming at me to check it. I remember the box of condoms by his nightstand, and I saw a key inside the drawer.

I push his bedroom door open and make sure to walk softly against the wooden floors. I open it and grab the key. My heart drops, and a cold shiver runs down my spine when I see Daegan move in his sleep.

I see his dragon tattoo and his back muscles move, but then he goes still. Holding my breath, I walk out of his room and hold the key tight in my hand to make sure it's tightly secured to the point it almost breaks my skin.

I'm praying and wishing to myself that it's the right key, and as soon as it glides in perfectly, like a missing puzzle piece, a small pop follows. I know I just unlocked something mysterious.

I push open the door, and I feel like I'm in a horror movie.

I let the door glide across the wooden floor until it softly hits the other side of the wall. I would have grabbed it before it collided, but the sight before me drained my blood until I ran cold.

There are photographs of me everywhere, pinned to every single wall. They go back to the first day I received a text message in Chrome Beans. I'm sitting there with my coffee and my book in hand. I'm at El Devine with my favorite cowgirl boots on with my friends. There are photos of me *sleeping*, photos of me with my ex-boyfriend, Jack, and photos of me with my mother. Photos of me *everywhere*. Walking to my car, at the gym, the grocery store.

Daegan? Is he? Is he the one who was stalking me?! Texting me? Leaving me black-painted flowers?

I'm trembling, shaking, the world crashing into itself like a dying star, and my soul shatters. This is insanity. This is crazy. Am I dreaming?

Are these side effects from him drugging me?

I pinch myself, rub my arms, and close my eyes over and over again to see if my horrid scenery will disappear. But when I open my eyes, nothing changes.

Something inside me decides to check his pockets. I head back to his room to check his pockets and find my hair. My curls. The same curls he texted me a photo of.

It's him. He's the one that's been watching me.

I start grabbing my clothes quickly but quietly. And just when I've put on my shoes, I'm opening the bedroom door. My heart thundering, and fear sets into every particle of my being.

I stand there, my hand on the doorknob, and I want to run.

But I'm paralyzed for some reason. The shock has caught up to me, and I feel like I'm about to fall over and faint, the nausea overpowering my movements.

"Alessia." He calls out for me.

"It's you, you've been watching me. The one who sent me those flowers. You cut a piece of my hair off."

"Alessia...don't do this. *Don't run.*"

PRETEND

I elbow him in the stomach, knocking the air out of his lungs, and a loud, pained grunt follows.

I take advantage and swing the door further open, bolting out as fast as I can, and start to run for my life.

46

Alessia

I'M SCRAMBLING, BANKING LEFT and right until finally I get a hold of my common sense and head towards his living room. I'm running barefoot, and remember that I don't have my car, phone, or wallet.

I let myself get consumed by our magnetic chemistry even though he did unspeakable things to get me here. He had me under his spell, and I forgave him too quickly. I let him fuck me. Hell, I chased that feeling of being wrapped into this delusional man, too.

And now?

Is he the one working with human traffickers? Did he turn in Ari and Grim for money?

Was he going to do the same to me?

My heartbeat races dangerously palpitating, and I have to think quickly. I run to his kitchen and I remember seeing handguns in almost every corner of his house. The man likes his firearms.

So, I look into the kitchen drawers and, at the same time, wait for Daegan to come out of the hallway to grab me or hurt me.

I lunge for his pantry, and to my surprise, I find a Glock 42. It's hidden behind pasta boxes, but still. The dark green design stands out, and I reach for it. I check if it's loaded and see that there's one bullet in the chamber.

"Alessia! Please, listen to me." Daegan begs, his dark falling over his bright eyes that are darkening with desperation. He grips the kitchen counter, and I raise the gun to him.

"Why do you have my hair in your pocket, Daegan?"

"Alessia, please put the gun down, baby."

"Why do you have pictures of me, Creature?!"

He stiffens like I had already shot a bullet through his chest at my words.

"Don't call me that. You've never called me by my operator name, so don't you start now!" He snarls. "Don't act like you're not in love with me because you know me, Alessia. I'm not here to hurt you!"

"I really don't know you, though." My lips tremble as I place my finger on the trigger. "Did you bring me here on purpose? Are you the one that's trying to capture me for money? To give me up for human trafficking? What? Was the money you got for Danny and Ari not enough? This was all a lie?!"

"NO!" He roars with disbelief like he can't register my accusations because they're too shocking.

"Then why have you been stalking me? How long have you been watching me?" I scream at him, putting up concrete walls between us with my tone.

He looks at me, and with a clenched jaw, a tear falls down his cheek. An unstable version of himself cracks and unfolds before me; this time, he's letting me see this version of himself.

"I'm not afraid to show you how much I love you anymore. I wasn't lying when I said you've consumed me, Alessia Sahara. Everyone calls me a freak, a blind robot that only knows how to shoot. But ever since I met you, I've let the dark parts of myself take over because it feels good to love someone who makes you feel like you belong in a world with an unforgiving system." He looks at me, and I'm about to break. I lower the gun as I listen to his voice tremble with his blatant, raw confession. "I...I don't know how to love you in a way that society deems normal. I'm not normal." He concedes with a heartbroken truth that rattles his deep voice. "Why would I want normal for us? Fuck what society tells me. I want you dangerously. Everything about you, all the time. Let me love you until the end of time in my own way."

"But..." I start, but he doesn't let me finish.

"I take my job very seriously. I go above and beyond the task, always. So when you were assigned to me by Ravenmore, it pissed me off. Nonetheless, I said yes because this team, this job, is the reason I breathe. At least it was the reason I breathed until I saw you for the first time. I watched you to find out who exactly Alessia Valentin is. I wanted to know who I'm going to be stuck with for the next few months...I had to know. So yes, you intrigued me. I fell for you hard, and I tried to snap myself out of it time and time again, but I failed. I'm not here to hurt you in the ways you're accusing me of."

But the memories of the text messages come back and make me want to hide again. I need time to think. I need space to figure out what my next step is. Everything is going at warp speed. I just got sent back home on my first deployment for fucking him. I raise the gun back at him, unsure of what to believe.

He did lie about being married.

PRETEND

He could be lying to me now!

"Daegan! It is you! You're the one who's capable of doing all this. You're a liar! You've lied to me before, and you're doing it again! You're the one everyone is looking for. It does make sense! This all started when you showed up on the Executioners team! All along, it's been you sending me these text messages! You even sent me text messages framing yourself at the shooting range in Iraq! Why would you do that? To make sure I didn't think it was you?"

His brows furrow, and his whole body stiffens.

"Alessia. When you deployed to Iraq, I stopped sending you text messages. That wasn't me." His towering frame tenses up, and he starts to walk toward me.

"Everyone warned me about you, Daegan! And I defended you over and over again! How could you do this to your team? *To me?* Don't fucking come near me!"

"Alessia, please, baby, let me touch you. God, let me fucking touch you, or I'll die if I don't."

His vicinity is suffocating, but I'm not sure if it's in a good or bad way yet. I'm still trying to process everything and protect myself. Something I've been failing to do.

He steps closer and is about to grab me as I step back. His hand reaches for mine, but he doesn't get to hold it as the tip of my gun touches his chest, and I feel like everything is in slow motion.

I lower my gun again, crying as I move, and he looks at me with so much intensity that it's intimidating.

Do I believe him? Do I hear him out? What do I do?

"Let me touch you." He tells me again, his gaze so serious and demanding that I think I'm going to fall apart. "Don't run. Trust me. Let me live by choosing to love my nightmares, my scars, my broken soul." He pleads. "No one has shown me that they're willing to accept my blackened heart after everything I've been through. Please tell me that I have found that in you, Valentine?"

He walks closer, and I'm hot and cold all over.

"I don't need a lamp. I don't need the fan off. Don't you get it, baby? I don't need anything in this world. *But I need you.*"

I fall apart and lower my gun slightly, but then a loud pop makes me jump. My bones rattle, and my ears ring as I watch Daegan's body fall to the ground, bringing me down with him. His eyes widen, and I grow cold and confused. Shit, did I shoot him on accident with my overdriven heart?

I didn't pull the trigger! What just happened?

Blood splatters and leaks everywhere on his grey kitchen cabinets. Daegan goes limp, and I don't get a chance to examine or even fucking breathe before I'm screaming. My hair gets pulled as I try to grab for Daegan as he lays in a small puddle of crimson, and it only grows by the second.

I'm scratching at the person who is dragging me by my hair, their hand gripped at the scalp, and I'm shrieking as my knees scrape the kitchen floor.

Then I feel hot breaths bite the skin on the base of my ear. "Now, how about that date, Alessia?" He coos cruelly.

That voice. That rough, menacing voice has me trembling.

Gabe.

47

Daegan

"**L**ET ME GO, GABE!"

Alessia's screams bring me back to life, and the adrenaline starts to pump through my veins. I push myself off the floor, and I laugh to myself. I look at the blood that is spilling out of my body, my blurred vision slowly stabilizing, and it makes me laugh harder.

Oh, what fun it will be to kill this man.

"I'm not leaving until Hannibal is lifeless!" He shouts back at her, and a loud slap rings out. She yelps and whimpers at his aggression.

Did he just fucking hit my girl?

I'm seeing red.

"You shoot me when my back is turned. What a cowardly move, Gabe." I call out over the counter. "You're dumber than I thought. You think I'm going to *let you* walk out of here alive? After hacking into my security system and interrupting date night with my lady?"

I went unconscious for a brief moment when I hit the door of the pantry from the devastating impact of his gun. Mother fucker has my girl in his grasp, and he's hurting her.

What I did to Frankie doesn't compare to what I'll do to Gabe if I get my hands on him.

When I'll get my hands on him.

"So Creature *can talk and take off his mask*. Let me see your pretty face." He taunts me as if I'll ever give in to a traitor.

"No, Daegan, don't!" Alessia begs.

"Shut the fuck up!" He does something to her again because she shrieks with agony, and I'm losing my patience.

"I still look better than you, Gabe." I shoot back. "I should have known it was you, but then I'd be giving an asshole too much credit for having the capability to fuck over Grim."

"Judge me all you want. I won't ever apologize for doing what I need to do to help fund—"

"Spare me your sob stories." I scoff, not letting him finish. I don't give a fuck what his reason is for trying to kill me. For working with criminals and almost getting Grim and Ari killed. There is no excuse in the world that would be valid for that. "You should have stuck to being a bartender. No wonder you got out of the Navy. You have a shit aim; this is a fucking papercut." He got me good, but he fucking missed any major organs. I plugged the hole with a kitchen paper towel that dropped on me. It won't last or stop the bleeding, but it buys me some time.

"I'm taking her with me after I kill you."

"No!" Alessia yells at him again. "Do you forget why everyone calls him Creature?" Alessia hisses in pain, and I'm wondering what the fuck he's doing to her behind the counter, but if I'm going to save her, I need to wait. I need to take the opportunity and tune out everything to get him where I want.

"They call him that because he has nine lives and doesn't like to die, but I'll make sure after tonight, he's run out of chances. You're going to come with me. Smiley promised me buckets of money for you being the detective's and admiral's daughter."

"You're not going anywhere with her," I promise him as I take the Glock that Alessia dropped from the floor. I hold it in my hands and check the chamber. It only has one bullet. Good. That's all I need to get the job done. I get my cell phone out and quickly text Graves our code of emergencies so he can get in on the fun and, at the same time, invite the police.

"I've always disliked you. And now I get to take the one thing that makes you talk...away. Say goodbye to your fuck buddy, Creature. You'll never see her again where she's going. I can come back and kill you later." He starts to move with Alessia in his arms. I can hear her fighting his hold, and I'm breathing heavily against the counters, watching the paper towel get soaked. I pull it out and wince, grinding my teeth from the pain before plugging a clean sheet of paper towels in it again.

"Let me go! Let me go, Gabe, ple—" A loud smack rings and the noises of Alessia struggling are silenced.

Motherfucker.

I hear him open the door, and I'm waiting. I tune out everything and Paint It Black plays in my head. I hum the tune while closing my eyes.

I spring upward, holding the Glock in my hand, and I only have a second to take in the sight before me, or I'm going to lose her. She's gone limp in his arms, blood trickling onto her forehead as he carries her out of the door in a chaotic manner like he knows if I catch him, he's dead. My sanity cracks when I realize he's using her limp body as a human shield.

Coward.

He's covering his head, where I desire to blow it off, and forcing me to shoot him while he's moving with her. I have to ensure I don't miss and hit the love of my life instead. I've done this many times with targets. They're moving, running, or in unimaginable positions, and I still get a headshot. This time, I'm forced to hit him somewhere else.

I raise the gun, and Gabe's eyes widen. He moves Alessia to cover his face more, and I don't hesitate a second longer. He's already out the door into the rain, giving me one chance. I take it.

I shoot, the bullet piercing his shin, forcing him to drop her, and he shouts in agony. His flesh gets cut open, spraying red everywhere, and I hum with satisfaction. My favorite color. He dropped his weapon along with Alessia's body.

I move toward him fast, and his eyes bulge because he realizes he's fucked. But the bastard gets energy from God knows where, and he sprints off of Alessia and fast limps farther outside. I manage to grab Alessia as she stirs but doesn't wake up. I pull her inside my house and hear a car door slamming with tires screeching following suit.

Gabe hopped in a getaway car, and I'm swearing every curse word under my breath as I shut the door. I lock it and pull her up to my chest as I sit against the wall, caressing her cheek. I check her pulse, and it beats slowly back. She's still alive. Gabe just knocked her out cold. Fucking bastard got away.

The sound of sirens can be heard in the distance, and my phone keeps going off, but I'm too distracted trying to wake up Alessia to notice or respond. She will wake up, and when she wakes up, I can think straight again. Right now, I'm seeing red, and all I want to do is hunt Gabe down until he's dead. Because whoever this Smiley person is won't stop. Gabe thought he could kill me and take Alessia with him, and now that he's still alive, he will always be a constant threat until he's arrested and these human traffickers are taken down.

But they just fucked over the wrong man because Graves is powerful. He'll find the ones responsible for the human trafficking rings and burn them all to the ground. I have no doubts.

I can feel myself growing cold, and I'm sitting there with Alessia in my arms, and all I see is my mother. I'm quiet, and I feel myself growing sleepy. The paper towel is soaked again, and it voluntarily falls out of my wound and onto the floor. Blood begins to fall out like a waterfall from me. I watch it run down my body. I'm going to pass out. I'm losing a lot of blood, just like that day in Iraq after I was stabbed in the back.

Everything makes sense now. Gabe used to be in the Navy and had access to a lot of things. He was the one who texted her at the shooting range, trying to pin it on me. The one who started the rumors of me being behind everything. He was the one who helped install the security system in Ari's home. The blood keeps falling out of my side.

Fuck. Did I get it all wrong? Did this motherfucker hit a major organ?

This scene is all too familiar, and I know what will happen if I don't get to a hospital within the next few minutes. I'm going to die, but at least I get to do it with my little valentine in my arms.

I look down at Alessia. The blood that ran down her forehead is clotted and dried. She looks so heavenly and peaceful, even though our situation is anything but easy. I kiss her sleepy lips as my heart rate slows down, the adrenaline that once filled my body is draining, and the aftermath of Gabe's gunshot wound reminds me of bloodcurdling pain in my side.

I press my lips softer to hers as a tear falls down my cheek.

"I love you, Alessia. I've never cared or loved anything like I do, you. I'm not sorry for falling hard, but I am sorry for breaking your boundaries. Isn't that what love is, though, Valentine? Is it love if you're not driven to the point of madness? Is it love if you're not willing to die for it?" I whisper, my voice fading with low blood pressure. I caress her cheeks, my knuckle brushing her cheek, and I no longer have control of my body. My hands fall to my side as Alessia rests her head on my lap. The sound of sirens grows louder, and I'm grateful they'll be able to care of her when I can't.

It's dark, quiet, and lonely. A memory of my mother playing the piano in our living room, teaching me how to play one of her favorite tunes, comes back, and I fall into the darkness.

Alessia doesn't answer me. She's still unconscious, and black shadows corner my vision. I just needed her to know one last time how much I love her...even if I didn't do it in the right way. My arms fall to the side, and I tilt my head back as I whisper one last sentence with a small smile on my face.

"If our game of pretending had this same outcome, I would do it again, little valentine," I smirk as I close my eyes for the last time.

48
Alessia

THE FIRST PERSON I see when I wake up is my mother. She's asleep on the couch, with messy blonde hair and a blanket that's up to her chin. Her head is tilted in a position where it looks uncomfortable, and I'm tempted to get up and move her, but I realize it's not that easy of a task. I try to move, but my muscles feel like jello.

How long have I been asleep?

I groan, blinking hard and steadily. I turn my head as the sirens from an ambulance attract my attention. Red and blue lights flicker fast in the corner of the room. It's late at night. I can tell by the window. The curtains are over it like a shield, but the blinds are open. The faint city lights in the distance are like small orbs. I need my contacts, I can't see well.

My beeping monitor beats regularly, and I'm trying to remember what got me here in the first place. I lay my head back as I try to focus on what led me here.

I stare at the turned-off ceiling hospital lights. Nurses and doctors run back and forth in front of me. I turn to my left, and a thick soreness strikes back.

Damn.

Then, it triggers everything.

Daegan took me to his house forcefully. He fucked me into another oblivion. Finding that room full of my things. He wasn't kidding when he said he was obsessed with me. And then Gabe shot him and held me hostage as he tried to kidnap me.

I heard everything he told me as he held me, but I couldn't blink or open my eyes. I couldn't respond when I only wanted to hold him back, even though I was confused.

Was it a dream? Was this all a horrible nightmare? Is he okay? Is he...*dead*?

I swallow; my throat is dry, and I want to get up. I need answers. And I need them right now.

The door to the room slides open, and a petite nurse walks in. She has long black hair, a beautiful heart-shaped face, and a smile that makes you feel like everything is okay.

I look at her name tag.

Ari Rider

"Ms. Valentin, how are you feeling?" She chirps with sympathy. After holding my hand for a few seconds, she goes straight to the laptop in the corner to plug in notes. The IV fluids bag is empty beside it. I have a port into my vein on my wrist, but I'm not attached to it.

"I—I'm okay. I think. Why am I here? Where's Daegan?" I ask as I groan. I sit up higher on the bed and look at her desperately for answers.

She looks at me with worry and presses on the keyboard.

PRETEND

"You're in the naval base emergency department. We've rehydrated you. You passed out and suffered trauma to the head. Thankfully, it wasn't too serious, but it was enough to make you pass out for a few hours. You're going to be okay, Ms. Valentin." She squeezes my hand.

"And what about Daegan?"

"Who?" She arches a brow, and her light brown eyes brighten with firm curiosity.

"Daegan Hannibal," I repeat.

"Oh, him," Ari frowns and sits on the bed. She grabs my hand again like she's about to give me the worst news of my life. She grabs the railing on the hospital bed and takes in a deep breath.

"Please don't say it," I beg.

"He's—"

"*Mija*...you're awake!" My mom exclaims, interrupting Ari. My eyes widen, and I shrink in the bed. "You're going to be okay, *mija*. You'll even get to be discharged by tomorrow morning. Now that we know it was Gabe, we're that much closer to shutting these assholes down and putting them in prison." She embraces me. Her cold arms hold me tight, and I hug her back as hard as possible, which isn't much because my muscles quiver weakly.

"You mean, you didn't catch him?!" I breathe out harshly with panic laced in my dry tone.

"No, I'm sorry, *mija*. He got away. But I'm confident we'll get him. From the investigation we did, Gabe is wounded, and he'll have to seek treatment at a hospital somewhere. We'll find him, I promise."

"What about Daegan?"

"I'm sorry, Alessia. He might not make it." My mom shares with me, grabbing my shoulder and squeezing it.

"Mom, don't tell me that, please don't tell me that!" I yell as my heart shatters and depletes into a puddle of misery. I can feel my vision blurring, leaking with hotness. It trails all the way down to my lips, and I wipe it away.

Ari stands quickly and grabs a box of tissues, handing them to me with blurry vision of her own.

"He's been in surgery. According to the paramedics, his friend, Graves, found him without a pulse, dead, but he worked on him vigorously and was able to get his heart beating again. He's...in critical condition. Right now, it's touch and go, but I'll come back with an update. If I must scrub in and bang on that operating room door myself to get you information, I will." Ari chimes in.

I nod vehemently, squeezing her hand.

"I've already talked to my husband. He's getting paperwork together to grant you a 60-day leave of absence. Get some rest. You'll be discharged soon from the hospital and—"

"I'm not going anywhere without Daegan." I cut my mother off, blinking more tears away. My chest tightens with despair.

He has to make it.

"He better make it so that I can yell at him. And tell him that he's crazy! To tell him that I'm upset with him for all the lies and deception." I shout at Ari and my mother like they're the ones responsible for everything wrong that's happened to me. Ari has no clue what I'm talking about, but I'm hoping she doesn't sedate me for my outburst that's pouring out.

My mom quiets down, and Ari listens with open ears. My mother stands and strokes the back of my head.

PRETEND

I close my eyes tight and suck in a deep breath. "I need to tell him that I love him. I love him despite the imperfections of how we got here. I don't care if our journey has been full of weird bumps. I love him."

It's the following day. Daegan's surgery is running longer than expected. Ari hasn't updated me, and I'm going crazy. I refuse to leave this hospital without him. My mother left home to shower, and she'll be back soon to take me back to her house. She doesn't want to leave me alone.

I'm folding my Jack Skellington blanket when someone knocks on the door. I turn to my left and see Kane.

I smile, and the thick rock in my throat forms. I start to tear up when I see Daegan's closest friend on the team. He's in his signature black leather jacket and beanie. He wears dark blue jeans, and his dark hair waves out at the corner of his patriotic beanie. He slides the door open fast, and I rush into his arms. He doesn't hesitate to welcome me in a warm, friendly embrace. He holds me tight, innocently.

"Alessia...how are you?" He murmurs against the top of my head. We're swaying back and forth as we hold each other. He pulls me forward to get a good look at my injury. He shakes his head when he sees the white bandage on my forehead.

"I'm okay! Nevermind me! I'm worried about Daegan!" I sniffle into his chest. Kane always feels good, smells good, looks good. He's always just...good, in the most friendly way possible.

"Creature's still in surgery, huh? Grim called everyone to the hospital. His wife works here and called him immediately, filling him in. We're all here, but I had to see you." Kane gives me one more tight hug before releasing me.

"Yes. I haven't heard anything. They're discharging me. I'm leaving soon, but I don't want to. If that's okay, I'll wait in the lobby with you guys."

"Of course, it's fucking okay. I can't believe Gabe is the one who was behind everything. I liked him for the most part. I didn't know him too well, obviously."

"Gabe was the one that shot him. He hacked into his security system and tried to kidnap me and kill him in the process."

"Piece of shit! I know he's still out there, but I'm sure we'll get him. Don't worry, Alessia."

"Excuse me." Someone clears their throat. An older feminine voice interrupts our embrace, and Kane and I separate slowly. "Hi, we've never met before, but I guess I should introduce myself." We both turn to the door, and a tall woman with black high heels, bright red lipstick, and bright green eyes walks in like she's on a mission.

I wipe away my tears, and Kane gives me space, letting my arms fall. The woman walks in front of us and stops by the vitals monitor.

She puts her perfectly manicured hand before me for me to shake. I take it and furrow my brows, puzzled by the awkward intrusion. How does she know me?

"I'm Stella Hannibal. And you're Alessia, right? My husband's girlfriend?"

49
Alessia

MY HEART DROPS. EMBARRASSMENT fuels my veins, and my cheeks redden with uncomfortable heat.

"*I'm going to be in the lobby.* Text me if you need anything." Kane brushes his beard and walks out. He closes the sliding door behind him, and I open my mouth to try and stop him.

"Don't leave me in here with her!" I scold him as I mouth the words, keeping my voice silent and tucked into my constricting lungs.

"I'm sorry!" He mouths back to me, whips his head forward with a shrug, and I flare my nostrils, placing my hands on my hips.

Oh, we're going to talk.

Again, he walks away when I need him. The first time was when Daegan threw me over his shoulders. The betrayal times two!

"Listen, I'm going to make this quick." I pivot on my foot slowly, rubbing my biceps cautiously.

She points to the chair, like she's demanding me to listen to her. I can't say I don't feel bad because I do. Technically, they're married, but if what Daegan said was true, they're separated and are allowed to date until their final court date. He isn't cheating. He never cheated.

"Listen, I didn't know he was married."

"Spare me the details, honey. I really don't care. I cheated on him and left him for one of my co-workers. We're going to our final court divorce hearing in just two weeks to finalize it. I've been with the other man this entire time, and he doesn't care. Daegan moved on. I'm glad he did when I couldn't help him how he needed to be helped, and for that, I take full responsibility."

Oh, thank God. She's not here to fight me.

"I—uh. Okay..."

"I didn't know how to deal with the constant missions and the constant deployments. I was lonely, and honestly, I was not a very good wife to him. We were together for only a few months, and then we got married. I'm not justifying my decisions to betray him or calling him horrible things in the past when I saw him after he was tortured."

So, Daegan was telling the truth.

"Why are you here?" I ask, biting my lips.

"I just wanted to ask you something." She says, her chin pointing out and her long lashes fluttering confidently.

She bites her lips, crossing her arms across her chest. She's in an all-white jumpsuit with jewelry all across her neck—expensive jewelry and perfume that can be smelled from two rooms down.

I shake my head politely. "Whatever it is, I don't feel comfortable talking to you about Daegan. Especially since he's not awake and—

PRETEND

"I want to ask you to leave him."

My heart drops.

"What?" I breathe.

"I regret leaving him. He might die, and it's making me realize that maybe I can put up with this military lifestyle...or maybe I can convince him to leave the teams and be a civilian. My ex-boyfriend left me. I'm single again. Our court date is coming up, and for the first time since we left each other...I want to contest it."

My mouth falls open slightly at her condescending words.

I breathe in deeply, and it barely releases the tension I have on my shoulders. "Ma'am. I..."

Who am I to tell her no? Who am I to tell her to fuck off? I can't do that. I won't be that woman who tells someone's wife to give up on her husband.

Her once polite smile turns into a deadly grimace of disgust. Unmasking her true feelings toward me. "Just think about it. I'm going to be here when he wakes up because I have no doubts he will. I'm going to take care of him. I suggest you leave, Ms. Valentin."

She walks by me, nudging her shoulder into mine, and I take her rude gesture with a grain of salt. I stand there, mortified with her and myself.

I stare outside the window, watching traffic fly by and people walk in and out of one of the other hospital buildings from across my room.

What do I do?

"Ms. Valentin! He's going to make it! He's still asleep, but he's alive. He made it through surgery." I turn around to see a bright Ari. She looks like she hasn't slept all night. Sweat on her forehead, reddened cheeks like she's been running a marathon, a pink cross necklace shines against the sun rays behind me, and she's still in a surgery cap.

I burst into tears as I hug myself. I sob hard, not caring if she sees me like this. A wave of relief hits me hard, knowing he's okay. He's alive. He's going to be okay. Ari runs toward me and crashes her body against mine. She hugs me tight, rubbing my back in circles.

"Is Mr. Hannibal your boyfriend?"

I don't say anything. I can't. I don't know what we are. I've never really known.

"You don't have to say anything. I'm married to a SEAL myself. Danny Rider is my husband and his team leader. He's going back to work soon, and I know Hannibal is one of the men he's in charge of."

I let her go. I smile while tears continue to pour down my puffed cheeks. The white flag I'm about to start waving back and forth haunts me. I need to do the right thing. I must.

"Ari, do you have a pen and paper?"

She pinches her brows together.

"I have a notepad and pen." She arches one brow, plucks a small pink notepad out of her scrubs pocket, and hands it to me with the Navy hospital brand pen.

I take the paper and pen in my shaking hands. "Perfect."

50

Daegan

I FEEL HER LIPS brushing against mine. I know these lips. They've been engraved into my fucking broken soul since I first touched them. I know every curve and the way she moves when our fleshes collide. I know these lips so well. The way they press, move, and the shape. I know how her bottom lip is slightly fuller than the top. And her taste. It's too heavenly familiar, and I will always willingly get lost in her.

But I can't move. I can't kiss her back. I can't talk. I can't tell her to keep going.

Alessia, please keep kissing me.

Because I want to drown in the way she touches me willingly.

Blood rushes down. My heart beat thunders, and still. I'm paralyzed.

Am I dreaming?

Then, just as fast as this undeserved blessing came, it vanished.

Why the fuck can't I move?!

Frustrated and helpless, I get lost in the black shadows again. The darkness swallows me whole, but instead of having nightmares about the time I was tortured, my dying mother, Dario, blood, and gore. I dream of Alessia.

Her voluminous tits, her goddess body, an angel, a gift, my little valentine. I dream of her and me on my go-to spot on the rooftop. When we watched all the stars twinkle against the night sky, making wishes on C17s and military aircraft.

My muscles, my voice, and my mind come alive. The dream I was in slowly dissolved, and I'm groaning. I feel the soft and yet rough fabric of hospital blankets beneath me. Pagers are going off, nurses are chattering about other patients and familiar voices of the assholes I work with.

"Hey, Creature's alive!" Kane celebrates. He leans on the wall with one foot. His black boot pushes off it, and he sits on the chair beside me instead.

"Damn, Creature. Do you ever die?" Grim stands, his arms crossed, and walks up and down on one side of the room, circling my vitals monitor like he's making sure I don't code. "My paternity leave is over, and I'm already wanting to extend it. What in the fucking world am I catching up on? Who'd you piss off?" He asks, and I groan. I reposition myself and hiss in pain.

Fucking hell, this hurts.

"Your mother." I retort, and Grim stops pacing. He gives me a 'Really?' expression and shakes his head.

"Are you going to thank me for saving your life?"

PRETEND

I turn to an amused, nonchalant Graves. My step-brother sits in the chair, not bothering to make eye contact with me, and I don't care to either. We're both like that.

"Thank you," I mutter through clenched teeth. "Fuck this pain." I groan and close my eyes, squeezing them tightly shut.

"You look like shit." Graves points out.

"Fuck you." I shoot back. I finally open my eyes after what feels like minutes, when it's only been seconds.

"No, thank you. I appreciate the offer, but I have a lady. A few, actually." Graves says politely, turning a page in his book casually. "But speaking of getting fucked, you're in hell, my dude. Your ex is here."

My stomach coils, and anger starts to brew in the pit of my stomach.

"I don't want to see Stella. How's Valentine?" I ask.

"*La hija del patron?*" Lopez scoffs out a laugh. A toothpick twirls in between his teeth, and he smugly smiles like he's proud of me. "*Ballsy*, amigo. *Very ballsy.* And this is why you're my favorite on the team. I even know my damn limits but *Ravenmores daughter?*" Lopez starts to whistle loudly, egging me on. I grab the pillow I'm lying on and throw it at him as he continues to cheer me on. He catches it just in time before it hits his face, and he chuckles.

"Step-daughter, fucker. Wipe that smile off your face, Texas, before I cut it off." I threaten. Lopez raises his hands, surrendering, and I close my eyes again.

"Hannibal! You're awake! Do you need anything? Are you in pain?" A nurse walks in, and I recognize her. Short, light brown eyes, long black hair. It's Grim's wife. She skips over to me, passing Grim as if they don't know each other, and she checks my monitor.

"I'm good, thank you. I would really like to get out of here, though." I concede as my entire body stiffens. A stabbing sensation vibrates where I was shot, and I wince.

"Awesome...well, you'll be in the hospital for the next few days. We have to ensure you're on the right track, and then we can send you home." She smiles, and Grim watches her like he's obsessed. It's the same way I look at my girl. "I'll come back in a little bit to administer more pain medication. I have to check on my other patients, but I'm so glad you're awake."

I nod, raise my hand, and thank her with a salute. She grins innocently, satisfied, and treads toward the door. Grim follows her, and just when she makes it outside the see-through sliding doors, he catches her by the hand and pulls her in for a kiss.

"I think I'm sick, Mrs. Rider. I need an examination, and I need it now, baby." He tells her in a low tone, but it's not low enough because the whole room hears him, and everyone knows he doesn't give a fuck where he "takes" Ari.

All of us turn away with bulging eyes, granting them space. I really don't care to see their public display of affection.

She blushes and pushes him off her chest.

"Damn it, Grim, don't you fucking dare do that again." Rooker scolds him in his fatherly, southern accent. He rolls his eyes, shakes his head, and turns his back on them.

Ari gives him one last goodbye kiss and walks away. Grim walks back into the room and pulls out his cigarettes. "I'm taking off now. I have to go back to my kiddos. They're with Ari's mom." He puts the cigarettes back into his pocket. Then he points a finger at me. "Make a full recovery, Creature. I need the best sniper in the entire military to be on my team. I'm confident we'll find Gabe and the other criminals that are after all of us." He orders me in an authoritative tone.

"Oh, they'll be found alright. I have no doubt about that." Graves whispers darkly with a mischievous smile. He's probably already gotten a hold of them, but I haven't been filled in. I haven't been filled on a lot of stuff, and I need to know where my little Valentine is at, and I need to know right the fuck now.

"And you are?" Grim asks him.

"Just another ghost on the wall. Don't worry about who I am." Graves tells him with a wicked grin.

Grim looks baffled and walks out, and Rooker follows him after we give each other a brotherly handshake. I swallow again, my throat dry and my body aching. Damn it, I hate being injured. I've got a death wish, no doubt about it. Two times already, I've escaped the Grim Reaper.

Kane gives me an unopened water to drink from. I take a huge gulp. "Is anyone going to tell me where Alessia is?"

"She left."

I grow hot with frustration when my ex answers me.

Lopez, Graves, and Kane look at each other, signaling that they're going to head out so I can handle this alone. Why is she here? I thought I changed my emergency contact to Graves when I was in Iraq. I know I did.

"I'm going to head out and get you some lunch instead of the hospital food." Graves closes his book, but he hands me a note instead of walking out. "Alessia made a full recovery. She just has a bruise and a cut on her head, but she's fine. She was discharged, and she's with Mrs. Ravenmore. She wanted you to have this. She said it was important to read it when you get discharged. Not now."

LEXIE AXELSON

I take a folded small piece of paper and hold it tight. Meanwhile, my ex stares at me with bitter eyes.

51

Daegan

"WHAT DO YOU WANT? How do you know she left? Did you say something to her?" I ask, throwing question after question. "Why are you talking to her? If you want answers, you should be talking to me."

"Daegan. You haven't seen me in almost a year. Let me take care of you."

"Stella. Why are you here? Let's get to the point. I'm already in hell and don't need to upgrade a tier."

"Daegan." She hisses. "I...I came here because this is the second time you've gotten hurt. I miss you. I'm worried about you."

"Why now?"

"I've always cared."

"Is that why you cheated on me and moved on with your co-worker? Is that why you called me a monster when I came back home because of my face?"

"I've changed. Things have changed." She grabs my hand, like she's trying to prove something to me and to herself.

I retract my hand slowly, and her smile falters.

"I miss you playing the piano for me. We can go back to that, you know?"

"Stella. I moved on. *You* moved on. It's been almost a year since we've talked, and now you want to see if we'll work out. Why? DAYS before we finalize our divorce?" I say with patience, somehow possessing my body.

I'm calm and collected, not bothering to raise my voice. This isn't worth it. Stella comes from money. I don't have any compared to what she has. Her boyfriend is a CEO of a well-known construction company globally. She always would get angry with me when I couldn't get her the designer things she wanted.

"I believe you threw my injuries, my job, and my less-than-impressive salary into my face, and that's why you left me. Do I need to make a list of all the reasons why we're getting divorced? To remind you that the real monster was you in designer clothing?"

"Daegan! I'm single again, first of all. It's given me time to think and figure out what I need to change. Please give us another chance."

I kiss her on the cheek, and she smiles with a flash of hope.

"Take your new, changed personality and find someone who loves it." Her bright green eyes fall to darkness. She stands from her chair with a face that could tear down buildings. She's sulking as she paces back and forth.

"You don't love me, Stella. And that's okay. You're lonely, and you think that if you show up here when I'm in this state, it'll put me in a place where I'm weak and take you back?"

She doesn't say anything. Instead, she rubs her bright, pigmented red lips together until it smears.

"Fine. No. I don't love you. You're right. But I do miss the way you feel."

"Stella." I snarl. I know what she's referencing—the sex we had together.

PRETEND

She pouts and then giggles, finally unmasking her true feelings. I knew this wasn't what she truly wanted. She walked in here after finding out that I may have found someone, and she wanted to ruin that because the man she left me for didn't want her anymore. Stella has always liked to manipulate situations in her favor. When I called it quits, I vowed never to let it happen again.

"Fine, fine, fine. I'm leaving. I'll see you in court in a few days to finalize the divorce." She walks to the sliding doors, but then turns around when her hand reaches it and that's when I find Dario in his wheelchair, my little sister, my older brother, and Graves waiting for me with bags of food in their hands. They wave at me, and Dario makes a '*yikes*' pose while Stella's back is turned and facing me.

"You risked your job. You put someone before your job—something you could never do for me."

After twelve days in the hospital, I am discharged. Another scar, another story on my body, a reminder I don't quit easily. God only knows why he's granted me so many chances but if I have one more chance at life, I want to spend it with one woman, and if she doesn't want me anymore...I'll accept it. But I won't ever love anyone else. I wasn't lying to her when I said she was it for me. I guess it's back to being married to my job. I fucked up. I know I did, but I hope she can forgive me, for her own peace of mind, not for mine.

I'm on my way home to tear everything down in that room Alessia discovered. She doesn't want me. I know she must not want me, and that's why she wrote me this letter. I'm holding it as Graves takes me home. I'm in the passenger seat of his Land Rover. The windows are rolled down, and I'm finishing up a cigarette.

"Doctor said you couldn't smoke."

I take another hit, inhaling the bitter taste, and it sinks into my lungs. I blow out the smoke out the window.

"I know."

Finally, I decide it is time to face the music. I honored her wishes and waited until I was discharged to open it. I open the crumpled, wrinkled letter and read.

Daegan,

I'm writing to you because I can't say goodbye in person. I can't look you in your eyes because I'll sink back into you like a snowstorm I don't want to be saved from. You're my anchor, Daegan. You're the light that shines through the grey, dangerous clouds that come to destroy me. On those days that the darkness overpowered me all year, you stood by me and went above and beyond to make sure I was okay, safe, and protected...always. This year, you've taught me a lot about myself. I hope that I've taught you things in return. Even though we agreed to do something that blurs many lines of my morals, I don't regret falling for you. I heard everything you said to me when you held me in your arms, when Gabe shot you, and I want to thank you for saving my life. There are no amount of words of gratitude that would be enough to explain that. The main point of this letter is to tell you this. Time can be a gift, it can heal, or it can make us go down a path we don't want to. And right now, I need time. You need time. So please...go do the good guy thing and let me go. I'll do the bad guy thing, and I'll leave.

~ Alessia

I fold the letter back up and put it in my jeans.

PRETEND

Fucking hell, Valentine.

I was already shot once. I don't need to be shot twice.

52

Graves

I THOUGHT WE WERE on the same page. My stepbrother and I had that in common. After Stella and his mother left him, Daegan stopped believing in love. He put up a wall after his wife called him a monster and cheated on him.

I don't think I've ever let myself be serious enough to even get close to that position where I dedicate myself to someone for a period of time.

I like my job. I like money. I like my cars. I like my mansion. I like sex.

I don't love.

Dylan Hannibal wanted us over for dinner tonight since he hadn't seen Daegan in years. Daegan hasn't seen him since Dario's injury that left him in a permanent wheelchair after being discharged from the military. Correction, he hasn't seen Dario's mother. My mother. Our parents are always together.

I love my mother, but the way she lives her life and the way I live mine has never aligned with her values and faith. We view life very differently. Daegan and I are similar in that way. Despite our parents living and dedicating their lives to the church, we have our own views on our religion.

Daegan hasn't wanted to talk since Alessia left him. After his mother killed herself while he was in the living room, he didn't want to talk to anyone for a long time, either. It took Dario and I years to get him to open up to us. Then high school rolled around, and we were inseparable. Daegan's older brother,

PRETEND

Dario, Daegan, and I were always up to no good. We all got matching archangel tattoos on our arms.

Then Stella came around. I never liked her, but she made him feel good for a period of time. She shed her skin, revealing she just liked to manipulate and control him because she could. She never wanted to be his wife. It was an impulse decision for her to marry him.

Our parents liked her. She came to church every Sunday. Her father donated buckets of money, and Daegan's father pushed him to marry her because she was Catholic. My mother liked her too.

Ever since Dario joined the Navy with him, my mother turned her back on Daegan. This started a rift between Dylan and her. She thought Daegan was a bad influence on Dario because he wanted to go to war and not become a Priest like Dylan.

When Dario was injured, it only fueled her hatred for Daegan more.

Daegan hasn't said anything since he read Alessia's letter. He wants her. He's been trying to find her and Gabe. El Devine has new management, and he's been there every weekend as if he's hoping she'll walk through the doors. It helps him feel closer to her, I guess.

He's been depressed, and I caught him drinking himself almost to the point of death one night. I was worried about him when he stopped returning my calls. I asked Kane and Danny if they'd seen or heard from him, but they hadn't.

I broke into his house, and I found him with a gun in his hand and an empty bottle of bourbon. He was sprawled out on his bed, fully clothed and barely breathing.

He can't find her.

And it's killing him.

I made sure to get him medical care, sobered him up, flushed the alcohol out of his system, and granted him more time.

He's gone back to work, and luckily for him, SEAL team Executioners haven't been called out for any mission yet. He's been volunteering for everything, going to work even when he's not needed, but the Admiral shuts him down.

The man is ruined.

If he's going to get deployed, he needs to have a clear head. He can't work like this.

We sit at a large table. Daegan's little sister is at the far end, sitting in front of her dad. Her back is straight, the respect she has for her father has made her want to be perfect. Her hands are placed on the napkin on her lap. Her light brown hair is tucked perfectly in pigtails. She's always liked to have her hair like that, and it's annoying.

Dylan looks more than pleased to see his son again. When he heard the entire family would be reunited tonight, he barbequed steaks and burgers. My mother, on the other hand, doesn't care to ask for Daegan. She didn't care that he got hurt overseas and that he was hospitalized here in the states...she resents him for what happened to Dario.

She's on her fifth glass of wine, and she can't stop talking.

"So, son. I'm happy to see you're recovering well." Dylan tells Daegan after he takes a bite out of his steak. His grey hair is short and gelled. He's wearing a white sweater and slacks.

Daegan nods and continues to cut his steak with a knife.

My mother scoffs with bitterness, and I clench my jaw.

PRETEND

"Daegan, what the hell did Stella want?" Dario asks after passing him salad. Dario doesn't like Stella either. All of us siblings don't. He doesn't hold what happened to him against Daegan. Never has and never will. But his mother is the one who looked after him and resented him joining the military in the first place.

Daegan grabs the plate from him and smirks. He shrugs, hoping his silence is enough. He doesn't want to talk about it.

The entire room grows quiet, and I look at my watch every five minutes because the awkwardness of this dinner makes me lose my appetite.

"Oh, we all forgot to pray. Everyone join hands." My mother clears her throat and reaches for Dario and Dylan.

I stiffen and look at Daegan. His grey eyes darken, and he stops chewing.

"I stopped praying after my mother died."

My mother's face reddens. The air turns thick. And I know she's pissed and, mostly, drunk. Dario stiffens. His little sister grabs Daegans hand and holds it softly. She squeezes it, and Daegan squeezes her hand back. Then, let's go.

My mother plasters the widest evil smile on her bright red lips. "I believe you should keep praying since your way of thinking almost got my youngest son taken away from me! My son doesn't get to walk again. But you? You can! We raised you all to be men of God. And now you want to divorce your wife, who is a woman of God, because of a mistake? You want to divorce her for that girl, don't you? Your boss's daughter? That whore?"

Daegan bangs his fist on the table, making the silverware and plates chime chaotic and loud. He stands, his jaw clenching as he scoots the chair back, and it hits the wall with a thud. His hands turn into fists as my mother bursts into bewildered laughter. She wipes her mouth with a napkin as her chuckles die down. She sinks into her chair as her smile falters.

"Kylie! That is enough. Daegan is my son." Mr. Hannibal scolds my mother, and I smirk.

What a hell of a family reunion.

Daegan stands there, breathing heavily, his chest heaving uncontrollably. Alessia is a sensitive subject for him. His nostrils flare, and he lets out a heavy breath through his nose like a bull and stalks off. He leaves the dining room and strolls toward the door. Dylan throws his napkin on his unfinished plate and jogs after Daegan.

"What is the matter with you, Mom? You need to move on. I'm alive, and that's all that matters." Dario grabs his mother's shoulder and shakes his head. She frowns and grows quiet, simmering in her own mess.

"Mother. Easy on the wine, will you?" I smile, amused by the entire interaction. She glances up at me but then quickly gets up from her chair to leave. She's too ashamed to hold my gaze.

I slug my suit jacket back on, stroll past everyone, and head out the door.

Daegan is waiting for me in the car. He's in his all-black challenger as his father pleads for him to stay. Daegan doesn't say anything.

I get in the passenger door and close it. I watch my father give Daegan something. But I can't tell what it is from the overpowering night sky. He takes it in his hand and puts it into his pocket.

"I love you, son. I don't know how many times I have to say it for you to believe it." Dylan pats the hood of the car twice and walks away. His shoulder slump, and his blue eyes water the entire time.

Daegan puts his car into drive and speeds out of the neighborhood.

PRETEND

I light a cigarette for him, and he takes it. He continues to drive in silence as Coldplay plays throughout his speakers. I prepare for another silent drive and silent weeks to come.

But then he lowers the music. He blows out the smoke and turns the steering wheel.

"Alessia left me. Just like my mother did."

53

Kane

I LOOK AT THE engagement ring I got my girlfriend. It's a natural diamond, an oval cut, that glimmers beautifully underneath the jewelry store lights.

I smirk, and my heart twinges as I hand it back to the store associate. She gives me a pained smile like she has an idea of what happened. I'm sure this happens a lot.

The memory of me returning home with flowers and the wedding ring box sitting in my pocket hits me.

I walk up to my girlfriend's front door, eager to see her little man I've treated like a son. In my other hand, I hold his favorite superhero toy. Before I left, he's been all about Batman, so I got him this before I showed up. As soon as my knuckle touches the doorframe, it pushes forward, and my breath hitches in my throat.

Weird.

I'm about to call out for her.

This was a turn of events. I wasn't supposed to be back home for another month or so, so I thought it would be a good idea to surprise her. I didn't notify her of my departure. I'm only here because I was to drop off Alessia and then return to Iraq and be with my team.

My girlfriend doesn't know anyone on the team just yet, so my unexpected appearance was locked in and ready to go.

Perfect moment to propose.

This was it. This was the moment that I thought about even as a teenage boy. I would commit to another soul with a promise never to hurt her. Never betray her. Never be selfish.

I was going to make a promise to cherish her and put her needs before mine. Something I was willing to do with someone else a year ago.

My heart thunders in my chest. I was going to propose to the girl who made me feel something after I destroyed myself, loving someone who never belonged to me.

The door glides open, and my heart rhythm starts to skip.

The sight before me is sickening.

My girlfriend is kissing the father of her child on the dining room table. His hands are on her ass as they make out. Their tongues slide in and out of their mouths. But the sun shining from behind me is on them like a spotlight into the horror that is my life.

This was supposed to be our moment.

I drop the red roses and toy, and they fall to the floor. I clench my jaw, hoping it conceals the burning betrayal that hits me in the chest and shatters my heart. The box in my pocket suddenly feels heavier than usual.

"Kane! What...what're you doing back?" She stops kissing him, and her ex-husband clears his throat and turns away from the door. He looks full of remorse...almost.

I scoff, and I put on a smile. The same smile I give in fucked up situations because no matter how shitty the moment is, I always try to stay positive.

I don't answer her. I'm a good man. I've worked hard every day to forgive myself for the mistakes I've made, and I know I'm strong enough to walk away from situations that only drag me down.

What hurts the most, more than the damn ring, more than the girl that I thought was for me...is her son. I will no longer be a part of the little man's life. I know she won't allow it.

"Goodbye, Rose," *I tell her as I close the front door for them, correctly this time.*

Anna, the store clerk, interrupts the memory.

"What happened?" She takes the ring from me. She holds it between her fingers, admiring it.

I give her a shrug. "Nothing much. It was going to go to the wrong girl...that's all."

"I'm sorry to hear that, darling." Her shaky voice slightly cracks from a dry throat. She holds my hand and gives it a comforting squeeze.

I smile. Even with my crappy luck with love lately, I still have hope that I'll find the one to fill the hole that Ari Alvarez left in my heart. "Don't be ma'am. I know one day...I'll find my girl."

Usually, I would call up Rider in a situation like this—even Alvarez. But Paul is gone. And so is Danny, in a way. I've lost the two closest men I've looked up to. I lost Paul to war. And Rider...well, I lost my brother because we fell in love with the same woman.

Rider is a leader on the team and even in life. He pushes people to their limits. And when they reach it, he makes them realize there's a new one...they just hadn't been challenged in ways they needed to be.

PRETEND

Here I am at home in the old room I shared with my brother while growing up. My mother still keeps it occupied with some of our things. I stare at the black wall with the Red Hot Chilli Peppers poster on my side of the bedroom. There's a framed photo of my graduation day when I became a Navy SEAL. I'm surrounded by my family while I stand there in the middle with my trident. I have so many brothers and sisters.

I was supposed to get out of the Navy. But I made the decision to stay in when Ari rejected me. It felt like the right thing to do.

Then my eyes catch the soccer ball in the corner. Ari gave me her soccer ball as a Christmas gift...right before she fell asleep on my chest from crying all night after we watched Scream together. She left a cute little note on it, scribbled on it drunkenly.

I smile and remember the night I kissed her at the military ball. She kissed me back. Even if it was for a second, she did. In that one second, my entire world stopped.

It was wrong. I hurt so many people. I'll never do that shit again.

I don't realize I'm balling my fists so hard until the circulation has been cut off, and the pins and needles sensation ripples. I let go and run a hand through my hair.

The memory is painful.

Fuck.

Will I ever love anyone else like I fell for her?

Suddenly, my phone buzzes. It's a text message. I pull it out of my pocket and grin at the name.

Alessia.

I sent her a text earlier, checking in on her and her mental health. She's filled me in on pretty much everything. She hasn't told me specific details, just that she left and where she is. She made me promise not to tell anyone—specifically Daegan.

I don't have many female friends, but starting this friendship with Alessia has been the most heartwarming thing I've had in a long time. I care a lot about her. She's a beautiful girl with a fun personality, and I'm glad we get to call each other friends. Even though I'm done with the personal security assignment, our communication has stayed consistent.

"Son!" My mom calls out for me from downstairs.

"Yes, mom?"

"Dinner is ready!"

I put my phone back into my pocket and head downstairs. My mom likes to suffocate me with her love and fill my belly with food until I can't move when I'm home. She's a mom to four boys. She can't help it. Two of them in which are SEALS.

"On my way!" I shout.

54
Daegan

Two Months Later

STELLA AND I OFFICIALLY divorced. I am fully healed and cleared to go back to work. Everything is back to normal. I'm set to deploy soon as the head sniper and go back out on missions with my team. This time, we're all going back out together. Grim, Cobra, Texas, and Bane.

Everything is falling back into place...except that I haven't seen Alessia since I held her in my arms as I bled out. I've gone to her house and her mother's and even asked if Ravenmore knew where she was. But no one will tell me. They don't want me in her life.

I can't find her. She won't answer her phone, and she has no social media presence. So, I've asked Graves to help me.

Ever since she left me, I've been wanting to do something I've been holding off since my mother's passing. My faith has been tested over and over all my life. But she makes me want to start praying again.

LEXIE AXELSON

I close the door to my guest room. Everything has been emptied out. All the photos of when I looked into her when she was first assigned to me are gone. Still, I carry the piece of her hair in my pocket.

My phone vibrates in my pocket, my heart jolts, and my chest tightens. Every time my phone alerts me, I'm a frantic mess, hoping I see Alessia's name pop up. She needs time, I get that. I'll give her time, but I need to see with my own eyes that she's okay.

I stop in my tracks after putting the last photo of Alessia in my drawer. I pull it out, and Grave's name reflects back. I sigh with a hint of disappointment and hit the green button.

"What's up?"

"I got Gabe, and he's singing like a damn canary."

Sure enough, I can hear Gabe's screams of agony in the background as Graves chuckles darkly.

"Keep it down, will you? I'm on the phone with the person you failed to kill." Graves shouts in the distance. My step-brother and I have the same humor.

A big weight comes off my shoulders. I roll my shoulders and swing my neck side-to-side until the bones pop. Motherfucker will rot in prison now. Still, I'm quiet, and my silence always speaks volumes to my step-brother.

"Do you want a piece of him before I turn him over to the police?"

I hesitate.

The thought of getting a hold of Gabe is thrilling and vengeful, but I don't want to give any more time to hatred. I'm saving it all. I'm saving all my energy until I see Alessia again.

"No."

PRETEND

I'm about to hang up, letting it almost fall off my ear, but then he encapsulates my full attention again when he shouts.

"Daegan, don't hang up...I also found Alessia."

55
Alessia

Present Day

It's a beautiful summer night on the beach. My toes are in the sand as mild waves wash up and soak them. My father went to Orlando with his wife and my little sister for her high school graduation. They wanted to celebrate at Universal, and I don't blame her. Fun rides and snacks always sound like a good time.

They left me alone for the weekend. My leave of absence is coming to an end and I appreciate they're letting me spend the last few days of it alone. I haven't been alone since I was attacked. Everyone in my family is scared for my life. They're scared Gabe will show up and finish the job…I dare him to. I've been sleeping with weapons to defend myself, and I won't hesitate to protect myself or my family.

PRETEND

It's dark out. The ocean waves are mostly black with a breeze that hits me over again smoothly. Feeling euphoric on my lotioned skin, and I can taste the salt on the tip of my tongue.

I wish I could stay here forever. There's just something about a beach and its environment that makes me forget about everything. I have to go back to work soon, and taking this time away from Bloomings has been refreshing. It's been giving me time to think and process everything that happened without having to worry about people trying to kidnap or kill me. To get away from a place where it was easier for those evil people to find me.

I'm in a summer dress, tempted to go for a midnight swim. The current is perfect tonight. Everything about this summer has been perfect except for the lingering hole in my heart. It's stayed a gaping mess, and I don't think it'll ever close...but maybe with more time, it will.

I've talked to Ravenmore multiple times. We're in talks to have me move duty stations to Italy. I've always wanted to go. I think it'll be easier for everyone and my safety to be away from Bloomings for a few years.

My phone rings as I sit on the sand. I pull it out and see that it's my mother. She never calls me this late. It must be something important.

"*Mija*, we got them. The entire human trafficking problem here in Bloomings is solved. Gabe is arrested, and all of the leaders, along with other service members who were a part of this. You don't have to worry anymore."

"Oh my gosh, ma, that's great."

"*Gracias a Dios.*"

"How's...?" I want to say Daegan, but I trail off and bite my tongue instead. "How's Henry?"

"He's great. Things are really intense right now overseas. SEAL Team executioners are leaving right now to go on this really dangerous mission...you didn't hear it from me."

We say goodbye, and I hang up, leaving my phone on a towel on the beach.

The water looks so peaceful, and I'm jealous of the ocean. I want to sink into it until I become one with it. Maybe it'll help me.

I start walking towards it until the water is up to my waist.

I wanted to go deeper when something from my left moves, and it looks like a human silhouette. Immediately, I think it's a neighbor. But that dragon tattoo. Those dark waves. Those bright grey eyes that look like they're glowing as the moon kisses them, making them glimmer and my heart doing a crazy dance.

How did he find me?

He's in the water with me. His shirt is off, scars, tattoos and all stalking toward me. Handsome and mysterious, Daegan is fully healed and closing the distance like he's ready to hunt me down. I walk back slowly, but his pace is too fast.

It's been two months. By my mother's words, I thought he was getting ready to deploy. I palm the water, keeping my arms above the surface.

"I told you to go do the good guy thing, Daegan!" I shout over my erratic heart and crashing waves. I'm referring to the letter I wrote him. He shouldn't be here. He should be in Bloomings.

"I thought about it, but then I realized the only time I want to do good guy things is when I'm with you." He shouts back, and I'm tempted to turn around and run back into my dad's beach house.

I look at the sage green two-story beach home with stairs contemplating.

"You're not running anymore. I won't let you."

He breaks me out of those thoughts when I realize he's right in front of me. I turn back to him, and he grabs my hand, pulling my attention from anywhere else. Saltwater drips down his chest, onto his abs, and down to his...God, I miss him.

"Daegan. I thought you were supposed to be getting ready for a deployment. You're not supposed to be here."

He smirks, his scars crease when he smiles devilishly. He picks me up and forces me to straddle him. I let him take me, my skin melts against his hard muscles, and my pussy immediately screams for him.

"How'd you know? Now, look who the stalker is." His snarky comment has me rolling my eyes and furrow my brows. I force myself to frown so I can hide the smile that wants to curve my lips. "You're right. I shouldn't be here. Show me how wrong I am." He teases me right before he pushes his lips on mine, and I kiss him back hard, fast, and messy. Our tongues are moving like we're becoming one. His hard bulge is right against my thigh, and I want to rub myself against it.

He breaks the kiss and whispers against my lips. He caresses my face with his giant, rough palms, and I do my best not to want to smother myself against him. My hands hold onto his back tattoo tighter.

"Daegan. We can't be together." I murmur while staring at his mouth that I've missed kissing so much. His beard is shorter, hugging his sharp jawline. He furrows his brows like he's in pain at my admission.

"You're mine, little valentine. Stop fighting it."

"I thought I was doing the right thing. I thought we both needed time." I concede, and he shakes his head.

"Do I have to fuck your doubts away? Do I have to mark you so you remember who you belong to? Do I need to fill you up with my babies over and over again? Do I have to have fucking marry you so every time you put on your dog tags, you'll have my last name? Do I need to buy the brightest ring so you'll know you're my wife and no one elses?" He grabs my jaw, opens my mouth, and then devours me with his tongue. We kiss each other hard, and I'm soaking everywhere at his possessiveness.

"I want all of those things and more." A tear falls down my cheek, and a hard wave crashes into our bodies. The cold sea bites our skin, but Daegan still holds onto me, not letting me move...almost like he's afraid I'll walk away again.

"Good. Now, put me out of my misery, baby. The only time I'm not hurting is when I'm inside you."

Daegan kissed me as he carried me back into my father's vacation home. It's like he knew exactly where to go and where my room was. At this point, I am already lost in him; I let my selfishness take over and let myself feel a glimpse of happiness that my soul so desperately needed.

"Fuck, I missed you. I missed you so bad, I wanted to kill myself. I convinced myself you didn't want me. But look at you. Look at how consumed you are by me like I am with you."

"Daegan." I breathe against his lips, but he doesn't let me say anything else. He keeps stealing my breath away with more detrimental kisses and I love it.

"This is what you do to me. Don't you ever fucking leave me again, or I'll make sure to tie you up and spank your ass until it's raw." He pulls on my hair as he kisses me, pushing himself harder against me. I'm still in my yellow dress. He pushes me into the small shower space and closes the glass door behind us. He grabs my dress by the collar and tears it open. My breasts fall out with small bounces, and he bites on the skin underneath my nipple as he throws it out, and it hits the tile floor with a loud smack.

I'm exposed, naked, and hungry for his taste.

"Get on your knees, and suck." Daegan growls, and I look at his pierced dick. Precome leaks from him already. He is so hard and ready for me that I'm on my knees in a split second, eager to take him in every way that I can.

The shower head runs down his back, and I oblige without hesitation. Our movements have been fast, ferocious, and anything but soft. I grab his already hard, thick cock, and I suck him hard. and just when I think he can't get any more massive, his cock thickens even more as I tongue him. I want to feel him. I want to stop hurting, too, and ask questions later.

56

Daegan

"**What does my dirty** girl want tonight? To be degraded? To be told how much of a needy slut she is or how she's such a good little girl? Do you want to be choked as you take my cock in your ass and cunt until you pass out?"

"Yes, baby. All of that, please." She purrs, licking her lips, and I pull the back of her head, and she opens wide. My dick twitches when she begs. I sink my cock into her soft, warm, perfect mouth like it's made to be in her body and only her body. She lets me fuck her throat, hard and rough, filthy and fast, just the way she likes it. She gags, sucks, and takes my cock down her throat without missing one beat. She massages my balls with her hands, and I groan, watching her suck me off.

The sounds of her sucking and gagging fill my ears like a beautiful tune. She smiles as she takes me in. She fingers her clit, and I growl. Her pussy should be in between my teeth, and I'm starving for her heavenly taste.

PRETEND

I pull my cock out of her mouth, and I grin, satisfied when I see that her lips are swollen, red, and puffy. She looks stunned, as if I took away something she's craving. She looks up at me on her knees, wide-eyed and lustful.

"Daegan, I want your come down my throat."

Fucking hell.

"Hang on to the shower head," I demand, picking her up from the floor and placing her body against the shower wall. This space is too small for me, but it's big enough to fuck my future wife in it. She holds onto the shower head as I devour her sweet pussy while I'm on my knees. She moans and fists my hair with one hand, trying to ride my tongue as she holds herself up on the wall.

Her legs are on my shoulders, and I sneak a glance at the goddess before me. Water from the shower head falls between her breasts and down her stomach. Her nude brown nipples are perfectly pointed and begging to be sucked on. I grab her breast as I continue to reclaim her pussy with my mouth.

"Daegan, fuck, Daegan, fuck!" She bellows out with divine pleasure.

I grin against her pussy when I see her close her eyes tight, and she begins to scream when I bite down on her clit, gently. Fuck she's amazing. Soft, needy, and dirty only for me.

I'm worshiping her like she's my savior.

"Daegan, I'm going to finish! I'm going to come!"

She arches her back and moans when her orgasm hits her. Her body trembles and pulls my hair harder as she rides out of the blissful cloud. But I keep going. I keep devouring her, not stopping until I get my own fill of her. Even though she orgasmed, it doesn't mean I'm done.

"Daegan, oh my God! Oh my God!" She tilts her head back and furrows her brows as she cries out when I continue to devour her sensitive clit. She's breathing hard as she continues to look down at me like she's going to break.

"I will always be the one you scream for." I smack her ass and palm it, digging my fingers into her skin, and continue to eat her out until she goes limp.

I turn off the shower and carry her tired body out of the bathroom. Her hair, body, and pussy is drenched. She kisses me tiredly as I whisk her away to her bed, wet and well tongue-fucked.

"Baby, we're just getting started for the night…for the rest of our fucking lives," I smirk with a depraved smile and eyes that hold limitless lustrous intentions to make her come. "Bend over."

She quickly gets on her hands and knees. Her ass is up in the air, her pussy dripping. I stroke my dick faster as I admire her two beautiful holes that I'm going to wreck for as long as we live over and over again for the years to come.

"Daegan, fuck me, please. Fuck me right now, I want your cock inside me." She begs. She holds her own breasts and watches me stroke myself.

"I want this body carrying my babies. I want to fill you up."

She bites her lip and blushes as I line myself with her entrance.

"Do you want me to go fast or slow? Do you want it sweet and hard or unremorseful?"

"Yes, please, yes." She chants over her shoulder.

"You want to watch yourself getting used, don't you?"

She bites her lip and my dick twitches. I push into her, and I growl at how tight and divine she feels.

"Fuck baby, you're so tight."

I start to pound her hard. The bed rocks, and the headboard hits the wall with each thrust. Her pussy surrounds my cock perfectly, tightly, over and over again, and I'm losing my mind. Every inch is getting to feel what heaven is like, and I'm already close to the edge.

She's so wet. So good. She's majestic and just for me.

"Has anyone touched you here since you left me?" I smack her ass roughly before I hover over her body. Her back is to my chest, and I lift her head by the base of her hair to respond to me as I keep fucking her. I lick her neck all the way to her cheek and hum.

The anger I felt when she left me consumes me again, and I want her to feel my pain. I want her to feel what I did when she walked away from me.

"No." She breathes out harshly.

I spank her again.

"Sorry, I couldn't hear you over me fucking your brains out."

Slap.

"I said—" She starts, but I don't let her continue.

Slap.

"Louder."

She fists the blankets, clawing at the bedsheets from how hard I'm drilling into her. I get off her back, and my hands dig into her waist. I squeeze her hips, marking her, as I continue to go in deep. Her breasts and hair are bouncing all over the place as I fuck her.

"No!" She yelps.

Slap. My palm smacks her ass again, and she flinches but re-positions herself.

"No, what little valentine?"

"No one has touched me! It's only been you. It will always be you!" She declares over our skin slapping.

I smile, satisfied, and push her face into the pillow. I ram into her over and over again. Then I feel her orgasm. Her pussy gets tighter, it clamps down on the head of my dick, and I'm gone.

"Open." I snarl through a clenched jaw. I flip her over until she's facing me. I stroke my cock, and I finish on her face. Streaks of come shoot out on her opened mouth and tongue. I'm on a high of nirvana and never want to escape it.

We're both breathing heavily as she takes it all in, and I hold her by the jaw as she welcomes it. I watch her swallow my fluids, and I move the head of my cock over the come that's on her cheek and the come that drips off her chin. I push it back into her mouth with my dick, and she smiles as I make sure she takes in every drop of me.

After making her come three more times, we fell asleep to the sound of the ocean. She feels like a new beginning. She feels like a fresh start after a horrible journey I thought would never end. I need her by my side for the rest of my life. If, after every training, mission, or deployment, I get to come home to her? It makes the fight that much more important.

I wake up after a dreamless sleep. Something I haven't had since I was captured, but my chest tightens when I realize she's not with me in bed, and I arch a brow. I sit up, throw the blankets off me, and stare at the v of my stomach, looking for her hand that used to be there.

I quickly find her. She's standing by the large open window with a baby blue silky robe that's open. Her perky full tits, her naked curves, and pussy are on display as she rests her back on the wall. Her robe barely goes below her tight ass, and her beautiful curls are messy. She holds a coffee mug in her hand like she's in her own world. Free and mesmerizing as the sea.

Alessia Sahara Valentin will be the ruin of me.

She's still unaware I'm awake. I glance at my watch on my wrist and see that it's five in the morning, and the sunrise is about to appear over the water. It's still pretty dark, but rays of pink, purple, yellow, and gold start to peak through.

I watch her take slow breaths. I don't want to interrupt this moment. Knowing she's mine, I need to soak it in for a bit longer. I rest my chin on the palm of my hand as I get lost in how peaceful she is. An ocean breeze flows past her, making her curls and robe fly, and I'm aching.

"Baby, come back to bed. I don't want to have to cut the eyes out of someone if they see what's mine."

She turns to me. She looks me up and down and stares at my already-hardened cock. I can't help it anymore.

She's mine.

All mine. All the time.

57

Alessia

God, this man is beautiful. I watch him with disheveled dark hair. His kraken tattoo moves as he takes in slow, steady breaths. His abs clench and unclench as he changes positions and sits on the bed.

"I'll always worship your body like it's my fucking religion," Daegan says in that same sexy deep voice I've become obsessed with.

I take a sip of the freshly made coffee with hazelnut creamer inside. I arch my brow and tease him to come forward. I let the robe fall to my feet, and he goes rigid.

"Come watch the sunrise with me. If you don't want anyone seeing me naked, come hold me." I swallow the warm coffee and hide half of my face with the mug as warmth swirls into my cheeks.

He smirks and gets out of bed. He stands behind me, snaking his hands over my stomach, and he pushes my back into him as he cups my breasts. He kisses my shoulder, and we watch the sunrise over the ocean water with infinite enchantment.

"You have ten beauty marks."

"Wha-what?"

"You have these cute little brown dots in parts of your body."

"I do?" I knew I had some, but I didn't realize there were exactly ten.

"Mhm." He kisses my forehead and grabs my face. He kisses my skin under my bottom lip where I know there's one.

"You have one here." He whispers against my cheek. Then he kisses a spot on my breast. "Here."

He moves to my neck, my lower back, my wrists, and my ankle, kissing every single spot until he gets in between my thighs and kisses the last one that's on my right leg. Every time he kisses me, I do my best not to melt and climb back into bed with him. I want to feel his beard tickle the inside of my thighs as he kisses me.

"Stella wanted me to leave the hospital. I—"

"I know what she told you, but Stella is Stella, and there's a reason why she's officially my ex-wife."

I'm silenced. It still doesn't change the fact that he was stalking me.

"I want my boundaries, Daegan. No more secrets. I mean it."

"No more secrets." He agrees before continuing. "I can't promise I won't love you any less than you deserve."

He tilts my head back until the side of my head rests on his shoulder, and he holds me by my throat as his tongue slips through my lips.

What is it about getting choked that fires me up?

"I'm not sure I can forgive you for stalking me." I break the kiss just as sunrise begins to shine on our faces.

"And that's okay. I can live with that. But I can't live without you. Do you know why I gave you one colored flower in a bouquet full of black ones?"

I shake my head, refusing to look at him. This feels weirder than catching Jack with Bailey. The taboo of it clings onto me like acid, burning layer into layer, and I can't bear to look at those eyes I've come to admire so much.

"Look at me. I'll say this once, but I refuse to live with any more regrets."

I look at him, and his eyes darken with pure intensity.

"You are the color in my black-and-white world. You are the single rose in a field full of them. You are the one notorious star in a sky full of them. You are the one soul I seek in a world full of them. Even if you can't see your worth, I see it. If you can't see the impact you have on me and everyone around you, I feel it. And I will remind you just how magnificent you are. As long as I wake up, you will know how uniquely beautiful you are each day and how profound my love travels for you. It is limitless, infinite, and unbreakable."

I'm soaking in his words as I melt into his arms. I want to open my mouth to say it back, but Daegan's watch chimes. He lifts it upwards until Grim's name appears on the little screen on his wrist with a text message. I give him the privacy he needs to read it. His body stiffens, and so does mine. I look away and stare at the waves crashing against the light brown sand on an empty beach. I close my eyes, enjoying the sound and moment of solace before he tells me anything.

This is what being with a man like him is like. I feel like I'm constantly holding my breath. This life of being with a special operator feels like drowning and then coming back up for air. They're coming and going at any moment's notice, and I'm not sure if I'll ever get used to it. All I know is I want to be with him.

"Listen, baby. I'm leaving on a mission. I have to be back in North Carolina and on a flight tomorrow night.

"Where?"

"You know I can't say anything."

I turn around and embrace him. My breasts brush up against his chest. "When are you coming back?"

Worry begins to fuel my veins, and I hold him like he'll disappear if I don't. He hugs me back, and I look up at him for the dreadful answer.

He's quiet. He clenches his jaw, and I frown. I place the mug on a small table, and my brows wilt together somberly. I raise my hand to touch his scars. He closes his eyes as I trail them for a few seconds before letting my hand fall back to my side.

He doesn't answer me. He opens his eyes, and his stare is cold and distant, as if he already wants to disassociate himself and go into work mode. He walks away to his jeans and pulls out a pack of cigarettes. He dresses himself in his pants and lights one up as he walks onto the balcony.

He passes me by, and the wall he likes to put up is all the way down again. There are a million thoughts running through his head as he rests his forearms on the railing. I stare at his dragon back tattoo with snarling teeth and bite my bottom lip as I watch him stressfully smoke.

"You can't tell me anything?"

He shakes his head.

"All the guys are going. It's going to be rough. It's going to be dangerous. It's going to be one hell of a deployment."

"They're all dangerous and bad." I point out from behind him while crossing my arms around my chest.

"I guess you have a point." He turns around and gives me a pained smile. A flash of his sharp canines briefly makes a presence, and he puts out the cigarette and watches me.

"I can't believe this all began when I asked you to pretend with me."

He pulls me by hand, and I stumble forward until I hit his chest.

"Where's your father?"

He tucks a piece of my hair back behind my ear.

I furrow my brows with curiosity. He's never met my biological father before.

"Why?"

He smiles, and his beautiful grey eyes are glazing with bliss.

"Because I want to ask for his blessing to marry my little valentine."

58
Alessia

Daegan holds me tight. He has his mask on. It's that same creepy sharp teeth signature smile on his mouth. He kisses the top of my head repeatedly before he pulls his mask up just above his mouth to plant one more see you soon kiss.

"I love you, Mrs. Hannibal."

"We're not married yet, Daegan." I scrunch my nose in defiance as I tip-toe to kiss his cheek. He grabs his bag full of equipment and throws it over his shoulders.

That thing has to weigh about a hundred or more pounds.

"You already are *Mrs. Hannibal to me*. I don't need a piece of paper to tell me that. Plus, I'm sure there's already a little Hannibal cooking in there." He points to my belly.

"Doubtful. Don't get ahead of yourself." I scold him.

I stopped taking my birth control when I first got home after my deployment. He may be right, but that would be fast, and I doubt a baby is growing. I've gotten two periods after I was attacked by Gabe. I expect my next one in the next twenty days or so.

I playfully nudge his chest away, but his combat boots are cemented to the floor. An airforce plane roars behind him, ready to take them where they're needed. Grim and Rooker pass by with their black masks, and Lopez and Kane fall behind me and Daegan.

"I love you, Daegan. Please be careful."

"Always am. I love you too."

"Creature! Let's go!" Grim shouts. I peek over my fiance's shoulder and see the most accomplished Navy SEAL. A huge scythe where his mouth is, but those blue eyes glow against his mask.

"When I come back, we're getting married, and you're going to meet my mother, Margaret." He tells me as he tucks hair behind my ear.

I suck in a breath as my heart flutters with heat.

Daegan turns to leave. He twirls his bullet as he stalks toward the plane, and I watch his favorite knife move against his belt as he closes the distance to the plane.

Kane walks by, and our eyes lock together for a second. His black mask is in his hand, clutching it tight. I stop him, grab his shoulder, and pull him in for a hug.

I care so much about Kane, and I know he feels the same way. It's a mutual relationship of friendship. His kindness and understanding will always be unmatched. He's become my closest friend.

"He won't tell me where you guys are going."

He hugs me tighter and then lets me go just as fast.

"I'm sure you'll find out soon with the type of clearance you have." He pats my head with his military-issued gloved hand.

"You have to tell me how you met this new woman of yours!"

Kane smiles littered with sunshine. He gives me a salute and starts to walk backward. The creases of his dark blue eyes are present, signaling that signature happy smirk.

"Yeah, about that..." his voice trails off with unease.

"Oh gosh, what?" I bark after him. He can't leave me on a cliffhanger like that. The *chismosa* in me wants to know his secrets.

"It's a long story, but I'll let you know soon. I'm going to leave now before Creature kicks my shit in for hugging you. See you, shortie!"

"Whatever!" I shout at his back.

"Kane! You were going to leave and not say goodbye?" A voice I know because of my time in the hospital rings through our ears. Kane stops, and it takes him a second to gather himself. I watch him turn around and face Ari Rider. She's in a beautiful red summer dress.

He stiffens but then relaxes. His aviator sunglasses are still on, and he grins with pure sunshine.

His cheeks flush a bit, and he stalks back to where Ari stands.

Every step he takes gets faster, and Ari holds out her arms in a friendly manner.

They embrace finally, and she tiptoes as he hugs her. She pats his back three times, and she smiles.

"Please be safe. Bring me back my husband." She pleads as they let each other go. Her brown eyes sparkle with genuine concern for their safety. I shouldn't watch them say goodbye, but it's quite literally happening a few feet away, and I wanted to see all the guys off.

"We always are. And, of course, I will." He reassures her as she holds his hands in hers.

"I've never stopped caring about you, Kane. You mean a lot to me. Just...be careful? He told me this was going to be a long deployment."

He lets go of her hand and clenches his jaw.

"It is going to be long."

He replies as he starts to walk backward.

"You haven't stopped caring about me...but I've never stopped loving you. I'm not sure I ever will." His smile is gone, his voice deep and full of emotion. He scoffs. Looking down at his boots as he walks.

She stiffens, and pain hits my chest.

Kane is always good. He is always happy. He is a good man who loves someone who belongs to someone else. I guess that's life sometimes. Not everyone gets to have their soulmate.

"Goodbye Ari Alvarez! I'll make sure that we both come back home, don't worry."

She relaxes a bit and smiles. He turns around.

Grim watches at a distance from the plane and Ari waves to him. She kisses her lips and holds out her hand in the air.

I watch Kane reunite with Lopez. Lopez twirls a toothpick. He's maskless and notices me watching all of them. They all have camo paint all over their faces, like they're ready to jump in and fight somewhere.

He winks at me, "*Adios bonita!*"

I pinch my brows together as I roll my eyes and purse my lips.

PRETEND

Always a flirt.

I watch them enter the plane before I give in to my journey back to the parking lot. I'm sitting in my car, listening to music while I watch the plane ascend into the sky. The airplane lights flicker, and the entire airfield vibrates from it taking off. It takes me back to the night we stargazed and pretended that the military aircraft were shooting stars.

Tears fall down my cheek because there's an ache in my chest. I know there's a hole in my heart that will remain until I see him again. The fear about loving someone who leaves constantly is that it hurts each time we say, *see you soon*. It doesn't get any better with time because there's always that dreadful reality that it can quickly turn into a goodbye when you least expect it.

I rest my forehead on the steering wheel and cry until my body physically can't take it anymore. After all the things I've seen when I was in Iraq, it's hard not to face the cruel reality of their job. With all the intel and information that would spill in, I now look at deployments and missions differently. I look at the Scarred Executioners differently.

These men are incredible, and I admire them.

59

Daegan

Three Months Later

"**W**HAT'S THAT?" Kane asks me as we gear up for the mission I've been waiting for since I was captured.

We found The Surgeon. The area is hot, but the Navy wanted to send the best of the best SEAL Teams to capture him...dead or alive.

I twirl a closed thick box from my valentine. I hold it with both gloved hands, and I'm tempted to shake it. My future bride-to-be is thinking of me. I'm going to tease her about this when I see her again.

I haven't talked to her in a few days. A few days ago, I texted her to let her know I was going out on a mission and that I would talk soon. She didn't respond but I'm used to it by now because of our schedules. The time difference is drastic. When it's daytime over here, she's asleep. When she's awake, I either don't have my phone, or I'm racked out. It's unbalanced but that was to be expected.

I lift it up so he can get a better view.

"A box," I reply.

He scoffs.

"Obviously, asshole," he spits with a smirk. Kane tucks a knife into his kit.

"I don't know. It came in yesterday. I haven't opened it yet."

I shrug. I tuck it back into my locker. I want to open it when I get back to the FOB. It's more of a motivation to fight harder. I get to come home to a mysterious gift Alessia shipped to me from back home.

"I wish I had an old lady at home to send me things," Lopez mutters under his breath while he twirls a toothpick in between his teeth.

"Maybe if you stop putting your dick in a different woman every week, you would have one." Kane chimes in while he holds his pistol, looking down through the sights. He has it aimed at the floor, and he squints at it.

"You know..." Lopez sits down beside me. "There is someone I think about. Someone who I always pictured myself settling down with. The house, the dog, some kids, even marriage. Somewhere on a ranch in Texas."

"Who's the poor girl?" I ask.

He chuckles.

"I call her mi mariposa. Her name's—"

"Lock it the fuck up. We gotta move." Grim cuts him off with a stern, deep voice. Grim's massive figure comes into view. His blue eyes glow against his painted face, and he's no longer Danny Rider. He's Grim, like the Reaper. He looks at me, then Kane, then Lopez. Rooker walks up from behind and stands side by side with him.

We are all still, listening with wide eyes and open ears.

I take one last look at my locker. I can't wait to open it after a mission fucking accomplished. I put any thoughts of Alessia and any other distractions locked away for the last time in the back of my mind before I transform into work mode.

It's done.

I take a deep breath in and relax my shoulders.

I have a dreadful feeling about this one...and I can't shake it.

Everyone has camo painted on their faces—shades of black, green, and brown disguise us.

Pure, thick silence consumes the room, and it's full of tension.

It's like everyone knows the Reaper is near, and we can't do anything about our future that has already been sealed.

"We've gone over the plan a hundred times already. We got this." Grim tells us.

"Hooyah." We all say synchronized.

Admiral Ravenmore walks into the room, and the atmosphere changes. Everyone knows I'm with his stepdaughter. It's been a couple of months since that day in his office when he asked me to promise to stay away from Alessia.

He's bitter about it and hasn't talked to me like he used to since.

Rightfully so. He knew I was married. It's something that'll eat me alive for not being honest with Alessia. But I never cheated.

Grim looks tensed up. We all have our armor plates on, gloves, kits, and our waists littered with weapons. We're ready to fight. We're ready to win.

PRETEND

We're swimming into the area. The HVTs are hiding on an island, and we're in the ocean. We make it to shore after agonizing minutes of swimming through strong currents. The black sea is an element even I know not to underestimate, but we all make it to land with all our limbs intact.

Grim takes the lead, of course. Other SEAL teams and Delta operators are on standby for QRF. But we're ready.

The sand is unforgiving. Our boots sink in, but we're vigilant and determined. We set up in the place Intelligence authorized us to. Lopez has comms ready. Slaughter, Rooker, and Grim get settled in their spots. We're in deep with the trees. Right away, it's my cue to get to work. As expected, there are enemies surrounding the beach. There are two of them, already aiming their weapons straight at us.

I take the initiative.

They're in my crosshairs.

Goodnight.

My finger is on the trigger as Grim calls my name through the mic. They all start to shoot at once, and I begin to hum.

"Creature."

"Already on it," I respond quickly.

I send it. I pull the trigger, and the kickback rolls into my shoulder.

The target goes down as the bullet pierces his face. Then the next one falls, and the next one. The silencer on my weapon made the shots quiet.

The world grows quiet. The sound of the ocean surrounds us. Insects and the wind rattling the trees is almost soothing. I love the outdoors, but right now...it's biting back, and the eerie sounds scream at us.

Something is wrong.

Something is very wrong.

Suddenly, there's shouting from a distance, and in a split second, we're surrounded by bullets. The enemy releases havoc, and we're pinned down in a spot with little fallback cover.

I keep spraying, hitting enemies left and right, but they just keep coming.

It's an army.

"Bro, what the fuck!" Lopez shouts and starts to radio in our location for support.

"I don't like this, Grim! I don't like it at all!" Rooker exclaims as we all return fire. The bullets look like mini fireflies through the darkness, but they're flying fast, and they're not missing a beat.

"Shit!" Grim shouts.

"What's going on? Talk to me, Grim!" Kane shouts into the mic. He's in the center of us all, and Grim is on the far left.

"I've been shot in the side." Grim rasps in the mic. "I'm fucking good, though. Keep fighting!"

Shots and more shots everywhere. They're coming from us and them.

"Damn it, that fucking hurts!" Rooker yells in pain. "I've been shot. I'm hit!"

"*Pinche mierda*! I'm shot too, brothers." Lopez agonizes from the far right. But he continues to radio in for support and doesn't stop returning fire.

PRETEND

I turn to Kane, and he has someone running up on him. He's the only one who hasn't been shot. I see two tall figures running up on him. Everyone else is busy keeping the threats away, but I've got his six.

Two bullets ring out from my rifle. First on the left side of his head and the second one on the right. Both bullets pierce through the wind, and they go down before they can grab him.

"Fuck, man, thank you!" Kane gratefully shakes. His dark blue eyes are wide and on high alert.

"Thank me with a beer later, loverboy," I tell him as my grip tightens on my rifle.

He smiles, laughs, and lifts his rifle to his shoulder to fire. But then I feel a bullet stab me in my leg, making me tumble over. I grunt from the pain. The bullet knocks the air from my lungs. The shot forced me to drop my rifle, and I laugh as I watch my favorite color drip out of me.

Fuck that hurt.

"Grim! Fucking move!" Kane's voice is laced with urgency. I look up as I try to catch my breath. Kane shouts at Grim and jumps to him. But it's too late. Grim gets shot on the far right side of his chest, making him fall over. Kane takes his spot when he pushes him with his arm, causing Kane to get shot in the chest two times.

Grim gets the energy from God knows where and grabs a grenade from his kit, and throws it a few feet away in front of us from where the shots came from. Loud pained groans follow, and it's a target hit.

The sound from the blast leaves us all with ringing ears. My entire world feels like it's going in slow motion. Smoke is everywhere but the fucking bullets don't stop.

"Give us cover, Creature! Kane is down. He's down! He's fucking down! Call for air support now, Tex!"

"They're on their way already! We have to hold our ground!" Lopez calls out.

"We gotta get back to the ocean!" Rooker orders us as he takes a round to his leg and then his side.

Shit.

He buckles over and grunts. He punches the floor with his gloved balled fist, pissed off. He growls in frustration. "Fucking hell!" He raises his rifle again and looks through his scope.

"How are we going to get to the water?! We're fucking surrounded!" Lopez shouts at Rooker as Lopez takes another shot in his arm. It sends blood spraying everywhere, and I hold my rifle up and take out five more targets.

We're all bleeding.

We are all in fucking trouble.

Grim drags Kane back to me. I look down and see that Kane's been shot straight through his plate and into his heart.

Shit.

"Slaughter. You keep on breathing, brother." I order him.

You're going to be alright.

We're all going to be alright.

He nods and grabs a hold of his chest. The blood is profusely leaking. He's covered in dirt, sweat, and blood. We all are.

Grim tries to help him, and I'm doing everything I can to breathe as another bullet wounds me in my side. A burning sensation runs through me, and I growl.

"Fuck." I spit out blood and shake my head twice.

PRETEND

I've been shot again, but I won't stop shooting.

Kane's voice makes me do a double take.

"Tell our girl I'll say hello to Paul for her." He struggles to talk. He's having short breaths, and it sounds like he's on his way to dying.

No.

No.

No.

"Don't you fucking dare make me tell Ari that! You're going to live through this, Kane. Don't make me tell her that!" Grim is in a full-blown panic. "You're my brother! Don't you go! Don't you fucking dare!" He snarls at Kane. I want to hear Kane's remark, but it never comes. I stop firing and take a moment.

Wake up, Kane. Wake the fuck up.

But he doesn't.

The reality sets in as hope fades to fucking nothing.

Grim's desperate to keep him alive, but Kane's already out. He puts pressure on his chest, and Kane's frozen. Grim watches him in disbelief, like he's in deja vu. This is the second time that I know he's had to watch one of his brothers die. Sadly, this is my fifth time, but this moment is hitting me harder. Grim's light blue eyes water, and I watch blood come out of his own chest. Something starts to come up my throat, and I taste iron. I spit my blood onto the ground and cough hoarsely.

Kane is the one I'm closest to on the team.

Alessia and him are close.

What the fuck am I going to tell her? Will I even get to come back home to tell her anything?

Kane is gone. His eyes are closed, and he's as pale as the moon that shines over us.

My heart aches. But the adrenaline keeps us going. It keeps us all going. We're all shot up and wounded on our way to hell.

"Grim!" I call him out, hoping it snaps him out of his thoughts. We stare at each other, thinking the same thing. The vein on his neck bulging in fury. We come to a mutual understanding as Lopez and Rooker groan from pain as they take on fire, just as they shoot back with their weapons.

We're all going to die here.

TO BE CONTINUED

What's next from Lexie Axelson?

Coming soon...

The Depraved Prince

A Dark Gothic Vampire Romance by Lexie Axelson

Acknowledgements

To everyone who continues to give my stories a chance, thank you. It means the world to me. I am eternally grateful to my readers. I hope I continue to write characters that touch your soul! If you enjoy reading my stories, please consider leaving a review. It is my hope to continue to grow as a writer in my author journey. Thank you to my husband, family, friends, ARC readers, street team, and book besties.

I can't do this without you guys. <3

About The Author

Lexie Axelson is a Hispanic author from South Texas. She is a military spouse and mother to two sons. She's a foodie who loves traveling, spending time with her family, and binge-watching horror movies. If she's not in a bookstore browsing, she's reading a book. Her passion for reading and writing started at a young age. And she hopes to bring more book boyfriends to your bookshelves!

Follow Lexie Axelson's socials for updates and more!
www.lexieaxelson.com
instagram.com/lexieaxelson
tiktok.com/@lexieaxelson
Join the facebook group!

PRETEND

facebook.com/groups/1718058931953720

Made in the USA
Monee, IL
27 October 2024

68773753R00246